ONE
DARK
NIGHT

TOM BALE

D0239008

bookouture

Published by Bookouture in 2018

An imprint of StoryFire Ltd.

Carmelite House
50 Victoria Embankment
London EC4Y 0DZ

www.bookouture.com

Copyright © Tom Bale, 2018

Tom Bale has asserted his right to be identified
as the author of this work.

All rights reserved. No part of this publication may be reproduced,
stored in any retrieval system, or transmitted, in any form or by
any means, electronic, mechanical, photocopying, recording or
otherwise, without the prior written permission of the publishers.

ISBN: 978-1-78681-705-1
eBook ISBN: 978-1-78681-704-4

This book is a work of fiction. Names, characters, businesses,
organizations, places and events other than those clearly in the
public domain, are either the product of the author's imagination
or are used fictitiously. Any resemblance to actual persons, living or
dead, events or locales is entirely coincidental.

CHAPTER ONE

He heard the car before he saw it: the high whine of an engine being pushed too hard. Glancing to his right, he caught a flash of movement through the trees and just had time to hit the brakes. A silver car burst from a narrow lane and careered across the road, the rear end skidding towards the front wing of their Peugeot 308.

Adam Parr could feel his car sliding a little; with so many wet leaves on the road, the tyres had lost some of their grip. A lot of stones and grit as well, washed out of the surrounding fields by weeks of rain. It was probably a stone that pinged up from the other car's rear wheel and struck the lights, but when he heard the shatter of glass, Adam's first thought was that the two vehicles had collided.

Beside him, Katy cried out as she lurched forward, then reflexively turned to check on the kids. Nine-year-old Freya and her younger brother, Dylan, had been engaged in an enthusiastic discussion about dinosaurs and asteroids, breaking off in midstream as the car came to a stop.

'We're okay, we're all okay,' Adam called out. Reassurance was the first priority, but there was also a surge of fury as the silver car, a Mazda 6, regained control and raced away.

That idiot driver could have killed us. Could have killed my kids…

'I'm not having that,' he muttered. He checked the mirrors and then accelerated, flashing his headlights at the Mazda.

'Adam?' After giving the kids a comforting smile, Katy hissed: 'Take it easy.'

'I am.' But spoken through gritted teeth, so he added a smile to prove it. 'Completely calm.'

And he flashed his lights again.

The Mazda gave no sign that its driver had noticed – or cared – and that took Adam's temper up a notch. They were on a narrow country lane that twisted and weaved through several miles of woods and farmland between the A275 and their home village of Lindfield, deep in the Sussex countryside. Traffic was usually sparse along here, though agricultural vehicles were not uncommon. Adam watched the Mazda disappear around a tight bend and half-expected to hear the boom of a head-on collision.

When that didn't happen he took the bend at the same foolish speed, and felt Katy's disapproval radiating out like a furnace. He didn't want to fall out with her, not after the pleasant morning they'd had. And she was right, of course: what was a broken light, in the scheme of things?

And yet…

He kept on flashing his lights, drawing closer as the Mazda struggled a little with the next bend, accelerated briefly and then began to slow.

'Adam.'

'He's damaged our car. He shouldn't be able to get away with it.'

In the back seat, tiny ears had pricked up. 'Was there an accident?' Dylan asked.

'Not an accident,' Adam said. 'It might have been a stone.'

'Which isn't really his fault,' Katy added quietly.

'Course it is. He's driving like a nutter, could have ki—' He remembered not to say it. 'That won't be cheap to fix, you know.'

'All right, but I don't think we should antagonise…'

She trailed off because the Mazda was braking sharply now. It pulled over, bumping two wheels up on to the narrow, muddy verge. An arm emerged from the driver's window, waving them past.

'What does he mean by that?' Katy asked.

'Dunno.' Only now did it occur to Adam that the other driver wouldn't necessarily know he'd thrown up a stone. He might be assuming that Adam was in a hurry himself, and had been flashing to get past.

As he slowed to a crawl, Adam felt his phone vibrate in his pocket: a distraction he could do without. He shifted to second gear and drove cautiously past the Mazda. The rear windows were heavily tinted, though he had a sense that the back of the car was occupied.

The driver was a young man, thin and pale with short red hair. The passenger seat beside him was empty. Did that mean there were kids in the back? It was shocking to think anyone would drive so recklessly with children in the car.

Adam pulled up just ahead of the Mazda. He looked in the mirror and met the driver's gaze, which seemed both hostile and slightly fearful. The man's head bobbed a couple of times – he must be listening to someone – then he turned to speak to whoever was in the back, punctuating the conversation with dramatic hand movements.

'Why don't we leave it?' Katy swiped at his arm as he went to open the door. 'Adam, please be sensible.'

'I just want to check what's broken.'

Maybe nothing, he told himself as he climbed out. He might have misinterpreted the sound, and with a fair collection of stone chips already present on the front of the car, it would be hard to pin any specific damage on the driver of the Mazda.

Freya delayed him a second, speaking from the back seat: 'Do we have to call the police?'

He smiled. 'No, darling. We might just need the details of their insurance company.' Turning to Katy, he said, 'Couple of minutes and then off home.'

Later, Adam would question whether he had really believed it could be that straightforward – and fool that he was, he'd have to say yes.

CHAPTER TWO

After shutting the door, he heard a soft thunk as Katy engaged the central locking. Not a bad precaution, though he couldn't really see the need for it.

He sensed the Mazda driver was watching, but chose not to look in that direction. Instead, trying to appear casual, Adam walked round to the front of the car. He scowled at the sight of the broken headlight lens, crouched down for a closer look and saw that a couple of the bulbs had been smashed.

Slipping the phone from his back pocket, he read the text that had just come in, deleted it, then opened the camera app and took a picture of the headlight.

As he straightened up he caught Katy's eye, and nodded grimly to confirm there was damage. His family were all staring at him, his wife tight-lipped and frowning, Freya and Dylan more perplexed than worried. No need to overreact, he reminded himself again.

He heard a noise, and saw the Mazda's door opening. The driver was tall and gangly, wearing grubby jeans and a denim jacket. He was muttering to someone within the car, his tone aggrieved and slightly petulant, like a teenager obeying under sufferance.

By now Adam was moving in that direction. He was glad of the phone in his hand – there was no better prop when you were feeling apprehensive – but he also had another practical use for it. Just in case things started to get heated.

'What's up, then?' the driver called, striding forward to meet him in the no man's land between the two cars.

'Why didn't you stop at that junction? You nearly wiped us out.'

'Didn't see it. Weren't no lines.' His voice was nasal, with a northern accent. He was probably in his late twenties, and twitching with nervous energy.

'When you cut in front of us, the wheels threw up a stone and smashed our headlight.'

The man gaped at him. 'And that's why you chased us?'

Adam nodded, determined to hold his ground when the other driver stepped closer. His eyes were wide, shining with a readiness for violence.

Staying calm, Adam said, 'We can let the insurance companies deal with it, if you give me your details.'

The man tossed his head as if he'd never heard anything so ridiculous, then half-turned, glancing at the Mazda. Adam shifted sideways for a better look and saw three people squashed together on the back seat, two men either side of a woman. She was a lot smaller than them, and her head was lolling slightly, as if half asleep, or intoxicated. One of the men had his arm round her neck, which didn't look particularly comfortable for him or her.

Adam felt a twinge of unease. It made no sense that the other man wasn't sitting in the front, to give them more room.

Why don't we leave it? Katy had said, and he'd known she was right. But he hadn't listened.

The driver turned back, shifting his stance to block Adam's view. Despite the cool weather, there was a sheen of sweat on his face. 'So how much is it gonna cost, then? Fifty quid? A hundred?'

Definitely something dodgy here, Adam thought. He wouldn't normally consider a cash offer until he had a quote for repairs, but maybe it wasn't too late to take his wife's advice. Better to avoid any sort of confrontation in front of his children.

'I guess a hundred will do it.'

The man gave a nervous gulp. 'Hundred, right. Wait here.'

He jabbed a finger at the ground, and the message was clear: *Don't move.*

Adam obeyed, but with the man's back turned he angled the phone towards the front of the Mazda. He'd set it to video, so it had recorded their conversation, and now it should be capturing a clear image of the registration number.

While the driver was leaning into the car, Adam checked on his family. Katy was watching in the mirror, and the kids had got up on their knees and were staring at him through the rear screen. He raised a hand, still trying to appear nonchalant, untroubled.

Until the scream.

It came from the Mazda. The woman had hurled herself forward, between the front seats, and was clawing at the steering wheel as the two men fought to restrain her.

'Help me!' she shrieked. 'Please help me!'

Standing by the car, the red-haired driver jumped as if he'd been tasered, then he recovered and chopped at the woman's arm, allowing her to be dragged back into her seat. One of the men clamped a hand over her mouth, and the other shouted, 'Dale, get in!'

Responding to the cry, Adam had automatically taken a couple of steps towards the Mazda before reality hit.

He was outnumbered three to one. There was no way he could take them on. But he had the registration number, he could get away, call the police from the car—

'*Please!*' The woman must have bitten the man's finger; as he swore loudly and snatched his hand away, she threw her arm out in a desperate appeal to Adam. 'They murdered my husband!'

CHAPTER THREE

Everything seemed to freeze. Only for a fraction of a second, but long enough for Adam to look into the eyes of the driver and know it was true.

Every instinct told him to flee, but his conscious mind resisted. What if he ran off and they killed her right now?

No. Getting his family out of danger had to be the first priority. These were clearly ruthless, violent men, and Adam was not.

As he sprang to life he sensed Dale turning, perhaps to come after him, but one of the men shouted, 'Get in, fuckwit!'

Adam dashed to his own car, pointing at the driver's door and praying that Katy would unlock it. She had turned towards him, her mouth open in horror. He heard the Mazda's door slam, and the engine revving. There was also a sound like another door closing, which didn't make sense, but there wasn't time to look back.

He skidded to a stop, grabbed the door handle and it yielded. *Thank God.*

'Adam, what's the matter? What are they—?'

'Can't explain,' he gasped, pulling open the door just as he realised the Mazda was hurtling towards him.

The driver was going to crush him against his own car.

Adam threw himself on to the seat, wrenching the door shut in such a panic that he caught his right ankle between the two plates of metal. He roared with pain as the Mazda flashed past.

Katy had cried out in response, perhaps fearing he'd been hit. His ankle felt like it was on fire. He was conscious of Freya and Dylan clutching each other, both distraught, but knew that comforting them would have to wait: first get them to safety.

'Call 999,' he said, trying to work out where to go. The best option was probably to turn round and head back to the main road, and then the nearest village.

He put the car into gear, only to register that the Mazda hadn't actually sped away. It had slewed to a halt across the road, blocking their path.

So turn around…

A second ago he'd dismissed a vague shadow, flitting past in the rear-view mirror. Now he caught movement along the passenger side. Katy, fumbling with the phone in her hand, yelled: 'Adam!'

Her door was opening.

Adam had the presence of mind to yank the wheel to the right and lurch forward, but the man had anticipated his actions, jumping on to the door sill and grabbing the roof with one hand. In the other hand there was a gun, which he shoved into Katy's chest.

'Stop the car or she's dead!'

Adam hit the brakes. He couldn't take the risk that the man was only bluffing. Besides, the road was too narrow to turn without several manoeuvres. Time enough to kill them all.

'Okay,' he shouted. 'I've stopped.'

Turning from Katy to his children, Adam knew he would never forget the sight of the raw terror in their eyes. The idea that he couldn't protect them was like having his heart ripped out of his chest.

'Drop the phone,' the man ordered.

Katy obeyed, shaking with fear. The man stepped on to the ground, jolting the car's suspension, and moved back to get a better view of them all. He was about fifty-five, short and paunchy with a bulbous nose and a long, greying thatch of curly hair. He wore cargo pants and a black leather jacket.

The gun was a silver revolver, clutched in a hand with the letters F-U-C-K tattooed on the knuckles. As with the red-haired driver, he had a northern accent; somewhere in Yorkshire, Adam thought.

'Hands in your laps, both of you. Leave the engine running.'

Adam and Katy complied, and saw now that the third man from the Mazda was running towards them. He was the same sort of age as the driver, mid or late twenties, with light brown hair and soft, pleasant features, but he spoke with a surprising degree of authority. Unlike the other two, his accent was local to the south-east.

'We're taking them,' he said. 'Two in each car.'

'Bloody hell, Jay—'

'Don't have a choice. You drive this one.'

'Total balls-up,' the gunman muttered. He waved his gun at Adam. 'In the back. Now!'

'What are you doing?' Katy cried. 'This is—'

She broke off as the younger one, Jay, took the other man's place on the passenger side, reached in and popped her seatbelt. Sensing that Adam was about to lunge at him, he snarled, 'We'll hurt your kids. I'm serious.' The venom in his voice belied his easy-going appearance: Adam knew that he meant it.

After dragging Katy out of her seat, Jay opened the back door and hauled Freya from the car. 'Not you,' he told Dylan, who was rigid with shock, tears streaming down his cheeks.

For Adam there was a level of helplessness that he'd only ever experienced in dreams. No matter what he tried – even if he sacrificed his own life – there was nothing he could do to save any of them.

He managed to fumble the door open and virtually fell out, his legs rubbery when he tried to stand. He began to turn, aware of the gunman crowding in on him, reeking of nervous sweat and nicotine, and was suddenly punched in the stomach. 'Too fooking slow!'

Partially winded, Adam was shoved into the back of the car and told to crouch in the footwell. 'Get the kid down, too.'

'But he's safer where he is,' Adam protested, indicating Dylan's car seat.

'Just do it!'

As Adam unclipped his son, there was a shout from Jay: 'Gary! Make sure their heads are covered. Use their coats.'

'You heard him.' Gary slammed the door and jumped into the driver's seat.

Dylan's coat was in the boot, having got muddy during a high-spirited game of chase, so Adam helped him remove his sweater while slipping off his own jacket.

He was half kneeling, propped against the rear seats. Bracing himself and Dylan for movement, he turned and saw his wife and daughter being bundled into the Mazda. One last pleading look from Freya, before Jay piled in after them and the car quickly reversed until it was straight, then roared away…

And immediately had to stop.

There was a tractor coming towards them.

CHAPTER FOUR

Gary swore, but still accelerated until he was tight on the Mazda's bumper. Both cars moved on to the narrow verge, scraping the bodywork against a few spindly trees.

The tractor was towing some equipment on a wide trailer, a line of cars trapped behind it. Gary turned in his seat and pointed the gun at Dylan. 'Don't even think of playing the hero,' he told Adam. 'You stay out of sight, or I'll put a bullet in the kid.'

Dylan gave a whimper of fear. Adam grasped his hand and hunched over, drawing his son as close as possible. He felt completely destabilised. How could this be happening, on a quiet country road in Sussex?

A couple of minutes earlier and the presence of these cars might have saved them. Instead, the tractor had held up the normal flow of traffic, and in doing so it had quite possibly saved those other motorists from becoming involved. A matter of seconds, that was all it came down to.

Adam could feel the tension in Gary, the willingness to shoot if anything went wrong. Perched up high, there was every chance that the tractor driver might look into the vehicles as he passed. If he did, would he notice the prisoners cooped up in the back?

Even if he spotted them, he probably wouldn't understand the significance – not unless he also saw the gun.

It was hopeless. But then, as the tractor rumbled alongside, Adam realised it could provide him with a vital diversion. While running to the car, he'd shoved his phone into his back pocket.

In such a confined space it wasn't going to be easy to retrieve it without Gary sensing the movement. But it had to be worth a try.

The tractor loomed in his peripheral vision. Peering from beneath his jacket, Adam saw that the driver was an elderly man, white hair sprouting from a flat cap and a Paisley scarf tight around his neck. He was staring straight ahead, presumably confident in his ability to get past, and didn't spare them a glance.

Adam contorted himself, arching his back to a painful degree in order to twist one hand towards his pocket. Dylan was curled up under his sweater, but kept sneaking a look at his father, desperate for reassurance that Adam could barely begin to provide.

We can describe these men. There's no way they're going to release us now.

His fingers brushed against the stitching along the edge of the pocket, then found the top corner of his phone.

The driver's seat creaked. 'Keep low,' Gary ordered.

The tailback of cars was passing now, one of them a lot more timid than the tractor. 'You got loads of chuffing room,' Gary muttered, and the Peugeot shifted as he found the biting point, ready to move.

Dylan looked up, and when he opened his mouth to speak Adam gave an urgent shake of the head: *not now.* He pulled the phone halfway out and had to pause, aware that his elbow was pressed against the back of the driver's seat.

'What?' Gary asked, sounding annoyed. Did he think Adam had said something?

And again: 'I'm not a chuffing mind reader. *What?*'

It must be someone in the Mazda, signalling to Gary, but he couldn't decipher the message.

As the car bumped back on to the road, Adam eased the phone out and nestled it in his palm. Call 999 or text some kind of emergency message? A call was more immediate, but Gary would quickly stop the car and overpower him.

It had to be a text. Adam was trying to come up with a brief, urgent message when Gary murmured, 'You want me to ring…?' He sounded like a bewildered contestant in a game of charades. Then, as comprehension dawned: 'Ah, shit. *Phones*.'

The car veered to the right as he leaned over, pawing at something in the front footwell: Katy's phone, which she'd been told to drop. It must be lying there, next to her bag.

Adam had unlocked his screen and was shielding the light with his hand when he felt Gary look round again.

'You got a phone?'

'Not with me.' Adam sounded too weak, too desperate to be credible.

'Don't piss me about.'

'I mean it—'

'You wanna play games?' Gary roared. 'Here's a fooking game for you.'

Seemingly without looking, he shoved the revolver through the gap between the front seats and pulled the trigger.

The boom of the shot was horrifically loud: both Adam and Dylan cried out and clapped their hands over their ears. The acrid chemical odour of the gun's propellant filled the car.

'Give me the phone, now!'

The words came through muddy and distorted. Adam knew he had to obey. As he rose, he saw Dylan's eyes roll up in his head; then, with a shudder, the boy collapsed.

'You shot him!' With a howl of pure grief, Adam dropped his phone and gathered Dylan into his arms. He was white as a ghost, but after a few seconds he stirred, moaning weakly.

'Didn't touch him,' Gary sneered. 'Bullet went through the back seat.'

Half crazed with fear, Adam carried on searching for signs of a wound. *If he's hurt, I'll kill Gary. I'll kill them all...*

But there was no blood, no obvious injury. Adam held his son close and felt him coming round. Even as he rejoiced that Dylan was unhurt, the sight of a neat little hole in the middle seat rammed home the truth. The danger was brutally real, and he'd just missed his one good chance to raise the alarm.

With an air of defeat, Adam tossed his phone on to the passenger seat and then slumped back in the footwell, Dylan lying dazed in his arms. He tried to tell himself to stay hopeful, but it was a struggle to believe that they would come out of this alive.

CHAPTER FIVE

It had been a gloriously normal morning. That was what Katy Parr couldn't get out of her mind. Gloriously, *ridiculously* normal.

A couple of years ago, at her suggestion, they'd joined the National Trust. She felt the children had reached an age where they could start to appreciate art, architecture, the beauty of nature, and Freya in particular was hungry to learn about history. Okay, there was some truth to Adam's jokes about how insufferably middle class it made them feel – not to mention prematurely middle-aged – but Katy didn't mind that. In her view, as the years passed and the children grew up, it would be important to have activities that still drew them all together as a family.

If they stayed together as a family, that was. Katy knew such things should never be taken for granted.

There were several National Trust properties within a short drive of their home in Lindfield, and the magnificent gardens of Sheffield Park were practically on their doorstep. This morning they'd enjoyed a slow walk around the lakes and along the tree-lined paths. After overnight rain the cloud had stayed low and oppressive, but even in the soft grey light the late autumn leaves were a riot of reds and golds.

Freya had carefully gathered a colourful bouquet of fallen leaves, while Dylan crept through the spooky groves of rhododendron trees, pretending to be a vampire. They'd visited the café, braving the long queue for coffee and cake; and if there was a single sour note to the morning it might have been the sudden appearance at their table of a wizened old lady, dressed as a fairy tale witch and proclaiming that in less than thirty minutes their lives would be hanging by a thread.

'Preposterous! We're only five or six miles from home, it's a journey on quiet country lanes, and this part of the world is as safe as anyone could wish for…'

There hadn't been a witch, of course. But this was the sort of scathing response Katy would have given to such a warning.

Even now, she was struggling to process the magnitude of the threat they were facing. Her ability to analyse, to be rational and calm, was repeatedly blocked by the monotone voice of denial. *This can't be real. It isn't happening.*

But it was.

Katy had been anxious from the moment the car burst into view. Watching the other driver, his jerky, hyperactive movements, had unnerved her all the more, and when she saw Adam's body language change – the way he'd turned and sprinted back to their car – a spark of rage had burned through the fear.

You had to be a man, getting worked up about something so trivial.

She and Freya had been thrown into the back of the Mazda and told to kneel on the floor. Katy had no idea what they were caught up in, though she had registered the presence of a woman on the back seat. She was probably in her forties, dark-haired and petite, her face deathly pale, her eyes unfocused.

Within a couple of seconds Freya had made a choking sound; the air in the car was a combination of sweat and tobacco and the foul stench of urine.

The driver gave an angry snort. 'Stinks, doesn't it? Carole there pissed herself.'

The woman barely reacted, but Katy could see it was true. Her dress and the leggings beneath them were dark with the stain.

The Mazda reversed, lurched forward and then jolted to a halt. Curses from the driver as Katy heard the heavy chugging sound of a tractor.

'Get right down,' Jay said, grabbing Freya's coat and hauling the collar up over her head.

'There isn't enough room,' Katy argued. 'Leave her alone.'

'Quiet.' He pulled off his own sweatshirt and draped it over Katy, who recoiled at the feel of it, the fibres warm and damp from his body heat and nervous sweat.

The car shuddered on to the verge and there was a roar from the tractor as it rumbled past, followed by what sounded like other traffic. Katy couldn't help but picture the lucky motorists, innocently driving along without a clue that these animals sat just a few feet away.

'Let's get going,' Jay said. Then he seemed to spasm. He squeezed Katy's shoulder. 'What happened to your phone?'

'I dropped it, like you told me.'

'And your husband's got one?'

It was so tempting to lie, but he wasn't likely to believe her. 'Yes.'

'What about the kids?'

'No. They're too young.'

'Course they are.' With a mocking laugh, he turned in his seat and gestured to the driver behind.

While he was distracted, Freya clawed at her arm and hissed, 'Is Dylan going to be all right?'

'I'm sure he will. Daddy's with him.'

'He'll be really scared, though. He's only seven.'

It nearly broke Katy's heart to hear such solemn, mature concern, as if Freya's two extra years meant she should be expected to take this in her stride.

'I know.' She gave a sad smile, desperate to add some words of encouragement and hope, but knew that nothing she said would ring true.

*

On the back seat, Jay was still gesticulating at the driver behind them. 'It isn't difficult, Gary. I'm saying *phones*.' Then a sigh. 'Thank Christ for that. Moron.'

Katy ducked as he turned back. His foot caught her painfully on the shoulder but she tried not to make any sound. Sneering, Jay draped the sweatshirt back over her head as if disgusted by the sight of her.

Because we're nothing to them. She reached for her daughter's hand and held it tightly. There was a sudden muffled crack, which seemed to come from directly behind them. Carole groaned and threw herself sideways. The Mazda swerved as the driver jerked in his seat, then yelled, 'Shitting hell, what's he done?'

Jay had also flinched, and was now turning again. Katy could sense the confusion in him, the barely suppressed panic. 'Fuck knows.'

'You think Gaz shot one of 'em?' the driver asked.

At that, Freya's whole body convulsed. Katy shifted as close as she could, and whispered, 'It's all right. Stay calm, Freya, please.'

After a few seconds she took the risk of peeking out. Jay was kneeling on the seat, signalling to the driver behind.

'Thumbs up,' he reported. 'All okay.'

Okay for you, Katy thought. But what about Adam? What about her son?

'This is seriously screwed,' the driver said. Unlike Jay, he had a northern accent, and a whiny tone. 'A total balls-up.'

'Well, it's done now,' Jay muttered. 'We've just gotta deal with it.'

A brooding silence fell. The driver was throwing the Mazda around and Katy felt nauseous. Where were they going, and what would happen when they got there? She was both desperate to know, and simultaneously couldn't bear to contemplate it.

She had a sudden recollection of news stories, where the survivors of a terrorist attack or some terrible natural disaster talked of the moment they'd made a deal with God: *Just let me get through this and I'll never ask for anything again*. Was that what she should be doing now, for all four of them?

It seemed unrealistic. Asking too much. But the idea of losing the kids was unbearable, and they worshipped their dad.

It's me, then. That was the deal Katy made. *I'll accept my fate, if it means the others can come out of this alive.*

She wondered if the same thoughts were running through Adam's mind. Probably. It was hard not to resent the way he'd reacted earlier, particularly as things were strained between them at the moment, but she had never doubted his love for his children. He'd die for them – just as she would – without a moment's hesitation.

All couples went through periods of restlessness, a creeping dissatisfaction and a longing to explore whether the grass was truly greener on the other side. Some marriages survived those periods, and some didn't. The secret, in Katy's view, was patience and effort, and she had blithely assumed that there would always be time and opportunities to fix anything that had gone wrong.

How foolish that seemed now.

CHAPTER SIX

At first Adam hoped to track the route they were taking. Although he'd been told to cover his face, he was lying in such a way that Gary couldn't easily check. Peeking out from under his jacket, his eyeline was restricted to treetops and sky, which didn't help much, but at least he had the advantage of knowing the area well.

The road they were on ran between the village of Lindfield and a retail outlet called Trading Boundaries, which they visited often for its café and art exhibitions. Using that knowledge, he was able to visualise most of the twists and turns, and was reasonably confident that they'd taken a left into Sloop Lane, heading south towards Chailey Green. After a few minutes they turned right: that had to be Nash Lane, in the direction of Scaynes Hill. The next right turn took them on to a much faster road, the A272, towards Lindfield.

Was it crazy to believe they were being taken home? Adam almost wanted to laugh at the thought. Then it occurred to him that Katy might have been forced to reveal their address. Were they going to be robbed, in addition to whatever else might lie in store?

He shuddered. *Don't make it worse by tormenting yourself.*

An unexpected left turn was followed by a series of manoeuvres that made little navigational sense, unless the driver was trying to throw off a pursuer – or confuse his passengers. That gave him hope. If their destination was being kept secret, perhaps that meant they were going to be released at some point?

Then again, it was hard to believe, given that Gary had so casually fired into the back of the car. That bullet could have easily killed one of them.

His train of thought was distracted by a groan from Dylan. Adam lifted the sweater off him just as he sat up and lurched forwards, spraying vomit across the back seat.

'Oi!' Gary shouted. 'What's going on?'

'I'm sorry, I'm really sorry,' Dylan cried, spitting and retching.

'Don't apologise. It's all right.' To the driver, Adam said, 'My son's been sick. Can we pull over and clean him up?'

'No. Get him back out of sight.'

'But he's upset, and I can't—'

'Do as you're told!' Gary roared. 'If I stop this car, it'll be to break every fooking bone in your body.'

After a long period of quiet, Carole made a wretched keening noise and began to whip her head from side to side. 'Let me go,' she moaned. 'Please let me go.'

'Stop it.' Jay gripped her by the shoulders and forced her to lie across his lap, her head pressed face down on the seat, where she continued to writhe, her breathing ragged.

Had this woman done something to bring such a terrible ordeal upon herself, Katy wondered, or was she every bit as innocent as they were?

A moment later, in a voice muffled by the seat cushion, Carole said, 'You didn't have to kill him.'

'Quiet!' Jay did something that prompted a squeal of pain from Carole.

Was it true? Katy nearly blurted the question. She remembered Adam's reaction, back at the car, and guessed that the woman had cried out something similar. It was because of this that they had been captured.

It was because of this that they might die.

She felt Freya shivering and squeezed her hand: another feeble gesture of support. There was practically nothing she could do to make her daughter feel better.

'Two minutes,' the driver muttered.

A moment later she heard Jay on the phone: 'Open up.'

Katy's stomach was roiling with anxiety as the car slowed and turned left, bumping over what might have been a drain cover or even a cattle grid, then came to a stop. A whir as the window slid down, and the driver said, 'Leave the gate. There's another car.'

'Another car?' It was the voice of an older man, registering shock. 'What the hell have you—?'

'Long story,' Jay cut in, and thumped the driver's seat. 'Get going.'

Katy was glad to know that Adam and Dylan must be coming to the same place, but it did little to ease the terror. Every nerve in her body seemed to be screaming, the adrenalin making her dizzy as she readied herself for the moment when she might have to make a life or death decision: to run or stay put, fight or submit, scream or be silent.

A splash of water and a clunk as the car went through a deep rut. The driver swore, yanking the wheel hard to make a 180-degree turn, then skidded to a halt.

Jay reminded them to keep their faces covered and their eyes shut. Then they were dragged out of the car and marched over what felt like a gravel path or driveway. Katy heard a door open, just in front of them, and an angry shout.

'Why wasn't she in the boot – and who in God's name are these two?'

It was a female voice, middle-aged and harsh with fury. The accent was estuary, Katy thought. London or thereabouts. The scent of perfume wafted towards her; something expensive, but designed to be used more sparingly than this.

'We had to bring 'em.' Jay's tone had turned sour, defensive.

'We kept their faces covered,' Dale added, as if trying to earn brownie points.

'And there was a complication,' Jay said, 'back at the house.'

'What sort of—?' The woman broke off. 'Where's Gary?'

A sigh from Jay. 'Let's get inside. There's a lot to explain.'

'You're damn right there is. Jesus fucking Christ, boys – you had *one thing* to do. One thing!'

The thud of footsteps receded into the building: the woman must have stormed away. Katy could sense that the men were intimidated by her, and she recognised the danger it posed. In a situation as chaotic as this, with tempers frayed, it wouldn't take much for a tragedy to occur.

CHAPTER SEVEN

Adam had no choice but to hunker down with Dylan, but he managed to find a tissue in his pocket and did his best to wipe the boy's mouth. With plenty of hugs and soothing words, Dylan stopped crying and claimed to feel slightly better.

According to his watch, it was ten to one when the journey came to an end. Adam thought they'd been in the car for about twenty or thirty minutes, and though they'd only driven on twisting country roads, that still meant they could have travelled perhaps fifteen miles in virtually any direction.

The car slowed, made a turn and stopped. He heard the window descend, and a deep male voice said, 'So who fucked up?'

'Not me, that's all I care about.'

'Now, now, Gary.' The man's tone was gentle, yet somehow contained a note of threat.

'Yeah, well. That kid finds a way to wriggle out of everything, but I aren't gonna be taking the blame for this.'

A grunt from the other man was followed by the squeak of hinges, then a metallic clang and the rattle of a chain: sounds that filled Adam with dread.

They were locked in.

The other man climbed into the passenger seat, bringing a pungent cloud of aftershave with him. The car moved away, bumping slowly over uneven ground.

'Who've we got, then?' the man asked.

'Bloke and his kid in here. A family of four, altogether.'

'Jesus. So it's waifs and strays we're collecting now?' Along with his disgust there was a hint of wry humour, as if he had experienced so much in his life that he was determined not to be fazed by anything.

'Big fooking error putting the lad in charge, Roger. But now he's made a mess I can bet it won't be him that has to clean it up, eh?'

The other man, Roger, grunted again, but said nothing more. Adam could only pray that Dylan hadn't understood the conversation, or what it might mean.

To Adam, it was sickeningly clear.

We're the mess that has to be cleaned up.

After the woman had gone, there was a moment of awkward silence. Even with her face covered, Katy could tell that the men were unsure what to do next, which told her a lot about the power structure here.

They were ushered up some steps and into the building, which stank of mildew and fast food. The floorboards were bare, stained and scratched from years of use. In some places the skirting had been torn off, and little piles of brick dust and rubble lay in the corners. Dampened wallpaper hung in finger-shaped strips, clawing at the floor.

With the front door shut, the coat was pulled away from her face and she was shoved into a large, carpetless living room with mould on the walls. There were no curtains, but dust sheets had been hung over the windows. In one corner part of the floor had rotted away, revealing a dark pit, like an open mouth. The furniture was limited to a couple of garden chairs and some plastic crates. The electricity worked, at least, because there was light from a single bare bulb.

They heard the clink of a bottle against a glass, then the woman walked in, sipping clear liquid from a tumbler. She looked older than Katy had imagined, late fifties perhaps, with masses of black, wavy hair. Her face was hard but handsome, with a slash of red lipstick and brilliant blue eyes.

After glaring at Jay, she raised her glass. 'So this is the lovely Carole Kirby?'

Flinching at the mention of her name, Carole asked, 'Who are you?'

'You can call me Maggie.' She wrinkled her nose. 'Did she wet herself?'

'Back at the house,' Jay said.

Carole raised a trembling hand to point at him. 'You killed my husband. Brian hadn't done anything. He didn't deserve...' She broke down in tears, and Maggie looked genuinely affected.

'Brian was innocent, that's true. I'm sorry for your loss.' She turned her gaze upon Freya, then Katy, and said, 'You shouldn't have been dragged into this, either.'

'Then let us go,' Katy said.

'I can't do that.'

'Look, we're not part of anything. We had a tiny bit of damage to our car, that's all. Whatever's going on here, it's nothing to do with us.'

Carole turned to stare as she registered that Katy was making a distinction between them. It hadn't been a conscious decision, and Katy saw at once how heartless it must seem... because it *was* heartless. But Katy had to put her children first, no matter what. And if Carole was their target, were the gang really likely to consider releasing her?

Maggie said, 'You see yourself as innocent bystanders, of course you do. Because of that, I'll try to make you as comfortable as possible.'

'That's not the point,' Katy said. 'We shouldn't be here at all. You have no right to keep us prisoner.'

A flash of anger transformed Maggie's face into something dark and malevolent. 'I can do whatever the hell I like, lady, and you'd better get that into your head before you make an enemy of me. Got it?'

Cowed by the intensity of her rage, Katy could only nod, and whisper, 'Yes.' She'd never seen someone's mood flip so dramatically.

Still glaring at them, Maggie murmured something to Jay and then strode out. Once she was gone, they were patted down by the two men. Katy objected as much as she dared to Freya being included, but in her case the search was cursory, and fairly respectful.

They were led into the hallway, from where Katy heard voices and the sound of a car door closing. Was that Adam and Dylan? Were they all right?

Jay opened a door next to the kitchen. Katy glimpsed a set of steps, descending into darkness. He leaned in and clicked on a light. 'Down you go.'

Katy blanched. Shook her head. 'No.'

Dale nudged Freya, who clung to her mother's waist. 'You either walk or we throw you down. Your choice.'

Still she could not move. This space reeked of danger: it was a cell, a trap. Go in there and they might never come back out…

It was Carole who reacted first. Touching her hair back into place, as if this might restore her dignity, she eased past Katy and peered into the gloom. A rickety-looking handrail wobbled as she grasped it, but she clung on and took the steps slowly.

'Go on, please,' Jay said. He had a soft, boyish face, with a rosy tint to his cheeks and clear blue eyes. If she'd met him in more normal circumstances, Katy would never have taken him for a vicious criminal. Appearances could be deceptive: she had to keep remembering that.

Taking Freya's hand, she steeled herself and led the way down. The handrail was almost useless, and some of the timber treads seemed to buckle beneath her feet. It was a relief – of a sort – to reach the solid concrete floor of this low-ceilinged cellar, weakly lit by a fluorescent strip light caked in dust and grime.

With the far end lost in shadow, Katy realised that this was a large space: probably thirty feet by twenty. The bare brick walls had once been painted white, and one was studded with holes where units and cupboards must have been removed. The remnants of various electrical fittings and some plumbing apparatus hung from the walls; a wastepipe of the sort used for dishwashers lay in a pile of gunk, and twin copper pipes emerged from the ceiling and came to an end halfway down the wall.

Most of the floor space was clear, but there was junk piled up at the darker end of the room: sacks of building sand and cement, a stack of plastic crates and offcuts of foam insulation, bound up in ancient cobwebs. A few clean patches on the floor indicated that some items had been removed quite recently, perhaps in preparation for today.

That theory was borne out by the presence of a thin plastic mattress on to which Carole had knelt. A coarse red blanket was folded beside it, and there was a bucket, a toilet roll and a bottle of mineral water.

Carole had covered her face with her hands and was sobbing quietly. Katy glanced at the steps and saw Jay at the top, staring down at them. Without a word, he retreated and shut the door. At last they had some privacy.

She drew her daughter into an embrace that almost suffocated her. 'I love you, darling. You've done so well, but I need you to go on being really brave. Can you do that for me?'

Freya was crying but managed a nod. 'I'll try.'

Katy was in no hurry to let go, and regarded Carole over her daughter's shoulder. The woman was still in shock, her skin almost bloodless, a tremor in her hand as she reached out and knocked the water over.

'What are they…? What is this?' she moaned, picking up the bottle.

It's for you, Katy thought. *They must have planned to bring you here.*

But she wasn't ready to be quite so blunt. Instead, she asked, 'Is it true, what you said about your husband?'

Carole groaned, clutching her belly as if she'd been struck. 'I wouldn't lie.'

Katy glanced at Freya; it pained her to have this conversation within her daughter's hearing. 'No, but… could it have been an accident or something?'

'It happened right in front of me.' Carole's gaze turned distant. She shuddered violently. 'It was the one on the back seat. Jay. He shot Brian in cold blood.'

CHAPTER EIGHT

The car pulled up and Gary and the other man got out. The back doors opened, with Gary issuing another warning: 'The kid's gotta shut his eyes. And you stay covered up.'

Dylan yelped with fear when the other man reached for him. He clung to Adam, crying and pleading. 'It's just for a second. It's okay, I promise.' Adam had to make these assurances without knowing whether they were true. It felt like a betrayal to wrench his hand apart from Dylan's, but it was that or risk his son getting hurt.

The men were in no mood to delay. Gary punched Adam in the kidneys as he tried to back out of the car. 'Get a move on.'

Dylan was calling for his father, and one of the men growled something that caused the boy to start howling. Blind and helpless, Adam was hustled over some rough ground and on to a concrete path, with Dylan and the other man right behind him. He stumbled up three or four steps and through a doorway into a building that stank of neglect and decay. Then a door slammed shut, his jacket was pulled from his head and he was allowed to stand free.

The other man was huge, perhaps six four, broad and bulky, with close-cropped greying hair and a bushy beard that only partly obscured a couple of scars on his left cheek. He looked to be about sixty, and his eyes were close set and hostile. He thrust Dylan forward and said, 'Quieten him down or we'll do it for you.'

Adam held his son tight, and managed to calm him enough to put his sweater back on. At the same time he tried to study his surroundings. He was sure they were in a rural location, and guessed this was an old cottage or farmhouse. From the cold, damp feel of the place, he didn't think anyone was living here permanently. More likely that these men were occupying it for a short time, and not necessarily with the permission of the owner.

As for the really important questions – who were they, why were they here, what did they intend to do with their prisoners? – Adam still had no idea.

Gary and Dale propelled them into a living room, where a middle-aged woman with dark curly hair was sitting on a fold-up garden chair, staring moodily into an empty glass. The other young man, Jay, was in the corner, riffling through Katy's bag.

'The husband and son,' she murmured to herself.

'Where are my family?' Adam asked. 'Are they all right?'

The woman studied him with cool blue eyes. She had a sunbed tan and careful make-up that couldn't quite disguise the creases and blemishes of a life hard-lived.

'You'll see in a minute.' She snapped her fingers. 'Phones.'

Jay gave her Adam's phone, and placed Katy's bag on the floor next to her chair.

'Where do you live?' she asked Adam. For a moment he was too preoccupied to answer: all he could think about was being reunited with Katy and Freya.

'Uh, Lindfield.' He saw the woman scowl, as though she didn't believe him. 'I promise—'

'Yeah, yeah. And where were you going when we…' She trailed off, gesturing at Dale in a way that made him squirm with embarrassment.

'On our way home.'

'Anyone there now?' the bearded man asked.

Will you be missed? That was what they were trying to ascertain, and Adam couldn't work out whether it would benefit him to lie.

The woman laughed at his hesitation. 'I'll take that as a no.'

Gary and Jay patted him down, taking a twenty and some coins from his pocket, as well as an old train ticket. They also removed his wallet and his watch.

'Quite a looker, isn't he, Roger?' she observed, and exchanged a sly, mocking smile with the bearded man.

Dylan writhed as he was searched, his face a mess of tears and snot. He was making a heroic effort not to cry, but when another sob escaped, the woman tutted. 'Nothing to blubber about, little boy. What's your name?'

Dylan turned predictably mute.

'Dylan,' Adam said.

She glowered. 'I wanted him to tell me. Why are you upset, Dylan? Don't you like it here?'

Bashfully, with his gaze fixed on the floorboards, Dylan shook his head.

'No? Well, I don't blame you. It's a shithole.' She snorted. 'But you're going to be a good boy for your Auntie Maggie, aren't you?'

Confused, Dylan raised his head, looking to his father for an explanation. *Is this woman related to us?*

'Answer me.' Maggie put a little more steel in her voice.

'You said a naughty word,' Dylan told her.

'True.' Maggie grinned. 'And plenty more where that came from, because I bloody *love* swearing!'

Suddenly bold, perhaps because he hated to be teased, Dylan said, 'I don't like you. You're nasty!' And he flung himself back into his father's arms.

Maggie, still pretending to be amused, held up Adam's phone. 'The code?'

At first he was grateful that her attention had switched away from Dylan, but then came the shock. They were going to read his messages.

He swallowed, and reluctantly told them. 'Double five, double six.'

Maggie tossed the phone to Jay, then delved into Katy's bag. 'And your wife's?'

'Uh, one-two-oh-five, I think.'

'Only "think"?' A smirk. 'Doesn't she trust you?'

Adam blushed like a teenager. 'Unless she's changed it, that's the code.'

Maggie tapped at the phone, and Adam saw the screen change when it unlocked. He wanted to ask how long they were going to be kept here, but felt that Dylan had already gone through enough trauma, without hearing what might prove to be a very distressing answer.

After a few seconds Maggie glanced up, flapping her hand as if irritated by their continued presence. 'That's it for now,' she said. 'Go!'

CHAPTER NINE

They'd been in the cellar for about ten minutes when the door rattled. Most of that time had been spent in dejected silence. Freya had cried herself out in her mother's arms, and now the two of them were standing in a calming embrace. Never mind that it was Sunday afternoon, and by now they should have been home and gearing up for a lovely roast dinner, the kids helping to prep the vegetables while they listened to one of Freya's playlists on Spotify; singing and dancing along to *Havana* or *Despacito*.

Funny in an ironic way, Katy thought, that this was precisely the sort of cosy routine that carved out the ruts which could one day overturn a marriage. Right now, wouldn't they give anything to be safely back in their little rut?

From their recent discussions, Katy had a good idea of the questions Adam was asking himself. *Is this all there is, all there's ever going to be? And if so, is it enough?* She'd asked them herself once or twice over the years, and the answers had always come back immediately, and in the positive. In Adam's case, she knew it might take a little longer, though she'd kept the faith that he would reach the same conclusion.

With Freya soothed, Katy tried offering comfort to Carole, but the woman barely responded. She was perched on one end of the thin mattress, with her head buried in her arms, a posture so hopeless that it drained Katy of energy. Instead of formulating a plan or even just working to keep their spirits up, she was overcome with dread.

There won't be a future because we're going to die, there won't be a future—

Then a clunk as the padlock was removed. The door opened and a strange bulky figure loomed in the doorway, blocking most of the light from the hall.

'Hold on tight!' said a voice, and Katy's heart leapt. Freya heard it, too, and both of them hurried to the foot of the steps.

'Adam!' Katy cried.

'We're all right,' he said. 'What about you two?'

'Yes. We're okay.'

She watched as he started down, gingerly descending the steps with Dylan in his arms. Katy put her weight against the handrail to lend it some stability. She guided him to the bottom and took Dylan, freeing Adam to hug his daughter. The children continued to cling to them while Katy and Adam held each other briefly and kissed.

'I love you,' Adam whispered. It was the first time he'd said it for a while, and even in these circumstances it caused a little jolt; he must have registered her reaction, for he added, 'And I'm sorry. Will you forgive me?'

'Forgive...?' For a moment Katy was expecting some dreadful admission, but he gestured at the ceiling.

'Being so hot-headed. It was a terrible mistake, but we can't afford to fall out over it. We have to put everything else behind us.'

'I know. If I was angry, it's nothing compared to how scared I was. We heard a gunshot and thought you'd been...' She shook her head; couldn't say it.

'The guy did it as a warning, that's all.' Adam cupped his hands against her cheeks, and kissed her again. 'We're going to get through this, I swear to you.'

It sounded like a foolish boast, even to his own ears, but Adam felt he had to say it. Just as he was compelled to play down the fact that Gary had fired into the back seat without looking.

He was still holding Katy when he spotted the cellar's other occupant, the woman from the Mazda whose outburst had set these events in motion. She was kneeling on a tatty-looking mattress, regarding him with a lonely, haunted gaze.

'That's Carole,' Katy whispered. 'She says they murdered her husband.'

Adam nodded, and took a couple of steps towards the woman, crouching until he was level with her eyeline. She had a delicate, elfin quality that in these circumstances made her seem even more vulnerable, as though she might shatter at the slightest touch.

'Carole? My name's Adam. Are you okay?'

She shook her head slowly, her mouth tightly closed.

'Are you hurt? Is there anything we can do for you?'

Another shake of the head. Adam glanced over his shoulder, saw Freya and Dylan in their mother's arms, and wished they weren't within earshot.

'Can you tell me what happened earlier, to your husband?'

Carole made a tiny choking sound. 'They shot him.'

Adam eased closer, sensing that he had to be careful, give her plenty of time. He also wanted to speak as quietly as possible, hoping the children wouldn't hear.

'Where was this? At your home?'

'Yes. In Bluebell Lane. We were…' She swallowed, then lifted her shoulders in a shrug. 'It was a normal Sunday. I was in the kitchen when someone knocked on the door. It was the… the innocent-looking one, Jay. Holding a parcel. As soon as I opened the door he stormed in. The others had been hiding beyond the porch. I couldn't… couldn't stop them…'

Her breathing was too rapid, panic rising as she relived the ordeal. Adam rested a hand on her arm, and to his surprise she launched herself forward and sobbed on his shoulder. After a minute or so, she sat back and began to speak.

'They took me into the drawing room. We have some quite valuable artwork, and there's a safe. I thought they would demand the combination, but...'

She paused, taking several deep breaths. 'They asked about my phone, my handbag. And they were making lots of noise, as though they didn't care if anyone heard. My husband must have realised what was going on... but he wouldn't have known they were armed. He was so brave. So brave.'

'He took them on?'

'Y-yes. They were saying I had to go with them – it didn't make any sense – but then he burst into the room, holding a golf club. We had burglars a few years ago, a couple of kids, and a golf club saw them off.' She sniffed. 'Not this time. Jay grabbed me around the neck, using me as a shield when he fired the gun. Brian was hit in the chest. He didn't stand a chance...'

Adam winced. 'What happened after that?'

'Bedlam. You could see at once that... that he was dead. The men started yelling at each other, and in the shock I passed out. I've no idea how long for, but when I came round they were carrying me to the car. They were still arguing as we drove away – I remember thinking that the driver would probably kill us all, the speed he was doing.'

'He nearly did.'

Carole wiped her eyes, and regarded Adam as if seeing him properly for the first time. 'That's how you came to be involved?'

'Yep. Dale almost hit us coming out of Bluebell Lane, and his car threw up a stone that broke one of our lights.'

He glanced ruefully at Katy, who was sitting with her arms around the kids. She was staring straight at him, her expression difficult to read, but he couldn't miss the hint of an accusation in her gaze. *You could have just let it go, and we wouldn't be here now...*

*

Carole went to pat his arm but didn't quite make contact. 'I'm sorry you got caught up in this. I shouldn't have called out.'

Adam tried to stay impassive, but the question worming through his mind nearly slipped out: *Why did you, then? You must have known I was powerless to help you.*

As if he had spoken, Carole said, 'It was instinctive, I suppose. But now, if anything happens to your family…'

He shook his head. 'I made the decision to go after their car.' He gestured at the ceiling. 'They're the only ones to blame.'

She gave a small, embarrassed smile. 'Thank you.'

To break the awkward silence that followed, Adam introduced Freya and Dylan, and Katy brought them over to say hello. These stilted attempts at normality were almost perverse in the circumstances, but Adam felt they had to make an effort.

Carole shifted even further to the edge of the mattress. 'Would you like to come on here? It's a bit better than the floor.'

As Katy encouraged the children to sit down, sudden noises overhead made them gasp: the thud of footsteps and the muffled sounds of an argument. Adam stood tall, the low ceiling only inches above his head, the paint shining with condensation like a layer of fevered sweat, and tried to work out what was being said.

Will we die here? The idea seemed to suck the air from his lungs.

Then Katy was at his side, murmuring, 'This doesn't happen, does it? Not here, where we live.'

'It's unthinkable. And yet we've got to deal with it.'

He examined his surroundings. The cellar was rectangular in shape, with the stairs midway along one of the shorter sides. The single strip light, caked in grime, illuminated little more than half the room. Adam conducted a careful search, hoping to find something they could use to escape – or at least to defend themselves. The remnants of some pipework interested him for a while, though copper was a relatively weak material, and in any case he couldn't see a way of prising it free of the brackets.

At the far end, behind the pile of junk, he discovered a hatch set high in the wall, that probably led outside. It had been crudely covered with thick timber planks, screwed tightly into the wall on either side. Even with the right tools, removing them would take a lot of time and physical effort, and it couldn't be done quietly.

Anything else? He started inching his way along the wall, touching and pressing the surface at different heights, hoping to discover a weakness. With large properties, the cellars often comprised two or more separate rooms, offering the chance to break through into somewhere that might have a way out.

'Adam.' Katy's voice was soft but urgent. He turned and saw she was staring up at the cellar door. In the silence he heard the clunk of a padlock as it opened and bumped against the timber.

CHAPTER TEN

Maggie Nolan was scared, but couldn't show it.

She showed anger instead, though not too much: even this bunch of halfwits might spot that her rage was intended to mask the fear. The first proper day of action: how could so much have gone wrong already? It felt like she was mounting a salvage operation before they were even afloat.

And Jay... Jesus wept, Jay...

'You shot him.'

'I didn't have any choice, right? He came flying at us, swinging what I thought was a sword.'

'A golf club,' Gary muttered.

'Yeah, but it looked like a sword.'

'And could still take your head off,' Dale said, earning a vicious look from Maggie.

'I'll get to you in a minute,' she growled. Back to Jay: 'He was supposed to be away.'

'Don't I know it?'

'So what did Carole say?'

'Couldn't get anything out of her. She's a basket case.'

'Great!' Maggie jabbed a finger at Dale. 'And how come we've got the fucking Partridge family in the cellar?'

Dale went crimson. 'It wasn't... I dunno how it happened.'

Maggie turned to Gary, who had been conspicuously quiet. 'He drove a bit wild, like. Cut someone up, and I think a stone broke the fella's light. He started flashing, driving on our tail.

Jay got worried about it drawing attention, so he told us to pull over.'

'Even then we'd have been okay.' Jay was on the defensive, and not happy with Gary for putting him there. 'Dale was talking to the guy when Carole suddenly screamed for help.'

'Why wasn't she in the boot?'

'Why'd you think?' Jay shot back, and Maggie clapped a hand over her face.

'You've brought the body here?'

'What else could we do?'

Roger chipped in: 'Couldn't leave it, to be fair. Say they had a visitor dropping by?'

'Anyway, we did our best to shut her up. She bloody bit me.' Jay showed her his hand, which had a semi-circle of red marks on the fleshy pad above his thumb.

'Get that disinfected,' Maggie told him. 'I don't want you ending up in hospital.'

Jay sloped off to the kitchen, where they had a small medical kit. Maggie took a gulp of vodka. Shouldn't be drinking this much, she knew. It would dull her edges, and allow her decisions to be swayed by emotion. But the alternative – cold sobriety – was more than she could bear.

'Right,' she said. 'Any good ideas for what we do with them?'

The Yorkshire contingent said nothing, though Gary made a pistol with his hand and pointed it at his temple.

Maggie glanced at Roger. 'Messy,' he said.

'It's *all* a frigging mess.'

'Certainly is. So shouldn't we give some thought to bailing out now?'

Maggie sighed, then shook her head. Of the four of them, it was Roger's wisdom she trusted the most, but she wasn't going to make any snap decisions.

'Gotta lose the car, at least,' he added. 'Fire or water. Otherwise, the tiniest trace of DNA and we're all up shit creek.'

Jay came back, a phone in his hand. That reminded Maggie: 'Any messages for Carole?'

'Not yet.'

'Maybe he knows hubby was home?' Roger suggested.

'Need to have a talk with her,' Maggie said.

'First, we've got to do something about this.' Jay held up the phone. 'There's a problem.'

The door opened and Gary came halfway down the steps. Adam felt a surge of hatred for the man who had fired his gun just inches from Dylan's head.

'Mum and Dad, you're wanted,' he said. 'Leave the kids here.'

'No!' Katy shouted, as Freya and Dylan instinctively clung to their parents.

Gary raised his hand, showing them the gun. '*Now.*'

'Do you need both of us, or can my wife stay with them?' Adam asked.

'Please,' Katy added. 'If they start to panic, it doesn't help anyone.'

Gary thought about it, then nodded unhappily. 'Come on, then.'

It felt like a victory to Adam, albeit a minor one. He quickly rose, trying to appear calm and fighting off the idea that he might never see them again. But his nerves betrayed him when he tripped on one of the steps, causing another flare of pain from the ankle he'd caught in the car door.

At the top he briefly considered trying to attack Gary and wrestle the gun from him, but that notion died when he saw Roger was there, too. Leaving Gary to lock the cellar door, Roger gripped Adam's arm and escorted him to the living room.

The woman, Maggie, was standing by the window, peering through a gap in the sheet that had been tacked over the window. There was no sign of the other two men, and Adam wondered if both were in disgrace after what had happened.

Maggie turned, frowned, and said, 'Where's his wife?'

Roger deflected the question to Gary, who had hurried into the room. 'The kids were kicking off. I can get her if you like…?'

'No.' She indicated one of the boxes. 'Sit.'

Adam complied, and felt Roger's presence at his shoulder. Gary shut the door, leaned back against it and crossed his arms. This felt horribly like the precursor to a beating, but if so there wouldn't be much he could do about it.

Maggie dragged a garden chair towards him, sat down and waved Katy's phone in his face. 'Your wife's had a message. Someone called Suzy, about a party.'

Party? Perhaps it was just the relief that no one had laid into him, but Adam almost grinned at the absurdity of the concept. Parties took place in the normal world; not in the terrible, twisted dimension they now inhabited.

Then he remembered: 'Oh, shit.'

'It's a mate of your son's?' Maggie said.

'Yes. And it's this afternoon.' He glanced at his watch, found only his bare wrist, then looked around the room in confusion. 'What time is it?'

'Doesn't matter. He's not going. But you need to send a reply. Tell her he's ill.'

'All right.' Adam held out his hand, but Maggie had more to say.

'Roger there is ready to step in. You try adding anything to the message and there'll be a price to pay, you understand?'

'I get it.' He took the phone, and for a moment felt sick with the desire to make a call for help. Here was the potential for rescue… and yet it couldn't be used.

With nervous, clumsy fingers he wrote a brief text, leaning awkwardly so that Roger could see the screen.

Hi Suzy, so sorry but Dylan has a bug and I don't think we can risk bringing him to the party. I know that Noah will be disappointed but I hope he still has a lovely time xxx

He showed it to Maggie, and at her nod of approval he was allowed to hit send. His heart ached as she took the phone back.

'What's going to happen to us?' he asked.

'Nothing. If you do as you're told.'

He couldn't help but look sceptical. 'So you'll let us go?'

'Eventually.'

'What does that mean?' He must have sounded too confident, for the query provoked a low growl from Roger.

'It means, *eventually*. When we've done what we came here to do.'

Which is what? It was the obvious question, but Adam understood not to ask. That was information he couldn't be allowed to have.

Maggie's thin smile acknowledged his discretion. 'We can't release you while there's any chance you might disrupt our plans.'

'How would we?'

'Don't be playing dumb with me, fella. I'm sure you're not just a pretty face.'

Adam felt a shiver of disgust at her predatory gaze. 'But after… whatever it is, we're free to go?'

Maggie nodded, but her expression didn't give him much reassurance. Despite the risk, he felt compelled to push for more.

'So even though we've seen your faces, we know your names…?'

Her face hardened. 'After this, you'll have good reason to say nothing, I can guarantee—'

She stopped abruptly, and looked down.

The phone in her hand was ringing.

CHAPTER ELEVEN

Once Adam had been taken away, it took Katy a while to convince the children that their father wasn't going to die. 'They're not going to hurt him,' she insisted, even while she feared that the opposite was true.

Dylan was the hardest to console. He lay across her lap, his head on her chest, and kept rubbing at his left ear. When she asked what was wrong, he said, 'It still hurts from when the man shot his gun.'

'Where was the gun? I mean, where was it pointing?'

'I don't know. But it was close to my head, I think. The bullet went through the back seat. It made me feel really funny, and I don't remember the next bit. I sort of went to sleep, and then Daddy was shouting, and he gave me a cuddle.'

This account, delivered in a sombre, quavering voice, nearly felled Katy. Dylan's description sounded far worse than the impression she'd got from Adam, though she could understand why he had played it down.

Beside her, Freya was chewing compulsively on a thumbnail. 'They kill people, don't they?' As she said it, she looked at Carole, who could hardly deny the accusation. 'So they might kill us.'

'Don't think like that.' Carole suppressed a shudder. 'They're bad people, but you haven't done anything wrong.'

She exchanged a quick, uneasy glance with Katy, as if expecting thanks for this gesture of support. Katy managed a brief smile, but the comment seemed to imply that Carole's husband *had* done something wrong.

Why did they kidnap you? she wondered. Why did you drag us into it?

What are you hiding?

It seemed to take an age for the phone to stop ringing. Only when it switched to voicemail did Maggie let out a breath. 'That was Suzy.'

Adam nodded. 'Her son and Dylan are inseparable. He'll be devastated that Dylan is missing the party.' This was a slight exaggeration, but he saw it was a chance to unsettle her, put a little pressure on.

She ignored him while she powered off Katy's phone. Adam kept his gaze on her. 'Can you at least give me an idea of how long we'll be here?'

'A day or two,' she said, and then swore, turning to look behind her. Adam's phone was on a packing crate in the corner, jumping as it vibrated across the surface.

'It'll be her,' he said, though he fervently hoped he wasn't wrong about that, recalling the text he'd deleted earlier. 'She'll want to find out how Dylan is.'

Roger snatched up the phone, just as it fell silent. They all relaxed, but as he walked back it began to vibrate again. 'Bloody hell,' he muttered.

Maggie pointed at Adam. 'You'll have to talk to her, make it clear he can't come. And put it on speaker,' she added.

'Same deal as before.' Roger gave him the phone. 'It'll be your kids that suffer if you try anything.'

Adam's mouth was dry. He might have been about to give a presentation or a speech. Moistening his lips, he connected the call. 'Suzy, hi—'

'Adam, I couldn't get through to Katy – about her message?'

'Yes. Sorry to let you down.'

'Oh, it's Dylan I'm worried about.' If she noticed how unnatural he sounded, she gave no sign of it. 'What sort of bug – food poisoning, do you think?'

'No idea, really.' Suzy Chadwick had a strong personality, and Adam realised that he couldn't afford to sound too vague. Better to use the truth, as much as possible. 'We went to Sheffield Park this morning, and he was sick in the car on the way home. It wasn't a pretty sight.' He forced a chuckle, and noted cautious approval on Maggie's face.

'Oh no, I can imagine. How awful!' Suzy's well-bred accent sounded laughably proper as it echoed in this cold, crumbling building. 'Noah will be so disappointed. Why don't you bring Dylan along, even if it's just to sit on the sidelines?'

'I don't think—'

'Because you know how they perk up once they're with their friends. He could leave at any time if it gets too much…'

As a successful recruitment manager, Suzy had a way of flinging out proposals that carried the force of a contractual obligation. Maggie was glaring at him, emphatically shaking her head.

'It's a l-lovely idea, Suzy,' he stammered, 'and thank you. But he's white as a ghost at the moment, and tucked up in bed.'

'Oh, the poor poppet.' There was a noise in the background, someone calling Suzy's name. 'Whoops, got to run. If he perks up, *pleeease* bring him along – and if not we'll drop by at yours afterwards, because he is *not* missing out on his party bag!'

And with that, she was gone. Maggie snatched the phone from his hand and clattered it against Katy's, as if deliberately trying to break them both.

'These gadgets do my fucking head in.'

'Call her back?' Roger suggested, though he didn't sound particularly enthusiastic about the idea. 'Or text her and make some excuse?'

'You heard what she's like. She'll come to our house, no matter what I say.' Adam played up his frustration, hoping this might somehow work to their advantage. 'In fact, I bet Dylan has told Noah what we've bought him, and he doesn't want to wait for his present.'

'Spoilt little brats,' Roger muttered. He took the phones from Maggie and said, 'What next?'

She wiped her face with her hands. 'Put him in the cellar. I need to think.'

Katy's thoughts were becoming increasingly morbid: imagining funerals, the clear-out and sale of their home. The effects of grief on her parents, on Adam's father, on their siblings and wider families, their friends and colleagues – all of whom, in time, would find their memories fading, until eventually some of them would have to be prompted with a question: *What was the name of that family...?*

The fear had become a physical pain, just below her sternum. She pressed a hand to it and groaned, and Carole gave her a questioning look.

'I'm all right,' Katy said, for the children's benefit. She was burning with questions for Carole, but most of them were too blunt to ask in front of Freya and Dylan. Instead, she tried small talk.

'What, er, what do you do?'

'Do?' Confused at first, and then: 'Oh, you mean work? I don't, anymore. I was a legal secretary when I met Brian. In fact, he was my boss. I'm his second wife. A horrible cliché, I suppose. He's quite—' She coughed. 'He was quite a bit older than me.'

Katy nodded as politely as she could. It would have been too easy to sneer, and now she'd got Carole talking about her husband she wanted to continue, in case there was an explanation to be had. But before she could speak again, the cellar door was unlocked.

The children automatically cringed, then gasped with delight as their father appeared. 'Daddy!' Freya bowled into his arms the second he reached the ground.

'I'm fine, I'm fine. It's all right.' Adam knelt down in front of Katy, and said, 'We'd got a couple of messages from Suzy. About the party.'

'Oh my god. I'd completely forgotten about that.'

'Me too.' He gazed sadly at Dylan, who looked confused rather than disappointed. 'Sorry about this. I know how much you wanted to go.'

'Doesn't matter.'

It ought to matter, Katy thought. Each wave of anger and bitterness was like raking at an open wound. They shouldn't be allowed to do this to her children.

'I had to call her, and say he was ill,' Adam said.

'You spoke to her? Were you able—?'

'Not a chance. The phone was on speaker, and one of them was standing over me.' He seemed irritated by her question, or perhaps by the burst of hope that had accompanied it. 'But you know what Suzy's like. Even when I convinced her that Dylan couldn't make it, she's insisted on coming round with a party bag later this afternoon.'

'To our house?' Katy sat back, scrambling to make sense of this development. 'What are they going to do?'

'I don't know. They brought me back here while they think about it.'

She mulled it over, picturing Suzy turning up at the empty house. When no one came to the door, she'd phone one of them, and what would happen then? Dylan was supposed to be at home in bed.

Finally, she said, 'I can't work out whether this is good for us, or not.'

'Neither can I.' Adam's pensive gaze switched to Carole, then back to Katy. 'What they did say is that they intend to hold us for a day or two, and then let us go.'

Katy heard the doubt in his voice but chose to stay hopeful. It was Carole who said, 'Do you believe them?'

'I'm not sure. I want to believe it, and I suppose that might be skewing my judgement.'

'Mm. I don't see them letting *me* go, do you?'

She'd mumbled so quietly that Katy wasn't sure if Adam had heard. Looking inward, he said, 'There's something they're planning to do, and whatever it is must be connected to you in some way. You or your husband.'

'Like what?' Carole's voice was cold, resentful.

'I don't know. Do you own a business? Or something they could steal?'

Carole looked too stricken to reply. Katy reached for Adam's arm and said, 'We were just talking about this. Her husband, Brian, was a lawyer.'

'Criminal law?' Adam asked. 'Do you think maybe he dealt with them?'

Carole shook her head. 'Brian was always in corporate law. For the past six years he's run the legal department of a telecommunications company. I don't see how he'd ever have encountered... people like this.'

'No. All right.' Adam sighed. 'But it sounds like you were targeted, and there must be a reason for that. Something in his private life – or yours?'

'It couldn't be Brian's first wife?' Katy asked, earning a sharp look from both of them; Adam was surprised, Carole offended.

'She remarried, lives in Portugal, quite happily. She got a very generous settlement.' Carole had reared up as if to go on the attack, then gasped as the cellar door was unlocked again.

This time it was Jay. He leaned down and took in their secretive little huddle, then zeroed in on Katy.

'Come here. Bring Dylan with you.'

Katy jolted upright, her heart racing with panic. 'What? Why?'

'The kid's going to the party.'

CHAPTER TWELVE

'Are you sure about this?' Roger asked, when Jay had been sent to fetch the woman and her son.

'Nope.' Maggie had known Roger for nearly thirty years, and was honest with him in ways that she could never be with anyone else. 'But what choice do we have? We can't afford for this friend to turn up at their house and wonder where they are.'

Roger spread his huge arms, as if framing the size of the problem. 'How about another text, saying they got called away?'

'After just claiming the kid's not well?' Maggie exhaled. 'Shit! I wish you'd come up with that idea before he spoke to her.'

'Didn't know their friend was such a pushy bitch, did we?'

She snorted. 'Let's see what the mother says. If she thinks her boy can keep his mouth shut, then we'll do it.'

'All right. But if we're still going ahead—'

'We are.'

'Well, then isn't it better to keep them all locked away, and out of contact?'

'Not really. We'll have no idea who might be trying to find them. And just think about it: a whole family goes missing, practically on Voronov's doorstep. To a guy as paranoid as him, one news report could be enough to ruin everything.'

'Yeah, I can see what you mean,' Roger conceded. 'Though it still comes back to keeping close. Being able to control them.'

'I think I've got it covered. I need to have a word with Gary—' She cut the conversation with a nod of her head; Katy and the boy were being brought in.

*

Dylan was disorientated, wobbly on his feet, and had to be helped up the steps, but at least there was a measure of relief to be out of the cold, gloomy cellar. Katy's mind was still in turmoil over what she'd learned from Adam. It had to mean a crime was being planned, but what was it – and how did it relate to Carole and her husband? She'd been sniffy about the idea of a connection to his profession, and yet Katy couldn't stop pondering.

Lawyers and criminals: the two went together, didn't they?

Maggie was waiting for them, sipping what Katy assumed was alcohol. All four of the men stood around the room, grimly appraising their prisoners. Under the fierce glow of their attention, Dylan buried his face in Katy's stomach.

'Do you think he's up to this?' Roger asked.

The question was directed at Maggie, but when she failed to respond, Katy said, 'How do you plan to do it?'

'You take him to the party,' Maggie said, 'just as you would have done normally. Where's it being held?'

'At a leisure centre in Burgess Hill.'

'And I assume you'd just drop him off and collect him?'

Katy swallowed. 'Yes, probably, but I think—'

'No, no. I don't want you staying there. What is it, an hour? Two hours?'

'Two.' Katy was stroking Dylan's head, trying to infuse him with enough confidence to relax his grip on her. 'But he's bound to be upset.'

'Can't be helped. What I want to know is whether he's able to keep quiet about this.'

Katy thought that was unlikely, but she feared the consequences of admitting it. Right now this seemed like a real opportunity to get away or raise the alarm.

'I don't know,' she said. 'I think it'll take some coaching.'

Maggie didn't look too pleased about that. She took a gulp of her drink, shut her eyes for a few seconds and gave a tiny shudder. When she opened her eyes, she had somehow taken on the persona of a severe but kindly acquaintance.

'I'm sure your husband has shared the news, but I'll explain it again. This whole thing is very… unfortunate. I'm sorry that you and your family have been caught up in it.'

Katy nodded stiffly. A couple of the men were standing in her eyeline and they didn't look sorry about anything; just angry.

'This is the deal,' Maggie went on. 'You've only got to stay with us for a day or so. Once our business is finished, you'll be released.' She sensed Katy's doubt and added, 'The names we're using aren't our real names. The cars aren't registered to us. This place, even if you managed to find it again, isn't connected to us, and after we're done we'll be going a long, long way from here.'

'What about…?' Katy began, then coughed, her voice struggling to form a question that might make these assurances harder to believe.

'Carole?' Maggie said, astutely. 'We don't have any reason to hurt her. Obviously in her case she won't be able to let things rest, but we're not too worried about that. Whereas you and your family won't have any reason to think about this ever again.'

As if it were that simple, Katy thought. But she had to hide her disgust, as best she could.

'All we need right now is for you to act normally. Take Dylan to the party, let him have fun with his pals and everyone's happy, all right?' Maggie beamed, but Katy produced only a tepid smile in response.

Could it really be that straightforward? Were they going to be released tomorrow, allowed to go home and pretend that none of this had happened?

*

'Can I have a minute with Dylan, please?' Katy asked.

Maggie hesitated before relenting. She stood up, nodding to the others. But before he left the room, Jay knelt at Dylan's side. 'Hey, fella. Can you tell me what sort of party it is?'

Dylan was mute, his face still pressed against Katy. 'Soft play,' she said.

'Yeah? That'll be fantastic. I bet you have pretend fights? Or playing soldiers?'

Almost despite himself, Dylan nodded.

'And who's best at climbing? Is it you, or… Noah?'

'No, I'm better than him.' Responding to the challenge, Dylan turned to face the man. 'And I'm a faster runner, though he says he is, but he isn't.'

Jay tutted. 'Some kids just don't like to admit it, do they?'

'He can throw further than me.' By now the others had filed out; with only Jay remaining, Dylan acquired a little more confidence. 'And he's better at football, though I do brilliant free kicks.'

'Do you now?' Jay chuckled. 'I was a goalie myself. Famous for my diving saves.'

He mimicked flinging himself sideways. Dylan didn't quite laugh, but he made a little gulping sound to signal amusement. Jay gave him a playful slap on the arm.

'You have a great time, okay? Forget about all this shi—' A pretend gasp. 'All this rubbish, I mean. Enjoy yourself, and perhaps save a bit of cake for your sister, yeah?'

Dylan nodded shyly. 'Okay.'

Jay got up and hurried out. Although his intervention had helped to settle Dylan's nerves, Katy fought off a sense of gratitude, telling herself this was probably just an act on his part.

And if it wasn't? Well, that would be even more frightening, she realised: to think that Jay might be capable of genuine warmth and kindness, and yet could still treat them with such inhumanity.

Now it was Katy's turn to kneel and face her son. 'Do you understand what you've got to do?'

Dylan nodded, biting on his lip. 'I don't want to go.'

'I know. But it's very important. You've been such a brave boy so far, and I need you to go to the party and play with your friends, but don't say *anything* about this.' She indicated the room around them. 'We have to keep it a secret, okay? A really big secret, and then tomorrow we'll be going home.'

'Have I got to go to school?'

Katy flinched. She hadn't even begun to think that far ahead.

'I'm not sure, yet. Let's just focus on the party for now, and keeping this a special secret. Agreed?'

She enfolded his hand in hers, kissed it softly, then blew a raspberry. He giggled a protest, and pulled away from her.

'All sorted?' Maggie was back in the room, Katy's phone in her hand. She had a message ready to send: *Dylan feeling better and says he wants to come. Is that okay?*

Suzy's reply was almost instantaneous. *Fab news! See you soon xxx*

'What time does it start?' Maggie asked.

'It's, uh, three till five.' According to her phone, it was now almost 2 p.m.

'Plenty of time, then.'

Is it? Katy thought. That suggested they weren't very far away. Nervously she said, 'We'll need to go home first, though.'

Maggie's eyes narrowed. 'Why?'

'To get the present for Noah. We can't turn up without it – otherwise Suzy'll want to come back afterwards to collect it.' She saw that Maggie was almost persuaded, and pressed on: 'Plus we need to get changed. Dylan was sick in the car, and we're both grimy from the cellar. People will wonder what's up with us.'

She was perhaps overstating it a little, and said no more. She could tell that Maggie was trying to work out if she was being played, but grudgingly the woman agreed.

'All right. You'll be going with Gary and Dale. One of them will be close by at all times, on an open phone to me. A single word out of place and the deal I've just made is off the table.' A flickering glance at Dylan, who didn't seem to be listening but probably was. 'Do I need to spell out what that could mean?'

Katy became conscious of her son's hand in hers, soft and clammy and gently writhing, conveying his desperation to be away from here.

'No,' she said.

CHAPTER THIRTEEN

All work and no play…

'Makes Holly a dull girl,' Holly murmured to herself. And she was right. Sunday afternoon and she'd been working solidly for some seven or eight hours.

Well, almost solidly. She'd broken off a few times, to send a couple of personal texts – somewhat inadvisably – and there had been that abrupt and very unwelcome ninety seconds of full-throated sobbing, which had threatened to morph into a panic attack, but otherwise it had been nose to the grindstone (whatever that was) for the whole of the Lord's day of rest.

She'd fired off dozens of emails and messages on social media to her 'minions' – as she not-quite-jokingly addressed them – issuing a torrent of instructions and criticisms and admonishments, always urging *more* effort, *more* dedication to the tasks that brought home their bacon. She now employed almost twenty subcontractors, based in various time zones around the world, whose job was to create or repackage content, plus a couple of editors and a whizzkid in viral marketing from upstate New York who accepted a grinding schedule and shit remuneration on the basis that he was being groomed to take her place in a year or two; maybe three at the most.

Viewed from the perspective of her website, you might assume this was an operation run from an upmarket loft-style office space in a newly gentrified district of London; instead the nerve centre was her modest two-bedroom apartment in Northampton. It was here that she took care of her own tasks: principally data analysis, and managing the key account relationships with the companies who employed her services to drive traffic to their sites.

And counting the money, of course.

Money, in Holly's view, had always been an exceedingly good thing. She'd devoted a lot of her life to acquiring and investing it – her current home was actually the smallest dwelling in a portfolio of eleven properties scattered across the country, and she was already at a point where the rental income alone could provide her with enough to live on.

At her current rate of progress she would be able to retire at fifty, or maybe even forty-five, and thereafter enjoy a sumptuous lifestyle on a good seven-figure fund. Which was fine and dandy, except for one thing.

She had no one to share it with. The men in her life had invariably let her down. They had left her, they had hurt her, they had died on her. Increasingly she had come to fear that hers was to be the fate of the last apple in the bowl: long past its sell-by date, its lustre gone; a dry, shrivelled, ugly thing that no one could possibly desire. This was the only conceivable future… unless.

Unless, somehow, everything changed.

Unless a miracle occurred.

And Holly, for all the hard-nosed logic and objectivity that she brought to her work, still found it possible to believe in miracles.

CHAPTER FOURTEEN

Adam had somehow expected Katy and Dylan to return before going to the party. In normal circumstances it was unthinkable that they would go anywhere without saying goodbye, but of course this was anything but normal. The gang couldn't care less about tender farewells.

When Freya grasped that fact, she grew surly and tearful, slumping down on the mattress with a deep sigh of resignation. 'They've gone, haven't they?'

'Looks like it.' Adam caught a sad, sympathetic smile from Carole as he put his arm around his daughter. 'It's good, really.'

'I don't think Dylan will enjoy it. Not after this.'

'I know.' Adam tutted; his daughter could be scarily perceptive. 'But hopefully he'll be able to forget everything for a couple of hours.'

'And afterwards, they're coming back here?'

'I believe that's the idea.'

'What about tomorrow? We've got school. And you and Mum will be going to work.'

'I don't know about tomorrow. They've said they'll let us go as soon as they can.'

'Why not now?' Her voice rose, cracking with emotion. 'It's not fair. It's horrible and I don't like it.'

'Freya, darling. You've got every right to be angry—'

'I want to go home!'

He caught Carole's eye again and felt embarrassed. His efforts to console his daughter were woefully inadequate.

'Let's all try and be positive,' she said. 'I'm sure that by tomorrow evening we'll be back home.'

Freya sniffed, and rubbed her eyes. 'And then we'll have to go to a police station, won't we, and be interviewed by a detective? Like on TV.'

'I suppose we will,' Adam said. 'Though it's probably not a good idea to talk about that while we're here.'

'In case they're listening?' Freya gestured at the ceiling. 'Will they shoot us if we go to the police?'

'No, no,' Adam said, and his promise was echoed by Carole.

'Your dad's right, though. Best not to mention the police.'

Freya started peering into the shadows as if someone might be down here with them. Leaning in close to her father, she whispered, 'When Mum's at the party, can't she get someone to call 999?'

It was a tantalising idea, and one that Adam kept thinking about. He'd hoped for a chance to discuss it with Katy before they went, so they could gauge the risks together. But how could he explain to Freya that she and Adam might be the ones to suffer if Katy were to raise the alarm?

Even if she managed to contact the police, she had no idea where they were being held. Maybe, if the police apprehended whoever was there with her, they might be able to get the location. But that was sure to take a while, and in the meantime the gang would realise something had gone wrong, cut their losses and flee... leaving three dead bodies in the cellar.

'I'm not sure Mum will be able to do that,' he said, 'but even if she doesn't, they'll be back here with us and we'll all go home together.'

Freya held his gaze for a moment, then nodded with a degree of sullen-eyed disbelief. A foretaste of the teenage years to come, perhaps, when she would no doubt challenge every word he said.

Reflecting on that, Adam knew that he would gladly – joyfully – take any level of adolescent rebellion, if it meant she survived this ordeal and reached adulthood, safe and well.

It felt like a good sign when her attention turned to more practical issues. 'Where are we going to sleep? And what about food, and a toilet?'

'We'll have to see what we can do to make it more comfortable. Pretend we're on a Bear Grylls show, trying to survive in the wild.' His grin teased a reluctant smile from her. 'Let's have a look round and see if there's anything we've missed.'

'Like an en suite bathroom?' Carole said drily, but Adam took the remark in good spirit.

'Yeah – or a drinks fridge with Coke and beer.'

Freya snorted. 'A big bag of Maltesers, and an iPad.'

Adam felt proud of his daughter for mustering some humour. Occupying their time in this way wasn't such a bad idea, although it was more about the distraction than the likelihood of finding anything useful.

Or so he thought. But in the shadows to the right of the steps, he discovered a curious panel attached to the wall. It was about three feet above the ground and measured about four feet square, formed of half a dozen tongue-and-groove timber slats. The slats were fixed with rusted flat-head screws at each end, and in places the wood was warped and split, and blackened with rot.

It was a cover, he realised. And you didn't fix a cover to a wall unless there was something behind it.

An opening?

Katy and Dylan were put into the back of the Mazda, with Gary squeezing in next to them. At least this time they were able to sit on the seats, although he still made them hunker down, and forced them to wear some makeshift blindfolds – strips of fabric cut from a grubby towel. Dylan snuffled quietly, too scared of Gary to cry properly.

Roger accompanied them along the bumpy track, then got out to open the gate. 'Watch your driving this time,' he reminded Dale, before seeing them off.

It was advice that Dale seemed to ignore, judging by the way they were flung from side to side on every bend. Katy quickly lost count of the changes of direction. With only her hearing to rely on, she guessed from the occasional roar of a passing car and the hiss of tyres through water that they were keeping to quiet country lanes.

After a few minutes of silence, Gary asked her about the venue for the party. Did it have CCTV?

'I suppose so.' Realising that cameras might deter him from coming in, she said, 'Actually, I think there's one at the entrance, and maybe a couple in the reception area.'

'How busy will it be?' Dale asked.

'On a Sunday afternoon? Probably packed.' She explained that the soft play was divided into four different zones, according to age and difficulty, and while it was possible to rent an entire zone for a party, the rest of the centre remained open to the public.

'Lots of people coming in and out, then?' Gary said. 'That'll suit us.'

There was silence again. Katy became aware of Dylan growing restless, twisting towards her and drawing up his knees.

'What's wrong?' she asked quietly.

Sounding deeply embarrassed, he whispered, 'I need to pee.'

Gary heard, and warned him: 'Don't be pissing in the car.'

'Think we're nearly there,' Dale said. 'Keysford Lane, do I go right along Stonecross?'

It took Katy a moment to realise he was addressing her. 'Er, yes, I think so.'

Gary muttered something, then reached over and tore the blindfold away. Dylan's was removed as well, and after making sure he was okay, Katy looked around to get her bearings. They were close to the Ardingly Road, which would take them into Lindfield from the north.

'There's a turn coming up on your left,' she told Dale. Dylan had started to groan, and was clutching his abdomen. 'Only a few minutes now,' she said. 'Just hang on for me.'

The sky had cleared since this morning, and bathed in late autumn sunshine the countryside was lush and leafy, and the village looked more picture perfect than ever. They passed the imposing Georgian symmetry of Lindfield House, followed by a medieval thatched cottage, and then the warm sandstone of the ancient parish church. The lime trees that had given the village its name formed a guard of honour along the High Street. Fallen leaves tumbled and swirled across the pavements; pedestrians were scarce, and paid them scant attention.

At Katy's direction they went right into Hickmans Lane, and after a couple more turns they were in Finches Place. The street where they lived. Where they ought to have been safe. Katy could see Gary growing ever more tense: this excursion carried a lot of risks for him and Dale, whereas for her it might hold some vital opportunities. She had to be smart enough to recognise them when they appeared, and courageous enough to take them.

She'd hoped for plenty of activity in her street: neighbours washing cars, sweeping up leaves or merely coming in or out of their homes. But she had no such luck. An Ocado truck was delivering groceries to a house a few doors away, and a car was turning out of the road at the far end, but otherwise there was no one about.

Perfect for them, and Gary acknowledged that with a grateful sigh. 'Nice house,' he remarked as Dale rolled past, then backed up, reversing on to the drive.

For a quick getaway, Katy thought.

CHAPTER FIFTEEN

Gary had her house keys in one hand, a phone in the other. 'You gonna give us any trouble?'

'No.' Katy released Dylan's seatbelt. 'Can we hurry? He's bursting for the loo.'

Dale was already out of the car and opening their door, smirking at his chauffeur's role. Katy and Dylan got out and made for the front door. Gary followed close behind, the phone at his ear.

'We're at the house,' he said. Then: 'All good.'

He passed Katy the keys. Hemmed in on the step, with Dylan moaning at her side, she could do nothing except unlock the door and let them in.

The Parr's house was semi-detached, with three bedrooms and a sizeable garden at the rear. Not an opulent property by any means, but certainly larger than anything they'd have been able to afford without a generous legacy from one of Katy's grandparents. As a result they lived in a house that was robustly soundproofed and screened with mature trees and hedges, in an area occupied by people who placed a premium on privacy and discretion. Right now, that made it the worst of all possible worlds.

As the door swung open Dylan barrelled inside. Dale made a clumsy grab for him but missed. 'He's just going to the toilet,' Katy cried, petrified that they were going to hurt him.

Dylan vanished into the downstairs cloakroom and shut the door. Would he lock it? she wondered. Would he think to climb out of the tiny window and seek help next door?

Then again, would she want him to do that?

In an agony of indecision, she entered the kitchen, trying to remember where she had left the present for Noah. Dale had stayed outside the toilet but Gary followed her, literally breathing down her neck. She cringed, then jumped as she heard the kitchen door shut behind him.

He was on her in a second, grabbing her hair and forcing her against the breakfast table, grinding into her buttocks. One hand gripped her neck, while the other pawed at her breasts. He was panting heavily, his breath like an ashtray that hadn't been emptied for days.

'Just a friendly warning,' he said, his lips grazing her ear. His smell enveloped her, suffocating in its foulness. 'Me and Maggie had a chat, and this is what we agreed.' His tongue probed her ear, while his fingers pinched her breast, trying to locate her nipple through her clothes. She choked with revulsion and tried to squirm away, but he had her pinned to the spot.

'You try anything while we're out – just one look or a word out of place – and there'll be a lot more of *this*.' His hand delved viciously between her legs. 'And not just with you, love. Think of little Freya.' He chuckled. 'Because she'll be first.'

The door opened. Gary quickly stepped back as Dale wandered in, with Dylan alongside him. 'Done a piss and now he wants a fucking drink,' Dale said.

Katy couldn't move for a second or two. She remained hunched over the table, head down, fighting the urge to vomit. There were tears in her eyes but she prayed that Dylan couldn't see them, or at least wouldn't understand what was wrong.

Gary noticed a glass on the draining board and ran the tap. 'Let's get the stuff and go.'

Katy took a couple of deep breaths and managed to compose herself enough to stand up straight. 'The clothes are upstairs,' she said.

Gary gave her a twisted smile. 'Lead the way, sweetheart.'

*

Dylan made to follow but Dale ordered him to stay in the kitchen. 'You can fetch the card and present,' Katy said quickly. 'I won't be long.'

Katy was shaking as she climbed the stairs. There was a strange, warped familiarity to her surroundings that came as a shock: the soft carpets, smooth walls, the fresh smells and clean surfaces: all so safe and cosy and welcoming, but now about as relevant as a movie set. After this brief visit, she might never see it again.

On the landing she was stopped in her tracks by the family pictures, which included some of her own pencil drawings of her children as babies and toddlers. But what truly pierced her heart were the official school portraits, complete with messy hair and twisted collars. The purity and innocence of their gap-toothed smiles caused an involuntary sob. She prayed that Dylan was too far away to hear.

With a growl of frustration, Gary nudged her forward. A bedroom was the worst place to be heading with a man like this, but Katy knew there was zero chance of him agreeing to wait outside.

The room had been left in its usual state of Sunday morning disarray; just a few hours ago the kids had piled on to the bed, loudly declaring that Mum and Dad had slept for long enough and it was time for the visit to Sheffield Park. As Katy now recalled, they hadn't actually been sleeping: quickly breaking apart, Adam had grumbled something about a morning glory going to waste – and *that* was something that didn't happen very often these days, either.

She removed her jacket and shirt, leaving a thin T-shirt over her bra. The intensity of his gaze made her decide to stick with the jeans she was wearing: no way did she want to take them off in front of Gary.

'If we're spending the night in the cellar, can I get some spare clothes for us all? And blankets, toiletries…'

'Some clothes. Nowt else.'

She nodded, deciding not to push her luck, and gathered jogging pants, T-shirts and thick fleeces. For herself, she put on a clean top and a long cardigan that would conceal the dirt on the back of her jeans.

She took a canvas bag from the wardrobe and stuffed the clothes inside, then turned to her dressing table. 'Need some underwear.'

'Hurry,' he snapped.

This was the tricky part. The dangerous part. She wanted his full attention, if only to perform an act of misdirection.

Kneeling at the dressing table, she opened a drawer with her left hand and pulled out a jumble of bras, shaking them at shoulder height until all but one fell to the floor. Then she rose slightly, turned and threw the bra towards the bag, while her right hand rested, apparently for balance, on the table.

Beneath her palm was a pair of nail scissors.

The bra had fallen short, and Gary instinctively stooped to pick it up, sniggering as he caressed one of the cups. He made a show of examining the label. 'Thirty-two D? Didn't feel that big to me.'

Katy scowled, but the taunt didn't really faze her. What mattered was that the distraction had worked, and she now had a pair of nail scissors tucked in the front pocket of her jeans.

She added knickers to the bag, and said, 'I'll need to get things for the children.'

Gary moaned about how long she was taking, but he didn't prevent her from gathering clothes from the other bedrooms, and he didn't try to accost her again.

Back downstairs, Dylan was waiting with Dale in the living room, both of them munching on chocolate digestives.

'Kid was hungry, and I'm bloody starving.'

Katy heard a burbling from her stomach and wondered if they would be fed. Dylan, at least, would get something to eat at the party.

'Can we take them?'

Gary had snatched the packet and was mashing a couple of biscuits into his mouth. He sprayed crumbs everywhere as he snarled, 'It's not a fooking picnic.'

Dylan almost broke Katy's heart by offering her the last piece of his. 'No. You finish it.'

'I want you to have it.' He insisted on putting it into her mouth as she crouched down to help him get changed.

'Thank you. Try to have something healthy if you can – and remember what I told you.' She gave him a serious look, praying he would be capable of seeing this through, but aware that it was probably asking far too much of him.

Shyly, Dylan stepped out of his jeans and into a fresh pair. Katy grabbed a packet of wipes and cleaned his face and hands, and for once he didn't squirm away from her. The tip of the scissors kept digging into her thigh but she ignored it; there would be far worse pain than this to endure before they were done.

At least she now had a weapon, a way of fighting back. But would she have the guts to use it?

CHAPTER SIXTEEN

Once Gary and Dale had gone there was a kind of lull, the other three just sitting in silence, as if their energy levels had dipped at the same time. Then Roger hauled himself up, lumbered into the kitchen and made tea. Maggie hadn't asked for it, didn't particularly want it, but she took the mug all the same.

After a sip, she said, 'Bit too much sugar.'

'Won't hurt.' Roger slurped his own, and handed a mug to Jay, who was staring intently at ones of the phones.

'Sneaky little bastard,' he muttered. 'Adam only fucking filmed us.'

'What?' Maggie asked.

'After we stopped the car. Dale got out and spoke to him, and the guy was videoing it.'

'Show me.' She beckoned him over, and he replayed the footage. The registration number wouldn't have helped Adam much, but there was a moment when the interior of the car could be seen, Carole enclosed between Jay and Gary on the back seat.

'See?' Jay said. 'If we hadn't brought them here…'

'*If* this, *if* that!' Maggie exclaimed. 'I'm sick to death of hearing it.'

'Raises a question, though,' Roger said. 'Do you really believe we can release the family?'

She gave a heartfelt shrug. 'The important thing is that *they* have to believe it. For now, at least.'

He digested this, and said, quietly, 'So we might have to kill them all?'

'I prefer not to think about it right now. But yeah, we might.' She felt Jay's gaze, and met his eye with her customary defiance. He went back to browsing through the phone.

'In that case, I'd better start thinking about the logistics,' Roger said wearily. 'A lot of blood and bodies.'

Riled by his tone, she said, 'Rog, I don't like the idea of killing kids any more than you do. But if it's necessary…'

'Yeah, yeah. I hear you. Disposal could be a headache, though. Better if they vanish completely.'

Maggie agreed. 'The key thing is that we don't get identified as being in this part of the country. That means losing all the phones we've used, the cars…'

Jay looked up. 'What about Gary, going to this party?'

'I sent him because he's not associated with us. Him and Dale are clean, from that point of view.' She couldn't resist a sly smile. 'Expendable, if need be.'

Roger whistled. 'As if we hadn't guessed how much this means to you.'

'Bloody right. And you both know why – we've burnt our bridges for this.' She sipped her tea, shuddered at its sweetness, and regarded Jay. 'Are you checking Carole's phone?'

'Every few minutes,' he said.

'Why hasn't he been in touch with her?'

Silence. Neither he nor Roger had an answer – and perhaps they guessed that, in her present mood, Maggie wouldn't welcome their theories.

They dispensed with the blindfolds for the short journey from Lindfield to Burgess Hill. It made the drive less disorientating, but did nothing to alleviate Katy's fears. There was so much that could go wrong, even if she made no attempt to call for help.

She had already decided not to try. She was sickened by Gary's assault, and convinced that the threat to Freya was serious. Fear for her daughter had loomed in her mind when, as they left the house, a neighbour over the road raised a hand in greeting while getting out of his car.

'Beautiful day!' he'd cried.

'Lovely,' Katy agreed, and left it at that. The neighbour was widowed, childless, a little eccentric, someone she'd always liked but frankly felt sorry for. Now she was weak with envy at the liberty that he took for granted.

Yesterday that was us, and we had no idea what was coming.

They were on the ring road to the west of Burgess Hill when Dale said, 'D'you want me to come in as well?'

'Nah, you stay with the car,' Gary said. 'We ain't hanging around.'

'So take this. It's easier to hide than your Ruger.' Dale wriggled in his seat and passed a neat black pistol over his shoulder. Katy gasped, thankful that Dylan was cuddled up to her and had his eyes shut.

In return, Gary handed over his silver revolver, tucked the narrower gun inside his jacket and winked at Katy. 'Don't give me reason to use it.'

The soft play centre was situated in one of the town's business parks, on a site that included an aerospace factory and a timber merchant's. The large car park, which ran along the front and one side of the building, was about two-thirds full. Most of the vacant spaces were at the rear, which was where Dale took them.

Gary produced a baseball cap and put it on, then gave her the bag containing the card and present. 'Act normal, like you're on your own. I'll be close by, but don't be looking at me.'

Katy nodded, though she felt sure she would appear anything but normal. How could the frenzy inside her not be apparent to the whole world?

Dylan had to be helped from the car. Heartbroken at seeing him so vulnerable, Katy gave him one more hug. She saw that Gary, wandering away from the car, was out of earshot, and said, 'I know it isn't easy, but try your best not to think about... *them.*' She kissed him on the forehead. 'Just enjoy the party, have a good time, and I'll be back for you in a couple of hours.'

'But I don't want to go,' Dylan said, in a tiny voice. 'I'm scared.'

'There's nothing to be scared about. Once you're playing with your friends, you'll forget all about this.'

'I won't.'

'Yes, you will. I promise.'

CHAPTER SEVENTEEN

Katy was consumed with guilt, not just because she was lying to her son, but because she was almost trying to indoctrinate him with those lies.

Of course he wouldn't forget about this trauma. Of course he was right to be scared.

But he nodded, just the same, and didn't resist when she led him towards the entrance. A boy from his class was on the way in; he smiled and waved, and Dylan shyly raised a hand in greeting.

'See?' Katy said. 'It'll be fun.'

Nevertheless her heart was pounding as she opened the doors and saw Gary positioned just inside the lobby area, a phone at his ear. He appeared relaxed, engaged in a conversation, and didn't give her a glance. There were half a dozen people queuing at the counter, and a lot of commotion coming from the café area off to the right.

Straight ahead and to the left were the different soft play zones, and at one of them Katy spotted a cluster of familiar adults, laden with gifts, and a bunch of excited kids hurriedly removing their shoes.

'Dylan! You made it!' A small boy with unruly blond hair came charging towards them. This was Isaac, one of Dylan's closest friends.

As Katy greeted him, she noticed Suzy Chadwick among the group, and there was a moment of eye contact. Reluctantly she pushed herself forwards, Isaac clutching at Dylan's arm as if confused by his lack of response.

'Noah said you might not be coming, 'cos you were sick?'

Dylan shrugged. 'Yeah.'

'But you're all right now?'

'He's a bit better, but needs to take it easy,' Katy explained.

She hadn't intended it as reverse psychology, but it had that effect: Dylan registered the concern on Isaac's face and said, boldly, 'I'm all right.'

'Come and see Noah.' Isaac tugged on his hand, and after a second or two Dylan allowed himself to be detached from his mother's grasp.

This was worse than the first day at school: Katy felt utterly bereft as he trotted away. But he didn't look back, and she had to remind herself to be grateful. This was good.

It would keep them all alive.

For a second she was stranded in the midst of these excited children and their parents. Everywhere she looked, people were smiling, talking, eating. It was all so happy, so safe and routine that she had a sudden desperate longing to scream for help.

I'm a prisoner. This man has taken my family. He has a gun...

The thought of it made her dizzy; she had to take a step backwards to regain her balance. It was so tempting, and yet quite unreal. Aside from the danger it posed to Freya and Adam, she felt sure that Gary wouldn't hesitate to shoot his way out of here if anyone tried to restrain him. She couldn't put other innocent lives at risk.

She also suspected that her pleas would be greeted with a uniquely English brand of embarrassment. How many people here would be appalled that she was making a scene? How many would ignore her, and look away?

Now she had to compose herself and find a convincing smile for Suzy Chadwick, who was tall and slender and always immaculate: Catalogue Mum, Adam liked to call her. The party's host hurried over and gave her a hug, before accepting the bag with the present.

'Aw, thank you so much for coming. Is Dylan all right?'

'I think so. He's been a bit subdued, but hopefully...' Katy shuddered as Gary dipped into her peripheral vision, muttering into the phone.

'Yes, I'm sure he'll be fine. Are you staying?' Suzy's tone was so bright and expectant that Katy feared there would be a battle to leave.

'Um, no. I thought Dylan might forget he's poorly if I'm not here to remind him.'

It was the lamest of excuses, but Suzy nodded in agreement. 'Of course.' Then she gave a conspiratorial grimace. 'Ghastly place, isn't it, but Noah adores it here!'

Someone brushed against her; Katy jerked violently, thinking it would be Gary, but it was Isaac's mum, Gemma Garvey. She greeted them both, and said, 'So glad I caught you, Katy. Look, I know this is short notice, but would you be able to take a commission for a portrait, to finish before Christmas?'

'Uh...' Katy was thrown; her work was just about the last thing on her mind. Recovering quickly, she said, 'I-I'll see what I can do. Can you send me the det—?'

'It's right here.' Gemma produced her phone and started to tap at the screen. 'It's a picture of my mum, but she doesn't know I took it. What I thought was that a pencil sketch would look wonderful.'

Katy had no choice but to wait, but her whole body prickled with discomfort. Her face must be bright red. Any second now someone was going to notice the state she was in and ask what was wrong... surely?

Suzy said, 'Anyway, I must dash. Let's catch up later.'

'Yes, I need to be going...'

'Oh, sorry, are you in a rush?' Gemma said. 'Ah, here it is! What do you think?'

There was a cough from just behind her; Katy felt sure it came from Gary but didn't dare look. She studied the picture on Gemma's phone, though nothing really registered.

'Email it to me in the highest resolution you have, and I'll see what I can do.'

'Can you? That'll be wonderful.' Gemma chuckled. 'I do feel guilty, though, because Becky was asking about something similar, so if I've jumped the queue…?'

Gemma waited, then gave her an odd look: expecting a laugh, Katy realised, but her mind had gone blank.

Another cough from just behind them; Gemma turned her head and found Gary standing uncomfortably close, half facing away and murmuring into his phone. She shifted away from him, giving Katy an opportunity to do the same.

'Yours'll be the priority,' she said. 'Is Becky not here today?'

'Um, I think she doubled up with someone.'

'Oh. What about Leah?'

Gemma looked round again, frowning. Gary had stayed where he was, but he seemed to be glaring at Katy.

'Not seen her. Did you want—?'

'No, it's nothing.' Katy touched Gemma's arm, willing her to stop speaking. 'I've really got to go. Sorry.'

She turned, veered around Gary and strode away, wondering if anyone would notice him following her out. As she pushed through the doors, holding them open for a couple of people coming in, she realised he wasn't yet behind her.

Could she run?

Not a chance. Because Dylan was in there, and she wouldn't dare leave him at Gary's mercy.

In any case, the Mazda was rolling towards the entrance, Dale braking as he spotted her. Reluctantly she went in that direction, opening the back door just as Gary materialised at her shoulder.

'Get in.' He shoved her along the back seat and climbed in beside her.

'All okay?' Dale sounded agitated. 'I didn't think it would take so long.'

'Nah.' Gary scowled at Katy. 'What were you talking about to that bitch?'

'She, uh, wants me to do a drawing for her.' She saw his lip curl with disbelief and said, 'It's my career – part-time, anyway. I work in a gift shop that sells my pictures, and I also take commissions from family and friends.'

'All right, Van Gogh. And who's Leah?'

'What?'

'You asked about someone called Leah.'

Katy felt like she'd been skewered. 'She's just one of the parents. We sometimes take each other's children to parties, so I was worried she might want…' She tailed off as he shook his head, already bored with her explanation. *Thank God*.

She sat back, pulled on her seatbelt and tried to steady her breathing. Because Leah wasn't just 'one of the parents': she was also a police officer. Asking about her within Gary's earshot had been a bigger risk than Katy had imagined – and all for nothing.

CHAPTER EIGHTEEN

Adam had plenty of things on his mind, but it was the panel that kept nagging at him. Knocking quietly had produced a clear echo, indicating that there was a void behind it.

He'd tried, very tentatively, to prise a couple of the slats away, but they hadn't budged. Then he'd pushed on them and felt the boards flex, though not as emphatically as he'd have liked. If he was right about the opening, he should be able to stamp and kick his way through, but when he raised that possibility both Freya and Carole looked horrified.

'They'll hear you,' Carole said.

'And then they'll come down to see what you've done, and they might…' Freya clutched at him and shivered with fear.

They were both right. Even if he could find a tool to prise the timber away from the wall, it was likely to make a lot of noise. And any damage he caused wouldn't be easy to conceal.

Wasn't it wiser – safer – to stay put? To trust in what Maggie had told him, and wait patiently until they were released.

Probably. But it didn't feel right.

When Freya started yawning, Carole suggested she curl up on the mattress. After a few minutes she seemed to be drifting, if not actually asleep.

Adam made another slow circuit of the basement, but found nothing he could use on the panel. He was aware of Carole watching with an expression that at times seemed almost scornful. Was it really so hopeless, this idea of his? Or was it simply that, after seeing her husband murdered before her eyes, she no longer had it in her to hope for anything?

He came back and sat down on the cold, dusty concrete. 'The road where you live, are there many houses along there?'

'Not really.'

'You didn't notice anyone suspicious over the past couple of weeks? Any unfamiliar cars?'

'No. It's very private, very quiet.' A little sob, choked off. 'That's what we both loved about it.'

'And you can't think of any reason why they'd target you or your husband?'

'Only to steal from us, which they could have done back at the house.'

'Unless they're after money from somewhere else?' Adam gestured at the mattress. 'It seems to me that this was planned as a kidnap, rather than robbery. Is there anyone they might be demanding a ransom from?'

'Just my husband, and he's... he can't pay anything now, can he?' Shuddering, she put a hand over her eyes.

'No one else?'

'No.' She sounded certain, but then dropped her hand, and he had the impression that something had occurred to her, only to be dismissed.

'There's nothing in your past life? No enemies from a business deal, maybe? Or a relationship?'

'I've told you, I have no idea. Can we please stop discussing this? I know how horrendous it is for your family, but...' She shook her head, unable to continue.

'All right.' Trying not to show his frustration, Adam got up and returned to the panel. He crouched and put one ear against the wood, vaguely hoping he might hear vibrations through the building. Instead he felt a tiny waft of cooler air.

Startled, and fearing that he had imagined it, he pushed against one of the slats until a thin shadow appeared where it slotted into the board above. He leaned close, and once again felt a stirring of the hairs on his cheek.

He looked up, exultant. 'There's air flow. It must be hollow behind there.'

Carole frowned. 'But doesn't it just go back into the house?'

'It's an internal wall, but it might give us access to one of the ground floor rooms.'

Carole still looked sceptical, but Adam wasn't deterred. Maybe they could find a way to sneak out, perhaps in the middle of the night.

The rattle of the padlock brought an end to his fantasy. He hurried to the foot of the steps and saw the door open. Katy was pushed through, holding what looked like a laundry bag. She stumbled down the steps and into his arms.

'Are you all right? How's Dylan?'

'He's okay, I think. Putting a brave face on it.' She nestled into him for a second, seeking comfort in a way that had become uncharacteristic of her. When she stepped back, there were tears in her eyes. 'At least one of us is safe,' she whispered. 'I wish he could somehow stay where he is, go home with Isaac or Noah…'

'I want us *all* to get out safely,' Adam said with determination. 'Didn't anyone notice that something was wrong?'

'Not really.' Katy described her brief conversation with Suzy and Gemma, while Gary had loitered nearby, apparently on the phone. 'He warned me that he'd be speaking to Maggie the whole time. If I did anything to raise the alarm, he'd warn her, and then someone here would…'

She couldn't say any more, but Adam understood. 'You did really well to hold it together.' He indicated the bag. 'What's that?'

'Some spare clothes for us all. I wanted to bring toiletries and blankets, but they refused.'

'You got this from them, at least. It's fantastic.'

'Oh, and that's not all.' With a secretive air, she checked that the door to the cellar was shut, then glanced quickly at Carole before carefully easing a pair of nail scissors from her pocket.

'Bloody hell. I hope you didn't take any risks?'

'Not really.' But she gave an involuntary shudder, and he could tell she was reliving something unpleasant. 'I saw a chance, and thought they might be useful.'

'Definitely. You're amazing.' He kissed her, then opened the scissors and examined the width of the blades. This wasn't just a viable weapon: it might also work as a makeshift screwdriver.

Katy touched his arm. 'We'll need to discuss how and when we might use them. We can't afford to do anything… reckless.'

Adam gave a rueful smile. 'I know.' He saw that Freya was stirring, and knew he had to leave it for now.

'Mum!' Freya stood up, hugged and kissed her mother, and said, 'Was Dylan all right?'

Katy nodded. 'He's fine. He went off with Isaac.'

'I'm pleased.' But she didn't look it. 'When it finishes, what's going to happen?'

'Well, I daresay I'll be going to get him.'

'And coming back here?'

Katy looked like she might burst into tears. 'I expect so, yes.'

Freya absorbed this with a sombre expression, then agreed to let her parents talk in private. Adam led Katy over to one side and asked, 'Did you get any sense of where we are?'

'Not really.' She explained how they'd been blindfolded, but then said, 'I don't think they took any detours on the way back, whereas on the drive to Lindfield I felt like they turned and double-backed a couple of times. It was just after three when I left the soft play centre, and when I got back here I sneaked a look at the clock in their car. It's about half past now.'

'So we're twenty-five, thirty minutes from Burgess Hill.' He asked her to estimate how long it had taken to reach their home.

'That wasn't as long, I don't think. Fifteen or twenty.'

He nodded thoughtfully, found a patch of floor that was covered with grime and used a finger to mark the positions of the two locations. He added a spot to the east, which he estimated as their abduction point.

'That first journey took about half an hour, maybe, but I suspect they were trying to confuse us. To have driven from Burgess Hill in the same sort of time means they have to be pretty close to where we originally encountered them.'

Katy, he could see, was doing her best to look interested. 'How exactly is that going to help us?'

'Right now, it isn't of any use. But it might be, if we can get out – or more likely if *one* of us can escape.'

'From the party, you mean? I don't think there's any chance of that.'

'No.' He stood up, and beckoned to her. 'Come and see.'

CHAPTER NINETEEN

Katy was puzzled by his sudden excitement, and wasn't sure how to react when he proudly indicated a section of the wall covered with grubby wooden panelling.

'I think there's a space behind it.'

'A space?'

'An opening. Don't you see?' His eyes were wide, imploring her to share his enthusiasm. 'So there might be a way out.'

'You mean a tunnel or something?'

'It's not impossible. I was trying to work out how to get these boards off, and the scissors could be perfect.'

She watched him scratching the rust off the head of a screw, then try to insert the scissors into the slot. In the silence, the scrape of metal on metal seemed hideously loud.

'What if they hear that?'

'They won't. Before this, I was tempted to give the panel a kick.'

'You'll get us all killed!' Carole protested, her voice more strident than it had been all afternoon. Freya looked terrified, and in that moment Katy could have slapped the other woman.

'I don't think that's very helpful,' she said through gritted teeth, forcing Carole to meet her gaze before nodding at Freya.

'No, all right. But who knows what they'll do if they catch him trying to escape?'

'I'm aware of the risks, believe me,' Adam said.

Although Katy had her doubts, she tried to be tactful. 'They do have a point.'

'I know.' Adam regarded the three of them in turn. 'I understand how you feel, but at least let me remove a couple of boards and have a look. Any sign of danger and I'll fix them back in place. It's so dark over here, they'll never notice.'

Carole issued a pensive groan, which seemed to signal that she agreed under sufferance, while Freya looked to her mother for an opinion.

'It's worth a try,' Katy said. 'If you can do it quietly.'

She left him to work on the panel while she focused on reassuring Freya. 'You heard what Daddy said. It's quite safe just to have a look.'

Carole was clearly listening, a surly expression on her face, and Katy wanted to snap: *Do you have any better ideas?* She had a feeling that a lot of things were being left unsaid, out of deference to Freya.

Adam toiled for what felt like fifteen or twenty minutes. By nature he was a patient, methodical worker, so it was unusual to hear him start to grunt and swear. She got up and joined him; resting a hand on his shoulder, she felt him flinch.

'How's it going?'

'Very slowly.' He switched the scissors to his left hand and flexed his aching fingers. He showed her where two of the screws were now protruding, but by only a fraction of an inch. 'They're not getting any easier to move, probably because the damp's made everything swell up. There are four screws to each board, and I'll need to remove eight or twelve of them to get in there.'

'Get in? I thought the idea was just to see what was behind it?'

Lowering his voice, he said, 'It depends. If it looks like there's a way out, I'm gonna give it a try.'

This news, unexpectedly, brought tears to her eyes. She leaned in to whisper: 'Don't you believe them, about letting us go?'

'I want to. But in my gut, I think we're too dangerous to them.'

Katy wiped her eyes, and nodded. That was what she thought, too.

Adam had another proposal. 'When you fetch Dylan, see if you can persuade them to let Freya come along.'

Katy raised her eyes in a question, but he said nothing more. She recalled the deal she'd made on the way here: *Let the others live in exchange for me.* Adam had done the same thing.

She held out her hand. 'Let me take over for a bit.'

She got to work, and quickly found out why Adam had been swearing. All but the tip of the blade was too thick to fit into the head of the screw, so any pressure caused it to slip out – and yet without that pressure, the screw wouldn't budge. It required strength but also the most delicate finesse.

After watching for a while, Adam went to sit with Carole and Freya, and Katy's thoughts turned to Dylan. The party must be about halfway through by now. She hoped he had managed to settle down and integrate—

The door rattled above her; in a panic she jerked away from the panel, dropping the scissors. She just had time to scoop them up and retreat from the wall when the door opened. Adam had jumped to his feet, and he stood beside her as Jay showed them the phone in his hand.

'Got a missed call from Suzy.'

Katy gasped. 'Dylan…?'

'Yeah. Come on up.'

She glanced at Adam, who put his arm around her shoulders. Katy leaned in for a hug and slipped the scissors into the back pocket of his jeans.

'Be careful,' he murmured, and kissed her cheek.

'You, too.'

*

Katy felt an immense, overwhelming dread as she climbed the steps. Even breathing was a struggle – and would be until she knew that Dylan was all right.

In the hall, Jay shut the door, then handed her the phone. 'Call her back. On speaker.'

Katy nodded. Her hand shook as she tapped at the screen.

Suzy shouted a greeting, but even that was almost lost in the background cacophony. 'Katy! Give me a second.'

They waited for the noise to recede, and then she was back, releasing a dramatic sigh. 'Sorry, darling, but Dylan has been unwell again. He's crying, wants his mum.'

'I'll come and get him.' Katy spoke without seeking permission: Jay glowered at her, but didn't object.

'It's such a shame – he really isn't his normal self. He's been say—'

'I'm on my way,' Katy broke in, terrified by what Suzy might be about to reveal. 'Thanks for letting me know.'

She ended the call before Suzy could speak again, and thrust the phone back at Jay.

'He'd better not have said anything.'

'I'm sure he hasn't.' She folded her arms across her chest and tried to project confidence. 'I need Freya with me.'

'What?'

'Dylan worships his sister. If he's ill or upset, she's the best person to calm him down – which is want you want.' She was trying to sound pragmatic, but knew there was far too much emotion in her voice. Adam's idea was a noble one, but if it worked and he was left alone here, she knew they might never see him again.

Jay gave her a long appraisal, as if weighing up the merits of her argument, and then reacted to movement. Maggie had appeared in the lounge doorway, and must have been listening.

'The girl's staying here.'

'But she could help,' Katy insisted.

'Tough. We're not having three of you out in public.' Maggie clicked her tongue, and nodded towards the cellar. 'Was this hubby's idea? Getting ready to play the hero, is he?'

Katy pretended not to understand, but she was blushing deeply. 'Who's taking me?' she asked.

CHAPTER TWENTY

As the minutes slipped by and Katy failed to reappear, Adam put the best possible spin on it, for Freya's sake.

'I expect she's gone to get Dylan. They'll be back soon.'

'Do you think he's poorly?'

'No. But you know how he gets with his friends – sometimes he overdoes it a bit.'

'What if he's told anyone about this?'

It was the question Adam had been dreading: he'd asked himself the same thing and failed to come up with a satisfactory answer.

'I doubt if he has. Let's try not to worry ourselves unnecessarily.'

In the circumstances it was understandable that Freya wanted him to stay close, but when Carole engaged her in a numbers game that required lots of mental arithmetic, Adam was able to resume his work. Growing more adept with the scissors, he found he could turn the screws a little more easily.

He'd also had another idea, but before he could give it a try he heard his daughter whispering urgently to Carole, who groaned in sympathy and said, 'Um, I think that's what the bucket is for.'

'I don't want to use that!' Horrified, Freya appealed to her father: 'I need the toilet.'

'I'm sorry. I know it's not pleasant, but I think the bucket is probably the best option.'

Better than inviting more contact with the men upstairs: that was what he meant, and Freya seemed to understand.

Carole helped him create a makeshift screen by standing the mattress on its side, propping it up with the bag of spare clothes that Katy had brought. They both retreated to the steps, promising to keep their backs turned until she was done.

'And don't listen,' she called.

'We won't,' Adam said.

'We'll talk,' Carol added. To Adam, she whispered, 'I keep thinking about what you said, and whether this is a… a kidnapping.' She shivered. 'But I can't think of any reason for it – especially when they've killed Brian.'

'Unless that wasn't intended? From what you said, it sounds as though everything happened very quickly.'

Carole gazed morosely at the floor, before finally nodding. 'I suppose that's possible. He wasn't even meant to be home this weekend.'

She said it lightly, but to Adam that sounded significant. 'Where had he planned to be?'

'Scotland. For golf. But his sciatica was bothering him. He didn't want to fly up there, only to find he couldn't play.'

'So it was a last-minute change of plan? The gang might have been counting on his absence?'

'Well… yes. But they'd have had to know about the trip, and I don't see how they would.'

'I assume he'll have mentioned it to people – friends, colleagues?'

Carole's expression grew dark, almost hostile. Adam sensed that he'd touched a nerve in some way, though he had no idea why.

He waited. After wrestling with some inner torment, Carole sighed. 'Oh God, I hate to admit this, because I don't believe it's connected in any way, but…'

'Yes?'

'I'm… I've been… seeing someone.'

*

It was the same routine as before: the blindfold, Gary beside her, Dale at the wheel. He drove faster this time, which should have meant a shorter journey, and yet to Katy it seemed to take an age. What had happened, exactly? How was Dylan feeling?

What had he said?

Once again the blindfold was removed when they were on the ring road. The first thing she noticed was that the sun was much lower in the sky; the afternoon turning to evening, and with that came the prospect of a night in captivity. A night in the cold, filthy cellar instead of a comfortable, carefree evening at home.

They were a minute or two away from the soft play centre when she plucked up the courage to confront Gary. 'I don't think it's going to work, having you standing so close again. My friend Gemma noticed you, and I think Suzy did, too.'

She braced herself for a violent response, but Gary only grunted. 'Your turn, lad.'

The comment was directed at Dale, who jerked in alarm. 'Why do I have to? It's not up to her.'

'No, but makes sense to have a different face in there.' A calculated pause, then: 'Or else I can call Maggie, tell her you don't want to do it.'

Dale muttered something that Katy didn't catch, and Gary sniggered.

The car park had cleared out, and they were able to reverse into a space opposite the entrance. Dale opened the door, took Gary's baseball cap and made a call.

'Just about to go in,' he murmured, and then, in a defensive whine: 'It were Gary who told me – so the woman's friends don't get suspicious.' He listened, scowling, and said, 'I won't.'

Gary smirked. '"Don't cock it up" – was that her message?'

He moved around the car and climbed into the driver's seat. Katy couldn't wait any longer. She set off at a brisk pace, leaving Dale to scurry in her wake. At the main door she turned and hissed: 'Not too close.'

'Shut your mouth.' Dale pushed past her and strode in, turning to scan the reception area as if looking for someone.

The party had moved to a roped-off section of the café, which otherwise was almost empty. Noah and about twenty of his friends were in high spirits, laughing and shouting and throwing soggy chips at one another. A small knot of adults had retreated to the far end, where Suzy was chatting easily to another parent, seemingly oblivious to the mayhem.

Katy felt her heart pounding as she spotted a diminutive figure sitting on a chair outside the toilets. Dylan, clutching a party bag in his lap, was leaning towards Gemma, who had her arm around him. She noticed Katy, and exclaimed, with obvious relief: 'Look, Mummy's here!'

As Katy threaded her way through the tables, she glanced back and saw Dale coming after her. Surely he wouldn't make it this obvious?

The panic was like a fist, blocking her throat, forcing its way down towards her heart.

Tell someone.

Beg for help.

At least Dylan will be safe, and so will you…

Dylan had stood, somewhat unsteadily, to greet her. Focusing only on him, Katy found the strength to sweep him into her arms. 'Hey, buddy, are you all right?'

His answer was a weak snuffle. Gemma smiled fondly, and said, 'He was sick, just after he started eating.'

'I shouldn't have brought him. It was a stupid idea.' Katy was so furious, she must have sounded half deranged. Gemma looked taken aback.

'Don't blame yourself. At this age, they can be fine one minute…' She cleared her throat. 'Before he vomited, he was very subdued. And there was an odd moment…'

Gemma hesitated, as if reluctant to elaborate in front of Dylan. Katy glanced round. Dale was about ten feet away, examining a display of snacks at the counter. Could he hear them over the noise of the party?

'Isaac invited him back to ours, you see, and he said he couldn't. When Isaac suggested getting me to ask you, Dylan said, "Mummy's not allowed."' Gemma gave an embarrassed smile. 'He said something really weird to Isaac, about "men with guns".'

She'd lowered her voice, but not enough to prevent Dylan from hearing. A sob burst from him, and he squirmed in Katy's embrace. 'I'm sorry, I didn't mean—'

'Darling, it's fine.' Katy had to speak over him or risk Dale picking up on the conversation. Squeezing Dylan tight, she grinned stupidly at Gemma, willing her brain to supply an explanation.

Don't be a coward. Tell her.

Another glance at Dale. He was pretending to be on his phone – or maybe he really was talking to Maggie, ready to give the word if she should speak out of turn.

Freya. They would assault her daughter.

Katy swallowed hard. 'It was a bad dream, last night.'

'Oh. I see.' Gemma didn't look entirely convinced.

'Yes, I wonder now if he had a bit of a fever – that often gives them nightmares, doesn't it?' She nodded, encouraging Gemma to buy it. There wasn't anyone in this room who could tackle Dale; not when he had a gun. Even the few seconds she'd need to describe the situation would give him ample time to get away.

And then Freya would die. Adam would die.

But Dylan will live, a voice inside her hissed. *And I will live.*

No. It felt wicked even to contemplate, weighing up the lives of her children, her husband. *I want us all to get out safely*, Adam had said, and she felt ashamed that she could view it any differently.

'Go on, you'd better get him home. Let's arrange a play date later in the week, shall we?'

Katy agreed. She turned away, realising that she ought to catch Suzy's eye to say farewell. She had the impression that Suzy – although still deep in conversation – was aware of her presence but choosing not to acknowledge it. Perhaps she was annoyed that Dylan had spoiled the party.

She'd only taken a couple of steps when Gemma said, 'Oh, you asked about Leah?'

Katy had to stop, turn and nod, even though Dale was now wandering in her direction, coming close enough to eavesdrop.

'William's here,' Gemma went on. 'His dad dropped him off, but he did say that Leah would be coming to—'

'No, it's fine. Wasn't anything important.' Katy blundered away, catching the edge of a chair and nearly toppling it over.

'I'm sorry, Mummy,' Dylan mumbled.

'Ssh. It's fine.' He was too heavy to carry much further; once they were in the lobby she set him down, and spoke in a whisper, close to his ear. 'You're not in trouble, I promise. But we need to be quiet about it now, okay?'

He nodded, fearfully. 'Are we going home?'

'I'm afraid not.'

'The brat hasn't opened his mouth, has he?' Dale was suddenly alongside them, glancing back towards the café.

'Of course not.' Katy hurried on, Dylan stumbling to keep up. She prayed he wouldn't say anything more.

Dale stayed with them, pushed through the door and marched towards the car. At the sight of the Mazda, Dylan began to cry again.

'Daddy and Freya are looking forward to seeing you,' Katy said brightly, as if this could compensate for where they were going.

Gary climbed out and opened the back door. He ushered them inside, cruelly snatching the party bag from Dylan's grasp and tossing it into the front footwell. The engine was still running, and once Dale took the wheel he moved off while they were fumbling with their seatbelts.

Then he jerked to a halt, forced to wait for a car coming in. A blue Audi. A woman at the wheel, with a child in a car seat in the back.

It was Leah. She registered that the Mazda had stopped, gave the driver a tiny nod, and then her gaze switched to the passengers before she rolled past and turned into a space. It was only a fraction of a second, but Katy thought she had seen recognition from her friend – or perhaps, as a police officer, she was simply taking note that Dylan wasn't in a car seat.

There was no time to signal or gesture, though Katy could only wonder at how frightened and desperate she must look. If Dylan had delayed them just a little longer, could she have grabbed him and run to Leah's car, screaming a warning that they had to get away?

It was pointless to speculate. And Leah had her other son in the back. Katy would have been putting them both in danger with no guarantee of saving herself and Dylan.

The Mazda pulled out of the car park and accelerated towards the main road. Gary produced the blindfolds and dropped them in her lap. He didn't bother to say anything: by now they knew the score.

They were prisoners again.

CHAPTER TWENTY-ONE

When she was done, Freya coughed to get their attention. She was crimson with embarrassment, despite their assurances that she had nothing to be ashamed about.

'Chances are, we're all gonna have to use it,' Adam said.

After putting the mattress back down, Freya surprised him by asking for the scissors. 'I want to try and help.'

Impressed, Adam showed her how to angle the blade, then he left her to work on the boards and sat with Carole.

'So this guy you're seeing, what's his name?'

'Alex.' She looked guilty. 'But none of this has anything to do with him.'

'I agree it's very unlikely—'

'Nobody knows about us, that's the thing. We've been so careful, so discreet. Alex insisted on it, just as much as I did. Absolute secrecy.'

'All right.' Adam pretended to accept her word, and made his next question sound like small talk. 'What does he do for a living?'

'Finance. That's really all I know.'

'And what's his full name?'

'Alex Barinov. He's Russian.' She watched him carefully, and Adam wasn't sure if he had fully suppressed an urge to grimace. 'He's fluent in English, as well as three other languages. He's very well-travelled, knowledgeable, amusing…'

'Rich?'

She seemed to shiver, then stared forlornly at the concrete floor. 'Very.'

'How old is he?'

She looked up, surprised by the question. 'Late forties – a few years older than me.'

'That means he was only a young man when the wall came down. So he's more likely to be a second generation oligarch – if he is an oligarch?'

Carole gave a fluttery laugh. 'I'm not sure what that means. You hear the word flung around so often these days.'

It felt like she was avoiding the question, but Adam let it go. 'Where does he live?'

'He has a place near Forest Row. That's where we meet…' Another laugh, this time with a bitter edge. 'This might sound peculiar, but I know very little about him. We agreed from the start not to delve into one another's lives. He's an intensely private person – and in that context so was I. He knows practically nothing about… about my husband—'

She choked up. Adam gave her a minute to recover.

'Is he married?'

'He says not, though I've no doubt that other women feature in his life.'

'How did you meet? And how long has it been going on?'

'Just over a year. I was in London for theatre and shopping with a couple of girlfriends. We had tea at the Dorchester and he was there for some sort of business meeting.' She blushed, as a teenager might when discussing a first date. 'I noticed him staring at me, but didn't imagine it meant anything. But then he sneaked a note into my handbag, asking me to call him.'

'Isn't it a coincidence that you both live in Sussex?'

'Not really. I think he has three or four properties in the UK, as well as several more around the world. Definitely something in

New York, and a villa in the Caribbean, because he talked about how we might be able to wangle a few days away.'

Adam frowned, trying to process this information, but his expression was misinterpreted.

'Believe me, I was just as confused as you are now. Why would someone as successful as that show any interest in a forty-three-year-old housewife with crow's feet and—'

'That's not what I was thinking. You're very attractive.'

'But you disapprove,' she shot back, brushing off the compliment. 'At your age, with a young family, it's so very different. And Brian and I… he was twelve years my senior, and we'd been together fifteen years. Initially he was so full of enthusiasm, living the fantasy of having a younger second wife. But it wasn't long before he slipped back into his old habits – golf, drinking and poker, with me in a distant fourth place.' She hauled in a sigh, and looked past him, unable to meet his gaze. 'He paid me no attention, not in the ways that matter. And I know that what I did was wrong, but I felt I was too young to give up on passion…'

'I can understand that.' He must have sounded a little too heartfelt, for she gave him a curious look; a kind of reappraisal.

'Really? Have you…?' A quick glance at Freya. 'No, forget it. I'm sorry.'

And then Adam was rescued – if that was the word – by the thud of footsteps in the hall. He turned to Freya, who hurried away from the panel and pressed the scissors into his hand. A moment later came the rattle of the padlock.

Katy kept replaying that moment of eye contact with Leah. Had she communicated anything of her distress? Would Leah wonder why she was accompanied by a grim-faced thug and driven away in the back of an unfamiliar car?

Perhaps – but it still wasn't going to do them any good. Katy probably had to be grateful that Gary and Dale hadn't picked up on it.

The journey back to their base was silent and tense; once again the blindfolds were kept in place until they'd been led into the house. Maggie was in the hall, arms folded across her chest. 'What happened?'

She was addressing the men, but Katy said, 'He was sick, but he's been a really good boy—'

Uncaring, Maggie spoke over her: 'Did he put us in danger?'

'Don't think so.' Dale's shrug was a little too theatrical for Katy's liking; he was also very red in the face.

'Sure?' Maggie asked.

'Yeah, yeah,' he gabbled. 'I stayed close as I could. No one seemed to be acting funny.'

'He didn't say anything,' Katy insisted, while Dylan clung to her, whimpering with fear as he understood that his conduct was under discussion.

'Let's hope not, for your sake.' Maggie smiled sarcastically at Dylan. 'At least it means no school tomorrow, kiddo.'

'Dylan likes school,' Katy told her, defiantly.

'I bet he does. Well, you're going to call in sick for both of them.'

'The same goes for you and Adam,' said Jay, who'd wandered out from the lounge. 'I take it you work as well?'

Katy nodded. 'Mondays I'm normally at a shop in Lindfield. But I'm not sure Adam can miss tomorrow. He has a very important meeting.'

'No way, lady,' Maggie spat. 'These excursions are doing my head in.'

She flapped a hand towards the door and followed Jay into the lounge. Dale unlocked the cellar, peered inside, then stepped back to allow them past. Dylan wriggled and tried to resist, and in a flash of temper that she immediately regretted, Katy snapped at him: 'Stop it, Dylan!'

'But I don't want—'

'Those steps are dangerous. Concentrate.'

Adam was at the bottom, with Freya just behind him. Dylan was coaxed down and jumped into his dad's arms. Both the children burst into tears, and for a minute or so the four of them were simply embracing each other.

Katy became uncomfortably aware of Carole, sitting apart and observing them with a half smile that conveyed an odd mix of envy and compassion.

When they broke away, and she'd persuaded Dylan to sit on the mattress with Freya and Carole, Adam said, 'Is he all right? What happened at the party?'

'Nothing serious.' She recounted what Gemma had told her. 'I think she was confused by his reaction, but not to the point of being suspicious about it. After all,' she added bitterly, 'who would ever imagine we'd be in this sort of trouble?'

Adam nodded at the ceiling. 'Did *they* get any hint of it?'

'No, thank God. The café was really noisy.' Her shoulders slumped, and she admitted to seeing Leah. 'Henry was in the back seat, but even so, if I hadn't already been in the car, I might have had a chance...'

'Ah, Jesus. Probably better that you didn't.'

'I know. But when I realised she might be there, and knowing she's a cop...'

'Katy, this is off the scale, compared to anything she'll have dealt with.' He shook his head, disapproving in a way that made her bite back an angry response:

At least I tried.

As if he'd read her mind, he said, 'A risk like that is only worth taking if both the kids can get away.'

'Is it?' Katy retorted.

He stared at her, wide-eyed, as if he couldn't quite believe what she'd said. 'Do you really th—?'

'I don't know,' she hissed, feeling both angry and ashamed. 'You're looking at me like I'm a monster for suggesting it, and maybe I am. But I'm reaching the point where the idea of saving one of our children is better than losing them both.'

'Then perhaps you should have done it,' Adam said sadly. 'Saved yourself and Dylan.' There was no mistaking the resentment in his voice, and he apologised at once. 'That was a shitty thing to say. I'm sorry.'

'Well, the fact is, I didn't do it, and we're back here now.' She pushed a hand through her hair. 'Anyway, it might be your chance next. Maggie said we all have to call in sick tomorrow, which is okay for me…'

'My strategy meeting!' Adam brooded for a minute. 'Even if they were to let me out, there's no way I'm doing anything to endanger you and the kids.'

She shrugged. 'You might have to.'

A glum silence, until Adam gestured at the wall. He showed her how he had managed to prise out one of the timber boards. 'I've had an idea, but I need your help.'

He pulled the leather belt from his jeans. Handing her the scissors, he directed her to use them as a lever, widening the gap enough to thread the belt in behind the board.

'What's that for?' she asked.

Grasping the ends of the belt in one hand, he pulled until it was taut. There was a creak of timber – not loud, but enough to make them both wince. Adam relaxed the tension, and they examined the wood. The board had come out another half an inch.

'See?' he said. 'The belt gives us a lot more leverage, but with a fraction of the noise.'

'You don't think they'd hear that?'

'I doubt it. Either way, it has to be worth a try.'

Katy considered what they had just been saying. How it was coming down to a slim chance of saving – at most – one or two of them.

'All right,' she said.

CHAPTER TWENTY-TWO

Adam might have sounded confident, but it was pure bravado. He had no idea what – if anything – was behind the cover. It also troubled him that he and Katy weren't really seeing eye to eye; nor were they facing up to the truth. He didn't think either of them believed that they were going to be released, and yet they couldn't quite acknowledge it to one another.

They sat with the children, but Adam quickly saw that Carole wanted to speak to him. He shifted closer to her.

'I've been thinking about a news story from years ago,' she said. 'Some bank robbers kidnapped the manager's family and held them hostage, forcing the manager to open the vault. I know Brian worked for a telecom company, not a bank, but perhaps they're after trade secrets, or some kind of intellectual property?'

'I guess it's possible,' he agreed, though she can't have missed his lack of enthusiasm for the theory.

'Going back over it, I'm starting to be persuaded that killing Brian was done in panic. I don't believe they expected him to be there.'

Adam felt she was correct on that point. They had come to the house for Carole, and no one else. The question was why, and Adam wasn't ready to rule out something in her own life, rather than her husband's.

'I think it might be worth pushing for more information.'

Katy, who'd been chatting with the children, shot him a worried look, and Carole said, 'I'm not sure if that's wise.'

'But if we can get a sense of what lies ahead, we can plan how to deal with it. And the only way to do that is by interacting with them.'

He looked from Carole to Katy; both of them not just unconvinced but scared – and undoubtedly with good reason.

Sighing, Katy said, 'What did you have in mind?'

Maggie held a meeting in the lounge. It was almost five-thirty and she badly wanted another drink. Her alcohol consumption had rocketed over the past few months, though she couldn't bring herself to care too much. Funny to recall how she'd once despised her dad, rocking back from the pub hours after his Sunday roast had been scraped into the bin; having to bear the brunt of his rage because Mum was off at one of her cleaning jobs, toiling all the hours she could because Dad had been fired again. Years later Maggie learned that the Sunday job had been bogus: her mum had been sleeping with a manager from the factory where she worked during the week, and he gave her money to back up her story. 'A gift,' her mother had insisted. 'Nothing more.'

How easily we fool ourselves, as well as others, Maggie thought. She regarded the men in her employment, and asked, 'Are you sure the kid didn't give us away?'

Dale shrugged, then shook his head. 'Don't think so.'

'We'd not be here now, would we?' Gary added.

'So I can believe what she told me?'

'Yeah. Except...' Dale made a gulping noise. 'There was a woman in an Audi, on the way in as we were driving out. Gave us a proper serious look – you know the way the filth do it?'

'You never said nowt about that,' Gary snarled.

'We were leaving by then. And it were only a second – it might not have meant anything.'

Roger glared at Dale but his anger, Maggie felt, was directed at her. 'Hope we don't come to regret letting the kid go to the party.'

It was Jay who came to her defence. 'Keeping the family out of contact could have led to people calling at their house. Ringing their phones. Notifying the cops that they've gone missing.'

'Exactly. What we did today bought us more time. It's not perfect, by any means, but it was a risk worth taking. And we succeeded, didn't we?' Maggie eyed Roger, inviting him to agree. 'Whatever garbage the kid came out with, the grown-ups aren't gonna give it much thought. What's important is that right now none of their friends or relatives are wondering where the hell they are.'

A few nods, and mutterings of support, but Gary said, 'If you ask me, the best thing would be to do them now, get it over with.'

'And have four more bodies to dispose of?' Maggie gave a scornful laugh. 'Or do we leave them in the cellar, while we're sitting around here for the next day or so?'

Gary looked down, mumbling something that might have been: 'Dump them somewh—'

He was interrupted by a tapping sound, gentle and strangely polite. From the cellar.

Maggie nodded at Jay. 'Find out what they want.'

Adam was knocking a second time when he heard footsteps. He glanced back at the others, clustered together on the mattress.

'Be careful,' Katy mouthed at him. Which translated as: *Don't do anything stupid.*

The door was opened by Jay. He looked relaxed, though there was a neat black pistol in his hand.

Adam had to clear his throat before he could speak. 'Can I talk to Maggie?'

'What about?'

'A few things. Tomorrow.'

Jay waited for more, but Adam was determined not to elaborate. After a few seconds, Jay flicked the gun in irritation. 'Come up.'

The tall one, Roger, was in the lounge doorway. He ushered Adam inside while Jay locked up. Maggie and the other two men were sitting in silence. There was no light seeping in around the makeshift curtains, and the room felt colder and even more gloomy than before.

'Thank you for letting Dylan go to the party.' It was hard to sound grateful in a situation like this, but Adam thought it might earn him some goodwill.

Maggie grunted. 'What do you want?'

'Well, some food and drink wouldn't go amiss.' He tried to grin. 'And a chance to use a proper toilet. That bucket might have done for one person, but not five of us. The children, at least, should be treated better than this.'

He was dry-mouthed, his heart hammering, and still Maggie regarded him as a cat would study a trapped mouse.

'And then there's tomorrow…'

'What about it?'

'I know you told Katy that we'd have to call in sick. She's okay with that, and it's fine for the kids, but I have a meeting that I've got to attend.'

Maggie looked dubious, and Roger said, 'Can't if you're ill.'

'Normally I'd agree.' Adam could feel one of his legs start to tremble, and tried to press more weight down on that foot. 'But this is vital to the business, and I'm quite a big part of it.'

'So they'll postpone it.'

'Till when?' This was precisely the response he'd been hoping for. 'If I can tell them Tuesday morning, it might just be possible…' He paused, but could see that Maggie wasn't about to give anything away. 'Even if I say I'm laid up in bed, they might require me to do the meeting via Skype. We did that once before, when my boss broke his leg.'

There was a heavy silence, until Jay spoke up. 'I could probably go with him, if there's no better option.'

Maggie sneered. 'And say what?'

Put on the spot, Jay stared at Adam with an expression that said, *Help me out here.*

Adam had to think fast. 'I could tell my colleagues that you're a friend of the family, interested in a career in marketing.'

Gary snorted. 'Like anyone's soft enough to fall for that!'

Adam kept his focus on Jay. 'I can give you some of the background, to make it convincing.'

'I don't think so,' Maggie said. And it was her opinion that counted, Adam knew.

'All right. But if they tell me to Skype, or one of them decides to come round and visit me, it creates a much bigger problem.'

She was still shaking her head, distractedly, and Adam didn't feel he was any closer to winning her over. His shoulders slumped in defeat.

'Well, that's all I wanted to say. At least you know…'

He was starting to turn when Maggie spoke: 'I'll think about it. Decide in the morning.'

'Okay. Er, can I ask when we'll be allowed to go? Is it tomorrow afternoon, tomorrow evening…?'

She jabbed a finger. 'Don't push your luck.'

Perhaps it was retaliation for his cheek, but Roger seemed to shove him as they reached the doorway, causing Adam to crack his elbow on the frame. It was still throbbing when he descended the steps into the cellar, but he was determined to show no sign of the pain to the others.

Katy jumped up. 'How did you get on?'

'They let me say my piece. Whether they'll act on it, I don't know.'

She lowered her voice. 'Did they believe you, about the meeting?'

'I think so. Maggie vetoed the idea of me going anywhere, but the young guy, Jay, suggested that he could come with me, so maybe he'll talk her round. He seems less afraid of her than the others.'

'And the ransom, or whatever it is they want?' Carole said tentatively.

Adam shook his head. 'Sorry. I didn't get the chance to ask about that.'

They shared a sip of water each, then he took the scissors and went to work on the cover. The need to explore the void behind it had become more important than ever. Far from being the backup plan, it might be the only chance they had of getting out of here.

Having seen Maggie's reaction, and her general demeanour, Adam was now convinced that the promise to release them was an outright lie, told only to keep them docile, easily controlled.

Once the gang were finished here, they wouldn't want any loose ends. And that invariably meant killing their prisoners.

CHAPTER TWENTY-THREE

'Cheeky bastard,' Roger muttered when he returned to the lounge.

'In his position, I'd probably do the same,' Maggie said. 'Takes some guts.'

'So what about food?' Gary asked, with a nonchalance that fooled no one.

Roger snorted. 'Hungry, are you, Gaz?'

'Probably time to sort out dinner.' Maggie gestured at Gary and Dale. 'You two can go. Any preferences?'

'How about a curry?' Roger rubbed his hands together. 'Something to warm us up in this shithole.'

Dale and Gary looked equally enthusiastic, so Maggie agreed. 'Go a fair way out – Crawley, maybe, or Redhill.'

Gary nodded. 'What about the lodgers?'

'Sandwiches will do for them.'

'And drinks?' Gary asked. 'Are us workers to be allowed any booze?'

His tone was loaded was sarcasm, because he knew she'd been on the vodka earlier. But they were facing a long, uncomfortable night, and she could do without a load of bitching and moaning.

'A couple of cans each.'

'And some chocolate,' said Roger, who had a notoriously sweet tooth.

'Watch your driving,' Maggie warned Dale. 'Even with cloned plates, we don't want to be drawing any attention.'

She handed over some cash, then realised that Jay hadn't said a word. He was staring intently at one of the phones, a funny little smirk on his face.

'Curry all right with you, Jay?'

His head jerked up. 'What? Yeah, fine.'

She waited until Gary and Dale had taken the order and gone, then said, 'Stick the kettle on, will you, Roger? And have a quick scout round.'

'Sure.' He understood he was being asked to make himself scarce.

Jay was still lost in his own world, a tendency that had always irritated her a lot more than it should.

'Whose phone is that?'

'Uh? Adam's.'

'Right.' She waited for more, but he'd already tuned her out. 'Care to explain what's so interesting?'

'Nothing, really.' He finally looked up. 'I've checked his calendar, and the meeting's booked from ten until one. Marked as important. So he's not bluffing about it, if you were worried—'

'On my list of problems, that comes in at a thousand and fiftieth.' She slapped a hand on her knee. 'How we ended up with an entire sodding family…'

'It's a mess. I'm still not convinced it's right to go ahead.'

'Jay, we've been through that more times than I care to remember. Anyway, what do you suggest – that we let them all stroll out of here?'

'No, but if those kids die, the police investigation will be relentless. There's nowhere on the planet we could hide.'

'I've known people get away with worse.' Ruefully, she shook her head. 'Abandoning everything now, what do you think's gonna happen when Voronov hears about Carole?'

'True. So we kill her, and leave both bodies at their house. Make it look like a violent robbery.'

'Voronov would know. Or he would assume. And then there'd be another attack on us, and no second chance of a negotiation.' She made sure he was paying attention, and said, 'I'm tired of it, Jay.'

'I know you are.'

'I want out. I want all of us out. Sipping tequilas on a beach, money in the bank, and well shot of this open sewer of a country.'

'If he comes through with it,' Jay muttered.

'It's in his interests.'

'People don't always—'

'I know,' she snapped. 'That's why we arranged the bloody insurance.' She waved a hand. 'So forget about Adam's phone – it's Carole's we need to focus on. Why hasn't Voronov been in touch?'

'Because he thinks Brian is around. Or he's busy getting ready for tomorrow.'

She made a humming noise to express her doubt. 'No. I think we need a chat with her, while the bozos are out.'

Katy agreed to help Adam remove part of the cover. Not because she thought it was a good idea, or likely to achieve anything, but because she hoped to minimise the noise. And Adam was determined to do it, with or without her support, which would have made her cross if it didn't scare her so much.

He doesn't think we're going to survive this. It's escape or nothing.

She couldn't discuss it with him, not while there was any chance of the children hearing. If that was the truth, it had to be kept from them until the last possible moment.

She felt a wave of fury so overwhelming that it blurred her vision and caused her to sway on her feet. She wanted to destroy the people who would do this to her beloved son and daughter. It was Sunday evening: right now they ought to be running baths, chasing down bookbags and homework, watching *Strictly* and debating the fairness of this week's expulsion, encouraging the kids to feel excited about the week ahead: seeing their friends, their favourite teachers, getting to play sports and paint and sing…

Once again, Adam looped his belt around the single protruding board, and then gingerly applied pressure, hoping to lever the rusted screws out of the wall. Katy prodded the point of the scissors into the gap, pushing down until she had enough of an angle to probe the brickwork around the first screw.

Their success was unexpected – the rawl plugs anchoring the screws abruptly popped out of the wall and the board swung free at one end, bending so much that it nearly split. Adam stumbled back, dropping the belt and frowning at the noise.

'Shit,' he breathed. 'If they heard that…'

Katy scooped up the screws and they set the board against the wall and shoved the fixings back into their holes. In the dim light, the panelling looked undamaged.

'You'd have to get close to see that it's loose,' she said.

Adam nodded. 'So we carry on?'

'Yes. But let me make a start – you reassure the kids.'

The force they'd exerted had already loosened the second pair of screws. After a couple of minutes with the blade, she'd brought the screws out far enough to push them from side to side, enlarging the holes in the brickwork.

The timber felt damp and almost slimy in her hands, and there was a smell of decay emanating from the space behind it. She signalled to Adam, who once again promised Freya and Dylan that there was nothing to be worried about. He joined her, his eyes widening in a question.

'I think it's ready to come out,' she said. 'If you take that end.'

Aware of how easily the wood might splinter – and be heard upstairs – they each grasped one end and kept the board more or less parallel to the wall, with Katy pulling gently on the fixings.

One of the screws jammed, then suddenly gave way, but this time they were ready for it.

They stared at each other for a second, the timber still in their hands, and then turned to the wall. The long narrow gap clearly revealed an opening, with bricks visible along the sides, and mounds of rubble and debris on the bottom. A few wisps of dust drifted out like smoke; clearly this space, whatever it was, hadn't been disturbed for many years.

They both crouched to look closer, but the interior was lost to darkness after only a few inches. 'Let's get another board off,' Adam said, 'and we should be able to see further in.'

A tap on his shoulder startled him. They turned to find Freya, holding hands with her brother, both of them gazing solemnly at the gap in the wall. Behind them, Carole remained on the mattress, hunched over and seemingly oblivious, trapped in her own private misery.

'Is it safe, Mummy?' Freya asked. 'What if the bad people come down here?'

'It's fine, sweetheart. We can hide it easily enough.'

'If they want us, they usually call from the doorway,' Adam said.

The second slat was easier to work on, because they could get their hands behind it, alternately pressing and pulling until the screws slid out of the wall. A few minutes of determined effort and it was off, and the board below that looked to have come loose at one end.

'If only we had a torch,' Adam murmured. He knelt down, tilting his head to squeeze through the gap and get part of his upper body into the space. Katy heard him blow a couple of times, then whistle quietly.

'What can you see?'

'Nothing.' He retracted his head, dust in his hair and eyebrows. 'But there was a bit of an echo. It goes back a long way, I reckon.'

'You can't be sure.'

'No. But it's large enough to crawl along. It has to be worth investigat—'

Footsteps overhead, and then a metallic sound. It was Katy who reacted first. Earlier Freya had told her how she'd had to urinate in the bucket, using the mattress as a screen. Now Katy moved fast, urging Carole to stand, then grabbing the woman's arm and hauling her up when she failed to respond.

'The bucket,' she said to Adam, who seemed to get what she had in mind. She was aware of more noise, the door being unlocked and opened, but couldn't spare even a fraction of a second to look up.

As Adam set the bucket down in front of the opening, Katy snatched the mattress and shooed him away.

'But I should—'

'Go!' She undid her jeans and pulled them down an inch or two, then crouched over the bucket with the mattress held in front of her, blocking the view of the panelling. There was a heavy tread on the stairs, and Katy suffered a flashback to the moment she'd been pinned against the table in her kitchen.

Don't let it be Gary…

A voice barked: 'Carole.'

It was Roger. And instead of waiting at the top, he was coming down, his head bent to avoid the low ceiling. He noticed Katy and scowled. 'What are you doing?'

'What do you think?' Adam answered on her behalf. 'Give my wife some privacy, will you, please?'

Roger glanced at her again, then returned his attention to Carole. 'We need to talk to you. Come on.'

Carole shrank back, clutching at Adam's arm. 'I don't know what you want from me. I can't help you—'

'Just come upstairs.' Roger was losing patience, and Katy knew that every second he was down here increased the danger.

'Go on, it's all right.' Adam gave her a quick embrace. 'They won't hurt you.'

Carole swallowed a sob, then made eye contact with Freya and drew herself upright, as if remembering the need to put on a brave face for the youngsters. Without saying a word, she walked past Roger and climbed the steps.

Katy shut her eyes against a similar urge to cry. Never had she seen someone look more like they were being marched to the gallows.

CHAPTER TWENTY-FOUR

Holly worked until all the natural light had bled from the tiny apartment and she was marooned in the solitary glow of her desk lamp. Outside it was reassuringly dark: this awful day, designed for leisure, had been survived, and she could now look forward to the bright bustle of Monday, and a new week.

She would have worked for longer if her vision hadn't begun to shiver and blur. Somewhere behind her eyes she felt the silvery twinge of pain that often preceded a migraine. After losing Simon so unexpectedly, she had been plagued by a succession of them, each one wiping her out for two or three days at a time.

She washed down her prescription painkillers with a gulp of cold tea and lay on her sofa, safely away from her workstation but not from her phone. Replacing one overlit screen with another, she raised it high and squinted at the messages she'd sent, scrolling through a pointless and predominantly one-way conversation.

Soliloquy: wasn't that what they were called? She was surprised to find just how many messages there were: under oath she would swear that she had toiled throughout the afternoon and barely touched her phone. And why did she sound so angry, so desperate, so despairing…?

That isn't me, she thought. It's not who I want to be. If I speak in that voice, it's because *he* makes me sound that way.

Her thumb was poised to send another – and she would commit herself to making it the day's final message; something self-deprecating, and gently apologetic – but then an incoming text ghosted on to the screen. A reply, a reply from him; and it made her smile and then laugh, and after that she was safe to turn on the lights and greet the evening, confident now that the migraine wouldn't attack – it wouldn't bloody dare, and neither would the black dog.

Suddenly, life was good.

CHAPTER TWENTY-FIVE

Maggie had to concede that Carole was a slim and sensual woman. In favourable lighting, with well-applied make-up and a fabulous outfit, she would no doubt be quite the stunner – for her age, at least. Right now, though, she looked drab and dowdy, her hair a mess, her face deathly pale and scraped of cosmetics. Only a trace of the sensuality remained, there in her eyes, in her mouth, in the way she carried herself.

Finding her had been a happy accident, after a chance remark that Voronov had a lady friend in Sussex, a lover that nobody beyond his inner circle knew about.

The Russian had never married, and was notoriously shy of publicity; virtually a recluse. In the time that they'd been forced to take an interest in the man – almost two years now – they'd caught a few rare glimpses of him slipping into a theatre, or a restaurant, and invariably he'd been accompanied by a young female companion.

There was a different one each time, but so interchangeable did they appear that Maggie had assumed they were only props. After all, a man of Voronov's nationality and background could never come out as gay. In that context, the discovery of his affair with a well-to-do Sussex housewife had come as quite a shock.

And, more importantly, an opportunity.

Maggie was sitting in one of the garden chairs, with the other right next to her. She tapped the seat. Kept her voice soft. 'Sit here.'

The woman obeyed. She was shaking with fright, and gave off an odour of nervous sweat; sweat and stale urine, along with the dust and decay of the cellar. It reminded Maggie of her mother's final weeks in a care home, rotting from the inside.

It was Carole who broke the silence. 'Please. I d-don't know what you want. M-my husband…'

'Like I said, I'm sorry about Brian.' Maggie rested a hand on the woman's knee. Carole shuddered, but didn't push her away. 'When this is over, maybe we can look at compensation for what you've been through.'

Carole bit her lip, then tried to speak. 'Th-that won't…'

'Bring him back?' Maggie tutted, as if commiserating, but Carole shook her head.

'It won't give me justice.'

The anger in her voice took Maggie by surprise. 'True. But then we never get everything we want in life, do we?'

Carole ignored the comment. She was weeping silently, snot bubbling from her nostrils. 'I can't help you. I know very little about Brian's employers. No one there is likely to listen to me.'

Maggie was amused by this, but said nothing. She found a tissue in her pocket and handed it to Carole.

'So I won't… I won't be able to get you a ransom, no matter what you threaten…'

'Who's threatening anything? I'm being very reasonable, aren't I?' Maggie waited for acknowledgment, but the woman wouldn't meet her eye. After blowing her nose, Carole tucked the used tissue inside her sleeve.

Maggie let her recover, then said, 'Why was Brian home this weekend? I believe he'd planned on a golfing holiday?'

'Who told you about that?'

'No one. We gained access to your house a couple of months ago. Top quality lock on your front door, but a lousy one on the back.'

Carole gasped. 'Nothing was stolen…'

'We were after information, and we found plenty – including your husband's desk calendar. The golf weekend was clearly marked.'

'He wasn't feeling up to it. His sciatica.'

'So it was a last-minute cancellation? Did that mess up your plans at all?'

'My…' Carole looked up, and seemed to read something in Maggie's face. Something she didn't welcome. 'Wh-why would it?'

'You tell me. It's a Sunday, not bad weather. Maybe you'd want to go out somewhere, meet a friend?'

'I had nothing planned. I don't know why you're asking, and if you won't say what you—'

'Alexander.'

A look of pure terror came into Carole's eyes. She blinked furiously and said, 'I d-don't know an Alexander.'

'Your special friend?' Losing patience, Maggie bared her teeth. 'We know all about it, Carole. The house in Forest Row? You're having an affair with Alexander Voronov.'

'No, it's—'

'He's probably given you a false name, but he's really called Voronov. He's a Russian businessman, or criminal – or both – said to be worth one point eight billion pounds…' She saw the blood drain from Carole's face, and finished simply: 'We want him, and you're here to make sure we get him.'

Carole opened her mouth but all that emerged was a quiet groan. Then her eyes rolled up in her head and she fainted.

Adam and Katy were keen to get back to work on the panelling, but had to persuade the children that it wasn't putting them in danger.

'Will you tell your brother a story?' Katy asked Freya. 'You're brilliant at that.'

'But what? I can't think of any.'

'You don't have to make one up. Something from a movie will do. How about *Frozen*?'

'You know that off by heart and back to front,' Adam said with a grin.

Freya gave them a put-upon face, but sat beside Dylan and held his attention with her description of the movie's plot, keeping her voice quiet but with plenty of expression, and sometimes making a creditable attempt at the characters' accents. Adam loved to watch her perform in this way, and thought she had real potential as an actress and a mimic, but his focus had to be on the task ahead of him.

'I wonder if it's a crawl space, used to access an old heating system or something.'

'In that case, it won't go anywhere,' Katy pointed out.

'Maybe not. But in theory, once you're through the wall, it ought to be possible to reach the floorboards. I noticed earlier that the ground floor is in a bad state. If we can reach a part where the boards are rotten, or missing altogether…'

'What – and pop up out of the floor like a jack-in-the-box?'

He tried not to be hurt by the sarcasm, but Katy sensed it and rested a hand on his chest. 'Sorry, it just feels like such a long shot. They're bound to hear something.'

'I'm thinking in the early hours. We're no threat to them down here, so at most there should be only one or two guys keeping watch.' He clenched his fist and rubbed it savagely against his cheek. 'No, you're right. It probably is a long shot. But I have a horrible feeling it's this or nothing.'

She knew what he was saying, and nodded grimly. Next came a question he'd been dreading. 'Does Carole honestly not have any clue as to why she's here?'

'Not really.' He must have sounded too reluctant to answer; Katy was expecting more, so he said, 'She did mention that she's been seeing someone.'

'An affair?' Katy's eyes widened in fury. 'You mean all this could be because she's been cheating—'

'Sshh.' A cautionary nod towards the kids. He ran through his conversation with Carole, and pointed out that the circumstances didn't quite fit that scenario. 'Normally it's the husband who goes crazy with jealousy. And maybe the Russian wanted Brian out of the way – but then why kidnap Carole?'

'Unless the Russian has got a wife? She'd have good reason to punish Carole…'

They shared a look, both of them struck by the same thought. Then Adam shook his head. 'Maggie as the wife of some Russian millionaire? I'm not sure about that.'

'Who is she, then? What's her interest?' Katy's gaze turned inwards, remembering something. 'When we were first brought in, Maggie greeted her a bit strangely. "So this is the lovely Carole Kirby?" That's what I think she said.'

'Like she knew her by reputation?' Adam was aghast. 'But what kind of lunatic would pursue a grudge on this scale?'

'Either someone who was treated really badly, or else a total headcase with a fixation on someone she can't have.'

The angry, sardonic tone left him in no doubt as to the comparison his wife was making. 'That's not fair—' he began, but she waved off his protest and gestured at the wall.

The third board was almost free at one end: soon they would be able to look inside. Aware of how close they were to falling out, Adam was only too grateful to end the conversation there.

CHAPTER TWENTY-SIX

Katy had to fight an instinct to withdraw into herself. She wanted time to process what she'd just heard; otherwise there was a chance that she would overreact, or make connections that didn't exist. And right now, this was more important.

She agreed that they should try to clear some of the debris from the opening and take a closer look, but not climb inside. 'It's filthy in there. If you come out covered in crap, they'll notice straight away.'

Adam looked round the cellar, as if searching for something to strengthen his case. 'But you brought spare clothes.'

'Still too dangerous. Let's wait to see if they bring Carole back soon.'

Adam huffed and puffed for a minute, but Katy held firm. On this sort of disagreement, at least, they were able to stay friendly.

Carefully they scooped out several armfuls of rubble and deposited it behind the sacks of dried-out cement, brushing off their clothes after each load.

When Katy leaned in for her first proper look, she was shocked by how tight the space was. If she crawled in on her belly, her head would be brushing the top of the brickwork. It reminded her that, early on in the relationship, Adam had confessed to suffering from mild claustrophobia, while she had always had a fear of the dark.

Right here, they had both things to contend with – not to mention spiders, and strings of ancient cobwebs coated with grime. And even worse…

'Won't there be rats?' she whispered.

'If there are, they'll keep their distance.' Adam indicated the house above them. 'It's the vermin up there I'm worried about.'

By now Katy estimated that Carole had been gone about twenty minutes. Had they taken her somewhere, or did they just want to speak to her?

Adam was still pushing to explore the crawl space. He put his head inside, then his shoulders. Katy grabbed his shirt. 'Please.'

'I'm not going any further.' His voice was muffled, but she could sense his excitement. 'I think I can see floor joists. And there's…' He grunted and stretched, one of his legs lifting into the air. Katy tugged on his shirt again and he extricated himself, clutching a handful of what looked absurdly like candy floss.

'Rockwool insulation. Someone's stuffed a load of it in there. I managed to move a bit and I think I could see some light coming in.'

As he brushed the dust from his shirt, he orientated himself and pointed to the right of the opening.

'I bet the house is on rising ground. Remember we had to climb steps to go inside? So this cellar is at the front, and the crawl space runs beneath the back of the house. I reckon the living room with the broken floorboards is over there. It could be a way out.'

Katy was unable to share his optimism. The thought of crawling in darkness beneath the floor, emerging into a room that might be guarded by a man with a gun, filled her with terror. Freya and Dylan would never manage it – and any panic, any noise, and they would all be dead.

Reading the doubt on her face, Adam said, 'I know it won't be easy.'

'Let's talk about it—' There was movement overhead. 'Shit!'

They grabbed the boards, slotted the screws back into their holes and prayed they would stay in place.

The door opened and Roger descended the steps backwards, guiding Carole. She seemed barely conscious, her head flopping forward with each step. Jay followed behind, supporting her weight and grimacing as the timber creaked and groaned.

'Whole thing could collapse,' he muttered.

'Nearly there.' Roger hit solid ground and reached out to grab Carole as she tumbled off the final step.

'What's happened to her?' Adam asked. He and Katy had rejoined the children, all four of them close together in a defensive group.

'Fainted,' Roger said. 'She'll be all right.'

They clearly weren't in any mood to elaborate, and Katy just wanted them gone before one of them glanced at the panelling. To her, the shadows between each board seemed glaringly obvious.

Before he turned to go, Jay offered a reassuring smile. 'Got some food for you in a bit.'

'Room service,' Roger added drily. 'How about that, eh?'

As they trooped upstairs, Katy and Adam both knelt at Carole's side. She had slumped on to the mattress, her eyes cloudy and unfocused. A thin line of spittle had dried between her mouth and her cheek. Her whole body was trembling.

'Carole?' Adam took her hand in both of his. 'Are you okay? Did they hurt you?'

She made a noise in her throat, but it was impossible to know what it meant. There were no obvious injuries that Katy could see, but the woman was clearly traumatised.

What did they ask you? Katy wondered. *Is this because you were cheating on your husband?*

Freya had gone on whispering to Dylan. Now she reached into the bag and brought out a fleece. 'Perhaps she's cold? She could wear this.'

'Good idea,' Adam said. 'Thank you, darling.'

They showed Carole the fleece, and without speaking she raised her arms and allowed them to put it over her head. Her movements were jerky, zombie-like, and Katy had the impression that she didn't really know where she was or who she was with.

It was a dreadful state to be in, but Katy's natural urge to sympathise was tempered by a gnawing resentment. Was it something as mundane and squalid as an illicit relationship that meant they were now all captives, facing a death sentence?

She wanted to scream at the injustice of it, and a fleeting glance at Adam must have betrayed her feelings.

'All right?' he asked.

Tight-lipped, she shook her head. 'Far from it.'

'What's—'

'Doesn't matter. Not now.'

Adam left it there. He was all too aware of Katy's views on infidelity, and it wasn't a subject he was keen to discuss. The priority had to be helping Carole as best they could – and perhaps finding out more about why they were here.

Even with the fleece, she continued to shiver. He gently placed his hands on her upper arms, and tried to massage a little warmth into her. 'What happened, Carole? Did they hurt you?'

'Not...' Carole blinked a few times, then shook her head again. 'Not physically.'

'But they questioned you?'

'About Brian.' Her hands danced above her lap, fingers writhing. 'Wanted to know... why he was home...' She was breathing too fast, gasping after every few words.

'Carole, it's all right. Deep breaths, like this.'

He exaggerated a slower rhythm; Carole watched him but couldn't mimic his actions. If anything, she was growing more agitated, a look in her eyes of utter devastation.

'Y-you were right,' she said. 'It is... it's Alex, Alexander...'

'You mean he did this?' Katy broke in. 'Your lover?'

'No…' Carole quailed at the anger in Katy's voice, and just before she dissolved completely she managed to say, 'He's their target.'

It was several minutes before she could speak coherently again. Adam sat with her, while Katy took the children to the far corner and helped them change into warmer clothes. They were both subdued, clearly shaken by Carole's emotional state, and Adam feared it would leave a lasting impression on them.

'He got in the way,' Carole said of Brian. 'That's what they told me. So you were right. It was me they wanted.'

Adam gained no real satisfaction from having his theory confirmed. 'I'm so sorry.'

'You can't be. Don't you see?' Her voice was a raw whisper. 'It means I'm to blame for all of this. For Brian. For you and your family.'

'You mustn't think like that. *They*'re the only ones to blame.' Adam shot Katy a warning look; imploring her not to disagree. Then he risked a delicate question. 'If Brian had gone away as planned, would you have been seeing Alex?'

'Not this weekend. He had other things…' She tailed off, and shut her eyes for a moment. 'That's what they wanted to know – so many questions about Alex. How often does he contact me? Did I tell him the golf weekend was cancelled? Had I intended to speak to him today?'

'What about Maggie?' Katy asked. 'Have you ever seen her before? Do you know her in any way?'

Her tone was still too brusque, prompting Carole to fold her arms in a defensive gesture. 'No, I don't.'

'So she's not Alexander's wife, or girlfriend?'

'No.'

'A family member, then – his girlfriend's sister, or something like that?'

Carole was shaking her head, and crying pitifully. 'Stop it. I can't deal with this.'

'Neither can we, Carole, but we're having to find a way.'

'Katy.' Adam frowned, but saw that she wasn't to be deterred.

'How is Maggie involved, then?' Katy pushed on with her interrogation. 'There must be a reason why she's targeted you like this, and I think you know what it is.'

'I don't! I swear to you, I don't!'

As Carole threw herself face down on the mattress, another voice yelled: 'Stop it! Stop fighting!'

CHAPTER TWENTY-SEVEN

It was Dylan. And for a moment after his outburst, there was a shocked silence.

'Oh God, I'm sorry. I'm so sorry.' Katy rushed to hug her son, but her apology was intended for them all.

'I hate it when you're arguing,' he said, sobbing against her shoulder.

'Me too.' Freya pointed at Carole. '*She*'s not the bad person, is she?'

Katy met Adam's eye, and shook her head. To her mind, there were nuances here that the others wouldn't understand – probably because in the circumstances they were irrelevant.

'No. She's not.'

A whimper from Dylan. 'My head hurts.' Katy was tutting in sympathy when he added, 'I'm cold and I'm hungry. I don't like it here.'

'Neither do we. But remember what we said about having to be brave?'

Now Freya's lower lip wobbled. 'It's hard to keep being brave. I'm scared, Mummy.'

We all are, Katy wanted to admit, but instead she gathered the strength to offer another assurance. 'Try not to be. Dad and I won't let anyone hurt you.'

The look she received in response made her want to shrivel up like a leaf in winter. Even at the age of nine, Freya was astute enough to know that this wasn't any normal situation, and that her mother's words were effectively worthless.

'They're bad people,' Adam said. 'They're planning to keep us until tomorrow, and then let us go. But I don't want any of us to be here for that long, which is why we've been trying to take the boards off the wall.'

'But is there a way to escape?' Freya asked.

'That's what we're trying to find out.' Adam gave Katy a hopeful shrug, and she nodded.

'Dad may have to climb inside, and see whether it leads anywhere.'

'Are you okay with that?' Adam asked. He moved over to the wall, and the others followed, watching as he removed one of the loose slats.

'Can I have a look?' Freya asked.

'Of course.' He removed the other slats, and allowed her to peer into the opening.

Dylan's tears had subsided; when he saw what Freya was doing, he broke away from his mum's embrace. 'I wanna look, too.'

'We have to be careful,' Katy said. 'The door could open at any second.'

She exchanged a troubled glance with Adam, then in unison they turned to look at Carole. They needed the mattress, to have ready as a screen, but that meant dislodging the woman, who was now curled sideways in a foetal position, her eyes squeezed shut.

Adam shook his head. 'We'll have to do without it.'

'Can you two go and sit next to Carole?' Katy asked. 'We won't be long.'

With the children out of earshot, Adam leaned close and whispered, 'I know it's frustrating, but try to go easy on Carole. I don't think she's far from having a complete breakdown.'

Katy said nothing, just plunged her fingers into her hair and pulled until the nerves in her scalp were on fire. She knew he was right, and it wouldn't do to shout or scream: *What about our children? What about their future, all the hopes and dreams we had for them, snatched away because of a single cry for help?*

Instead, she kept to practical issues. 'Don't go in too far. Remember what they said about bringing some food.'

'Do you believe that?' He snorted. 'More likely they were taking the piss.'

'Maybe, but we can't lose sight of the risks. If you get caught—'

'If I get caught, they'll probably kill me.' Adam hissed the words, his mouth so close that she could feel the exhalation on her cheeks. 'But you know what? If we stay here and do nothing, this time tomorrow I reckon we'll all be dead.'

The darkness was almost absolute, with only the merest suggestion of light far ahead and to his right. Adam had always hated to feel constricted, but reminded himself that to be imprisoned here for another day should give him far more reason to be afraid.

As his eyes began to adjust, some vague shapes gradually formed, along with an impression of horizontal space. Wriggling forward a few more inches, he tentatively reached out until both arms were fully extended at the sides. He couldn't feel any obstacles, other than more debris and tufts of insulation. That helped to quell the panic.

Plenty of room in here, he told himself. *You're not trapped.*

At this point his upper body was through the opening, but his legs were sticking out. Despite what he'd agreed with Katy, he decided to crawl another foot or so.

He shuffled forward, lifting his stomach in an attempt to reduce his contact with the dirt. Probably futile: the air was choked with dust, and the ground beneath his hands was so grimy he couldn't tell if it was concrete or beaten earth.

Another shuffle, and his knee caught the edge of the brickwork. Katy warned: 'Not too far!'

He acknowledged her with a grunt, but continued to advance. Again he put his arms out to the sides, but this time swept them in front of him as well – and one hand hit something: a hard, rough surface. Shifting forwards and turning partially on to his side, he patted his hands against what he guessed was a brick pillar or supporting wall. He tried to visualise the rooms above, and decided that this could be the wall between the kitchen and hallway.

Given that he was now virtually on his side, it made sense to roll on to his back, though in doing so his shoulder scraped against a thick timber joist. But it was worth enduring a little pain; with his vision attuned to the darkness, he could make out the pattern of floorboards, laid across a joist that was just a few inches above his face.

He ran his fingers along the underside, and then tried an experimental push. The board didn't yield, and there was no gap, no light coming in. There must be a floor covering above him, unlike in the living room.

If that was the only way out, it would rely on the gang choosing somewhere else to sleep tonight. If even one of them stayed in the lounge, there was zero chance of sneaking past.

Recalling Katy's jibe about a jack-in-the-box, he felt deflated. He tried to wriggle backwards, intent on searching the floorboards for other weak points, but was interrupted by a gasp from Katy, and then a long, strange rumbling noise – not rumbling, so much as gurgling.

At the same time he heard footsteps, the boards creaking directly above him. Then he registered the smell – it was curry – and understood that the noise had come from his own stomach.

'Adam! Quickly!'

The aroma was intoxicating. Adam's body convulsed as he understood what it meant. He tried to get on to his front, knowing it would give him more leverage, but he was too close to the joist; his arm jammed and he was stuck.

He'd never felt such terror. His lungs seized up and his heart went into a frenzy, black spots bursting in front of his eyes. Katy hissed another warning but it meant nothing. He couldn't move. And now they would enter the cellar and find him here and shoot him while he was helpless.

CHAPTER TWENTY-EIGHT

Katy saw his legs bucking desperately and realised that somehow he had got stuck. There was movement above them, and a muffled burst of laughter. They didn't have long.

'Hold still,' she urged him. 'Flatten yourself down.'

She couldn't understand why he'd turned on to his back, but better now that he stayed that way. 'Grab Daddy's foot,' she told the kids, while she took the other foot and pulled. It was like a scene from some grisly fairy tale, summoning her children to help save their father from the ogres.

At least there was progress. Adam slithered forward a few inches, and she could hear him scrabbling to push himself along. His legs emerged and now his upper body was lying across the brick-framed opening, with enough room for him to turn and back out.

But there wouldn't be time to replace the wooden slats. Katy turned, and hissed at Carole: 'We need the mattress.'

Though she'd managed to half sit up, Carole was in no state to respond quickly. She let out a moan, and then a shriek as the padlock bumped against the door.

Adam stood unsteadily, his face pale beneath smudges of dirt. The fleece he'd put on over his shirt was filthy, and Katy yanked it up and off. She was astonished by the sight of Freya and Dylan propping the loose boards against the wall, trying to conceal the opening.

As she balled up the fleece and tossed it into the corner, there was another worry: 'The scissors?'

Adam pointed to the floor beside the mattress. 'There.'

This time Carole came to life, sliding them beneath the mattress just as the door opened. Adam was still rubbing dirt from his face as Katy ushered the children away from the wall.

They were clustered next to Carole when Gary tramped heavily down the steps, holding a carrier bag. Spotting Adam, he paused on the third step and swung the bag towards him. Adam had to step back to avoid being struck in the stomach, then he hastily grabbed the bag as Gary let go. A couple of packets of sandwiches tumbled out.

'There you are.' Gary chuckled as Katy stepped forward to pick them up. Then he noticed Carole. 'What's up with her?'

'She's been like this since you brought her back,' Katy said. She wanted Gary to focus on her; if he looked too long at Adam he might notice the wooden slats against the wall.

'No one touched her,' Gary protested.

'Well, she's in a bad way.' Adam had now shifted towards the others. 'She needs to be somewhere more comfortable than this.'

Gary only sneered. 'Tough. Be grateful we're feeding you.' He turned to leave, sniffed the air and paused.

Katy's heart nearly stopped. Had he felt a draught, or caught some sort of odour from beneath the floor?

'Smell that?' He smacked his lips. 'Fooking lovely curry for us, and a beer to wash it down.'

Cackling to himself, he tramped upstairs. Katy let out a huge sigh. She could take any number of gibes if it meant he hadn't spotted the crawl space.

There were five packets of supermarket sandwiches, along with a large bag of Doritos and a bottle of Pepsi. They shared the food out equally; Dylan said he still felt sick, but he munched on a handful of Doritos and agreed to consider eating the sandwich later.

Carole barely reacted when they set the food at her side, and she didn't engage with their attempts to turn the meal into a kind of picnic. Adam and Katy did their best to act as though it was pleasurable to eat like this, kneeling on a dusty concrete floor in a dimly lit cellar – an adventure, something out of the ordinary – but they couldn't blame the kids for looking unconvinced.

It was getting colder. Soon they would all have to use a single bucket for a toilet, and then find a way to huddle together and try to sleep. Even if that proved possible, they would awake to a second day of captivity, with no idea of what might lie in store for them. And that uncertainty, the terrible fear of the unknown, couldn't be minimised, couldn't be concealed from the children forever.

Adam finished his sandwich in a matter of seconds and was still ravenous. He wouldn't countenance eating anything else, but caught Katy eyeing the food they'd passed to Carole, which lay untouched.

'Hey,' he said gently. 'It's best if you try to eat something.'

Carole moaned, and shook her head. 'My fault. It's all my fault.'

'No. They're to blame, not you.' He shifted closer, took one of her hands in his. 'You're freezing.'

He motioned to Katy, who scowled when he took the blanket. He wrapped it around Carole's shoulders, but she hardly acknowledged his presence. He found himself checking her face, but there was no physical paralysis. Her condition was emotional – severe shock – although no less serious for that.

Katy was supervising the children as they drank some of the Pepsi. Whether deliberately or not, she had moved to put herself between them and Carole, as if to shield their view of the poor woman. It also meant she had her back to Adam, which seemed like a deft way of conveying her indifference.

His resentment flared, then died just as quickly. This was another danger, he realised: the tension causing them to misinterpret the simplest of gestures.

He opened the packet of sandwiches and held one out for Carole. 'Please try to eat. Even just a few mouthfuls.'

After staring at the limp bread with a look of confusion, she accepted it, took a small bite and chewed mechanically.

'Well done,' he said. 'It'll help a bit.'

Her shoulders jerked in a shrug. 'You have the other one.'

'I'm fine. Better if you save—'

'I won't eat it. Please.'

Conflicted, he glanced at Katy, who must have been listening. She looked round and said, 'You might as well.'

He felt guilty. It didn't seem right to eat more than anyone else. Then again, later tonight it might fall to him to get them out of here, crawling beneath the floorboards and then running for his life, possibly while carrying one or both of the children in his arms.

It was devoured in a couple of bites, while Carole nibbled at a corner of her sandwich. Suddenly her eyes welled up with tears. A few lumps of soggy bread tumbled from her mouth. 'I killed Brian. I betrayed him.'

'Carole, no—'

'I did. Because of Alex. I can't…'

'What?' He leaned forward in alarm, but her gaze was distant, unfocused.

'I can't feel…'

'Can't feel what, Carole?' He placed his hands on her shoulders. Just minutes ago she'd been ice cold; now a feverish heat was pouring from her skin. Staring through him, she only repeated the same phrase, over and over again, the words slurring to a quiet mumble while the tears rolled down her cheeks.

'I can't feel… I can't feel… I can't feel.'

CHAPTER TWENTY-NINE

It was a day of fuck-ups, big and small. Dale swore he gave the correct order to the curry house, but somehow they'd got a missing chicken bhuna, and far too much rice. For a good five minutes Maggie could hear them squabbling like children.

'Just divvy it up, and stop fucking arguing,' she shouted from the lounge.

She was pouring another vodka when Jay slouched in, a paper plate piled high with rice and not much else.

'I wouldn't mind, but he didn't even get my Peshwari naan. It's cheese.'

'Christ almighty, does it really matter?'

Roger was next, carrying two plates and muttering about a piss-up in a brewery. Maggie took the plate she was offered and said to Jay, 'You can have some of this.'

'Nah, it's fine,' he said, in such a grumpy tone that Maggie had to shut her eyes and pray for the strength to cope.

'Are they coming in?' she asked of Gary and Dale.

Roger shook his head. 'I told 'em to eat in the kitchen.'

'Useless tossers,' Jay added.

'They're serving a purpose,' Maggie said quietly. 'Anyway, it's Carole we need to discuss. And Voronov.'

Jay tore off a hunk of naan bread and sniffed it suspiciously. 'Why not get her to message him, if you're that worried?'

'I might do that,' Maggie agreed, but Roger was wrinkling his nose.

'For all we know, he may have texted her just before we turned up, and she deleted it. Or perhaps she'd already warned him that Brian was home?'

'That's not what she said – and I don't think she's in any state to lie to us.' Maggie looked at Jay for confirmation. 'Do you?'

'No chance. She's a nervous wreck.'

'Tell you the truth, that worries me more,' Roger confided. 'Voronov might not take kindly to what we've done to her.'

'He won't have to know.' Maggie let out a sigh of exasperation. 'Am I the only one to see we might have the *opposite* problem?'

Jay must have decided the cheese naan was to his taste; he was shovelling in another piece when he frowned at her. 'What?'

'A lack of contact could mean he's cooled on her. Without that relationship, she doesn't offer us any leverage, if we need it.'

'But that's the thing – *if* we need it,' Roger said. 'We've got a deal agreed. This is just insurance.'

'Look,' Jay cut in. 'It's done now, and like you say, we don't know how valuable she is. Voronov might have moved on, found himself another milf, or he might be crazy about her…'

'What's your point?' Roger asked.

'If Carole's only here as insurance – and possibly worth fuck all – it might be better if we didn't use her. Better if Voronov never gets a hint that she was kidnapped.'

Maggie had lifted a forkful of chicken biryani into her mouth; chewing with little enthusiasm, her appetite fled as she saw where Jay was going. 'In case we have to kill her?'

He nodded. 'I think you're in denial here. Her husband was murdered—'

'And who by?' Maggie reminded him.

'Yeah, yeah. Anyway, there's no way she'll keep quiet about that. She can't – because the cops will suspect her of doing away with him.'

Especially with a lover in the wings, Maggie thought, which gave her the germ of an idea.

Roger cleared his throat. 'Surely that doesn't matter? Once the deal's done, we're out of here for good. New homes in the sun and all the rest of it...'

'No, he's right,' Maggie said, with heavy regret. 'Cleaner all round if Carole dies, too.'

'But Voronov can't know,' Jay said. 'Even if the relationship has run its course, he'll go insane if he finds out we killed her, especially when he's just handed us a small fortune. That's meant to be the peace settlement, and here we are launching a whole new war...'

Jay emphasised his words by flapping the remains of his naan bread, which suddenly resembled a scalp. Maggie felt her stomach roil.

'He'll know. It's too much of a coincidence – Carole and her husband found dead at the same time we come to Sussex to do a deal.'

'He might *suspect*, true. But he won't be sure.' Jay sounded pleased with himself. 'And better still, we might be able to pin their deaths on someone else.'

'Who?' Roger asked, but Maggie just laughed, feeling better than she had in hours. That germ had just taken seed elsewhere.

'Who have we been talking about?' she asked.

Roger frowned at her. 'Voronov...?' His confusion slowly gave way to a beaming smile. 'Voronov!'

'It's bloody perfect,' Maggie agreed. 'You devious little rat, Mister.'

Jay bowed his head. 'Gives him a lot more to think about.'

'Okay. But how do we make it stick?' As ever, Roger was one for the practicalities.

'Gotta get some DNA,' Jay said. 'That should be possible, as we'll be meeting him face to face. Then we take both the bodies back to the house.'

Maggie shook her head. 'Transport Carole alive, and kill her there.'

'Fine. By that point we've got our cash, which you can bet Voronov is furious at having to hand over—'

'Even though it's peanuts to him,' Maggie put in.

'Yeah, but he still won't like it. He'll probably be harbouring thoughts about coming after us, tracking us down. In the meantime, waiting just around the corner for him...' Jay clapped his hands together. 'Boom! He's in the deepest shit of his life.'

Maggie tried to tamp down her excitement; it sounded slightly too good to be true. 'We still need a bit of distance. If we get lucky, the bodies won't be discovered for a few days.'

Jay nodded. 'Exactly. And we can whack up the heating to accelerate decomposition. Makes it harder to pinpoint the time of death.' He caught Maggie's astonished glance and said, 'I saw it on TV – *CSI* or something.'

'That's important,' Roger said. 'Especially as there's gonna be a difference of more than twenty-four hours between Brian's death and Carole's.'

'It's not just that,' Jay said. 'For all we know Voronov might have alibis for a lot of this weekend. The vaguer the time of death, the harder it'll be for him to prove he couldn't have done it.'

'But will they have his DNA on file?' Maggie asked.

'I doubt it. That's where a little anonymous phone call comes in.'

Roger almost choked. 'We point the law in his direction?'

'Very slick.' Maggie pondered it. 'What you're forgetting is that he's well-connected over here – not at the same level as in Russia, but still enough that he might wriggle out of it.'

Jay didn't think so. 'We all hate the cops, but they're not as bent here as in a lot of places. And the politicians in Britain are cowardly wankers – happy to suck up to the oligarchs when they're posing as legitimate businessmen, but any hint of scandal and they'll drop him like a hot brick.'

'Potato,' Maggie said. 'The phrase is "hot potato". But I think you're right.'

'Very shrewd,' Roger added. He'd cleared his plate, and now wiped his hands on his jeans. 'Even if he manages to escape a conviction, the case will keep him bogged down for months, if not years.'

They grinned at each other, sharing a second or two of mutual congratulation before the peace was disturbed by a heavy thumping on the cellar door.

Gary looked in on them, a tin of Carling in his hand. 'I take it you heard that?'

Maggie nodded. 'Find out what they want.'

CHAPTER THIRTY

At the sound of movement beyond the door, Adam nervously moved down a step. He blew out a breath and filled his lungs, praying this wasn't a bad idea.

Katy hadn't been particularly supportive, agreeing only because she feared that Carole's worsening condition would upset the children. She didn't believe their captors would do anything to help.

'They don't care about her,' she'd hissed to Adam, and it hadn't been necessary to add: *Or us.*

Gary opened the door. His face was flushed, and there was a blob of curry sauce on his shirt. 'What?'

'Carole has a high fever.' Adam turned sideways, making sure he was still blocking Gary's view of the panelling, and gestured at her. 'Her speech is rambling, and she's disorientated. She needs medical help.'

'That's not happening.' But he took a long look at Carole, who was hunched over, shivering and muttering to herself, one stray foot juddering uncontrollably. With a sigh, he turned and spoke to someone in the hall: 'Watch the door for a second.'

Dale appeared in his place, gun in hand. He glared at Adam, who trudged down the steps and gave Katy a hopeless, apologetic glance.

'It's the right thing to do. I still think that.'

Katy was sitting between the children, both of them hugging her for warmth and comfort. Some of the fight seemed to have gone from her eyes, so it didn't really surprise him when she nodded wearily. 'I know.'

Gary lumbered into the lounge. 'He's saying Carole needs a doctor. Reckon she's feverish, disorient-disoria—'

'I get it,' Maggie snapped. 'How does she look to you?'

'Like death warmed up.'

'Perhaps she's claustrophobic?' Jay suggested.

A snort from Roger. 'You'll be pointing out how we're abusing their human rights in a minute.'

Jay didn't rise to the taunt. 'Maybe she should sleep up here?'

'Go and get her,' Maggie told Gary. 'Give him a hand, will you, Rog?'

She stood up and stretched, her knees and spine popping. Without being asked, Jay gathered the paper plates and took them out to the kitchen. For a moment Maggie was alone in the room. She wandered over to the makeshift drapes and carefully peeked out.

They had chosen this place well. The nearest settlement was a couple of miles away, the source of a vague orange glow in the south-westerly sky. The house stood on a plot of some twenty acres of neglected meadows and exhausted arable land; as Maggie understood it, a battle was underway between NIMBYs and the developers who proposed to build dozens of homes. Right now they were stuck in limbo, with nobody caring that the house was slowly crumbling into the ground. It was the perfect place to hide out.

She stared at what she knew to be a copse of trees, close to the house, but the darkness remained impenetrable. It made her shiver. She was a city girl, born and bred, and at some deep, primitive level she feared the absence of light and sound, of buildings and vehicles and people.

And funny, she thought, how isolation could make you feel either vulnerable or secure, depending on your mindset.

Carole was brought in by Gary and Roger, their arms linked with hers and holding her upright, her feet scudding across the floorboards. She wasn't wearing shoes, and her tights were almost shredded around her toes. Her head was bowed, her chin nearly touching her chest, and her arms were curled inwards, hands clasped together and clutching her stomach.

She looked like someone who'd just suffered a beating, and since Maggie was confident that no one had touched her during the past six or seven hours of captivity, that seemed to indicate a problem.

They came to a stop. When Gary pulled his arm free Carole promptly collapsed, falling sideways until Roger managed to take the extra weight and lower her to the floor. Carole's head jerked upwards as she landed, legs splaying out in a very indelicate pose, her dress riding high on her thighs. She was wearing a baggy, shapeless fleece over the dress, which Maggie guessed had been given to her by Katy and Adam.

'What's wrong, Carole?' she asked.

The woman mumbled a short reply, which none of them understood. A sudden metallic crunching noise made her yelp. Gary had just crushed the empty can of lager in his hand.

'Two each, right?' he said. 'Anyone want—?'

'Not now,' Maggie answered for them. 'Take a look round outside, will you?'

Gary frowned. 'Is there something up?'

'Precaution. Off you go.'

The truth was that she wanted him out of her sight; the man was driving her insane. She didn't like the way he smirked as he ambled away, or the sarcastic laughter a moment later, when he rejoined Dale in the kitchen.

Moving closer to Carole, she knelt carefully on the bare floorboards, nodding at Roger to back off a little. There was no reaction from the woman, whose head was slumped at a painful angle, her hair falling across her brow and covering her eyes. Her body was trembling, and one foot worked like a piston, a frenzied release of nervous energy.

Maggie grabbed the foot and squeezed it hard. Carole squealed, pressing her arms even tighter into her belly.

'Are you hurt, Carole? Is something wrong with your stomach?'

A whimper. Her skin felt scorching hot. Perhaps Jay had a point: it might be best if she slept up here, where they could keep an eye on her.

'We have some painkillers, if that's what you need?'

There was movement, a sullen shake of the head. But at least she was listening.

'Can you look at me, please, Carole? I need to talk to you. About Alexander.'

Slowly the head came up. Carole's eyes were bloodshot and leaking tears, and the skin beneath them was dark and puffy.

'Wh-what about him?'

'How many times a week do you talk to each other?'

Carole winced, as though it was a taxing question. 'It... I don't know... Not every week. Not if he's away, or if B-Brian...'

Maggie nodded briskly. 'So it wasn't regular. When did you last see him?'

'Three... three or four weeks ago.'

'In Forest Row?'

'London. A hotel.'

'And you didn't set another date?'

'We don't... That's not how it works.'

Maggie glanced at Jay, who had Carole's phone in his hand. He was swiping the screen, a thoughtful look on his face.

'There's a contact here. Alyssa. But no messages or picture. Probably the code name.'

Jay didn't look up in time to see the flash of terror in Carole's eyes, but Maggie spotted it.

'Relax,' she said. 'You've got nothing to worry about.'

'You killed my husband.' Her head dropped again.

'In self-defence. And that's not what we're discussing here.'

Carole's knuckles were white, her hands writhing and pushing as if trying to burrow inside her abdomen. Maggie wondered if it was appendicitis or something: Christ, wouldn't that be typical of their luck?

'We might need you to send him a text. Or a WhatsApp. Which one would—?'

'*No.*' The reply was forced out between clenched teeth.

'Listen to me, Carole. You're going to help us, and that starts with pulling yourself together.'

The woman's head snapped up. 'I won't do it,' she snarled. 'I won't be used as bait.'

Maggie let out an involuntary laugh. 'That's not what you are…' She faltered, distracted by something trickling between Carole's fingers. 'You're bleeding. What have you done?'

Carole was at first surprised, slowly gazing down at her lap as if she thought Maggie was bluffing.

'I…' she began. She sounded baffled, yet also strangely serene.

Then she sprang.

CHAPTER THIRTY-ONE

Carole hadn't intended to draw blood. The tension had grown so unbearable that without realising it she'd pressed the tip of the scissors into the fleshy base of her thumb, harder and harder until it pierced the skin.

But it was good. She welcomed the pain, for the clarity it brought.

She was gripping the scissors like a dagger, with her left hand wrapped around her right to make absolutely sure they couldn't be seen. To stop herself from shaking she was having to press both fists into her belly; in this position it wouldn't take much for the scissors to penetrate her stomach.

She'd considered it, briefly, but knew the blades were too stubby to cut deeply enough. All she'd get was a nasty, painful wound that stood little chance of killing her.

The neck was a better option. And with that, an idea came to her.

She felt bad about Adam and Katy, depriving them of a vital tool. She felt even worse for their children: condemned to death, almost certainly, by an accident of fate.

But it wasn't about them anymore. It was about finding a response to her own pain. Her guilt. Atoning for her sins.

Starting with this.

She launched herself forward with the surprise that comes from a genuinely spontaneous action. Her body was weak and fevered, but somehow that didn't matter. There wasn't much energy or coordination required to slip the scissors into a slightly better grip, while swinging her right arm round in an arc that brought her fist parallel to Maggie's throat.

She felt the tip of the scissors make contact, but only for a fraction of a second. Her movement had been too fast, a wild swiping attack that couldn't do any real damage. Maggie jerked backwards and lost her balance, toppling to the floor. One hand went to break her fall, while the other rose to her throat. Carole spotted a bead or two of blood appearing, a trickle rather than a flood.

But it bought her some time. For a second or two no one moved, all of them trying to make sense of what had happened. How had she done that? Was she a danger to them?

The answer to the latter question: *not in the least.* These men could overpower her in a heartbeat, but by the time that occurred to them she was up and running.

She'd reached the hall before the first panicked shout came from Maggie: 'Stop her!'

A glance at the front door told her to forget it. There were heavy bolts at the top and bottom. No good making for the back door, either: the ginger one was in the kitchen, glugging from a can of beer.

He reacted to Maggie's cry by turning towards the hall. For a moment he was staring straight at her, his mouth gaping open. The can fell from his hand and beer started frothing on the floor.

Her only option was the stairs. The treads were bare timber, cracked with age and neglect. Splinters tore at her soles but she barely felt them. Suddenly the pain had gone, the tiredness had gone; she felt more alive than she had in a very long time. Probably since that first afternoon with Alex, in fact, and the glorious realisation that she was still a woman, a sexual creature, that she could desire and be desired.

Now the passion was for something else entirely.

A voice yelled, 'Don't shoot!' That was from the bearded one, Roger. She could hear them running after her but didn't look back. Someone must have raised a gun, and her heart sank with the understanding that they wouldn't use it.

They wanted her alive. So she could lure Alex into a trap.

It was dark on the landing; several doors nearby were shut, and she couldn't see a light switch. On instinct she ran along the passageway, drawn by the softer grey glow of an open doorway at the far end. To reach it she had to leap over a hole where part of the floor had collapsed, and she caught a glimpse of the room below. Could have fallen through the ceiling and killed herself; even in this madness she was able to smile at the irony there.

From behind her came heavy footsteps. 'One at a time,' someone shouted, 'or else the fucking stairs'll give way!'

Could she be that fortunate? To be gifted a few extra seconds to get this done?

The room at the end of the landing was as dilapidated as the rest of the house. A large sash window looked out on a pitch-black night. There was a crack running vertically through the lower pane, and the rotted remains of a velour curtain lay on the floor. As her eyes adjusted to the darkness, she scanned the room and realised there was nothing in here that could help her.

Except the scissors. They were still gripped in her right hand. The slick and sticky texture of the blood between her fingers was a bizarrely pleasant sensation, but there was still an intense revulsion to overcome if she was to proceed with what she'd half considered doing, ever since she'd thought to sneak the scissors out from beneath the mattress.

The neck. Plunge the blades into your neck.

Her reasoning was clear. She couldn't save the innocent family being held prisoner in the cellar, any more than she could bring her husband back. The guilt was unbearable; impossible to live with.

She had no idea what Alex might have done to attract the attention of people like Maggie and her accomplices, but Carole was determined that she wouldn't be used to ensnare him. She would not be a pawn in someone else's game.

A bright light came wavering along the landing. 'Carole, what are you playing at?'

The voice belonged to Jay, the one who'd killed Brian. A young man who, if he chose, could present himself as well-mannered and charming; like one of those good-looking, cheeky tradesmen that a woman of a certain age might fantasise about. It had to be an illusion, of course: beneath the surface lay a monster.

She moved back, out of sight of the doorway. She didn't think he'd seen her, but he knew she was here.

'For Christ's sake, Carole. You'll hurt yourself.'

I hope so, she thought. She raised the scissors and placed the tip against her neck. Finding the right spot. The carotid artery, wasn't that it? Something that, once ruptured, would cause her to bleed out quickly.

Jay again: 'You're being silly. Come back downstairs and we'll listen to what you have to say.'

He sounded like the exasperated parent of a young child. Funny. She'd have loved to have children, but it just wasn't to be. One of those things. But she was glad now: it meant there were very few people who'd feel the loss deeply, if at all.

The light came floating into the room. Jay was in the doorway, using the torch from a phone to locate her. She saw the gleam from his eyes, and the shock as he registered the scissors, now held a few inches from her neck. Ready to punch through the flesh.

'Carole, don't do this. You can't.'

Her hand was trembling. Tears falling. Because she knew he was right.

She couldn't do it.

Behind him, one of the others said, 'Have you got her?' At that, Jay took a cautious step into the room and Carole turned and ran. Ran as hard and fast as she could manage in half a dozen strides and threw herself head first through the window.

She heard the crash of the glass and felt a rush of cold air, a crazy confused mass of sensations all numbed by terror; blood pouring through her hair and down her face, her limbs vaguely trying to twist and find a way to land safely, but she resisted, fighting the survival instinct with every last bit of courage, not even placing her arms out to protect her head and then, finally, it was done. She was free.

CHAPTER THIRTY-TWO

Katy was in no doubt that they'd heard glass breaking, but less sure of the noise that followed, a distant low-pitched thud that might have been an impact.

She and Adam had been exchanging puzzled glances for the past few minutes, as they tried to make sense of the activity overhead. After the shouts and running footsteps, both of them were dreading the moment when the padlock rattled and it was their turn to be in the spotlight again. But so far it hadn't happened.

And then came a sudden shriek of rage, unmistakeably from Maggie: '*Fuuuck!*'

'What do you reckon?' Adam whispered.

Katy gave a quick shake of her head. The last thing she wanted was a debate in front of the children.

Too late. Whether or not it was in response to her dad's comment, Freya tugged on Adam's arm. 'What's happening?'

Then Dylan: 'They're not hurting her, are they?'

'I don't think so.' Adam sounded unsure. They were both finding it harder to maintain any kind of cheerful facade, and Katy couldn't blame him when he added, fretfully, 'I hope not.'

Maggie had gone out to the kitchen, where there were paper towels and a rudimentary first-aid kit among their supplies. She used a hand mirror to examine the wound to her throat. It was about what she expected: a minor nick to the skin, but another inch or so to the side and a little deeper, and it could have been serious.

She moistened a paper towel and dabbed the blood away. Checked her reflection again and was happy that no other treatment was necessary.

Roger, Dale and Jay were blundering about upstairs. Hearing Jay's voice, she went out to the hall and waited for him to bring Carole back down. An almighty crash made her cry out and grab the newel post.

Jay appeared moments later, almost stumbling in his haste to descend the stairs.

'What the hell was that?' she asked.

'You won't believe it.' He shook his head. 'She dived out the window.'

'Dived?'

'Yep. Just threw herself out, head first.'

Maggie blinked a couple of times, as if to check whether she was dreaming. No such luck. A sudden overwhelming fury filled her lungs; she opened her mouth wide and yelled: '*Fuuuck!*'

Jay winced, leaning out of range in case she tried to slap him. 'She might still be alive,' he reminded her, and eased past, heading for the kitchen.

The stairs creaked. The other two came down, both looking stunned. Roger indicated her throat. 'You okay?'

'Fine. It's this…' She threw her arms up in frustration, but Roger made a shushing noise and pointed towards the cellar.

Behind him, Dale was bobbing on his heels and trying to suppress a smile, as though this was all some big, exciting game.

'Go and help Jay,' she barked.

'Gonna be a mess.' He sucked his teeth. 'All I got to see was her feet, going out last. Like something from YouTube.'

Maggie waited till he'd gone, then muttered in disbelief, 'Fucking YouTube…'

'Dickhead,' Roger said.

Footsteps in the kitchen: not Jay but Gary. It took Maggie a second to remember that she'd sent him outside. He registered the look on their faces, started to speak then broke off as Jay appeared.

'Well?' Maggie asked him.

'You'd better come and see.'

Katy stood at the foot of the steps, listening hard. The murmur of voices was coming from the hallway; Maggie and one or two of the men. The tone was urgent, angry, confused.

She kept her gaze on Adam, who wore the same look of desperate concentration. So far it had been in vain: they had no idea what was going on.

He was crouched by the mattress, an arm round each of the children. Freya was shivering, despite three layers of clothing, and Dylan had tears in his eyes. Above them, the voices faded and there was silence.

Katy crossed her arms and hugged herself tight; she wasn't intentionally signalling a lack of comfort from Adam, but perhaps that was how she felt.

'Callous bitch, aren't I?' she said quietly.

'No. I don't think that at all.'

Katy shrugged. 'It's not that I don't care about her wellbeing. I do. But it's so hard to ignore the trouble that *we*'re in – and it's all because of whatever's going on in her life. Because of her cry for help, when she must have known there wasn't anything we could do.'

'I had the same reaction, but let's be fair – if you were in a situation like that, would you be thinking rationally?'

'I hope I'd—' She stopped short, then shook her head. 'Probably not.'

A face-splitting yawn from Dylan diverted their attention, and set Katy off. 'What time do you think it is?' she asked Adam.

'Dunno. Nine, ten o'clock?'

'Past their bedtime, in other words.'

The boy's shoulders slumped. 'I want to go home.'

'Please, Dylan. We've been through this.'

Fortunately, he was too tired to argue. As Katy organised where and how they would sleep, Adam roamed the cellar, kicking at the bags of cement and peering at the old packing crates.

'I don't think there's anything else we can use,' Katy said.

'That's not why I'm searching.'

His tone was blunt, so she didn't push for an explanation. Moving the mattress slightly, a thought struck her. She lifted the end where Carole had been sitting. 'Have you got the scissors?'

'I thought you had them.'

'No. They were under here.' Gently, she urged the kids to stand up and lifted the mattress completely.

Adam joined her, stared at the floor and shook his head. 'Don't say Carole took them?'

Along with the concern, was there also a hint of admiration in his voice? To Katy, it felt like a betrayal. *I could have been raped by Gary, and I took that risk to snatch the scissors from under his nose.*

'You see? She's only thinking of herself.' She choked back a sob. 'Those were ours. She had no right.'

Adam looked rueful, as if it was only now occurring to him that they'd been deprived of a valuable weapon. 'I don't know how she had the presence of mind. She looked completely out of it.'

'Unless she's been exaggerating?' Katy hadn't wanted to admit that some of Carole's behaviour had struck her as a little theatrical.

'Crap.' He blew out a sigh. 'I wonder what she was planning?'

Katy looked up at the ceiling. 'More to the point, has it worked?'

CHAPTER THIRTY-THREE

Outside there was just enough light to find her way. Off to the side, a waterlogged lawn led to the trees that were still enveloped in darkness. Recalling her unease this afternoon, Maggie had to wonder if it had been a premonition of sorts. She had little time for superstition, omens, portents, didn't really believe in any of it – except when she did.

She followed Jay round to the back of the house, along a concrete path strewn with bricks and off-cuts of wood. In the years before the planning application there seemed to have been several half-arsed attempts to remodel the house, all of which had left it in a worse state than before.

At the rear the light wasn't so good, but Maggie told Jay not to use the torch. 'Don't want to risk attracting attention.'

Jay's grunt had a note of sarcasm. Did he think it was because she was squeamish, and preferred not to see?

In fairness to him, a moment later she understood why he might have thought so. Carole had landed on a wide concrete terrace. From the hideous angle of her head, it was clear she had broken her neck. If that hadn't been fatal, her torso had come down on a heavy timber planter with a decorative zigzag pattern around the top. Carole's lower spine appeared to have been crushed, and judging by the amount of blood and gore, the sharp wooden tips of the planter had ruptured her flesh.

Jay held the back of his hand against his mouth and took deep breaths. 'It's like she's impaled on that thing. So unlucky to hit it.'

'It's not *her* luck I'm interested in.' Carole's eyes were open, but not yet dull or cloudy. Maggie thought she could still read the pain in them. 'Who'd jump through a window to get away?'

'It wasn't about getting away. I think she intended to kill herself.'

Catching a silvery gleam, Maggie crouched and spotted a pair of nail scissors, still clutched in Carole's hand. 'Where the hell did she get those?'

'She didn't have them earlier, I'm sure of it.'

'Katy!' Maggie fumed. 'When they went to fetch the present for the kid's party, she brought back clothes.'

'So it's Gary that screwed up again.' Jay leaned over and spat on the grass. 'Are we gonna talk to her?'

Maggie shook her head. 'I don't want the family knowing about this.'

'So what, then?'

'It's not gonna be pleasant, but she'll have to be moved. Stash her inside, next to Brian.'

'But look at the mess. Can't we bury her or something?'

'On a site that's earmarked for development?' She gave a scornful laugh. 'No. We're taking them home tomorrow, remember?'

'We're not still going ahead with that...?' He faltered when she turned on him.

'Listen to me, Jay. This is twice you've fucked up. Anyone else would be begging for forgiveness, and here you are, trying to tell me what to do.' Maggie poked him in the stomach, hard enough to make him groan. 'Don't push it. I'm on a short fucking fuse right now.'

Adam helped Katy make things as comfortable as possible for the children. Huddled together on the thin mattress and wrapped in the blanket, he thought they might just be able to get some sleep. Without the extra clothes that Katy had brought from home, it would have been far too cold.

'You did well,' he said, aware that the loss of the scissors had stung her badly. She nodded brusquely but said nothing.

To his astonishment, Dylan was asleep within seconds, his features as soft and relaxed as if he were tucked up in bed at home. Freya's eyes were heavy, though she fought it for a while. 'What about when Carole comes back?'

'I'm sure she won't mind you two having the mattress,' Katy said.

'Grown-ups can sleep sitting up,' Adam said. 'Like Grandpa after Sunday lunch.'

That seemed to do the trick. A few minutes later she drifted off, and at last they could talk freely. Adam sat on the second step, purposely leaving enough room for Katy to sit beside him. He caught the momentary hesitation before she came over.

'Do you think we'll see Carole again?' she asked.

'Depends what she did, I suppose. But if she wasn't as ill as she looked, and she tried to escape…' He studied Freya carefully, wanting to be certain she was asleep. 'I think it's more likely they've killed her. That crash sounded violent.'

'If that's the case, then we have no way of…' Katy trailed off, fists bumping angrily against her knees. 'All we can ever do is speculate. We don't actually know anything.'

'To be brutal about it, there's only one question that matters. If something's happened to Carole, what does it mean for us?'

'You still think they'll kill us, rather than let us go?'

'I want to be wrong about that. But it's what we've got to prepare for, yes.'

A brooding silence. Then Katy said, 'I'm surprised they haven't come to punish us. For the scissors.'

'Perhaps Carole didn't get to use them. Or perhaps they think she had them hidden on her the whole time.'

He didn't voice the third possibility. Perhaps the punishment was coming, any minute now…

CHAPTER THIRTY-FOUR

Maggie stayed close while they moved the body inside, partly to supervise but mostly to demonstrate that she had the stomach for it.

Jay had been right about the mess. Tomorrow, in daylight, someone would have to wash the patio down. By then, she imagined that various animals would have taken their fill of the blood. Rats, foxes, and whatever else lived out here in the wild.

'Let's hope it pisses down tonight,' Roger said. But Maggie knew the forecast was mostly dry, with an outside chance of showers. Even the weather wouldn't play along.

One thing they'd thought to bring was plenty of plastic sacks. Trussed up, the woman was a lot easier to deal with. Bulky, but clean. An awkward parcel, rather than the remains of a human being.

They deposited her in what was probably once a dining room, nose to tail with hubby, who'd been brought in hours ago and was similarly wrapped and ready for the journey. Maggie was itching to be rid of them, aware that their presence made this the most dangerous night of her life.

'As soon as we have a time and a place for the meeting, a couple of you can shift these back to the house.'

'Gonna be busy,' Jay pointed out. 'If I'm taking Adam to his office.'

'You won't be. It's too difficult to control.'

'Personally, I think it's worth the risk.'

'The way I'm feeling right now, I'm tempted to stick a gun into that cellar and do away with the lot of them.'

The same point was made when they convened in the living room. This couldn't be classed as anything other than a crisis meeting, and despite his status as a hired hand, it turned out that Gary had plenty to say.

'First off, no way did Katy get those scissors when I were with her. I watched her like a bloody hawk.'

'While she was getting undressed,' Dale sniggered.

'That's right enough. Who wouldn't?' Unfazed, Gary addressed Maggie again: 'It's for you to decide if you're going ahead with this plan of yours, but one thing's for sure: that family can't be seeing the light of day again.'

Dale seemed to shiver, pretended he was stretching and said, 'Is that you volunteering, then, Gaz? Kids as well.'

'I can do it.' He kept a steely gaze on Maggie. 'It'll cost you, though.'

Roger cleared his throat. 'If it needs doing, we'll do it.'

Jay was last to turn in her direction, one of the phones in his hand again. '*Does* it need doing?'

Maggie felt the pressure on her, but was determined not to be swayed by it. 'I haven't decided yet.'

'I think we're in danger of forgetting what's important,' Roger chipped in. 'The meeting tomorrow.'

'Exactly,' Maggie said. 'Yes, Carole was here to give us a bit of insurance, but her value was never clear cut. In any case, Jay's come up with a better use for her and Brian.'

She described the proposal to implicate Voronov in a double murder. Gary looked suspicious. 'When did this come about?'

'While you were getting the food,' Maggie said.

'By killing herself, you could argue that Carole's saved us a job.' Roger gave a grim smile.

Unimpressed, Gary pointed to the floor. 'You can get all the DNA in the world from the Russian, but you ain't gonna make it stick if you leave the other prisoners alive. They'll know what really happened to Brian and his missus.'

Maggie sent Jay a fleeting glance, which was all Gary needed to read her uncertainty. He crossed his arms across his swollen belly and said, 'Seems to me it's time for a renegotiation.'

'What?' she snapped.

'I signed up on the back of your reputation, but it's been one balls-up after another. Only fair that our fees take account of that. I want another fifty per cent for me, and twenty-five for Dale.'

Maggie pretended to find it funny, though inside she was seething. 'Can't do that.'

'You'll have to,' Gary said. 'Or we'll walk.'

Jay sneered. 'You wouldn't be that crazy.'

'Try me.' Gary tapped his jacket, where the shape of his revolver was impossible to miss. 'But let's keep it friendly, eh?'

Another hour had passed, or maybe longer, and still Carole hadn't returned. The cellar grew colder, the air dank and moist; Katy could taste the mildew when she breathed. The thought of the spores settling on her tongue was revolting, but the issue of their long-term health was hardly relevant right now. Immediate survival was all that mattered.

When Adam started to move some of the crates and bags of cement, Katy feared that the noise would disturb the children. Adam didn't disagree. 'I don't think it can be helped. But I'll be as quiet as I can.'

Now she felt all the more despondent that she couldn't be honest. Concern about waking the kids was only a side issue; what really scared her was that his plan was necessary.

'Let me help,' she said. 'I'll do the crates.'

Adam stacked about a dozen bags of cement on the floor beneath the crawl space, with a gap between that and the wall that should give them just enough room to squeeze past and climb in. Put a few crates next to the pile and the opening would be concealed, at least from a cursory inspection.

While they lifted and carried, creeping past the children like cartoon burglars, Adam confessed to doubts about his idea.

'It's bothering me that we might not find a way out. Say the rooms are all occupied, or we can't find a weak spot in the floor?'

Katy, who thought one or both scenarios was very likely, could only shrug. 'Then we come back here, and hope for another chance tomorrow.'

'Yeah.' He studied the opening. 'I'd like to think we could hide in there, maybe fool them into thinking we've escaped some other way…'

'They'd find us in no time. They're bound to notice that this stuff has been moved.'

'Not necessarily. It's only junk.'

Katy thought he was being optimistic, but took a slow look around the cellar. 'Maybe if we did something about the light?'

'Good idea,' he said, though he sounded glum, as if the discussion was forcing him to admit that their efforts were futile.

'The bigger problem will be convincing the kids to go in there. It's pitch black, filthy, cramped. At their age I'd have been terrified of it.'

'Do you think?' he asked sadly. 'Maybe we'll just have to explain what's at stake.'

After staring forlornly at the wall, he grabbed the fleece he'd been wearing earlier and used it to scrape away cobwebs and clear a path through the debris. He climbed in until only his feet were visible, then shuffled out, his hair and face blackened by the dirt he'd raised. When he grinned, his teeth glowed white in contrast.

'Better than it was.'

'Thank you.' She managed an anxious smile. 'And you're right. If there's no other choice, they'll have to do it.'

He raised his head towards the ceiling, and they both listened for a minute. Voices could be heard, very faintly, from the direction of the main living room. Then a creak of floorboards from the other side of the house.

'I wish we knew what time it was,' Adam said. 'They must be planning to sleep at some point.'

'Depends what's happened. Anyway, better for the kids to get plenty of rest, so they're fresh and ready to go.'

The phrase made her flinch, and squeeze her eyes shut. *Ready to go: who am I trying to kid?* But when she opened her eyes, Adam was gazing at Freya and Dylan, and seemed to be drawing encouragement from her words.

'I guess we should try to do the same,' he said. 'Doze a little, at least.'

She nodded, and they sat down on the floor beside their sleeping children. Katy pushed her body against his and tried to share as much of her warmth as she could. Adam squeezed her hand and tipped his head to touch hers. 'A couple of hours, then, and pray it goes quiet up there.'

Katy was silent. *He still believes*, she thought. He still believes we're going to find a way out.

And with a churning in her belly, and anguish in her heart, she asked herself: Does it make me a bad person if I don't agree? Am I a failure? A coward?

Or am I a realist?

CHAPTER THIRTY-FIVE

Maggie suggested that she and Gary speak alone, in the kitchen. She caught a raised eyebrow from Roger and winked to signal that she'd be okay.

The Yorkshireman lumbered in, tapping a cigarette from its packet as if to make clear he was only pausing as a favour on his way out for a smoke. Maggie rested back against a unit. There was a sharp knife six inches from her right hand.

'You're being well paid, Gary. Don't get greedy.'

'Bollocks. I know how much this is worth to you.'

'So what? You're contractors, remember. The value of the deal is down to me. I'm the one who has to sit there and look Voronov in the eye.'

'But you need me and Dale to help you act the part.'

Maggie's splutter of laughter was all the more wounding for being completely genuine. 'Oh, Gary...'

'Try and do it without us, then.'

She shook her head, and switched to a conciliatory tone. 'If it all goes well, there'll be an extra ten G for you, and—'

'Twenty,' Gary cut in.

'Ten. And five for Dale.'

'Two for Dale. Twenty for me.'

'Ten and five. I'm not haggling with you, any more than I'm going to spread the word about that night in Sunderland.'

Gary's face lost some colour. 'What?'

'Couple of years ago, wasn't it? You had a threesome with a young tart and her fella, and I heard you got *very* interactive with them both.'

'That's a damn lie!' Gary advanced on her, fists raised, then thought better of it.

'Doesn't matter to me, what you get up to in bed.' Maggie wrinkled her nose at the sour, oniony smell of his sweat. 'But your pals back home don't have a lot of time for these "alternative lifestyles", do they?'

They were interrupted by Jay, holding one of their phones. 'Xavier.'

This meant the conversation with Gary was over. Glowering at Maggie, he muttered, 'Ten and five,' and went outside for his cigarette.

Jay handed her the phone. 'You agreed a raise?'

'Only what I'd already costed.' She opened the message, her heart beating fast. It said: *I can call you in five minutes.*

They waited in the kitchen. 'You think Gary's gonna be a problem?' Jay asked.

'Nah. I don't blame him for trying it on. We got his services for less than I was willing to pay, and he probably knows that.'

She turned and ran the cold tap. The ancient pipes gurgled, belching air. She held her hands under the flow, enjoying the not-quite painful sensation of cold. Then she rinsed her vodka glass and filled it with water and drank, and wasn't put off by a vaguely metallic flavour that probably meant something toxic in the plumbing.

The phone trilled. She picked it up and said, 'Yes?'

'Maggie? Ah, good.' The Belgian's tone was calm enough, but Maggie could detect some tension beneath the surface. Little wonder, given the risks he was taking.

'Do you have the location yet?' she asked.

'Unfortunately, no. His secretary will contact you tomorrow morning.'

Maggie flashed a worried look at Jay, who was leaning close enough to hear. 'I was hoping you'd get that information to us ahead of time.'

'Not possible, I'm afraid. But you are in place, yes?'

'We're here, but that isn't much use if he suddenly suggests another part of the country.'

'No, no. It will be Sussex, I am certain of it.'

'I hope so. Is he in Forest Row tonight?'

A hesitation, then a low chuckle. 'You know how he fears an ambush, of any type.'

So that's how we're playing it, Maggie thought. Which was fair enough: she hadn't told Xavier the precise location they'd found, nor did he know about their decision to abduct Carole.

'How much warning will we get?'

'I anticipate he will want to meet within one hour of the call. Perhaps two hours at most. And remember, when the location is divulged our people will already be present. There will be no opportunity for, uh, dirty tricks.'

'It never crossed my mind,' Maggie lied. 'We just want a guarantee he's going to play it straight.'

'Rest assured,' Xavier said. 'Expect a call no later than eleven.'

Maggie cut the connection and stared at Jay, who said, 'At least it's not cancelled.'

'Means going in blind, though.'

'Yeah. But it is what it is. Can't blame the man for being paranoid.'

Maggie nodded reluctantly. 'It's how you stay alive.'

Adam's head jerked up. Katy had just spoken, and he realised he must have fallen asleep.

'How long's it been, would you say?'

'God knows.' A shiver ran through him. 'Sorry, think I dozed off.'

'Don't apologise. I did a bit, too.'

They listened for a while. The house was quieter than before, though there were still occasional footsteps.

'I heard a woman's voice,' Katy said. 'But I'm pretty sure it was Maggie, not Carole.'

'If she was all right, they'd have brought her back here by now. Don't you reckon?'

'Maybe.' Then a sigh. 'I know I've been… hostile towards her. I feel bad about it now, knowing they might have hurt her.'

'That's not your fault. And like you said, she's cheated us by taking the scissors.'

She nodded. 'What annoyed me, if I'm honest, is the way you seemed to be more interested in her experiences, her point of view, than you were in mine.'

'That's not—' he began, too loudly; beside them, Freya groaned in her sleep.

'It reminded me of Holly, and how you always bend over backwards to see her side of things.'

'Do I?' He swallowed awkwardly. 'I've always tried to be fair…'

'But there are situations where things are so unequal, it isn't right to be fair. It's not appropriate.'

His laugh sounded slightly false to his own ears. 'I don't have a clue what you mean.'

'Well, I'm your wife, your partner of fourteen years, the mother of your children. Holly is a former girlfriend, who you dated in your early twenties. Would you say that we have an equal right to your time and energy?'

'Look, she seemed to be in a bad way, and I did my best to help her. It was a few messages, that's all.'

'And she's left you alone since then?'

'Yes,' he said, but only after a microscopic hesitation.

'She had no right to seek you out, not after all these years, and God knows how many other relationships.'

'It was two or three, and I think each one did more damage than the last.' He tutted. 'Anyway, we've had this conversation before. You have no reason to be jealous of Holly, and there was no ulterior motive. I just tried to do what I thought was right.'

'Yeah. Like chasing after a car because it accidentally caused a stone to break one of the lights.'

He looked away, stung to his core. 'You'll never know how much I regret that. I'd give my life if it meant you and the kids could get out of here.'

There was a sombre silence. Adam realised they ought to be concentrating on identifying any sounds or movements in the rooms above. Then, in a whisper, Katy said, 'After this – if we get out of here – we need to have a proper talk.'

'About?'

'The future. You and me. Holly.'

'There's nothing to discuss where she's concerned.'

'I think there is. By making the effort to help her, you might have led her to believe she's still in with a chance.'

'I'm sure I haven't.'

'It's what she thought last time.'

'Well, it's different now.'

It was a lame response, and he was expecting to be picked up on it when Katy simply shrugged and said, 'The other thing is Canada. We need to consider it again.'

'Really? You were dead against it.'

'I know. But this has changed everything.' She gestured towards the ceiling. 'Even if a miracle happens – they let us go and we merrily stroll out of here – do you honestly think we'll be able to put it behind us?'

'I…' He realised he had no good answers. 'Well, it might take a while.'

'They know where we live, remember? Two of them were in our house. And Gary—' Her voice choked. 'He threatened me…'

Adam read the meaning in her face and went cold. 'What did he say? Did he do anything to you?'

'It doesn't matter.' She wiped her eyes. 'The point is that we may never feel safe, and in that case perhaps we should look at a drastic change.'

He looked her in the eye, and saw she was sincere. Back in the summer he'd been approached by an ex-boss, now running his own agency in Vancouver; there were plans for dramatic expansion in the next two years, and he wanted Adam to consider heading up a branch of the company. There was no pressure on him to make a quick decision, and he'd promised to think it over very carefully. But Katy had been vehemently opposed, on the grounds that they shouldn't be abandoning her parents, or depriving them of contact with their beloved grandchildren; not to mention uprooting Freya and Dylan from their settled, happy existence in Britain.

It was very different for Adam: his mother had died when he was nineteen, and after a second marriage failed his father had steadily retreated from the world and rarely had any meaningful contact with them. But it would hardly be a surprise if this ordeal had altered the equation from Katy's perspective.

And perhaps, given her comments, another reason lurked at the back of her mind: that emigrating to Canada would remove Adam from the clutches of an erratic and potentially troublesome former girlfriend.

With a sigh, he said, 'Okay. We shouldn't rule anything out.'

'Not that I think we'll escape,' Katy admitted. 'I want to believe it, but I just… I just can't.'

Nothing Adam could say to that: he was done with pep talks for now. Instead he concentrated. 'It's gone very quiet up there. We ought to think about…'

She gripped his arm. 'Let's wait a bit. Please.'

He frowned, aware that her reluctance could easily feed his own. It was such a dangerous thing to try, and might achieve nothing. And yet it had to be attempted, didn't it – if only because the alternative could be worse?

'All right,' he agreed. 'But not much longer.'

It was gone midnight when Maggie oversaw the arrangements for getting some rest. Gary and Roger would keep a watch until two, Maggie would take over till five, and then Dale and Jay from five till eight – 'Or whenever we all wake up.'

It wouldn't have escaped Gary's notice that he and Dale were given separate shifts, each accompanied by someone Maggie trusted. She'd said as much to Jay before they rejoined the others. 'I don't want us sleeping in the same place, either. Can you find somewhere upstairs?'

Jay nodded. 'Sure. Do you think he's up to something?'

'Not really. Though I wouldn't rule out him and Dale doing a runner.'

'If they try it, do you wanna stop them?'

'Good question.' She snorted, and saw her breath condensing in the frigid air. 'I doubt if any of us will get much sleep. It's freezing.'

'The family have been quiet this evening. Should I check on them?'

'Don't bother. It'd be doing us a favour if we woke up tomorrow and found they'd all died of hypothermia.'

'Still tempted by Gary's idea, then?' He made a gun with his fingers.

'It's hard to avoid that conclusion, if we want to come out of this clean, and safe.'

Jay tapped his bottom lip. 'Looking at the stuff on his phone, this meeting of Adam's is a big deal. I reckon I could go with him, without too much risk – but not if you're intending to top them all.'

'I'll need you for Voronov.'

'This is in the morning. Voronov probably won't be till the afternoon.'

'No, but…' A yawn overcame her. She felt sapped of energy all of a sudden. 'We'll sleep on it, yeah?'

'Okay.' She could see he wasn't happy postponing the decision, because of what it said about her state of mind. They had an important job to do, and it required focus, determination, clarity of thought. Right now, she was all over the place.

Well, fuck it, she thought. This morning the objectives had been simple enough. Establish their temporary base in Sussex, make the cellar ready for a single prisoner, abduct Carole while her husband was absent and keep her safe in the event that some leverage was needed, to counter the risk that Voronov might renege on the deal at the last minute.

Instead, it had all gone to shit. Carole was dead, her husband was dead, and they had four more potential victims to worry about. Six bodies, when there should have been none.

Never mind Gary doing a runner, Maggie thought grimly. *If I believed in fate I ought to be getting the hell out of here myself.*

CHAPTER THIRTY-SIX

Katy slept, though she was not asleep. She knew she was in the cellar, a prisoner, trapped down here with her family. But she was also at her parents' house, cold and tired and miserable because there was a party arranged, or some kind of gathering – were they about to go away, to Canada, perhaps? – but she wasn't up to it, didn't want to socialise. She was desperate to sleep, and in any case she wouldn't dare be seen by anyone. Not till she'd washed her hair and found some clean clothes, at the very least.

But the first guests were already here, including a girl from school who'd possessed an unerring ability to make Katy feel inferior. *Let's see how you like it to be upstaged*, she thought, because according to her mother Beyoncé had accepted an invitation, and she might be bringing Jay Z along as well. 'So hurry yourself up,' her mum urged—

A gentle shake of her arm and Katy opened her eyes and the dream, once obliterated, was wiped from her memory.

It was Adam who had woken her. 'Time to go.'

'Is it? I mean—' She felt nauseous, disorientated. 'Did you sleep any more? How long has it been?'

'I don't know. But they've turned in for the night, I'm sure of it.'

He stood up and reached out to help her. She allowed herself to be brought to her feet, wincing as her muscles complained.

'Do you honestly believe we can get out?'

He spoke so quietly that she virtually had to lip-read. 'I think they're going to kill us. It's this or nothing.'

She glanced at Freya and Dylan, still knitted together and fast asleep. She had to blink away tears to see them clearly.

'All right. Let's do it.'

Adam knelt down and touched his son's shoulder. 'Hey, fella. Time to wake up.'

A strange, unexpected calm had descended on him. He felt energised and alert and ready to do whatever was required to save his family. This would succeed or it wouldn't: either way, it had to be attempted.

Dylan stirred, then began to moan. Adam hurriedly covered his mouth. 'Sshh, Dylan. It's all right. It's just Dad.'

The noise woke Freya, who turned, blinking in dismay. 'What's happening?'

'We're gonna try to get out of here,' Katy told her.

Adam might not have phrased it like that, but he couldn't blame her. Freya didn't react, though he was sure he could see her thinking: *Will it work?*

It took a minute or so before Dylan was calm enough to get up. Shivering, he clung to his mother. 'What time is it?'

'We don't know for sure. The middle of the night.'

Adam moved across to the wall and studied the opening. 'Best if you go first,' he said to Katy.

She looked stricken by the idea. 'Why?'

'Because whoever's in last is probably the most vulnerable, if they hear something and come down to investigate.'

She thought about it, then shook her head. 'Doesn't matter. I don't know where we're going. You should lead.'

'Are you sure?' He hugged her, and they kissed. After the earlier tension between them, he felt they were back in tune again, bound together by their commitment to Freya and Dylan.

He crouched down and looked at each of his children. 'I know this has been horrible for you, and what we're doing now might be even worse. But it won't be for long, okay? Mum and I need you to be incredibly brave again, and very, very quiet.'

'So the bad men don't hear?' Dylan queried.

'That's right,' Katy said. 'We've got to treat this like a great big adventure.'

The boy nodded, but Adam didn't think he was fooled. Freya certainly wasn't; her hands trembled as Adam explained the sequence.

'I'm going in first. Freya, you follow, then Dylan, then Mum. There's plenty of room, and although it's going to be dark, remember that Mum and I are right there with you.'

With the pep talk over, he put his head and shoulders through the opening and paused to listen. The acoustics were different in here, and it was possible to pick up little creaks and thuds that wouldn't be audible in the cellar. Any movement overhead produced some sort of reaction in the structure of the building.

Earlier, while Katy had dozed, he'd been aware of someone moving above them and had concluded that at least one of the gang must be staying up to patrol the house. He hadn't let that knowledge deter him, though he felt guilty about keeping it from Katy.

He braced himself and wriggled forward, lifting his feet off the bags of cement. Once through the wall, the space opened out, though it didn't grow any lighter. It made sense that some of the rooms would be in darkness, if the gang were trying to sleep. A positive development, just as long as they could prevent the kids from panicking.

He was about to move again when something made him freeze. Not a sound, so much as a vibration. He cocked his head, and heard a tiny click, so faint and far away that it might have been his imagination.

He waited twenty, thirty seconds. *Stop finding excuses*, said a voice in his head. *You have to do this.*

The next sound was closer, still quiet but easier to distinguish. The soft tread of footsteps, quite different from before.

Then a second set. Light steps, accompanied by a shuffling, scraping sound.

Shit, he thought. *Why aren't they sleeping?*

'Adam?' A hissed question from Katy. 'What is it?'

He pushed himself back a few inches, intending to climb out and explain what he'd heard. They couldn't go ahead with it – not now, at least. Perhaps in another hour or so…

Something moved, just a couple of feet away from him, down here in the void. He jerked away, almost hitting his head on the brickwork above the opening.

Then heard it again: definitely close by. A rat?

He felt revulsion, even as his rational mind processed the sound and decided that it was too regular; not scrabbling claws but a kind of tapping.

He waited, heard the next one and this time eased a little closer. It was the impact of something on the grimy, rubble-strewn ground beneath the house. A dripping sound.

He squinted but the darkness gave him nothing. He reached out, blindly, and something struck the back of his hand.

He recoiled as if stung, moved backwards until his lower body was out of the crawl space and there was enough light to see what was on his hand.

A sticky drop of blood.

Maggie had been a restless sleeper for most of her adult life, due to a variety of causes. Her kids, first when they were babies, then because they were teething, and then – in what seemed like no time at all – when they were running amok until the early hours and crashing around her kitchen with the munchies. Her husband, a chainsaw-snoring drunk who brought into their marriage a succession of police raids. Then there was the ever-present fear of retribution from various feuds – such as this one with Voronov – and the difficult, unsatisfying adjustment to an empty bed, caused by a succession of prison sentences, and then by widowhood.

So with that in mind, and given the present circumstances, it should have been impossible for her to sleep so soundly that she could be caught out.

Waking in a rush, she sat up, heart already thrumming, registering sound and movement and danger. The lounge was in darkness but there was a little illumination from the hall. Enough to make out the moist gleam from the eyes of the man who held a blade to her throat, while someone else pressed a thick cloth over her mouth and nose.

Suffocating, she writhed in panic and tried to cry out, but could already feel her strength ebbing away. As they pinned her to the floor, it felt as though she was melting into a useless liquid. She dimly heard a shout from the next room, followed by the unmistakeable stutter of automatic gunfire: four or five shots in one rapid burst, and then a heavy thud.

CHAPTER THIRTY-SEVEN

Katy could tell that Adam was spooked by something, but didn't know what. She moved the children back to give him space to climb out, and saw he was wiping one hand against the other.

'I think—' he began, then broke off as the cellar door shifted in its frame, as if being quietly tested. A tiny clunk as the padlock moved with it.

'They're coming in!' Katy breathed.

But now there was silence. For a second or two they waited, unsure what to do. Then, from further away, came a shout, followed by a burst of gunfire. Even muffled by distance, and the walls between them, there wasn't any doubt.

Adam's eyed widened. He glanced down at his right hand; Katy followed his gaze and saw something smeared on it.

'Get in, quick.' He saw her confusion and added: 'Not to escape. To hide.'

Another shout from upstairs, then heavy running footsteps. No one was creeping around anymore; it was just panic and confusion.

Katy leaned through the opening in the wall and hauled herself into the crawl space. She wriggled on her belly, drawing up her feet when she felt one of the children being lifted in behind her. Realising that she didn't have to face forward if they were only hiding in here, she crawled a little further and then curled up and managed to turn, just as Dylan whispered, 'It's dark.'

'I know, but don't be scared.' She found his hand and guided him closer while shuffling backwards to make room for the other two. 'We'll all stay together.'

Next in was Freya, and Katy whispered guidance: 'Reach for Dylan and hold on to his foot.' She was still moving backwards, her body scraping over rubble and filth. Something brushed against her ear and she nearly screamed, but realised in time that it was just a strand of the insulation material, sagging from between the floor joists.

Upstairs the sounds of chaos continued: running, shooting, cries of anger and pain.

'What are they doing?' Freya asked.

'I don't know,' Katy said, but she had an idea: some kind of battle.

She could just about see Adam as he climbed in, almost blotting out the light from the cellar – and with that she remembered.

'The light!'

Adam's nerves were screaming. At any moment he expected the cellar door to crash open and men with guns would finish them off.

It sounded like there was a war being fought overhead. For a fleeting moment he had considered that it might be the police, storming the building, but he'd seen enough TV documentaries to know that they would identify themselves as armed police, and he'd heard no such warning.

A door slammed hard enough to shake the ceiling. Adam helped Freya climb in and was preparing to follow when he heard Katy say, 'The light!'

At first he was confused; then he remembered their conversation earlier. He grabbed a plastic crate and set it down beneath the light. It creaked and sagged beneath his weight, but held for long enough to wrench the fluorescent tube out of its fitting.

The cellar was plunged into absolute darkness. He stepped down, heard Freya moaning softly and headed towards her voice. In his panic he forgot about the bags of cement and blundered into them, feeling a burst of pain in his knee.

'Dad!' Freya whispered.

'I'm here.'

Time seemed to have slowed down, every second containing a whole lifespan of risk. He managed to set the crates in position, then clamber into the opening. As he shuffled forward he heard frightened gasps and whimpers from his children. The darkness seemed to intensify every sound. Were they loud enough to be heard in the room above?

He realised that the noise had abruptly ceased. No voices, no movement.

'Sssh,' he whispered. 'Very quiet.'

He could no longer hear the dripping sound. He reached out in the direction it had come from, and tentatively patted the underside of the floorboards. His fingers came away tacky; the blood had stopped flowing and was drying now.

Are they all dead? he wondered. Was that too much to hope for?

Then a quiet creak. He tracked cautious footsteps passing above him and into the hallway.

Next came the rattle of the padlock. A heavy clunk, as if it had been examined and then dropped. A murmured voice, impossible to identify. Then more steps, and a metallic scritching sound. Adam thought his heart was going to stop.

The padlock was opened and tossed aside. When it landed, the impact sent a shudder through the floor, and an answering spasm of terror ran through the four bodies clustered beneath the house.

Someone was coming for them.

CHAPTER THIRTY-EIGHT

Jay had found a small bedroom that didn't reek of mildew. Unlike most of the others, he'd thought to bring a sleeping bag and a travel pillow, which meant he could stay reasonably warm and comfortable.

He'd brought Katy Parr's bag upstairs, along with both of their phones, and for a while he amused himself by scrolling through their messages, their photos, burrowing deeper into their lives even as he wondered if tomorrow those lives would end.

Then his eyes grew heavy and he dropped Adam's phone into the bag, checked his gun was close enough to grab in an emergency, and surrendered to his fatigue.

As he slept, part of his brain stayed alert, taking note of the various movements from below. With two of them keeping guard, there was nothing sinister about footsteps in the hall, or even the sound of the back door quietly opening and closing. Jay was confident that any tread on the stairs would register as a sign of potential danger, and he'd wake in time to react to it.

But it was something else that woke him: possibly a shout, though his sleep-addled brain took a couple of seconds to process it. He struggled to recall who was taking the first stint on guard duty – Gary and Roger, wasn't it?

He was trying to decide if it had been one of their voices he'd heard when the shooting started.

*

A jolt of adrenalin propelled him to his feet, gun in hand. He stepped out of the sleeping bag and listened for movement on the stairs. He could hear more activity from below, but nothing that made sense. Why hadn't Maggie taken charge? It ought to be her voice rising above any others…

Unless she'd been right about Gary, and he was trying to take control. But what Jay had heard was automatic fire, not the single shots from a revolver.

He pulled his trainers on and crept towards the landing, using what little illumination came in from outside. It had been brighter than this when he'd gone up; a light from the kitchen had been switched off, which made no sense.

He still wanted to believe this was a stupid disagreement that had got out of hand, but raw instinct told him it was a lot more serious. As he reached the top of the stairs there was a blast of gunfire; he jerked back, and only just stopped himself from screaming.

He was peering in the direction of the muzzle flashes, which had come from a smaller living room next to the lounge. Because of that, he nearly overlooked the dark figure standing in the hall, just to the right of the stairs. Then someone else strode out of the living room and muttered to the stationary figure. The voice was gruff and unfamiliar, and it was too dark to see either of them clearly, but Jay caught a gesture that made sense. The man was indicating the stairs.

Jay took another step back. He had no idea who these men were, and knew he couldn't win a firefight against automatic weapons. Time for discretion here: live to fight another day.

He moved back to the bedroom, grateful for the darkness and his knowledge of the layout. One of the men started to climb the stairs, moving slowly. Jay understood that he wouldn't have long, but he did still have a chance to get away.

Remembering to avoid a section of damaged floor, he crossed to the window. The route took him past his bedding, where a lumpy shadow caught his eye. Katy's bag, which could so easily have tripped him and betrayed his location. Dizzy with relief, he picked it up.

The window was a sash, previously gummed up by years of neglect. Fortunately, he'd opened it earlier in the evening, to check what could be seen from this side of the building. At the time he'd noted that the ground below the window was on a slope, a muddy lawn with only ten or eleven feet to fall.

He put all his strength into pulling the window up. It rose with a heavy grinding noise, loud enough to carry through the house, but hopefully it wouldn't be easy to pinpoint.

Having shoved the window open, he stuck a leg out and twisted, hampered by the gun in one hand and the bag in the other. The window slipped a couple of inches, hitting his shoulder, and he swore under his breath. Ducking his head, he leaned sideways and swung his other leg out. From the landing came the crack of breaking wood, and then an angry grunt; the man had stepped on a rotten floorboard.

Jay glanced down. Satisfied that no one lay in wait, he shoved the gun in his pocket and dropped the bag to the ground. He gripped the window frame and let his arms take his weight, his feet scuffing against the outside wall. A bird hooted from a tree nearby, almost like a warning, just as he felt a cool draught from within the room. The bedroom door was swinging open.

He pushed himself away from the wall and let go, already drawing up his knees and spreading his arms, ready to drop and roll. The impact was hard but bearable; his ankles and knees came out of it undamaged, although his right hand got caught beneath his body, bending painfully at the wrist.

After rolling once he sprang up, grabbed the bag and ran. His immediate priority was to find cover, and then consider the next step; maybe sneak back to the house and use the element of surprise to deal with the intruders…

His speed was limited by the darkness, though the moon had risen and was filtering some light through a thin layer of cloud. After half a dozen steps it registered that he couldn't feel the weight of the gun in his pocket; it must have fallen out when he jumped.

He faltered, half turning, but couldn't see much chance of finding it. That meant going back to the house was no longer viable.

Running away was the best option – the only option – and hadn't he known that from the start? It was why he'd grabbed the bag, though right now he'd gladly swap it for a set of car keys.

He heard a shout. The words were muffled or perhaps spoken in a foreign language, but the meaning was clear: they'd spotted him.

He sped up, trying to duck and swerve while also studying the contours of the ground. He saw trees up ahead, just a few yards away now, and he was almost there, the first leaves brushing against his face as he heard the shot and felt a searing pain in his side. A spray of blood burst from under his arm and he let out a shriek, blundered through the foliage for a few more steps, then tripped and went down, landing with such force on the wound that he passed out.

CHAPTER THIRTY-NINE

Adam heard the steps creak as someone descended, then stopped. What were they doing?

Very slowly, he tried to ease on to his side, hoping to curl his body into an L shape and be able to look back through the opening. But even the smallest movements risked giving him away: the sound of his foot scraping against the brickwork might be fatal. All he could do was twist his neck as far as it would go, ignore the screaming pain in his tendons and hope for a glimpse of the cellar. If he was about to be hauled out of his hiding place, he wanted to have some warning.

Maybe they won't look any further, he thought in desperation. Maybe he could convince them he was alone...

He realised that the darkness had softened. The opening was revealed as a pale grey square; beyond it, a beam of light intensified as it swept in his direction.

The man had a torch, and was searching for them. Adam strained to catch the sound of his breathing; even a cough or grunt might help identify which member of the gang it was.

The light dimmed, but did not go out. Heavy footsteps scuffed the concrete. A soft impact and then a rasping noise as the plastic mattress was kicked aside. Now the roaming light was back, brighter than before. Adam could almost feel the man's confusion, his curiosity as he studied the stack of crates.

Then he took a step towards them.

Would he try to drag them out, one by one, or simply open fire into the crawl space? Adam knew he had to spread himself across the opening and hope to absorb as many shots as he could, praying that the bricks and timber would offer some protection to Katy and the children.

More creaking on the steps, and a guttural voice that he couldn't place. Just one word, which might have been, 'Clear?'

No answer from the man in the cellar. The light was still playing upon the crates. Adam felt Freya's leg begin to twitch and was sure she would have to flex it, or let out a cry of pain.

Then the man made a noise in his throat, a single syllable reply that made no sense to Adam. But the torch beam slid away as the man climbed the steps and left them in total darkness again.

Were they safe?

That was what he wanted to believe – but it felt like tempting fate even to consider it. So he waited, still frozen, expecting to hear the familiar sounds of the door closing and the padlock fitted back in place.

Instead there were urgent footsteps, then silence.

And something else: a wash of cool, fresh air, unlike any of the other draughts they'd felt. Adam thought he knew why, but how long until he could find out?

A minute or two passed before Katy broke the silence. 'Do you think they've gone?'

'Maybe,' he whispered back.

At this, Freya let out a whimper of pain. 'My leg's got cramp.'

'You did really well, both of you,' Adam said.

'I want to get out,' Dylan moaned.

'I know. Not too long now.'

Easy to say, Adam thought. Should they wait five minutes? Ten? Half an hour? That seemed absurd: they didn't even have a way to measure the passing time.

The house above them wasn't entirely still; there were various creaks and sighs. Natural caution told him to stay put until he was absolutely certain. On the other hand, if the property had been abandoned, who was to say it was permanent? Imagine if they waited too long, and the gang returned...

He didn't think he'd made a conscious decision, but when Katy hissed his name he realised he had moved, sliding his feet towards the opening.

'Wait here,' he whispered. 'I'm going to check.'

Katy was just as conflicted. She was too far back to see or hear anything in the cellar, but she understood from Adam's reaction that someone had come looking for them, and had presumably given up.

But why? If it was one of the gang, where on earth did he think the family had gone? And if it wasn't one of the gang, but someone else...

She didn't want to dwell on that, not now the house was deathly quiet again. The police wouldn't have come in and then left like this.

Adam moved suddenly, telling the rest of them to wait. Was it too soon? Katy couldn't say, but she didn't object when he slowly wriggled out of the crawl space.

'Can we go?' Dylan asked. He was pressed tightly against her, and had been weeping, mutely, for the entire time they'd been hiding.

'Soon.'

'Is it safe?' Freya asked, fearfully.

I hope so, Katy thought. She said, 'Daddy's gone to check.'

He was back sooner than she expected – thankfully – just as she was tormenting herself with the thought of him being cut down in a hail of bullets.

'Freya, you first,' he hissed. Katy urged Dylan to follow his sister, and she crawled out after them, not daring to speak until Adam had reached in and guided her through the opening.

'Take it carefully. It's still pitch black out here.'

'How far did you go?'

'Just to the top of the stairs. There isn't much light, and I didn't want to…' He trailed off, waiting until she was on her feet before adding, 'I think it's bad. Really bad.'

The children were just to the side of the opening. Katy found them by patting her hands over their faces, as though playing a party game. Dylan grabbed her and wouldn't let go, so she asked Freya to follow behind him, while Adam led the way.

'Be careful not to trip,' he warned them. 'Especially on the steps.'

It struck her that they would make a comical sight, shuffling in single file around the bags of cement, but there was nothing amusing about the situation they were in. The urgency ran through her like an electric current. At any moment a light could snap on, guns could take aim and fire.

Climbing the steps, all concerns about putting too much weight on them was forgotten, blotted out by the terror of ambush. On this worn and ancient timber it was impossible not to make any noise. If anyone had remained in the house, they would hear the family coming up.

Adam entered the hall, checked in both directions and then ushered the children out. As Katy followed she realised she could now see the others, though only as vague grey shapes. There was a thin bar of light leaking from a room at the end of the hall, where the door was ajar.

Adam was staring at it, too. Was someone in there?

She sniffed. Listened carefully. Then Dylan sniffed, too.

Katy squinted in the dark, and made out the moist gleam of Adam's eyes. He'd reacted to the same thing.

'That smell,' she whispered.

'Yeah. Is it…?'

'Petrol.'

Adam took a fraction longer to identify the smell, and at first he attributed it to one of the cars outside, perhaps wafting in on the breeze.

There was enough illumination to see that the front door was bolted shut. The fresh air was blowing from the kitchen, so he gently steered Freya and Dylan in that direction.

In the silence, with all his senses on high alert, the quiet click caused a jolt of panic. It came from behind him. He glanced back, just as a small yellow light flared and spread across a dark bundle in the centre of the lounge.

Bodies – two or more – doused in petrol and now running with flame.

'Go!' Adam cried, aware that the other three had also turned to look.

The fire raced across the floorboards towards them and entered the hall. Katy had grabbed Freya's hand and pulled her into the kitchen. Adam hoisted Dylan over his shoulder just as the first tiny flames licked at his feet. Stamping them out, he reached the kitchen, where a large window had been left open.

Katy went for the back door. Adam had intended to move cautiously, in case any of the gang were waiting outside, but that idea was now redundant. They had to escape the fire.

It was too dark to make much sense of the landscape around the house. Adam followed Katy and Freya as they stepped out and ran a few yards across an uneven lawn.

'What about the car?' Katy asked, then answered herself. 'Don't have the keys.'

'Nope,' he gasped. 'First we hide, then work out what next.'

She pointed to her left. 'Trees over there, I think.'

'Perfect.'

His half-formed plan had been to get his family to safety, then return to the house for their keys and phones. The fire had put paid to that. What he couldn't understand was why they hadn't been pursued by whoever had set it.

The first line of trees must have been deliberately cultivated to provide an impenetrable screen: they were narrowly spaced and entwined with a mass of small branches almost to ground level. Adam and Katy crouched down and pushed their way backwards through them, drawing the children in after to protect them from the whiplash of the branches.

Within a few feet the trees opened up enough to stand. It was pitch black, and the ground was boggy: two reasons not to go any deeper. Adam said as much to Katy, who hugged him close and whispered, 'Do you think we're safe here?'

'We should be.'

They both crouched again, embracing the children, and looked back towards the house. All they could see was an indistinct shimmer of light as the flames leapt and danced in the windows.

Would anyone spot the fire and raise the alarm? This place was obviously somewhere remote, so the flames weren't necessarily visible. But it didn't matter. Adam tried to push away the anxiety and let the relief flood in.

No one had chased them. No one had shot at them. They'd escaped the cellar, and fled from the fire. Now they were free, well hidden, and only had to wait for help to arrive...

So why did he continue to feel so vulnerable, so scared?

He puzzled over it for a minute, during which time no one spoke, or moved, and the only sound was their breathing, which gradually became slower and less harsh as they rested, and calmed, and regrouped.

And then Adam understood what was spooking him.

The breathing.

CHAPTER FORTY

He could hear someone else, not too far away, trying to breathe very quietly. It was hard to pinpoint the location of the sound, or even listen for any hint of movement, because little gusts of wind were rustling the leaves. A predator could be creeping up on them and they would never know it.

He leaned close to Katy. 'I think we need to—'

And broke off, as she flinched. Because there was another sound in the distance.

Sirens.

'Coming here?' Katy whispered.

'Must be. In any case, we should…' He didn't want to spell it out, didn't want to scare them all over again. Help was on its way, wasn't it?

A small branch snapped, across to their right. Adam felt Katy's body lurch in fear, as his did the same. Before he could speak, she said, nervously, 'Just a squirrel. Or a badger?'

Maybe it was. But Adam knew they had to get out of here. The sirens were growing louder, though still a fair way off.

'Come on.'

He held hands with Freya, made sure Dylan was with Katy and then they got down and crawled through back the undergrowth. Branches clawed at his face and leaves caught in his hair, a spider's web snagged on his cheek and deposited something foul into his mouth, but he focused on the way ahead, and kept checking that Freya was close behind him.

They reached the lawn, and no one seemed to be following. Adam led the way along the edge of the trees, not daring to stray too far into the open. The house was fully ablaze, ugly black smoke pouring from the windows. A lot of noise inside, as things burned and broke and collapsed. Because of that, it took a moment to realise what they *couldn't* hear.

The sirens had stopped.

With the fire throwing out enough light to see, Katy frowned at him. 'Where have they gone?'

Just as mystified, Adam shrugged, bitterly imagining the cops racing towards some mundane traffic incident.

He led his family past the house, towards a large parking area, and saw what he thought was their Peugeot, along with the Mazda and another vehicle. The driveway curved around and down a slope, vanishing into darkness. Adam couldn't make out the boundaries of the property, or identify where a road might run, but he could see two lots of pulsing blue lights, blinking in and out of sight as they wove around the twisting country lanes.

'There they are.'

'Thank God.' Katy heaved a sigh of relief, and told the kids, 'Won't be long now.'

Adam remembered how Gary had stopped at a gate when he'd brought them in. From here he couldn't see it, but he didn't want any more delays.

'Wait here,' he told Katy. 'I'm going to open up for them.'

Katy watched him dash away and clutched the children tighter. There was little doubt that the blue lights were heading towards them, and their height against the hedgerows made her think they were police cars. That made sense: the fire probably hadn't burned long enough to come to anyone's notice.

It started off as an idle thought – someone must have called in about the gunshots – and then filled her with terror. *If that's an armed response team, and Adam comes running out of the dark as they pull up…*

'Kids, I need you to stay here! Don't move.'

There was a startled protest from Dylan, which she hated to ignore. But this couldn't wait. She raced after her husband, unsure whether to shout or keep silent, settling for a pantomime hiss that Adam would never be able to hear.

Skittering down the slope, she saw headlights probing the foot of the drive, where a wide metal gate stood open. Adam had almost reached it when she called out again. 'Stop!'

He turned. 'What is it?'

'They might have guns.' She caught up with him, grabbed his arm and propelled him back towards the house. 'Go and stay with the kids. Trust me.'

The first police car turned in a few seconds later. It was a BMW X5. Stepping into the range of its lights, Katy raised her arms and stood completely still. She wanted it to be immediately evident that she posed no threat, though it was far from certain that this was the right thing to do. She was shaking with fright.

The car stopped. From the passenger side a uniformed officer got out, a gun in his hand.

Katy's voice was strained and shaky. 'Please help us, we were abducted, and locked in a cellar. My husband and children are up by the house. They don't have guns.'

To her own ears it sounded like a pathetic babble, but the policeman's expression was one of intense concentration. 'We had a report of shots fired. Are you saying—?'

'There were people with guns. I think they've gone.'

'Think?' This was from the driver.

She nodded. 'We heard a lot of shooting, then nothing. We waited, I don't know, ten or fifteen minutes. The cellar door had been left open. We didn't see any sign…'

She tailed off as a second car pulled up behind the first. She took a deep breath, and realised she didn't feel quite so wobbly or afraid.

'And the fire?' the driver asked.

'That started as we left the house, but we didn't see anyone.'

'Okay,' said the first cop. 'Keep your hands raised. I'm going to pat you down, check you for weapons.'

He sounded apologetic, but Katy felt a wave of gratitude and relief. 'I understand.'

He moved quickly but cautiously. From up close, she could see he was about thirty, and looked slightly anxious. His search was brisk and efficient, and when it was done the driver joined them. 'And your family are by the house? How many people?'

'My husband and two children. A boy and a girl.'

'And no one has weapons of any sort?'

'No.' Given permission to call them, Katy turned, nervously, and shouted, 'Adam, it's okay. Bring the kids.'

The driver moved away to confer with the officers from the second car, one of whom cast her gaze over Katy, and said, 'Does anyone need medical treatment?'

'Um, I'm not sure. I guess if there's anyone still alive in the house…'

She heard one of the cops say, 'Call it anyway. I think we're looking at a major incident.'

There was a sudden loud crash and the fire, which had dwindled a little, roared back into life. A new column of smoke poured from one of the upper windows.

Adam materialised from the shadows, carrying Dylan in one arm and gripping Freya's hand. A couple of the cops moved towards them and quietly explained the need for a search. Adam nodded, and encouraged Dylan to get down and stand still. Both children complied, looking dazed and white-faced with shock. There was no celebration, no overt emotion at all; as if none of them knew how to react.

It struck Katy that this must be a consequence of exhaustion. She was also aware that, while this terrible ordeal was finally over, a new ordeal was very likely just beginning.

'Wh-what time is it?' she asked the female officer.

'Two twenty-three.' The woman looked concerned. 'I'm afraid you won't be able to leave just yet, but you can all wait in one of the cars. There's ambulances on the way, to get you checked over. When did you last eat and drink?'

Katy found she couldn't respond; this sudden kindness, clashing against the day's cruelty and aggression, had brought tears to her eyes.

The cop touched her arm. 'Don't worry. I'll see what we can do there.'

'Thank you.' Katy tried to smile, and relax, and enjoy the sensations of freedom and safety. But she couldn't shake off a conviction that, after this, their lives would never be the same again.

CHAPTER FORTY-ONE

Adam hadn't wanted to let Katy do this on her own, but he'd seen how determined she was. Rushing back to join Freya and Dylan, he'd understood what motivated her. If you had armed police responding to an unknown emergency, turning up at a burning house in the middle of the night, there was probably a greater chance of an overreaction if the first person they encountered was a man – especially one as filthy, dishevelled and stressed as Adam was right now.

Which didn't mean that Katy wasn't in danger herself, so it was an enormous relief when the call came to join her. Dylan was incapable of walking, so Adam found the extra energy from somewhere to carry him, while assuring Freya that they were safe, and would soon be able to go home.

A couple of the officers patted them down, and then Katy took Dylan. One of the cops asked Adam to confirm that, to his knowledge, there was no else on the property.

'I don't think so. But after we escaped from the house, we hid in the trees until we heard sirens. And I think there might have been someone else in there.'

A gasp from Katy prompted the officer to turn her way. 'I heard something, like a twig snapping,' she said. 'I assumed it was an animal.'

'Maybe,' Adam said. 'But I thought I could hear someone breathing.'

The cop nodded. 'Okay. We'll check it out.'

He asked Adam to describe the layout of the property, and the route they had taken when they'd run from the house. They were interrupted by the arrival of two more police cars. As the personnel began to assemble, Adam overheard talk of inner and outer cordons, and the need to secure the scene before the fire brigade could go to work.

'Two pumps, about five minutes away,' one of them reported.

'This sounds like a stupid question,' Adam said, 'but where are we?'

'A couple of miles west of Chelwood Gate. Do you know it?'

'Yes. We're not too far from home, then.' Adam explained that they'd had their faces covered on the way here. They were probably only five or six miles from where they'd been taken.

After a few minutes of breathless activity there was a sudden lull, when the family were no longer the centre of attention. Without a word being spoken, they formed a tight cluster, Adam and Katy crouching face to face with the children between them, all too stunned to do anything except cherish the physical bond, and the fresh air and open space around them.

It lasted perhaps thirty seconds, but it was enough for Adam to feel some energy trickling back. Then they were led to one of the patrol cars. Katy and the children sat in the back, and Adam took the front passenger seat. A couple of cops busied themselves in the lane, and another remained by the gate, talking on his radio, while half a dozen more spread out and approached the house, guns drawn, and using flashlights to guide their way.

Katy shut her eyes and rested her head back. 'I hope we're not here too long.'

Adam agreed. 'Best try to nap.'

It was advice which Dylan had already taken. He was curled up sideways on the seat with his head in Katy's lap. Freya was yawning fiercely but wouldn't quite give in to sleep.

'It's all right now,' he told her.

'But is it? I mean, do we just go home, and back to school, and everything's like normal again?'

Both he and Katy couldn't help a rueful smile at the disbelief in her voice.

'Well, not school tomorrow – *today*, rather.' Katy squeezed her hand. 'Let's just see, shall we?'

Adam nodded. 'It'll take some time to get over. There's a lot we'll have to talk about, and of course the police will want to take statements—'

'But what about the people who took us?' she asked. 'Where are they now? Will the police be able to catch them?'

'Honestly, you mustn't worry about that,' Katy insisted, drawing Freya into an embrace.

'Your mum's right,' Adam said. 'No one's going to hurt you, or any of us. We're safe.'

Snuffling, Freya wiped her nose and gave him one of her looks. 'Do you promise?'

'I promise,' Adam said, and forced himself to ignore the uneasy glance he got from Katy.

This might not be true, but the kids had to believe it. That was what he told himself – otherwise they might never recover.

A couple of fire appliances turned up, but were halted in the lane by the officer manning the gate. It was a few minutes before he received a message on his radio and waved them through. Katy assumed this meant the site had been declared safe. The gang had fled.

She and Adam watched the fire engines negotiate a path through the police cars, and up the driveway. There were several vehicles parked on the patch of rough ground in front of the house, including their own. Not a lot of space, but one of the appliances managed to get reasonably close, and soon they had a couple of hoses directed at the house.

'I doubt if there's much left to burn,' Adam muttered as brown smoke continued to pour from the building.

'Or identify,' Katy added quietly. Checking that Freya was now asleep, she said, 'How many bodies, do you think?'

'No idea. I saw two, at least, but that was only a glimpse of one room.' He sighed. 'Freya was right about how… incomplete this feels. Who did this to us? Who's dead and who's still alive?'

Katy gazed at the activity around the house, armed police and firefighters clustered in little groups. 'Don't you think they intended us to die in there?'

'Probably. What I can't understand is why one of them came down to find us, but didn't react when we weren't there.'

'Unless he worked out where we were hiding, and knew the fire would take care of us?'

'Yeah. But why not lock the cellar door?'

'Thank God he didn't.'

'I know. But it's bloody odd, isn't it?'

'Remember they'd have been in a hurry to get away.' She pondered, then said, 'That click we heard – I wonder if it could have been some sort of timer?'

'Yes. That would explain why no one followed us out.' He looked grim. 'Trouble is, the fire will have destroyed all sorts of forensic evidence. It'll make it much harder to catch them, or to get any convictions in court.'

Katy sighed. By now she had expected a sense of elation at the fact that they had all managed to escape, unharmed, and yet the reality turned out to be just more of the emotions that had plagued them throughout their captivity: anxiety, doubt, fear…

CHAPTER FORTY-TWO

Next to arrive was a man of about forty, with short dark hair and a neatly trimmed beard. He wore tailored black trousers, a navy blue shirt and a quilted coat. He climbed into the driver's seat, introduced himself as Detective Inspector John Branning, and said that he would be leading the investigation into whatever had taken place here.

'All I know at the moment is that a distant neighbour reported multiple gunshots – which is why the armed response vehicles were despatched – so if you can shed any more light on this, I'll be very grateful.'

Adam nodded, while fighting off a yawn. Branning succumbed to one himself, and said, 'Though I do appreciate that you're probably exhausted. All I need right now are the basic details.' He took out a voice recorder. 'I'm going to use this, if you don't mind, because it's a lot easier than taking notes.'

They were about to get started when a uniformed officer tapped on the window. 'Ambulance is here.'

'Okay, thanks.' The recorder went back in his pocket. He climbed out of the car and he and a couple of his colleagues spoke to the ambulance crew.

Then he opened the passenger door and said, 'Slight change of plan. Realistically, it'll be a while till I can get a proper look at the house. In the meantime, the paramedic has suggested we take you to the Princess Royal. She thinks she can sort us a private room with a bed for the kids, at least for the rest of the night.

It'll be a lot more comfortable, and I can do the debrief there. That good with you?'

Adam glanced at Katy and guessed she was thinking the same thing as him – *I'd rather be at home* – but this was a lot better than sitting in a police car all night.

'Yes, please.'

Katy had vivid memories of attending the Princess Royal hospital in Haywards Heath in the middle of the night. When Freya was eight months old they'd had to rush her to Accident and Emergency after a chest infection turned so severe that she was vomiting up water and struggling to breathe. It still made Katy shudder to think of how slowly the minutes had passed in the over-lit, uncomfortable waiting room, but what she cherished about that night was how extraordinary the doctors and nurses had been: calm and friendly and utterly dedicated to their work.

On this occasion, the staff were just as solicitous, but the surroundings immeasurably better. Having entered via the A and E, they were directed to the second floor, where a nurse showed them into a room with a bed and several chairs.

The children, both still asleep in their parents' arms, were gently placed on the bed. DI Branning went off in search of refreshments, while a young Australian doctor checked them over, starting with Katy, and then Adam. Katy suspected that Branning had had a discreet word with the doctor, for she didn't ask any questions beyond their age, background and general health.

'You're both dehydrated, and you look a bit beaten and bruised,' she told Adam. 'But there's nothing here that requires treatment. All the vital signs are good. Just drink some water, and try to rest up.'

Freya and Dylan were lying back to back, fast asleep on their sides, Dylan's nostrils bubbling a little with each breath. Gazing at them, the doctor sighed. 'Is there anything on Earth more beautiful than the sight of children sleeping?'

'Will you need to wake them?' Katy asked.

'They look fine to me. Let's give them a couple of hours. In the meantime, if you have any concerns, I'll be just along the corridor.'

Now, finally, they were alone. There was a brief hesitation, a shyness, almost, in Adam's gaze, and then Katy relaxed her shoulders and opened her arms, inviting him into an embrace.

'Oh, Christ.' Adam gave a muffled sob. 'I don't know why, but believing we're safe is almost as hard as believing it happened to us in the first place.'

Katy fought back tears of her own as she felt a spasm of relief run through his frame.

'We're safe,' she agreed, 'but are we okay?'

'The doctor seems to think—'

'Physically, yes. I mean emotionally…'

He shrugged. 'There'll be time to take care of that. Therapy, I suppose, if we need it.'

And then Branning was back, and somehow he'd rustled up a couple of coffees, four bottles of water and some packets of sandwiches, not dissimilar to the ones they'd been given in the cellar.

Suddenly ravenous, they fell upon the food, while Branning looked on with a sympathetic smile. He was itching to begin: the voice recorder had reappeared, and he also had a notepad balanced on his knee.

After confirming the basic details – their names, address, dates of birth – they began with the outing to Sheffield Park, and what should have been a short, uneventful journey home to Lindfield. Adam's face reddened when he explained that a stone had damaged their car.

'I reacted like a dick, to be honest.' He went on to describe how a foolish confrontation with the other driver had exploded into something far more deadly.

DI Branning was very interested in Carole, and slowed their account while he took down as much information as they had about her and her husband.

'He was murdered at their home, you say? So the body could still be there?'

'I guess so,' Adam said. 'I've no idea what they did with it.'

Although he couldn't supply the Kirbys' address, he knew the road she lived in, and Branning made a call to one of his colleagues, asking them to check it out immediately.

They resumed their account, sharing the narrative, each of them occasionally interrupting to add a detail or clarify something the other one said. If Branning found it confusing, he didn't say so, and his expression grew ever more sombre.

His ears pricked up at mention of the birthday party. 'If we've got any of these guys on CCTV, it'll be worth its weight in gold.'

'I persuaded them to take me home first,' Katy said. 'We had to collect a present, and change our clothes…' She trailed off as she registered how Branning was staring at her.

'They went to your house? Actually inside?'

Katy nodded, even as she experienced a sinking feeling. 'Yes.'

'How many of them?'

'Two. The one we knew as Gary, and Dale, the driver.'

'Right.' Branning's tone had turned regretful. 'I'll have to get a forensic team out there first thing in the morning.'

'So we can't go back home?' She sent Adam a despairing look. More than anything she'd been longing to take a shower in her own bathroom, to sleep in her own bed.

'Sorry. Given the extent of the fire where you were kept prisoner, there might be far more valuable evidence at your house.'

'We'll have to find somewhere else to go,' Adam said wearily.

Branning nodded. 'Only for a day or so. Perhaps check into a hotel, or if you have any family you can stay with…?'

Adam exchanged a glance with Katy, who sighed.

'I don't suppose we have any choice, do we?'

CHAPTER FORTY-THREE

Clive and Laura Cotterill lived in a smart four-bedroom house on the western edge of Lewes. Clive was sixty-three, and still worked long hours for the small engineering firm which he and a colleague had set up more than thirty years ago. Laura, a year younger, worked for East Sussex County Council as a senior manager in the finance department, and was just as reluctant to retire.

They were good people who lived busy, active lives. Both loved to hike over the Downs, and Laura was a keen paraglider who often flew from nearby Mount Caburn. Clive was passionate about football, supporting both Lewes FC and Brighton and Hove Albion, whose Amex stadium was within walking distance along the A27.

Adam liked his in-laws a lot, and always enjoyed their company. They were adored by their grandchildren, and had been a godsend for babysitting over the years. The only problem was that Clive – and to a slightly lesser extent, Laura – had a tendency to fuss, and worry, and offer unwanted advice. Most of this was directed at their daughter, so it was Katy who dreaded having to admit to any sort of problem, however minor.

And this was far from a minor problem.

'They'll have to know at some point,' Adam said. 'Might as well get it over with.'

'But we haven't come to terms with it ourselves yet.' Katy looked embarrassed, having this conversation in front of DI Branning. 'I just feel so drained. I don't know where the energy will come from to deal with their reaction.'

'I could have a word with them, if you like?' Branning said, before adding, 'It's probably better for the children, to be in more familiar surroundings. Compared to a hotel…'

As Katy nodded reluctantly, Adam gave her a wry smile. 'You could pretend to be asleep and I'll carry you inside.'

Another reason to go there, he pointed out, was that his in-laws kept a spare key to their house, which the police could borrow.

'That would be great.' Branning had earlier warned that the possessions taken from them by the gang – keys, phones, wallets and so on – were unlikely to be returned quickly, if at all. Anything that hadn't been destroyed by the fire would be retained for forensic analysis and possibly kept as evidence.

Adam said, 'I suppose we'd better get our bank cards cancelled, just in case they were stolen by whoever set the fire.'

'The gang?' Branning queried.

'I don't know. The more I think it over, the shooting we heard had the feel of an ambush, somehow, rather than just a fight.'

When they gave their initial account, the detective had been troubled by Adam's suggestion that at least some of the gunfire might have come from outsiders – how else to explain the brief search of the cellar?

'It can't be ruled out,' Branning had conceded. 'But if you didn't see the gunmen, and the voices were too distant to identify, we'll have to start with the assumption that the people who abducted you were responsible for the shooting, and the fire.'

Now the conversation was interrupted by a sharp cry from Dylan. With a sob in his voice, he called out, 'Mummy! Daddy!'

They both jumped to their feet. Dylan was clawing at the sheets, but still asleep. Katy was closest, and laid a hand on his brow. 'Sshh, it's all right. Mummy and Daddy are here. It's just a nightmare.'

She glanced at Adam, who knew exactly what she was thinking: *Is this the first of many?*

Katy had to wake him before he calmed down. He wiped his eyes, surveying the room in confusion. 'Where are we?'

'In a hospital. We're all safe.'

'Do we have to go back to that place?'

Katy shook her head. 'Never, ever.'

By now Freya had woken, too, and was staring shyly at Branning. 'Can we go home?'

'Not just yet,' Adam told her. 'But we might go to Gran and Granddad's, how about that?'

'Okay,' she said, sounding slightly more cheerful.

Branning said, 'Now they're awake, why don't we ask the doctor to check them over, and then I'll drive you to Lewes.' He glanced at his watch again, and yawned. 'It'll be barely 6 a.m. when we get there – is that too early for your parents?'

'They're normally up around half six, I think.' For a moment Katy looked aghast. 'But what do we say? How do we even begin to explain it?'

The detective offered a gentle smile. 'It won't be as difficult as you think. And you're strong people, I can tell that. Survivors.'

Katy had butterflies as the police car turned into Southdown Avenue and climbed the short hill towards her parents' house. *You gave me such a wonderful upbringing, and here I am, about to pile on a lot of misery and stress.*

The potential consequences of this experience were starting to loom large in her mind. Dylan's nightmare was probably the least of it; as a family they might need years to get over the effects of imprisonment and danger – if they got over it at all. There was no saying what impact it might have on their relationships, on work and school, on issues of safety and trust.

Freya and Dylan had fallen asleep again in the car. DI Branning parked on the drive, and Katy got out first, to prepare the way. The early morning light was drab and grey beneath a layer of cloud, but the air was milder than the day before, fresh and fragrant.

There were no lights on, so Katy tapped quietly on the front door, not wanting to startle her parents. After the second knock, a curtain moved upstairs and she glimpsed her father's face, pale and worried.

The door opened a few seconds later, and his anxiety had already gone up a few notches. He wasn't a tall man, but he was wiry and strong, and right now every muscle seemed to be tensed in anticipation of disaster.

'Katy, what are you doing here? Is that Adam? Who's the man in the—?'

'Police,' she blurted. 'He's a detective. We're not in any trouble – we're all okay, no one's hurt – but we can't go home right now.'

'Clive? Is that Katy?' Her mother's feet came into view as she descended the stairs, tying a robe around her waist.

Clive stepped back, looking bewildered. 'Yes, but with a policeman…'

Laura slapped her hands to her cheeks. 'What's happened? Are the children—?'

'They're fine, honestly. I can explain in a minute, but first I want to get the kids into bed. Is that all right?'

'Of course.' Laura stopped and looked hard at Katy. 'The spare room's virtually ready for them.'

As she turned to go back upstairs, Clive said, 'Were you burgled?'

'It's a lot crazier than that,' Katy said. 'Two minutes, and then we can talk.'

Adam was already lifting Freya out of the car. She stirred, opened her eyes as they crossed the threshold and gave her granddad a sleepy smile.

'Hey, beautiful.' He brushed her cheek with a kiss. His eyes were glistening with tears. Despite being barefoot, clad only in jogging pants and a T-shirt, he insisted on fetching Dylan. DI Branning was standing by the car, and the two men exchanged a slightly awkward greeting.

Katy held the door open for him. Dylan nuzzled into Clive's shoulder and moaned softly on the way upstairs. Branning stepped into the hall and smiled at her.

'They seem to have reacted pretty well, but I'm still happy to explain it for them, if you'd like?'

'No.' Katy shook her head. 'We'll take care of it.'

She fetched the spare set of keys and returned to find him taking in what he could see of the house.

'Much nicer here for you all,' he said. 'Needless to say, we won't be revealing this location to anyone.'

Katy was momentarily appalled, assuming he meant that the gang might be looking for them. Then she realised he was probably referring to the media.

'I see. Thank you.'

'The family liaison officer will be able to give you a lot of advice on the practical day-to-day handling of a situation like this. But you don't need to worry about it now. Just make sure you get some rest.'

The stairs creaked and Adam came down, rubbing his eyes and yawning. 'Freya's still awake but I've persuaded her to stay in bed. Your mum and dad are getting dressed.'

'Better put the kettle on, I suppose.' Katy was about to offer Branning a drink when his phone buzzed. With an apology, he read the message, and they could see from his face that it was serious.

'Fire's out, and the house has been declared safe enough for my guys to have a look round – on the ground floor, at least.'

Katy swallowed hard. 'What did they find?'

'Four bodies. With the possibility of more – upstairs, or hidden away somewhere. But four bodies that we know of.' He looked a little shaken, as if only now appreciating the scale of the case he was investigating.

Katy glanced at Adam, both of them puzzling over that number, and he said, 'Any idea of their identities?'

'Nothing yet, I'm afraid.' Branning checked his watch. 'I'm off home for a shower, change of clothes, kiss my wife and daughter, and then I'll be heading over there.' He stifled a yawn. 'Like I said, try to get some sleep. I'll be back later in the morning to update you and discuss where we go from here.'

They nodded, shook hands, and Katy instinctively gave him a hug. 'Thank you,' she said. 'A few hours ago, I don't think either of us would have dared to dream that we'd be here, safe and unhurt.'

Branning looked taken aback. 'My part in that was minimal, but it's what happens from now on that matters. Keeping you secure, and dealing with any... aftershocks.'

He slipped out of the house, and Katy shut the door and automatically drew the security bolt across. She thought the detective's last comment had been slightly cryptic, but Adam summed it up plainly enough.

'What he's saying is, it isn't over.'

CHAPTER FORTY-FOUR

Adam knew how much Katy was dreading this first conversation with her parents, so he diverted them into the living room while she was in the kitchen, making tea.

Clive wore a fixed, stoic expression, and gripped his wife's hand tightly as they sat down together. Laura held a tissue, which she was dabbing at her eyes.

'This is so silly,' she said. 'I feel like I'm in pieces, even though I don't know what's wrong.'

'But we know *something* is,' Clive said through gritted teeth.

Adam nodded, cleared his throat, and said, 'Yesterday morning we took the kids to Sheffield Park. On the way back, there was… an incident.'

When he reached the part where Katy and Freya had been dragged from the car, Clive emitted an audible moan and fled from the room.

'He's all right.' Laura wiped her eyes again and waved at Adam to continue.

Clive returned a couple of minutes later, along with Katy, and gave out the hot drinks. Both had been crying, and there was a grey pallor to Clive's face that Adam found alarming.

He and Katy stumbled over the rest of their account, thrown off course by numerous interruptions. Laura and Clive couldn't be expected to listen in the same calm, professional way that DI Branning had done, and Adam did his best to sympathise, but he also found it incredibly wearying.

'Oh my word,' Laura kept muttering. 'Those poor children. Those poor children.'

Clive veered between shock and fury – 'They ought to bloody swing for what they did to you' – but mostly he looked poleaxed.

And then Katy snapped: 'Dad, Mum, all this hand-wringing isn't going to help. For the sake of the children, we've got to play it down rather than keep hammering home how terrible it was.'

'No one's suggesting—' Clive started.

'I know, Dad. What I mean is, get all of this emotion out of your system now. Because when they wake up we need it to be as normal as possible.'

'That's easy to say,' Laura pointed out, 'but we'll hardly be able to ignore what's to come. The police investigation, a court case…'

'That's true,' Adam said. 'There's probably all sorts of turmoil that we can't avoid, but if we can at least keep their home life as ordinary as it used to be.'

'Yes,' Laura said, in a newly decisive tone. 'We understand that, don't we, love?'

'You're going to stay here today?' Clive asked. 'I'd better make some calls, get Andy to open up…'

'No, Dad. You need to go to work. Both of you.'

'But we can't,' Laura said. 'We want to help.'

'And you are,' Adam cut in, before Katy said something less conciliatory. 'But the immediate priority is to grab some sleep, and the police will be back to speak to us later. There's no point in you two missing a day's work.'

It took a little more argument, but finally they were persuaded. Laura went up to shower, and made the bed in what had once been Katy's room. By seven o'clock they were finally alone, though Katy wanted to keep the door open, to listen out for the children in the room next door.

'Haven't been this late to bed since our clubbing days,' she joked as she slipped beneath the duvet.

'And we didn't do it that often then.'

'No. We were lightweights.' She wore a sad smile, snuggling against him, face to face. They kissed, and what started as something perfunctory became long and intense, like a celebration of survival.

Then Katy broke away. 'I'm sorry. I'm too tired for anything more.'

'Me too. Do you think you'll sleep?'

'I hope so.' She rolled on to her back, and stared at the ceiling. 'Do you know what my dad said, when he came out to the kitchen?'

Adam felt a twinge of something – excitement, dread, he wasn't sure. 'What?'

'He gave me a hug, and said, "After a thing like this, you'll want to get away, won't you?"'

'Away? Like a holiday?'

'No. He meant leaving here, the UK. Moving to Canada.'

Katy expected more of a reaction than she got; Adam just grunted, said, 'I can't think about that right now,' then turned over and was asleep so quickly that she wondered if he was faking it.

She was fretting that she'd never relax enough to sleep when there was a distant tapping sound and she felt movement beside the bed. She went to open her eyes and found them crusted with sleep.

Confused, she rubbed them clear and saw that Adam was up, and pulling on the jogging pants that Clive had loaned him.

'Where are you going?'

'DI Branning's here. It's twenty to ten.'

'*What*? It can't be!'

'I know. I was out like a light. You must have been, too.'

'But I don't really feel like I've slept.'

He suggested she take her time. 'Have a shower. I'll get them sorted with coffee.'

'Them?'

'There's someone else with him. Another cop.'

'Wait a second.' She reached for his hand, sat up and drew him in for a hug. 'Actually, I do feel better for that.'

'Me too. More positive about everything.'

'And look…' She cleared her throat. 'I'm sorry for how I was with Carole. And sorry for doubting you.'

'Forget it. We were both under enormous stress.'

That felt like a slightly graceless dismissal of her apology, but Katy knew she had to let it pass. They weren't always going to be comfortable discussing every aspect of their captivity, and each would have to respect the other's feelings.

Together they looked in on the children, who were both sound asleep. Then Adam went downstairs and Katy treated herself to what felt like the extraordinary luxury of a hot shower. For how long would such everyday experiences take on an extra degree of pleasure? she wondered.

Her mum, who was only one dress size larger, had told her to help herself to clothes. Katy went for jeans, T-shirt and sweater, and decided to use a touch of make-up as well.

The visitors were in the kitchen extension, sitting at the oak table. All but one of the blinds were drawn, and a thin drizzle was drifting through the garden.

Adam had brewed a pot of coffee and was making a second round of toast. DI Branning, who had also changed clothes and looked noticeably more alert than when they'd last seen him, was busy devouring the first round.

He introduced his colleague as Constable Zoe Ripley, their family liaison officer. She was about thirty, a strong-looking woman of medium height, with short dark hair, a snub nose and a naturally wry expression.

She stood up to shake hands. Her grip was like steel, and Katy tried not to wince. Branning smiled. 'Before joining the police, Zoe was in the army for several years, and has also worked as a close protection officer, so you couldn't be better looked after.'

'Not that we're expecting any trouble, mind.' Zoe had a Nottingham accent, and a deceptively relaxed manner; her placid gaze seemed to miss nothing.

Katy opted for tea and a slice of malt loaf, and joined the others at the table. Branning said he had various things to report: 'Starting with what's most important to you.'

After discussion at what he described as 'the very highest level', it had been decided that the police were going to say nothing about a family having been held captive at the house. 'For now, at least – and for as long as we can manage it – your part in this incident will be kept secret.'

'Really?' Adam sounded stunned, as well as grateful.

'Chances are, word will leak out eventually. But by the time it does, we hope to have identified the bad guys and put them away.'

Zoe said, 'So you get a decent breathing space, without having the media camped at your door.'

Branning nodded. 'We were lucky, in a way, that it happened in the middle of the night. By the time the first reporters got to the scene, you'd already been taken to Haywards Heath, and there was more than enough going on at the farmhouse to keep them busy. We're satisfied now that there are no more than the four bodies we found earlier.'

'Have you been able to identify any of them?' Katy asked.

'Just two,' Branning said. 'A male and a female, who we're reasonably sure are Carole and Brian Kirby.'

They both gasped. 'So Carole is dead?' Katy gave Adam a sorrowful look, before asking, 'Do you know how?'

'Not exactly. But it was extremely unpleasant.' The detective grimaced. 'Brian died from a single gunshot wound. We located their home address, and found evidence to support what Carole had told you. We believe the body was transported to the farmhouse in the boot of the Mazda.'

'At the same time they abducted us?' Katy was horrified. When she and Freya had been thrown into the car, there had already been a dead body in the boot.

'And the other two bodies?' Adam asked.

'Both male,' Branning said. 'They were in a different room to the Kirbys, and they'd been severely burnt. I'd hoped to have some photographs to help identify them, but there was nothing useful.'

'Plus it's not fair to show you that sort of material,' Zoe added.

Adam shrugged. 'I'm willing to take a look.'

'We can tell that one of them was short, overweight, probably had a lot of tattoos.'

'Gary,' Adam said, looking to Katy for confirmation.

'We did wonder. The other is tall, quite thin, a young man, I'd say.'

'Dale?' Katy said. 'Dale or Jay.'

'Well, we're running the names and descriptions that you gave us through our databases. Nothing so far, which suggests that they *were* using aliases – as they claimed to be – but maybe we'll get lucky with the DNA. Frankly, I'd be gobsmacked if none of these individuals has any prior convictions.'

'What about the cars?' Adam asked.

'Stolen, with cloned plates. Again, there's forensic evidence still to be collected.' He reached for another piece of toast, then changed his mind. 'On that subject, we hope to have your home examined and released to you by this afternoon.'

'And we'll be safe to go back?' Katy asked. 'Even with three of them potentially still out there?'

'We don't see any likelihood of reprisals. Right now this gang, whoever they are, will be preoccupied with staying out of our reach.'

'But it's still a reasonable concern,' Zoe said. 'If you've got somewhere for me to crash, I can stay over for a couple of nights.'

'By which time we may have them,' Branning said. 'The fact is, most criminals aren't very smart. Given the chaos this lot caused, I doubt if it'll take long to find them.'

Katy was cheered by this, but Adam, in a cool tone, said, 'And what if it's not them?'

Zoe gave him a sidelong glance. 'Not what?'

Branning frowned. 'So far we haven't found anything to indicate the involvement of… other parties.'

'But it's early days,' Adam reminded him.

'Absolutely. And of course we'll look into Carole's background, for any sign of this affair you mentioned.'

'That was the key to the kidnapping.' Adam was vehement, and looking to Katy for support. 'Wasn't it?'

'Well, it's what Carole seemed to think – though we weren't present when the gang spoke to her.'

This had Adam fuming, but Katy felt it was more important to stick to the facts.

'If that wasn't the reason for taking her, what was it?' he asked.

Branning shook his head. 'The investigation is a few hours old. At this stage there are always far more questions than answers.'

'Tell them about the other discovery,' Zoe said.

'Ah, yes. We found your bag, Katy, and it seems to contain both your phones, a purse and a wallet. It's all with forensics at present, but as soon as I can get it returned to you…'

'That would be great, thank you,' she said. 'Where did you find it?'

'Uh…' Now he looked uncomfortable. 'In the trees, roughly in the area where you told us you'd gone to hide.'

'We didn't have the bag,' Katy blurted, but Branning raised his hands.

'I know. There was evidence of blood on the ground nearby.'

'So someone *was* hiding near to us?' Although his suspicions had been vindicated, Adam looked sick, and Katy knew why.

They hadn't been safe after they escaped from the house. Would they ever be truly safe again?

CHAPTER FORTY-FIVE

At 10 a.m. Holly was woken by a text. Normally she muted the phone, especially after a session at her desk that had seen her finally log off and collapse into bed shortly after four, by which time her eyes had mutated into shards of glass.

But after last night she wanted to know at once if he got in touch again. She wasn't completely sure that he would, especially after edging on to such dangerous ground. In the cold, drab light of a winter Monday he could well come to his senses (as he might see it) and that would no doubt entail a period of silence.

But here he was. It had to be him, because virtually no one had her mobile number. She used email for friends and acquaintances, and the landline for her mother.

Already there was a tingle as she sat up in bed; an image of him right here, between these sheets. Between these legs. Ha!

But no name in the display. An unfamiliar number.

Shit.

Holly took issues of privacy and security very seriously, especially as she knew how easily most online barriers were breached. She had a miserable old Samsung whose number she supplied when some form of verification was required. But no chance of her proper number cropping up on some tawdry marketing list…

Growling beneath her breath, for she knew she wouldn't get back to sleep, she dabbed the message open and read – and scrolled – and read.

And jeez. Turned out it *was* him, gone all nefarious and sneaky-beaky. And with such an honest, fervent tone, it made her heart beat faster. Warmed her to her very core.

The message ended with a plea, a question. Could she do it?

In a world now supercharged with positive vibes, she ran through a few schedules in her mind; it would mean stepping away from the grindstone, but wouldn't anyone argue that she ought to be doing that a bit more often? Let New York boy take up the slack for a while.

Pretending to weigh it up while she leapt out of bed and ran for the shower, busy listing all the small tasks of defoliation that represented the base camp of her beauty regime. *You're kidding nobody, pal.*

Are you gonna do what he's asked?

Oh hell, yeah.

CHAPTER FORTY-SIX

The morning passed in a blur. Katy phoned the school to say the children had both gone down with a bug and would be off for a day or two. That reminded Adam of his strategy meeting – an event which had dominated his thoughts for weeks but now seemed pathetically trivial.

Pretending to be ill wouldn't cut it, so he concocted a story of a cousin, who lived alone, succumbing to a life-threatening stroke. He phoned his boss and endured a difficult conversation, resisting the urge to be brutally honest: *My family nearly died, and do you know what? Compared to that, my career means nothing.*

Instead he asked for the minutes to be emailed to him. 'I'll review them and get back to you with my comments tonight. Gotta go – sorry, Ray. The doctor wants to talk to me.'

After they'd eaten some breakfast, DI Branning took them through the entire ordeal in greater detail, referring to his own notes to double check and verify their initial account.

Around eleven the children woke, a little bewildered to find themselves at their grandparents' house. Dylan in particular was confused as to whether yesterday's experience had been real. Tempting as it was to say otherwise, Adam reluctantly confirmed that it had happened, but it was over now, and they were safe.

Not that he completely believed that, but he said it just the same.

There was another round of breakfast, with the kids devouring scrambled eggs and bacon. Then more of Branning's colleagues arrived, and he explained that the whole family would need to provide fingerprints and DNA samples, to eliminate them from the various searches.

Katy asked for a quiet word with Adam, and they briefly discussed the question of giving consent, before agreeing that it would be ridiculous to refuse. Upon their return, Branning said, 'You can take legal advice if you wish, but we do need these samples.'

Adam shook his head. 'We just want to confirm that we're not suspects.'

'Well, in my eyes there's about a zero-point-one per cent chance that the two of you faked an abduction and committed four murders, then set a house on fire and hung round with your young children to wait for us to arrive.'

Adam managed a grin. 'Put like that...'

Once it was done, Branning and the others departed, leaving just the family liaison officer, Zoe, who quickly built a rapport with the kids, showing them various martial arts moves and talking about her life in the army, which had included tours of Iraq and Afghanistan.

Katy's mum popped home during her lunch break, bringing cakes and donuts, and smothering the children with affection. They virtually had to prise her away, but she wouldn't go back to work until they agreed that Freya and Dylan would stay over tonight.

'Or all four of you, if the house isn't available. But these two need a few treats.' Beaming at the children, she said, 'I've spoken to Granddad and we're both taking tomorrow off. We can go out, wherever you want.'

A detective constable called Emma Morgan came by at about two, bearing gifts in the form of Katy's purse and Adam's wallet and watch. The handbag itself was being retained for further examination.

'Can you both check that all your cards are there?' she asked. 'We need to know if anything's missing.'

'Just cash, by the look of it,' Katy said. She'd had about eighty pounds in her purse. Adam wasn't so sure, but thought he'd had a twenty and some coins.

'Sorry about that. We'll need to add it to the statement. There may be a chance to recover some—'

Katy made a dismissive gesture. 'Compared to what could have happened, it's nothing.'

'No, I suppose not.' The DC gave a tentative smile. 'We're nearly done with your car, as well. John's going to arrange for it to be driven here.'

'Fantastic, thank you,' Adam said. 'And our phones?'

'Uh, not yet. In fact, may I ask for the codes to unlock them?'

Adam couldn't hide his unease, so he converted it to displeasure. 'Is that really necessary?'

'I'm afraid so. They were in the gang's possession for a number of hours, and I believe they were unlocked?'

Katy nodded. 'You think they used our phones?'

'It is possible—' Morgan began.

'Why?' Adam snapped. 'I mean, they had their own phones.'

'True. But we have to check.'

Giving Adam a severe look, Katy said, 'That's fine. How long will you need them for?'

'Hopefully only a day or two. Everything's being fast-tracked like you wouldn't believe.'

'Okay.' Adam offered a conciliatory smile. 'Sorry, but you know how it is, not having your phone…'

'Oh God, yes. Like having your arm chopped off.' DC Morgan was smiling, but Katy wasn't.

Katy knew that Adam was worried about something.

*

When DI Branning returned for his third visit it was twenty to four, and the strain was showing in his face.

'Shift should have ended by now,' he admitted in response to Katy's question. 'I was aiming to get here sooner, but there's a lot happening at once.' He raised his eyebrows. 'That, and I was followed from the station by a couple of journalists. I've just detoured through Lewes to get rid of them.'

Adam's reaction was to head for the window, but Branning assured him there was nothing to worry about. 'As an extra precaution, I parked round the corner.'

Earlier, overcome by a morbid curiosity, Katy and Adam had watched a couple of different news channels, and done some searching online. They found numerous reports, beginning with a fairly sketchy description of bodies found at the scene of a house fire near Chelwood Gate, in East Sussex. Further details had been added during the morning, and the one that drew more intense coverage was the announcement that four people had been murdered at the property, and that these deaths pre-dated the fire.

By early afternoon one phrase in particular was beginning to crop up on Twitter: *gangland incident*. There was widespread shock that such brutality could occur in the heart of the Sussex countryside, though some of those commenting made reference to shootings in Cumbria, Hungerford and of course nearby Chilton, the scene of a vicious killing spree almost a decade before.

Not long before the detective arrived, Katy took a careful prowl around Facebook and found a link to the story with comments from local people, suggesting that two of the victims were a wealthy Sussex couple, who'd been snatched from their home and murdered when they refused to hand over passwords to their online accounts.

'It's just gossip, speculation,' Branning said when she mentioned it. 'And mostly inaccurate.'

'Not the core information,' Katy said. 'At first it was a gangland thing. Now there's a local couple involved. How long till someone gets a whisper about us?'

Branning couldn't look to Zoe for help; she was in the garden with Freya and Dylan, playing a hybrid game of rounders and cricket.

'I'll do my utmost to keep you out of it. I can't guarantee I'll succeed, or that someone won't force my hand. But if I can buy you a few days, there's every chance the media will have their feast and move on.'

'In search of fresh victims,' Adam muttered. He'd grown increasingly moody all afternoon, and Katy sensed that a confrontation of sorts was now unavoidable.

'It's a bit annoying that you've had to keep our phones. And that you're going through them,' she added, with what Adam might have interpreted as a meaningful glance in his direction.

'They'll be returned as soon as possible, and again I can assure you of our discretion. We're only interested to see whether there was any activity while they were held by the gang.'

'Do you know any more about them?'

'It's coming together, bit by bit.' Branning leaned over and removed a laptop from his bag. 'Firstly, we've traced the owners of the property. It's been unoccupied for years, after most of the land was sold to a neighbouring farm. The owners have no idea who might have been staying there, but anyone scouting the area would have seen that it was empty.'

He set the laptop on his knees, and after tapping a couple of times he turned the screen in their direction. It showed a frozen image that Katy immediately recognised: the car park of the soft play centre in Burgess Hill.

Branning clicked on the mouse pad and the images moved in a series of slightly jerky frames, showing the Mazda gliding into a space towards the rear of the car park. The driver remained in his seat while three passengers got out.

Katy was shocked to see herself looking remarkably composed as she led Dylan towards the building; she recalled how frightened she had been, and how certain that someone would pick up on that fear. Instead she looked just like any other parent, perhaps a little tired, delivering their child to a party.

The detective switched to a camera in the lobby, which captured a clear image of Gary's face as he strutted in ahead of them, apparently on the phone.

'This is the one you knew as Gary, yes?'

Katy confirmed it, and Branning told her that they had plenty of useable footage from inside the centre. 'We can see him loitering close by, sending you a lot of suspicious sidelong glances. Suspicious in retrospect,' he amended, in response to her bleak expression. 'I daresay nobody had any reason to challenge him at the time.'

'I kept hoping.' Katy stared down at her lap, where she found her hands were writhing together. 'Or should I have told someone? It was such agony, not knowing what to do – because he had a gun, and because Adam and Freya were still prisoners…'

'You did the right thing,' Branning said. 'You mustn't feel any guilt whatsoever – either of you.' He looked from Katy to Adam, who nodded uneasily. 'It's incredible how well you held it together.'

He moved on to footage from the second visit, where a camera in the café area caught Dale nervously ducking his head as he pretended to study the food counter.

'That's "Dale", yes?' Branning put the laptop aside. 'So far these are the only two that we have on camera. A neighbour of the Kirbys' has CCTV, and we've got a glimpse of the Mazda as it passes en route to their house, and again making a quick getaway about fifteen minutes later. On both occasions there's no clear view of the occupants.'

'But do you know who they are?' Adam asked, with a touch of impatience.

'These two, we think we do. Turns out they used their middle names. Frank Gary Harding is from Bridlington, though for most of his career he's worked in Leeds.'

'Career?' Katy echoed. 'Doing what?'

'Doorman. Drug dealer. Pimp. And a bit of hired muscle for various lowlifes in West Yorkshire.'

Katy had shuddered at the word 'pimp', and both men registered it. Branning took a sip of the water he'd requested in place of more tea or coffee, and went on: 'The skinny guy is Tyler Dale Shipway, from Sheffield. Only in his mid twenties, but a stack of convictions for vehicle theft, joyriding, assault – oh, and causing death by dangerous driving. That was at the tender age of fourteen.'

They both gasped. Branning said, 'Latterly he's been involved in drug dealing, and he's worked alongside Gary on a couple of occasions. To be honest, you won't find many people mourning their deaths.'

'I'm sure,' Adam said in a heartfelt tone.

Branning pressed his hands together and put them to his face; a praying gesture that signalled deep thought, or a contentious subject – or both.

'So here's what we have. These two men, Dale and Gary, both based in the north of England, both known as freelancers – they're the only ones exposed to CCTV and situations where witnesses might identify them. And they're the only members of the gang found dead. What does that suggest to you?'

Katy shrugged. She had no idea what he was getting at, but guessed that they weren't going to like it.

'Tell us,' Adam said.

'Well, since you've told us that the other three members of the gang had south-east accents – and since those three appeared to be calling the shots – it seems fair to assume that they hired Gary and Dale just for this operation. Yes?'

Adam groaned, and folded his arms across his chest. 'So they were expendable?'

'Maybe not to start with. But once things had gone badly wrong, and you guys got caught up in it, perhaps there was a conscious decision to let those two take the risks in public, knowing they were going to be dealt with when it was over.'

Katy nodded. 'Makes sense. So you think Maggie had them killed, and then started the fire?'

'Right now, it's a pretty compelling scenario.' Branning turned to Adam, inviting his contribution.

'I just don't see why they'd cut and run like that. Yes, we snarled up their plans, but they gave every sign of sticking around for some kind of meeting or event on Monday.' He glanced at Katy, who nodded in support. 'And why murder Carole? She was valuable to them. Some kind of bargaining chip.'

'With this mystery Russian?' Branning queried, in a cryptic voice.

'Yes,' Adam said. 'He's the key to this, and I don't know why you're not doing more to find him.'

'I'll come to that,' Branning said calmly. 'But you mentioned Carole? I'm afraid it's not clear cut that she was murdered.'

CHAPTER FORTY-SEVEN

'What?' Adam almost spat the question out, but DI Branning was unperturbed.

'We think her death could have been an accident. Or she might even have taken her own life.'

Katy made a gulping noise, and quickly covered her face with her hands.

'I'm sorry,' Branning said. 'Are you okay hearing—?'

'Fine, yes.' Katy nodded brusquely. 'Go on.'

The detective hesitated for a moment, then took a deep breath. 'Her body wasn't as affected by the fire as the two in the lounge. She had a broken neck and a number of devastating puncture wounds to her lower body, consistent with a heavy impact. The search around the house revealed corresponding damage to a wooden planter on the patio – along with a lot of blood, and large fragments of glass from the bedroom window above.'

'So she jumped?' Katy's voice was weak with shock. 'She jumped from the window?'

'On purpose?' Adam asked. 'Or did they throw her out?'

'We can't be sure, but I think more likely it was of her own volition.' Branning leaned back in his seat. 'Of course, we don't know if this was a desperate bid to escape, or maybe just a desire to… end her misery.'

Or a bit of both, Adam thought. Recalling his own turmoil, he was conscious that he too might have reached a point where any action, no matter how self-destructive, was preferable to an uncertain fate.

'She took the scissors.' Katy looked sadly at Adam. 'Perhaps she'd made a plan to get out, and carried it through?'

'We may never know for sure,' Branning said. 'But you can see how this changes the dynamic? If she was their bargaining chip – as you've suggested – then they were left with nothing.'

Katy was nodding gently, buying into it. 'So they cut their losses?'

'Yep. Eliminated the hired hands, whose loyalty might not have been guaranteed, and then did a runner.'

'But they left us alive,' Adam pointed out.

'Albeit in a burning house.'

'Someone opened up the cellar. Why do that?'

Branning shrugged. 'A last-minute attack of conscience? Maybe one of them unlocked it, only to find you were missing. With time running out, they couldn't stay and search, so they got out of there.'

'Which means –' Katy shot a nervy look towards the garden – 'we're unfinished business.'

'Not necessarily. They've covered their identities fairly well so far. I don't know if we'll get any viable DNA or prints from the house, and the cars they left behind are giving us the opposite problem – a messy stew of DNA from God knows how many people.'

'Hold on. Are we supposed to be reassured by the fact that you might struggle to find them?' Katy asked, and the detective only smiled, ruefully.

Adam had other concerns: 'Going back to what you just said, it sounds like you accept there was some kind of deal being set up, with my "mystery" Russian.'

'Oh, it's feasible that there was a plot, and that their target was an unknown party—'

'Not unknown. She told me his name is Barinov. Alex Barinov.'

'He doesn't exist. There's no super-rich Russian of that name in the UK. And so far we haven't found any kind of communication between Carole and a secret lover.'

'He's got a house near Forest Row.'

The way Branning smiled, he might have been humouring an idiot. 'I have someone checking the ownership of the larger properties in that area, but wealthy individuals frequently make their purchases via shell companies or trusts. It gives them privacy, and I daresay a load of tax advantages as well. Short of knocking on every door and showing them a picture of Carole…'

'Well, can't you do that?' Adam snapped.

'Not with the budget available for this enquiry. Because frankly, Carole's affair is irrelevant. After she died, they abandoned whatever scheme they'd concocted. Chances are that this Barinov, whoever he really is, will never have a clue what lay in store for him.'

Adam had opened his mouth to object before his brain caught up. He promptly shut it again, and slumped in his seat.

On the face of it, DI Branning was right.

'We'll go on looking, and of course we'll be delving into Carole and Brian's lives in great detail, in the hope of finding a clue to the kidnappers' identities.' He spotted Adam's doubt, and said, earnestly, 'I'll keep an open mind, I promise.'

Next came an update on the situation at their own house. The forensic team had been delayed and might not be finished until later this evening.

'Not a problem,' Katy said. 'We're happy to stay here tonight.'

Branning was thanking them for their patience when Freya and Dylan burst in, complaining that it had become too cold to play outside. Katy checked the time and was shocked to find it was nearly five o'clock.

'Well, I'm pretty much done. You have my number, if you think of anything. And Zoe will be here till six, though I'm sure she'll stay longer if you'd like her to?'

Katy exchanged a glance with Adam, and said, 'No. We'll be fine.'

'Good. I'll try to leave you alone in the morning as well.' His phone buzzed as he stood up. He read a text, and said, 'Car's outside.'

Katy didn't understand until they reached the hall. She opened the front door and saw their Peugeot on the drive. DC Morgan handed over the keys and addressed Branning: 'I think I'm coming back with you?'

'Yep. Just got the message.' Branning called out a farewell to Zoe, who was loitering at the far end of the hall, then he and Morgan hurried away.

Katy shut the door and felt a wave of relief. The keys in her hand were another step on the road back to normality. Next up, hopefully, would be the return of their phones and the option to go back home.

Adam went outside to check the damaged light, and said he would call a guy he knew, who worked at a garage in Haywards Heath, and see if they could get it fixed, perhaps tomorrow morning. 'Otherwise we're gonna get pulled over if we drive anywhere.'

In the kitchen, Katy put the kettle on, and was joined by Zoe. After a little awkward conversation, the liaison officer said, 'Look, I realise how unusual it is to have a stranger around, and I'm certainly not here to make things more difficult. If you want me to stay late tonight, that's great, but equally if you'd prefer some space…?'

Katy nodded. 'I think we probably would, if you don't mind?'

'Not at all. I'll leave you my number, and you have John's as well.'

She said goodbye to the children, both of whom rushed to give her a hug. It was a sign of how well they'd bonded, and a gratifying sight.

After seeing her out, Katy felt a stab of fear the instant they were alone. What if Maggie and her men were somewhere close by, waiting for just this opportunity?

'Tom can do the car first thing,' Adam reported back. 'Dunno what I'm going to say if he notices the bullet hole.'

'Let's ask my dad. He might be able to get something for it.'

She called her father before he left work, then as a family they settled in the lounge, all four of them squashed up on the sofa in a warm, affectionate tangle of limbs.

At last Katy felt some of the stresses melting away. This terrible experience hadn't broken them. As individuals they were resilient, and as a family they would survive.

Not just survive, she thought. *Flourish.*

They had a pleasant half hour together before her parents came home. Clive had brought a tub of filler, some sort of epoxy resin. They moved the Peugeot into the garage, and he and Adam were busy for twenty minutes, first cleaning the upholstery where Dylan had been sick, then filling and sanding the hole in the bodywork.

'Just needs painting,' Adam said, 'but it's far less noticeable now.'

Her parents were adamant about taking the children out tomorrow. They debated possible destinations in the kitchen while Clive knocked up his famous bolognese, ably assisted by Freya and Dylan, and finally they agreed on Port Lympne, a safari park in Kent.

Laura was planning to put the children's clothes through the washer dryer once they were in bed. Katy had washed hers and Adam's clothes this morning, which her mother insisted on ironing.

Dinner was ready by half six, and at Clive's suggestion they ate off their laps in the lounge while watching a superhero movie on Netflix, chosen by Dylan. Afterwards, as Freya grew bored and started surfing on the iPad, Katy overheard Laura urging her granddaughter to search online for ideas for Christmas presents.

'I've already got a list,' Freya said.

'Doesn't matter. Add more to it,' Laura said, ignoring the look she got from Katy.

There were three flavours of ice cream for dessert, and Clive had also bought a box of chocolates. In despair, Katy followed Adam out to the kitchen when he went to load the dishwasher.

'This is totally over the top,' she complained.

'I agree, but I can see why they're doing it. I also know what they'll say if we object.'

'"It won't do them any harm",' Katy said in a mimicking tone.

'What's that?' The door swung open and Clive was there, holding an empty bottle of wine.

Blushing, Katy shook her head, while Adam hurriedly spoke up: 'Delicious meal. Thank you.'

Her dad wasn't fooled. 'We'll get them to bed soon. Why don't you two wander along to the pub? I'm sure you could benefit from some time to yourselves.'

Katy looked at Adam, who might have been about to protest, and said, 'That's not a bad idea. Thanks, Dad.'

'It's nothing. The way I see it, we can do a fair bit to help the kids move on from this.' Clive gave them a serious look. 'Whereas, in your case… it's really only the two of you that can help one another.'

CHAPTER FORTY-EIGHT

Adam reflected on his father-in-law's words as he and Katy walked towards the town centre. Sound advice though it was, he couldn't deny that he felt uneasy about the prospect of an open, honest conversation with his wife. When it came to acknowledging what they'd been through, he still needed more time to analyse his own feelings before he was ready to discuss them with anyone else. He thought it was likely – if not certain – that Katy felt the same.

The fallback, as ever, was to talk about the children instead. Katy started with another protest about the way her parents were spoiling them.

'And what about missing out on school? If they're having a day out tomorrow, do we send them back on Wednesday?'

He shrugged. 'I'd assumed they might need longer. Why don't we see how they are tomorrow night and review it then?'

'All right. There's also the issue of what they tell their teachers and friends. I'm not happy with the idea of asking them to lie – and in Dylan's case, he's bound to let something slip.'

'With his imagination, they'll probably assume he's making it up.'

'That wouldn't be fair to him. And if we don't want them to lie, then we have to inform the school ourselves, so they're aware that there might be… reactions to it.'

'I dunno. They're good kids, and pretty level-headed. Seeing them interact with your mum and dad, I don't get the impression—'

'It's far too early to know.' Katy's tone was abrupt enough that a couple of people on the opposite pavement turned to look. She offered a quiet apology.

Adam sighed. 'No, I get what you're saying. A lot of problems ahead.'

They decided on the Pelham Arms, which was the closest pub on the western fringes of the High Street. It was a cosy, welcoming establishment that dated back to the reign of Charles I. It always amazed Adam to think that people had once gathered on this spot to drink and gossip during the English Civil War.

Hoping he wasn't facing something quite so tumultuous this evening, Adam waited until they'd found a table to ask: 'So what do you really want to talk about?'

Katy shook her head, as if confused by the question, but he'd caught a flash of anxiety.

'Canada?' he queried.

'I think we *will* have to discuss that, but…' Her expression hardened. 'What's on your phone that you don't want the police to see?'

'What?' He tried to laugh. 'Who says there's anything?'

'Adam, please.'

'I mean it. I just don't like the idea of strangers combing through my phone. I've got work stuff on there, important emails—'

'Porn?'

'No! Of course not.'

She appraised him carefully. 'Okay, it's not porn. So what is it?'

Adam couldn't break her gaze, but nor could he look her in the eye and deny it. He took a quick, fortifying mouthful of beer, and said, 'Holly's still messaging me.'

Katy felt her heart race at the mention of that name. 'What sort of messages?'

'Look, I didn't tell you all the details about her last relationship. The reason it ended was because the guy died. A car accident, apparently.'

'Oh.' Katy was unable, yet, to offer condolences.

'She's been in a really bad way. Working too hard. Drinking too much. Back on medication, then off it again.'

'So the same as last time?'

'Worse, probably. She's been maintaining that her life might as well be over, and she doesn't know why she bothers to get up in the morning... all the usual stuff.'

'Right.' Katy found his unemotional tone a little jarring. 'I take it you sounded more sympathetic to her than you do now? Have you met up with her?'

'God, no. I'm not interested in—'

'Where's she living – still in Northampton?'

'I assume so. That never came up.'

'So what does she want from you?'

'Just... like you say, a bit of sympathy. Someone to rant at, who wasn't going to pick up the phone and get her sectioned.'

'A shoulder to cry on, then?'

'Not literally. It's just a few texts, back and forth.'

'Last time, as I recall, she wanted a lot more than that.'

Adam dipped his head. 'But she didn't get it.'

'She nearly ripped our marriage apart, Adam. And to know she's going through the same routine again, and you've lied to me...'

'Because I knew it would upset you. That's the only reason.' He gazed into the middle distance. 'The last few days she's been texting too often – and there were some I just deleted without replying.'

'I bet the police have a way to recover them.'

She said it partly to gauge his reaction, and was slightly heartened when he only shrugged. 'I'm sure they do, if they need to be that thorough.' He downed the rest of his pint and stood up. 'Same again?'

Katy's wine glass was still half full, so she shook her head. While he was at the bar, standing with his back to her, she observed him carefully, as if some aspect of his body language might reveal whether he had been completely truthful.

She realised there was no way of knowing. She either had to trust him… or not.

When he turned back, slurping at the beer to stop it spilling, she decided to set the matter aside for now. There were other things she wanted to discuss.

'I can't get over the fact that they found our stuff in the trees. When you talked about hearing someone close by, I was praying you were mistaken. To think we could have blundered into them…' She took a sip of wine, trying to quell the alarm that was rising within her. 'Who do you think it was?'

'One of the gang, I suppose. I'm worried there's a whole other element to this, and DI Branning doesn't want to know.'

'To be fair, his theory makes a lot of sense. Carole died, so the gang cut their losses and ran away.'

'I agree, up to a point. But why did someone come down, shine a light round the cellar, and not call out to us?'

Katy blinked rapidly, unconsciously trying to avoid going back to that place, even in her memory. 'Perhaps because it had all gone horribly wrong, and the house was about to go up in flames?'

Adam was consuming his beer with a fierce concentration, as though he regarded it as necessary rather than pleasurable. 'I know what Carole told me. After talking to Maggie she was convinced it was all about this guy, Alex. He was the key to the whole thing.'

He was getting angry, not raising his voice but speaking in a low-pitched growl. Katy leaned back in her chair to put more distance between them.

'Maybe it was. But if she tried to get away, and ended up dead, it makes a lot of sense that they would ditch their plan. And if "Alex" gave her a false name and can't be traced, what are the police supposed to do? Spend a fortune chasing some phantom, instead of searching for Maggie and the others?'

Adam's glass was now empty. He set it down with such delicacy that it made her think he wanted to smash it, just to release some frustration.

'You're probably right.' He stifled a belch. 'Shall we go?'

Outside they found the temperature had dipped, enough for their breath to emerge in brilliant white clouds. The sky was clear overhead, and there was virtually no wind. As they crossed the road into Warren Drive, the high flint walls of Lewes prison seemed to glow in the moonlight, like some imposing Dickensian backdrop. Wood smoke tickled Katy's nostrils, and she sneezed a couple of times.

'Bless you,' Adam said, with a trace of irony, and linked his arm through hers.

Her dad had insisted that she take his phone with her, so they wouldn't be out of contact. An incoming text made them both jump.

She read the message. 'One of the cops has just dropped the spare keys back. Apparently we're fine to go home any time we want.'

'That's good.' He paused, as if to see whether she would disagree. 'Tomorrow morning, while the kids are out for the day?'

Katy nestled against him, briefly resting her head on his shoulder. *I can trust him*, she told herself. *Holly isn't going to come between us.*

'I'm worried about how it's going to feel,' she said. 'Stepping inside the first time…'

'I can understand that. Do you want to tell me what happened?'

'Not really.' She felt embarrassed, almost ashamed, which was not only ridiculous, but unjust. 'When we went into the kitchen, it was only me and Gary. He pushed me against the table and… well, got a bit physical. He threatened to rape me if I tried to raise the alarm.' She shuddered. 'But not just me. Freya.'

Adam groaned. 'The bastard. But that makes it even more incredible that you got the scissors from under his nose. I'm in awe of you.'

'Don't say that. I feel like it's tempting fate to take any sort of pride in how we handled it.'

Adam was surprised. 'Really? Why?'

'Because there are still so many issues to confront. Getting the kids settled back at school. The police investigation. The chance of the media finding out about us – and maybe one day a court case.' She wiped her eyes. 'It's so hard to believe our lives will ever get back on track, and I'm worried that we may end up having to emigrate, whether we want to or not, just to have any chance of normality ever again.'

CHAPTER FORTY-NINE

Adam realised the beer had gone to his head, on top of the wine he'd had with dinner. It made him feel a little brash, and aggrieved that Katy seemed so reluctant to buy into his theory. On the other hand, she hadn't torn his throat out when he told her about Holly, so he had to give her credit for that.

What he'd omitted to say was that the messages had got a bit silly, and far more flirtatious than they should have done. Some of them he'd ignored – like the ones that suggested he ought to jump on a train to Northampton and bang her brains out. Others he had skirted round, often deliberately misunderstanding their intent, but there were a few where he'd responded in kind, with jokes and flattery and a certain willingness to act as though there was still something between them.

Bloody stupid, reflecting on it now. And even half-pissed, he cringed to imagine how it would look if DI Branning and his team recovered the deleted texts and read some of the things he and his former girlfriend had said to each other.

Then again, it had no bearing on this incident, and surely the police had a duty to be discreet about such things?

Approaching the house, they could see a single light on downstairs. Katy unlocked the door and they crept inside, only to hear a creak on the landing. Clive appeared, wrapped in a dressing gown, and whispered: 'Kids were zonked by eight o'clock, and we've decided on an early night. Good news about the house, eh?'

'Yes,' Katy agreed, but in a distinctly muted tone.

Adam thanked his father-in-law again for their help today, and followed Katy into the kitchen. He assumed she wanted to continue the conversation, but after filling a glass of water, she said, 'Last night has really caught up with me. I'm off to bed.'

He checked his watch; it was only ten past ten. 'You okay if I stay up for a while? I told Ray I'd take a look at the minutes of the meeting.'

'Don't get in too deep, though. You must be shattered.'

'Yeah. And not quite with it. So if I write any notes, I'll review them in the morning before I send them!'

The comment earned him a smile, and a peck on the cheek. 'Night.'

He contemplated the kettle before settling on water himself. Rather than use the iPad, he moved to the tiny office area, which was barely more than an alcove between the dining room and kitchen.

A nudge of the mouse woke the desktop computer. Adam opened a web browser and brought up Hotmail. After entering his password, he clicked to open a new tab and quickly scanned Google news. The sidebar contained some local headlines, including one from the *Argus*. INVESTIGATION CONTINUES AFTER FOUR BODIES FOUND.

This was the same headline as earlier, but when he opened the link he saw a new subheading: LOCAL COUPLE CONFIRMED DEAD. The article now identified Brian and Carole Kirby as being among the victims. An unnamed police source had suggested that the incident had begun with a home invasion, and that detectives were still trying to ascertain why the couple were taken to the empty farmhouse.

A botched robbery that escalated into kidnap and murder, according to the author of the piece, who also speculated at length about the identity of the kidnappers. Clearly the police were still offering very little solid information, but Adam couldn't see them getting away with that for long.

Unwilling to waste any more time, he switched back to Hotmail. The Inbox had loaded and there were two emails from his boss, both with attachments. The message that caught his eye, however, was from Holly Wolstenholme.

Adam gasped, reeling back in his chair, then he glanced over his shoulder as if fearful that Katy would be standing there. It felt like a kind of sorcery – as if by discussing Holly tonight they had conjured this new communication from her.

Of course, the real explanation was simple enough. She'd been texting him yesterday morning, and had probably grown impatient when he failed to reply. He peered at the screen. The email had been sent at six o'clock this evening, and there was just the one. For Holly, that was quite restrained.

There was no subject, and what he could read of the message began: *Adam, are you there?*

With a nervous sigh, he clicked on the message. It said: *Reply to me as soon as you get this. VERY IMPORTANT!*

He took a sip of water, and foolishly checked once again to make sure he was alone. He had no reason to feel guilty, so why was he acting like this?

He was inclined to ignore the message, then realised it was better to communicate by email, rather than have more and more of her texts stacking up for some nosy police technician to read. He typed a short reply:

Hi Holly, having problems with my phone but all good here. Are you okay?

After sending it, he opened the first of Ray Pascoe's emails and saw that he'd been sent the minutes, along with a couple of spreadsheets. If he opened one of these now, he'd probably be here until the early hours, just as Katy had warned.

A new message appeared. His heart sank as he pictured Holly at her desk, fully prepared to work – and chat – the night away. This one was just as succinct, but a lot more shocking:

I know what happened Sunday. Are you all safe?

A minute or two went by, perhaps longer, while Adam stared at the screen in confusion. Just nine words, which he read over and over, and still they refused to make sense.

Then he jerked forward, grabbed the keyboard and wrote with manic speed:

What the hell do you mean? WHAT DO YOU KNOW, AND HOW?

He hadn't noticed that he'd hit the caps lock by mistake, but he was in no mood to re-type. He clicked on *Send* and sat back with his arms crossed, his breath whistling angrily through his nostrils.

The reply was almost immediate:

Don't shout! I know this must be a shock. Are the family safe?

He almost growled at the screen. This was a typical feature of her conversations, aided by the distant nature of a written exchange. She would consistently ignore his questions while bombarding him with her own.

Better to talk in person, he thought, but he sent one more email, composed with a little more consideration.

Yes, we're all safe, but I want answers to my questions and a proper explanation. Otherwise, no more contact.

She must have barely had time to type a reply, because it was here within seconds.

Ooh, someone's cross. Sorry, Adam, I know this is a mindfuck, but we have to meet. Tomorrow, OK?

This time he did let out a growl, and had to make a conscious effort not to bash the keyboard as he typed.

No, Holly, not OK. Tell me what's going on.

He stared at the screen. Thirty seconds. A minute. He was beginning to think it was a bluff, or some kind of sick joke, when her response came in.

Has to be f2f. Lives depend on it. I can't say any more. The Skyway Hotel, Dunstable, 1 p.m. tomorrow. DON'T TELL ANYONE!

He spent a long time considering how to respond – or whether to bother at all. She had to be kidding him, didn't she? There was no way she could know about this.

Finally, he wrote:

You can't expect me to drop everything on the basis of these emails. If you think you know something important, tell me what it is.

After he'd sent it, he immediately regretted the high-handed tone. Holly was liable to retreat at the merest hint of an overbearing attitude. Retreat – or explode. Adam doubted that she would make any allowance for the frustration she was causing.

Sure enough, there was no reply. After ten minutes of refreshing the page, he decided on drastic action. It meant using his in-laws' phone, which he felt guilty about, but he had to get an answer.

He dialled Holly's mobile number from memory – aware that this feat alone would have disgusted Katy – but all he got was a message informing him that the phone was switched off.

Of course it was. Adam wasn't sure if she had a landline, and in any case he didn't know her exact address to look one up.

Back to the computer. He waited ten more minutes, then weakened and sent another email:

Please, Holly. What's going on?

Then he surfed on news sites, reading with little interest of political upheavals and economic developments and sporting triumphs, and somehow it got to midnight and still she hadn't replied.

The Skyway Hotel, Dunstable, 1 p.m. tomorrow.

If Adam wanted answers, that was where he had to go.

CHAPTER FIFTY

It was probably the best night's sleep she'd had since becoming a parent. Katy woke at just after seven and felt blissfully refreshed. Birds were chirping outside, and the light against her eyelids had a quality reminiscent of childhood; it confused her for a moment, until she blinked a few times and everything came rushing back.

She was at her parents' house, sleeping in the guest bed in what had once been her childhood bedroom. Adam was squashed in beside her, his knee resting against her thigh. This morning they would be returning home: the first phase of a journey back to some kind of normal life.

Except for last night's admission that he was still in touch with Holly. And either he was being disingenuous, or just naive, but Katy recognised that the woman had but one purpose in mind.

She wanted Adam back.

The sound of activity downstairs was a welcome distraction. Katy slipped from the bed, grabbed her clothes and got dressed in the bathroom. Entering the kitchen, she was taken aback to find her parents and her children happily tucking into cereal and toast, all of them bright and cheery and wide awake.

'How long have you been up?'

'About half six, I think it was,' Clive said.

'That early?' She eyed the kids. 'You're not usually this lively on a Tuesday morning.'

'It's because we've got the day off,' Freya informed her.

'Yeah, and we're gonna see tigers, and gorillas!' Dylan waved his spoon in celebration, flicking droplets of milk over his grand-dad, who only laughed, and then dodged the cloth that Laura threw at him.

'You're like kids yourselves,' Katy muttered, as always slipping into the role of boring grown-up while her parents seemed to regress.

But she couldn't deny how wonderful it was to see the children so happy.

She poured two mugs of coffee and carried them upstairs. Adam was awake, if groggy, and sat up when she placed his drink on the bedside table.

'What time did you come up?' she asked.

'Uh?' he said blearily. 'Not too late.'

'No? You look…'

'What?'

Haunted, she thought. But she only shrugged, and said, 'I must have been out cold.'

'Yeah, you were.' He sighed, pulling at his face as if trying to rearrange his features.

'Set for today?' She offered a nervous smile. 'Freya and Dylan are already hyper about Port Lympne.'

'That's good.'

His gaze turned distant. This might have been the right moment to ask him again about Holly – was there really nothing more to it than what he had told her? – but Katy couldn't bring herself to do it. Today threatened to be hard enough as it was.

After taking a sip of coffee, his hand trembled as he put the mug down. He lay back and let out another shuddering sigh.

'Are you sure you're all right?'

'Oh, couldn't be better.' He gave a little mocking laugh, then shut his eyes.

Katy wasn't in the mood for conflict, so she left him to it. Pausing on the landing to drink her coffee, she saw her daughter trudging up the stairs.

'Hey, Freya. What's up?'

'Nothing.' But her glum expression said otherwise.

'You're excited about today, aren't you? It's a chance to enjoy yourself, and put all the… nasty stuff behind you.'

'Yeah, I know. But Granddad said they'll be taking us home tonight. To *our* house.'

Katy tried to smile. 'That's right. But Dad and I will be there all day, making sure it's ready for you.'

Freya sniffed disparagingly. 'Those men know where we live. What if they come back to get us?'

'They won't, darling. Honestly.'

Freya didn't look convinced. 'Can Zoe stay?'

'Um…' Katy was thrown off balance. 'We can ask her, if it'll make you feel better?'

'I think so.' Nodding thoughtfully, Freya eased past. 'Got to brush my teeth.'

'Okay.' Katy stroked her daughter's hair as she went by, and marvelled at how smoothly she could lie when the well-being of her children was at stake.

I don't know if it's safe, Freya. And I'm scared, too.

Adam, shamefully, had pretended to be asleep until Katy got up. He'd woken to an instant recollection of the email exchange with Holly, and couldn't face any sort of interaction with his wife until he'd had time to review it again in his mind.

Whatever benefits he might have gained from a good night's sleep, he was still at a loss to explain the emails. How could Holly possibly know anything? And what would be her motives for lying?

He was saddled with confusion, and had only one choice to make: either ignore her and forget it, or go to Dunstable and meet her as requested.

When Katy brought him a coffee, she could tell there was something wrong. Hopefully she put it down to apprehension about returning home. He knew that should be his focus for today: helping his wife to overcome her fears, and vanquish the traumatic memory of Gary's assault.

Once he'd finished the coffee he got dressed and joined his family. He'd checked his reflection in the bathroom mirror, and couldn't see any obvious sign of the shock that he'd had last night, though there was certainly evidence of the stresses and strains of the past two days. A few more grey hairs, a wrinkle or two that seemed deeper than before. Mostly it was visible in his eyes; he would have to make a conscious effort not to look inward, where the demons lurked.

Fortunately the children were in high spirits, and their irrepressible energy powered him through what might otherwise have been an uncomfortable encounter with his in-laws.

Then Clive nodded towards the alcove. 'I see someone was working last night.'

Adam could only nod dumbly, stricken by a sudden fear that he'd forgotten to log out of Hotmail.

Clive chuckled. 'Don't look so worried. I was just as bad at your age. Couldn't leave the business alone for a minute.'

'Who says you're any better now?' Laura observed.

'Well, I think today's outing is proof of that.'

Adam smiled at his father in law's mock indignation, and running with the workaholic theme, said, 'Actually, I just need to check something now.'

Katy was talking to Dylan about the wildlife he'd be seeing today, and she didn't seem to pay him any attention when he sidled into the study area and brought the computer to life.

He saw that he had indeed come out of Hotmail, but since the home screen was right in front of him, he quickly logged in again, hoping for a new message from Holly – ideally a full explanation, or else an admission that she'd been playing games.

There was nothing; just the usual rash of semi-junk emails from retailers and pressure groups. It seemed that Holly really did expect him to come running.

He heard footsteps: Freya was approaching, and the open honest affection on her face acted as a rebuke. He logged out, then casually deleted the history while chatting with his daughter. She wanted reassurance that they were safe to go back home.

'Honestly, Freya, there's nothing to worry about.' He grasped her hands, looked into her eyes and told probably the biggest lie of his life. 'It's over now, and we're all going to forget it ever happened.'

CHAPTER FIFTY-ONE

Her parents were ready to depart by eight thirty. Katy and Adam found themselves hugging the children as if they were going away for a month, rather than a day. Clive chided them for it, even though they all knew he would be exactly the same.

Kissing Katy on the cheek, he said, 'We'll bring them home about five, sixish.'

Home. It had turned into a scary concept. But once her parents had left, there didn't seem to be any good reason to delay their return – especially as they first had to get the light fixed.

Adam reversed the car from the garage. Katy approached it, nervously, and examined the repairs to the rear panel. He and her dad had done a good job, but when she got into the passenger seat and looked over her shoulder, the sight of the hole in the upholstery made her gasp. The bullet had gone through the rear seat as effortlessly as it might have gone through her son, her husband—

She moaned, bowing her head. Adam leaned over and gave her a hug. 'Are you okay? Do you want to go back indoors?'

'No. I'll be fine in a minute.' She took slow, deep breaths, and tried not to think about how she and Freya had been wrestled from this car less than forty-eight hours ago.

Adam was tentative with the controls as he drove away, perhaps because he was reliving his own experience. She made no comment about the route he chose – along the A27 towards Brighton and then north on the A23, coming off at the A272 for Haywards

Heath. It involved going miles out of their way, albeit on major roads, but crucially it meant avoiding the sort of twisting country lanes that they had driven along on Sunday.

Katy sat in silence and gazed out of the side window and tried to clear her mind of thoughts. She sensed no desire for conversation from Adam, which perhaps signalled a bleak day ahead. Which of them would be first to weaken? she wondered, before realising she had the question back to front.

Who would be strong enough to acknowledge that they needed to talk?

The garage in Haywards Heath was busy at the start of the day. After checking the car in, they wandered along to a nearby parade of shops, still not saying much. Fortunately it only took about twenty minutes to replace the broken light. When they returned to sort out the paperwork, Adam's friend Tom was at the counter, and of course it was natural for him to ask how the damage had occurred.

'Another car threw up a stone,' Adam said.

'Bastard. Did he stop?' He looked from Adam to Katy; they both shook their heads.

Adam said, 'I flashed, but he didn't seem to notice.'

'Should have run the twat off the road.' Tom sniggered, failing to notice their horrified expressions. 'Hope you got his number, at least?'

'We did,' Katy said. 'But I'm not sure how far we'll get with that.'

'Just one of those things, isn't it?' Adam said blandly. Katy wanted to sob at the thought that so much pain and anguish could have avoided, if only he'd adopted this tolerant approach on Sunday.

But it wasn't really true to his character, and even Tom seemed to look surprised. 'I'd be bloody livid, mate.'

Then another customer sought his attention, and it was with a measure of relief that they slipped out of the workshop and drove away.

Katy was convinced that this relief would be short-lived, but when they reached Lindfield it was to find that the house, in all important respects, was unchanged. A little colder than normal, which might be why they both shivered as they crossed the threshold. And there was an odd smell in the air, or perhaps a combination of odd smells; Katy heard Adam sniffing as she followed him along the hall. Then again, strangers had been tramping in and out, and no doubt the forensics team had used various equipment and chemicals.

A tour of the house revealed only minor disturbances to the lounge and their bedroom. It was the kitchen that had been subjected to the most thorough search for evidence. Katy could tell that the worktops had been wiped down, though there were still traces of silver fingerprint powder on some of the cupboards and on the door, close to the handle.

She stared at the table, remembering what had gone on in here and ready to confront any negative reaction to it. Gradually her breathing slowed, and she could no longer feel her heart thudding in her chest.

'Okay?' Adam asked, cautiously.

'I think so. But I'm glad the kids won't be here till later. I want to make it feel more "lived in", if I can.'

He nodded in agreement, but looked shifty, almost afraid. 'I hate to say this, but I could do with going into work for a few hours.'

So that was why he'd been a bit antsy this morning. 'Because of the meeting?' she asked.

'Yeah. But I won't, if you're not comfortable being here on your own?'

She made a sucking sound with her lips. 'I'll be fine. And Zoe said she could come over any time.'

He gave a tentative nod, perhaps embarrassed by the implication that the family liaison officer might care more for Katy's well-being than he did. 'You're definitely sure about this?'

'Yes. Or do you want me to persuade you to stay?' She grinned, but Adam seemed to shudder.

Still he hovered, then said, 'Do we still have your old phone?'

'I think so. Why?'

'Thought it would be easier for you to reach me.' He snorted. 'Plus I feel lost without one.'

She found the phone, which they'd used in the past as a backup when one of the others had broken. It had a pay-as-you-go SIM card with about ten pounds loaded on to the account.

'Battery's probably dead,' she said as she handed it over.

'I'll start charging it now, and finish at work. Gonna have a quick shower.'

She listened to his weary tread on the stairs, unsure whether to trust her instincts that something wasn't quite right. The meeting he'd missed was undoubtedly important, and she could see the value in getting back on track as quickly as possible...

And yet.

She busied herself in the kitchen, washing up the crockery that was in the dishwasher. It was twenty past ten when Adam trotted down, wearing clean black jeans, a white shirt and a tailored jacket.

'Feel much better for that.' He hugged her, and Katy thought she felt the dampness of a tear against her cheek; it must have been his hair, still wet from the shower.

'What are you going to do this morning?' he asked.

'Tidy up, then wander into the village and get a bit of shopping.' She slapped her hands against his chest, pushing him away. 'I'll be fine. Don't worry about me.'

'All right.' A kiss, soft and slow and solemn. 'I love you.'

She nodded, but the same phrase caught in her throat, so all she could say was, 'I hope so. Don't be away too long.'

CHAPTER FIFTY-TWO

Adam felt dreadful as he left the house. He was sure that Katy was suspicious of him, and she had every right to be.

That was partly why he'd taken the old phone. He didn't want her trying to contact him via the office.

There was another reason, too. Once he'd stopped to refuel the car, he rang Holly's number. Still no response, but this time he was directed to voicemail.

'Holly, it's Adam. I've had to borrow a phone. Call me when you get this message.'

He left it at that. Better not to demand an explanation, or reveal that he was on his way to Bedfordshire. This, he hoped, would put the ball back in her court.

It was now twenty to eleven, which gave him more than two hours to get to Dunstable. That should be enough time, although a lot would depend on the state of the dreaded M25.

With the phone charging via the car's USB port, he reached the A23 and headed north, still hoping that Holly might call and put a stop to this wild goose chase. But in his heart he doubted it would happen; even after all these years, he knew her too well.

Once she'd gained the upper hand over him, it wouldn't easily be relinquished.

They had met during his first proper job after university, working for a vast multinational ad agency with offices in central London.

Holly, who was also a graduate and two years his senior, had been assigned to help him settle in.

At the time Adam had been in a fairly casual relationship with a fellow student, Shona, who'd opted for a job in her home city of Birmingham, on the understanding that they would regularly spend weekends together.

Adam couldn't recall exactly how it had happened, but within a couple of months he was no longer in contact with Shona, and spending every spare minute with Holly. The one oddity, as Adam had seen it, was that Holly insisted on keeping her own rented flat, even as things got serious. Although she wanted a long-term relationship, she didn't seem interested in buying a home, or even in pooling the savings they'd make by renting a single place together.

It was only later – two years later – that he learnt the truth. Far from being rented, her spacious apartment in Crouch End was actually a legacy from a wealthy aunt. She owned it outright, and hadn't wanted Adam to know about her relative prosperity, much less to share in it.

But that information had been eclipsed by a far more damaging discovery: she'd had a brief but intense affair with one of their colleagues, Greg, an arrogant, middle-aged senior account manager who never failed to smirk when he and Adam passed in the corridor.

Holly had pleaded for forgiveness, and had he been a little older and wiser, Adam might have acquiesced. But prior to these revelations he'd been thinking seriously about proposing to her, which made the betrayal much harder to bear. When he saw a job advertised at a small but ambitious firm in the mid Sussex town of Haywards Heath, he had opted to make a clean break. A new job, a new home – and within a few months, a new girlfriend in Katy, whom he'd met in a bar called Orange Square, close to his office.

He'd met Holly just once more, while in London on business, a few months into his relationship with Katy. Holly had declared that she was a changed woman: drinking less, off the weed and the coke, exercising more and pledging to remain faithful. She had tried to persuade Adam that he and Katy were just a fling, the same sort of deal she'd had with Greg. Now that they had both got it out of their system, they could talk about marriage.

Adam had put her straight, politely at first, but they ended up having a blazing row in the middle of a packed coffee shop. After that, there was no further contact for nearly eight years, though he heard through mutual acquaintances that she was in a settled relationship with a builder who'd done some work on her apartment.

As painful as those moments had been at the time, they were accompanied by plenty of happy memories, and more importantly, a clear conscience. Adam was a lot less inclined to revisit the next chapter in their drama.

He wasn't sure of the exact date, but Dylan had been a baby and Freya a delightful but demanding toddler, plagued by a succession of chest infections that frequently kept her awake and left her parents frazzled and worried sick. On the rare night that she didn't plead to come into their bed in the early hours, they could usually count on Dylan to wake them two or three times instead.

He'd encountered Holly at a conference on SEO optimisation in Seville: three blissfully undisturbed nights in a snazzy air-conditioned hotel. They spotted one another during a seminar, and afterwards Adam was chatting with a small group of delegates when she joined the gathering. He could hardly walk away, and in fact he was shocked to see the change in her. She appeared to have aged by more than a decade; her hair was greying, she'd put on weight, and there was a sort of wounded expression which seemed to be permanently imprinted on her features.

When they had a moment to talk alone, her manner was so subdued and apologetic that he had felt a rush of sorrowful affection. However illogical, it was hard to shake off a sense that he had let her down in some way, that he ought to have saved her from what, it transpired, had been a viciously abusive relationship with the builder.

'It's not your fault. It's no one's fault but his. And mine,' she had added ruefully. 'I made my choice.' A beat of silence, which he recalled even now, because of the intensity of her gaze, and the question it had asked. Then she'd said, 'And you made yours.'

They had slipped away to a quiet restaurant and toyed with pasta and drank far too much red wine. As she recounted the awful string of humiliations, the manipulation and deceit and violence, Adam found himself promising to help her in any way that he could. Of course she was welcome to email him, or text, or perhaps even chat on the phone when it wasn't too awkward. He was less sure about meeting up – 'Only for coffee,' she insisted – but didn't rule it out at some point.

Back at the hotel, waiting for the elevator, she had slipped her fingers between his, and said, 'There's nothing I'd like more than to sleep with you now. Nothing on Earth. I know that I can't, but will you kiss me?'

A fateful question. He didn't think he could refuse her a single kiss. Didn't think it at the time, and he didn't think it now, six years later, as he sped up and slowed down, cut outside dawdling motorists and was passed on the inside by drivers more impatient still. He pictured her on that night, sexily drunk and exuding desire; her lips, as she moved closer, so enticing, and the hopeful, hungry gleam in her eyes…

It was a long kiss, conducted privately, as they ascended to the seventh floor, and when the lift juddered to a halt and the doors opened, against all the odds they were both incredibly strong. They broke apart, and he said, 'This is mine,' and she said, 'Yep,' and that was that.

He walked away, didn't look back; Holly continued to her room on the ninth floor and the next day she was gone.

But it didn't matter. With that kiss, in her mind at least, a commitment had been made.

There were no great delays on the M25, other than the usual snarl-up on the notorious stretch between the M3 and M4 junctions. He was on the M1 for only a few minutes before the junction for Dunstable loomed ahead. He turned on to the A5183 and followed it for several miles through pleasantly undulating countryside, bathed in late-autumn sunshine.

The road was dotted with low-rise chain hotels aimed at business travellers or budget-conscious families, and the Skyway was clearly out of the same mould. It was situated on the edge of a big construction site, and Adam had to pause for a couple of lorries to pass before he could turn into the car park.

It was ten to one. He unplugged his phone and checked for messages. Nothing from Holly.

He sat for a moment, fuming. Even after coming all this way, he still doubted the wisdom of going in there, letting her jerk him around like a puppet.

The texts had begun a couple of days after he returned from Seville. At first they were manageable: friendly, but not too friendly. He had responded in the same vein, was careful not to flirt or refer to that moment in the lift… and yet he had chosen to say nothing to Katy about their encounter.

One day he'd mislaid his phone, and by the time he found it there were over a dozen texts, getting increasingly angry, as well as an email which set out, with clinical fury, all the reasons why Adam needed to end his marriage and return to the only woman who truly loved and understood him.

That email had been copied in to Katy, via the website where she advertised her artwork.

Adam shuddered at the memory of how close he'd come to losing her. For all that he might have been tempted to stray, Adam had a cautionary tale in the form of his father, who'd initiated the break-up of his own relationship, almost certainly with short-term pleasure in mind, only to spend years in miserable isolation before he fell in with a woman as selfish and misanthropic as himself. In the meantime, Adam's mother had worked herself ragged to compensate for his father's absence, before dying of cancer in her forties. Without that break-up, Adam felt sure his mum would still be alive today.

As a result, he was determined not to play the villain in his own family. It had taken months to repair the damage and rebuild trust, and throughout this time Holly had continued to contact him, never to an extent that it could be construed as harassment, but just enough to keep him on edge.

Then, abruptly, it stopped. He dug for news and heard various rumours: a near fatal overdose, a move abroad, a new partner. The truth, which he'd learned only a couple of months ago, was a less dramatic combination of all three.

The overdose had never been more than a calculated cry for help. The move abroad was a temporary secondment – and then only to Amsterdam – and the new partner was actually a man she'd originally dated at sixth form college.

His phone buzzed. A text from Holly: *Room 228.*

He stared at the building in alarm. Was she watching for him through binoculars?

Of course not. He was just such a sap that she had predicted he would be here, right on cue.

He got out and trudged towards the entrance. He thought about calling or texting Katy, but that might only invite awkward questions.

He'd envisaged that they would meet in the bar. The hotel had a large open-plan lounge area next to reception, as well as a restaurant. Surely she wasn't going to try anything stupid?

He took the stairs, happy to work his legs after two hours in the car. The elevator would bring forth unwanted memories.

If she opens the door in her underwear, I turn and walk away.

He was clear on that, crystal clear, when he tapped on the door. But he had butterflies. His palms were sweating.

A few seconds passed before the door opened. Initially, there was relief: Holly was fully dressed – in jeans and a silver top – so that was okay, and somehow a transformation had occurred since their encounter in Spain. Her hair was shorter and darker, her eyes and skin much clearer, and she'd lost some weight. She looked far more like the Holly he'd dated in London, all those years ago.

'Adam, come in, come in.' She was practically vibrating with excitement as she beckoned him inside and then stepped back, leaving him no choice but to catch the door. 'Sorry about the cloak-and-dagger arrangements, but this is so, like, monumental…'

'What is?' he asked, as the door swung shut behind him.

He followed her into the room, relieved to see there was only a single bed, and it was cluttered with a laptop and a couple of empty pizza boxes.

A couple?

She turned back to him, grinned and pointed over his shoulder, at the figure now stepping from the bathroom to block his exit.

It was Jay.

CHAPTER FIFTY-THREE

Katy stood at the lounge window, watching Adam drive away, and asked herself: *Do I believe he's going to work?*

After some thought, she decided she wasn't certain. There was an easy way to check: give it a little while and then call the office and ask to speak to him.

She could do that, but what would it say about the level of trust? About the state of their marriage?

No. She wouldn't submit to paranoia – about Adam, or Holly, or anything else. But she allowed herself to check that all the windows and doors were locked – only sensible in the circumstances – and then got busy. She cleaned the kitchen thoroughly, tidied the lounge and the bedrooms and then dusted and vacuumed the entire house.

She worked with manic intensity for more than two hours, not pausing for a moment, never giving herself time or space to dwell on anything unpleasant. Once it was done she felt exhausted, in a good way, and deeply satisfied. It wasn't about the cleaning, she understood. It was about laying ghosts to rest.

After taking a shower, she wavered briefly. Enough time had passed that it wouldn't be unreasonable to give him a call, ask how he was getting on…

The other temptation, growing by the minute, was to check his Hotmail. Both their passwords were saved on the family computer, so it wouldn't be any great act of espionage.

No.

She was hungry, but also in need of fresh air, and distraction. She found the old handbag that Freya used for dressing up games, collected her purse and keys, put on her coat and went out.

Adam recoiled at the sight of the man who had held them captive. This was beyond a nightmare. Beyond anything his brain could deal with.

Staggering backwards, he bumped into a dressing table and used it to steady himself. Jay's hands were raised, palms out; he had a wryly apologetic smile, and didn't seem to present any immediate danger. Adam glanced at Holly and realised that she, too, was quite relaxed, not at all troubled by Jay's presence.

Of course not. She must be in on it – whatever 'it' was.

She'd lured him here.

'What the hell is going on?' he asked, the words catching in his throat.

'It's cool,' Jay said. 'No need to get worked up.'

'*What*?' Adam looked to Holly. 'You know who this man is, and what he's done?'

She nodded. 'Please, Adam. Just hear him out.'

'He killed someone! He's a murderer.'

'I know about that. It was a mistake.'

'Self-defence,' Jay added.

Adam turned back and saw he'd moved slightly closer. Jay's posture wasn't threatening, but Adam didn't intend to let his guard down for a second. It earned him a scathing look from Holly.

'Just chill out, will you, and listen to him.'

'No, *you* listen. This man is part of a gang that abducted us. Held us prisoner, locked up in a filthy, cold cellar—'

'He's told me everything,' Holly interrupted. 'Until last night, he thought you must be dead. He was worried about you all.'

She sounded genuine, though to Adam it was a ludicrous idea. Why would Jay feel any concern for them?

'Look, Adam. I can see this is hard to take.' Jay backed up, then sat on the floor beside the bathroom. 'Why don't you let me explain what happened, and why I'm here.'

Adam said nothing. Jay might have retreated, but he was still blocking the only escape route.

Then he felt a hand on his arm. Holly, calmly insistent, pulled him towards the bed. He perched on the corner, and flinched when he felt her hand trail affectionately across his shoulders. She moved behind him and took the seat at the dressing table.

'How did you get involved...?' Adam began, but then the answer came to him. 'My phone?'

She nodded. 'I texted you a few times on Sunday afternoon, and you replied – well, I thought it was you, but really it was Jay.'

'He pretended to be me? And you're not bothered by that?'

'Damn right I was, at first. When he asked me to meet him here, and I was expecting to see you... my instinct was to run out and call the police. But he begged me to listen – which is what you need to do. Please.'

'I did this because I had to.' Jay spoke in barely a whisper; it made him sound chastened, respectful, but for all Adam knew that was merely an act.

'A fight for survival calls for desperate measures,' Holly said. 'And that's what we're talking about here.'

Jay nodded. 'The thing at the Kirbys' was horrible. Brian came running at me and I panicked. I think even Carole knew it was self-defence.'

'Not really,' Adam snarled. 'You'd burst into her house to kidnap her – and now she's dead, too.'

'Yeah.' Jay's voice sounded heavy with regret. 'She went crazy, lashing out with some scissors. She ran from us, but for some reason went upstairs. We only wanted to keep her close for a day or two, and she knew that, but she…' He shook his head, shuddering at the memory. 'She threw herself out of the upstairs window. Didn't even try to land safely. It was… fucking dreadful.'

'But you have to accept responsibility for that,' Adam said. 'You, Maggie, and the others.'

Jay looked away. Holly reached out and gripped Adam's arm again.

'Honestly, if you'd seen him yesterday afternoon, searching online for news of what had happened. He was sickened by the thought that you might all be dead.'

When Adam only grunted, Jay said, 'I'm surprised nothing's made it into the media. I take it the cops decided to keep things quiet?'

'They thought we'd be safer that way. Because of the danger that you might come back for us.'

'It's not us you have to worry about,' Jay said darkly. 'How did you escape? The whole place went up in flames.'

'We'd found a hiding place. A crawl space in the cellar. After the gunshots, someone came down – I assumed it was one of you. Whoever it was, they thought the cellar was empty so they didn't bother locking the door when they left.'

'I'm glad. The news reports say four bodies, including Carole and Brian – is that right?'

Adam nodded, but another question had occurred to him. 'We ran from the fire, and hid in the trees. I thought I heard someone close by – and that's where the police found my wife's bag.'

'That was me,' Jay admitted. 'I heard something, too, though I didn't realise it was you. If I had, maybe I'd have given myself up.'

Adam felt his insides go cold. 'Who did you think it was?'

'The men who attacked the house. The men who started the fire.' Jay looked to be on the brink of tears, a shocking sight in the circumstances. His voice quavered as he asked, 'The other two bodies – who are they?'

Disorientated by his obvious distress, Adam frowned. 'Don't you know? The police think it's Gary and Dale – that's the names we knew them by, at least.'

Jay blew out a sigh, and used a thumb to wipe his eyes. 'Makes sense,' he muttered, but didn't elaborate.

'The theory is that the others killed them and did a runner. That's Maggie, Roger… and you.'

Jay shook his head. 'We didn't kill them. And I barely got away. A bullet clipped me.' He eased sideways, and Adam noticed the bulge of what must have been a bandage beneath his T-shirt.

'What about the other two?'

'I've made some calls. No one's seen them. If their bodies weren't at the house, it means only one thing. They've been taken.'

'By who?' Adam asked. He could see Jay struggling to keep a grip on his emotions, and said, 'Is it this mysterious lover of Carole's – Barinov?'

Jay confirmed it with a nod. 'He's got them. And he won't stop there.'

CHAPTER FIFTY-FOUR

Adam had a brief, bittersweet sense of vindication at hearing his theory confirmed, but it was eclipsed by a growing dread. At the same time he realised that his fear of Jay had abated; he didn't appear to pose any immediate threat.

'His real name is *Voronov*. Alexander Voronov,' Jay said. 'And we were crazy to take him on. He was always two or three steps ahead of us, and we never had a fucking clue.'

'So why do it? You must have known the risk – that you'd be exposed when it came to collecting a ransom.'

'There wasn't any ransom, and we didn't take Carole to blackmail Voronov. She was there for insurance. Once the deal was done, we would have released her, unharmed. The same with you and your family.'

'I need to hear a lot more before I decide whether to believe that,' Adam warned him. 'I ought to be calling the police right now.'

'That's what you want to do, is it?'

Adam indicated the door. 'Am I even free to leave if I want?'

There was a despairing sigh from Holly, which didn't do anything for his mood.

'And you,' he said, turning to face her. 'You're harbouring a fugitive. You could end up being charged as an accomplice.'

'Ooh – exciting!' Holly made a sarcastic smacking sound with her lips.

'I mean it.' He looked back at Jay. 'Or is she your prisoner, too?'

In response, Jay climbed slowly to his feet. Adam tensed, but he saw how the younger man winced, then turned his back on them, reaching for the door. He pulled it open and stood to one side.

'If you want to leave, I'm not gonna stop you.'

'Adam, this is stupid,' Holly exclaimed, but Jay shook his head.

'Nah, let him decide. We knew there was a chance he'd react this way.'

'Can you blame me?' Adam wasn't sure how he'd been put on the defensive. He got up, wanting to call their bluff, and took a couple of steps towards the door.

'You can leave,' Jay said quietly. 'But if you call the cops, I won't wait around for them to arrive.'

Adam nodded stiffly, and marched out of the room. He could hear a TV playing loudly nearby, and a burst of music from someone's phone at the far end of the corridor.

He and his family had escaped from the cellar, and that was meant to be the end of it. He should go down to the bar and call the police. Let Jay – and Holly – take their chances. This man Voronov was their problem, not his.

The door stayed open, Jay out of sight behind it, while Holly regarded him with a heavy-lidded gaze. He stared at her for a moment, that oh-so familiar pout and the eyes, deep and dark, that never failed to grab his attention.

But the Russian was the key. Hadn't he told DI Branning he was certain of that?

'Fuck it,' he said, and strode back in. He no longer knew whether he was thinking straight, or making decisions based on emotion rather than rationality. But he wanted to hear more.

Holly's face was transformed by her smile. 'Thank you!'

'Never mind that. You have to tell me exactly what's going on,' he said sternly. 'And I want to know why I'm here.'

'Fine.' After shutting the door, Jay folded his arms and leaned nonchalantly against the wall. 'The second bit is simple to answer. I need your help.'

Katy had intended to call in at the gift shop where she worked, drawn by the appeal of being amongst friends in a safe, relaxed environment. But yesterday she'd had to lie about needing time off to look after the children, and while she could pretend that Adam or one of her parents had stepped in to help, she simply didn't have the energy to sustain the charade.

And this was only the beginning. If Freya and Dylan were to be coached into keeping quiet, there would be any number of occasions when the truth might accidentally slip out.

The first test arrived much sooner than she anticipated. She'd gathered some grocery shopping at the Co-op, then hurried out and turned the corner, only to find Gemma Garvey strolling towards her, walking her excitable black terrier.

'Katy, hi! Did you get the photo of my mum?'

'Sorry?' *For the commission.* Katy had asked it to be emailed. 'Ah, I haven't had time to check…'

'Never mind. How's Dylan – is he back at school?'

'No, still off.' Katy felt heat rushing to her face and was glad of the dog's interest; as it pulled on the lead she knelt to make a fuss of him. 'Freya's down with the same bug. Adam's just popped home, which gave me a chance to do some chores.'

She hefted the shopping bag to illustrate her point, and rose to face Gemma, who was tutting with sympathy.

'Poor Dylan really wasn't himself at the party.' Her mouth formed a circle: 'Ooh – did you ever get hold of Leah?'

'What? Oh, no, it wasn't anything important.'

Gemma looked surprised. 'Only you seemed a tad stressed.'

'Did I?' Katy produced a laugh. 'No more than usual.'

'I must admit, I was quite on edge myself while we were talking. Because of that weird man.'

Katy faked confusion, but felt she must be horribly unconvincing. 'What man was that?'

'You must have noticed him. Fifty-something, short and fat, wearing a ridiculous baseball cap.' Gemma was studying her face for a sign of recognition. 'He kept looking over at us in a really creepy way – and he even left at the same time as you. I nearly said something, only I got distracted by the kids.'

Katy offered a smile, which probably looked more like a grimace. 'Good job you didn't. I wasn't even aware of him.'

She managed to withstand another minute or two of small talk, which the dog interrupted by trying to bolt towards a squirrel. They exchanged hurried farewells, and then Katy was free and could let out a shudder at the thought that Gemma might have intervened on Sunday. Picturing Gary under pressure, challenged by a bossy young mother and suddenly pulling a gun on her…

But he hadn't. And he was dead now.

Her heart was racing, just the same. She tried to calm it by focusing on the present. This was the first real test of her cover story and she'd come through unscathed. That was a positive thing, wasn't it?

Yes – until she reviewed the conversation and saw the implications. At some point soon, Gary's mug shot was likely to pop up on the news, whereupon Gemma would recognise him and wonder what he'd been doing at the soft play centre. And why he'd shown so much interest in Katy.

She felt sick. They could try all they liked, but their secret wouldn't be staying secret for long.

CHAPTER FIFTY-FIVE

Adam took Jay's answer to be sarcastic, so he responded in kind.

'You need my help? Well, I can drive you to the nearest police station. I can even speak up in your favour if you admit to your part in this, and give up the real identities of your accomplices—'

'That's not what he meant.' Holly rapped her knuckles, crossly, on his shoulder. 'You're being childish.'

'Well, forgive me. But I'm struggling to deal with a request for help from a man who terrorised my family.'

Jay spoke up. 'I've said I'm sorry, but now we need to move on. There isn't much time.'

'You're right. The police will find you soon enough. If Voronov poses a threat to my family, and you claim to be on our side, then you'll give yourself up, and tell them what you know about him.'

'He's untouchable. Too well connected.'

'I don't believe that.'

'Don't you? London is the number one destination for Russian oligarchs, gangsters – whatever you want to call them. For years they've been buying up property. They use British tax havens to hide the billions they looted from their own country, and the authorities here don't give a shit as long as the money keeps rolling in.' A caustic laugh. 'So if Voronov chooses to wipe out a few lowlifes, he'll do it without any fear of the consequences.'

'You're not a lowlife,' Holly said, oozing compassion for Jay.

Disgusted with her, Adam said, 'He means Gary and Dale.'

'Not just them,' Jay said. 'And I only used that word because it's how you see us. You, the police, society in general. And it's definitely how Voronov sees us.'

In a prim voice, Holly said, 'Jay's told me a lot about his upbringing, his family. If you knew about their lives, you'd understand some of the choices they've had to make.'

Jay raised a hand to stop her. 'I don't think Adam's impressed with the social worker routine. Shame – I had him down as a bleeding heart liberal.'

'Maybe I was, till the first time someone aimed a gun at my children.' Adam glared at Holly. 'I still can't fathom why you've taken his side.'

'Because it's *your* side too. Which he'll explain, if you just listen.' He was turning away when she said, quietly, 'And because of Jill.'

'Who's Jill?'

'Jill Margaret Nolan. *Maggie.*' Jay's cheeks tightened as he clenched his teeth. 'Voronov's got her, along with Roger – who doesn't have a middle name and couldn't be arsed to make one up.'

He paused again, and pinched his nostrils; fighting back tears.

'If he only wanted them dead, he'd have done it at the same time as Gary and Dale. And if the cops have searched the property and not found any more bodies, it means Voronov has taken them so he can kill them slowly.'

Adam frowned. 'So, once again, why did you try to blackmail someone as dangerous as that?'

'It didn't start out that way. This was more of a… a feud. And for what it's worth, I never thought we should try to take him on. But it wasn't my decision to make.'

'Voronov's going to torture them,' Holly said. 'Maybe for days.'

Adam glanced at Jay, who nodded. 'He'll do it to get information, as well as for the pleasure of it.'

Given how Maggie and Roger had treated his family, Adam still wasn't inclined to exude sympathy. 'What sort of information?' he asked.

'He'll want every tiny detail about our operation. What we planned, whether we had inside help – which we did,' he added. 'A guy on his staff, who's probably already dead. Voronov will be brutal in getting revenge against anyone who was involved in this.' He tapped a thumb against his chest. 'With me at the top of his list.'

'That's why Jay has to stay away from any of his known contacts,' Holly said.

'Yeah. Though that won't stop them pulling Maggie apart to find out where I am.'

'Why Maggie?' Adam asked. 'Because she was in charge?'

'Partly that,' said Jay. 'Partly because she's my mum.'

Back home, Katy made herself a sandwich and went online. She had a quick look at some news sites, but didn't particularly search for updates on their own story. After checking her emails, it occurred to her that they might have messages on the landline phone, given that they couldn't be reached on their mobiles.

Sure enough, there were several, including a chatty one from her dad on Sunday evening, hoping they'd had a good weekend. Suzy Chadwick had called, thanking her for Noah's present and hoping Dylan was on the mend. And there were two from a colleague of Adam's, expressing concern that he hadn't responded to their texts, and was he okay?

That made her wonder how Adam was faring at work. Whether his excuse for missing the meeting had been accepted, or whether he had weakened and given them the truth. Even the brief exchange with Gemma had illustrated how difficult it was to lie, consistently, and not be caught out.

The doorbell made her jump so violently that she nearly fell off her seat. Until then she would have said she was fairly relaxed about being in the house alone.

Evidently not.

It was probably a neighbour, or perhaps DI Branning or one of his team. She checked through the lounge window to find a stranger: a woman in her late forties or early fifties, tall and well dressed in a Burberry trench coat and a dark grey fur hat. The small bag over her shoulder was possibly a Gucci.

Her face was narrow and pale, and dominated by bold red lipstick and a pair of dark glasses. She rang the doorbell again, then knocked for good measure. Katy thought about ignoring her, but had a feeling this visitor would be persistent.

Taking a deep breath, she marched into the hall, unlocked the door and opened it halfway, stepping into the gap and making sure her feet were close to the threshold.

'Mrs Parr? Katy, isn't it?'

'How can I help you?'

The woman smiled, but without seeing her eyes Katy couldn't tell what it meant. She sensed the woman looking her over and felt shabby and unimpressive in comparison to her visitor, who might have stepped off the red carpet at an awards ceremony.

'My name is Veronica Pierce. Ronnie, for short.' A card was brandished, which had photo ID and confirmed the name, as well as an occupation: journalist. In a cut glass accent, she said, 'I'd like to talk to you, if I may, about some of your recent experiences.'

She knew: that was immediately clear. Katy felt a surge of anger that someone had sold them out.

'I don't know what you mean.'

The smile twisted a little, as if at a cruel joke. 'Forgive me. Your face says otherwise. But please hear me out – I have no desire to put you or your family in the spotlight.'

'I'm sorry, this isn't making any sense—'

'Katy, hush. My story will be written, with or without your cooperation. My intention was to focus on the Kirbys, Carole and Brian, but I can, if I wish, widen the scope.' She removed the glasses; her eyes were pale blue, and shone with mischief and cunning. 'You were at the farmhouse near Chelwood Gate, where the bodies were found. I want to hear your experience.'

Katy took an involuntary step back, but the woman didn't attempt to exploit it. She didn't need to do anything as crude as poking a foot inside.

It was clear to them both that she had won.

CHAPTER FIFTY-SIX

Adam felt he had to reassess the situation, and at least give the impression of a more conciliatory approach, now that he knew it was Jay's mother who was facing a slow, agonising death.

'I'm sorry. I understand why you didn't want me pointing out that you brought this on yourself.'

'Oh, it's true enough. And I know you don't owe me a thing.'

'Then why ask for my help?'

'Because there's no one else,' Holly said. 'And I believe Jay's a good man at heart.'

'But he deceived you, bringing you here under false pretences.'

'That's a trivial point, compared to what's at stake.' She sounded exasperated, and spoiling for a fight.

Jay cleared his throat. 'Look, as it turns out you got lucky at the farmhouse.'

'Because we hid,' Adam pointed out. What he meant was: *no thanks to you.*

'Yeah, but next time you might not be so lucky. You have to understand that collateral damage, even when it's little kids, means nothing to a man like him.'

'There won't be a "next time",' Adam said hotly.

'So you hope.' Jay stalled another objection, and said, 'Let me tell you how it was. Sunday night, I woke to chaos and realised we were under attack. I was upstairs, and I had your wife's bag, with the phones. I managed to get out, but they shot at me as I was running over the lawn, and a bullet clipped my side. Only a shallow wound, thank God, so I was able to get to the trees and hide. I made a note of Holly's number on my phone – and took all the cash I could find in the bag.'

'He'll pay it back,' Holly added.

'Yeah. Once the fire was well alight, I knew I didn't have long to get away. I headed across country and then holed up in a barn for a couple of hours, near to some village. In the morning I got the first bus to East Grinstead, and then a train to London. I knew Voronov would be after me, so I couldn't go anywhere near home. I had no idea who was dead or alive, but I had to assume the worst.'

As if energised by the drama he was describing, Holly started to pace the room. 'In those circumstances, wouldn't you risk a little deception?'

Adam could only shrug. 'Go on,' he said to Jay.

'I sent her a text. I had no idea if she'd buy it, or agree to come here, so I made a few calls. No one had seen or heard anything of Roger or Maggie, and their phones weren't picking up.'

'You said you got a train to London,' Adam pointed out. 'So why come here?'

'I'd worked out where Holly lived, and thought it would be more tempting if she didn't have to travel far. I'd also started thinking about where Voronov might have gone, if he had taken any prisoners.'

Adam gave a start. 'You mean he's near here?'

Jay shook his head. 'I'm not talking about really close.'

'Okay, but if you have any idea where he might be holding them, you have to tell the police.'

There was a sad smile from Jay, while Holly stood in front of him, hands on her hips. 'You just said yourself, he's a fugitive. Of course he can't go to the police!'

Jay tapped off the arguments on his fingers. 'One, they'll come after me rather than him – I'm an easy conviction, compared to

Voronov. Two, I can't offer any evidence, so it could take days before they do anything. Three, even if they catch him red-handed, he has the connections to make any problems go away.'

'See?' Holly swatted playfully at Adam's head. 'Right, I need a breather, and some food. Hungry?'

'Starving,' Jay said.

'Pizza? Burgers? Sandwiches?' She was looking at Adam, who suddenly realised how gassy his stomach had become.

'Anything, thanks.'

She grabbed her bag, and for a moment Adam couldn't quite believe that Jay would permit her to leave. Once the door had shut behind her, he asked, sarcastically, 'Has she fallen for you or something?'

'Would you be jealous if she had?'

Adam ignored the retort; it served him right. 'I just don't get why she'd help you.'

'You mean, "What's in it for her?" Perhaps that isn't how she sees the world?' Jay wore an expression of sly amusement. 'Then again, I don't know her as well as you do.'

'I haven't seen her for years—'

'She was your girlfriend once. She's played an important part in your life... then and now. Holly and Katy,' he mused, with a playful smile. 'Not to mention those two gorgeous kids. You've been a very lucky man.'

'I don't want to talk about my family,' Adam growled, but it was an aggression borne of guilt. If Katy knew he was here, and who he was with...

'I'm sure you don't. But this affects them, too, I'm afraid.' Jay saw that he had Adam's full attention. 'We're all in Voronov's world now, and there are only two exits. One is to go out in a box.' He swallowed hard, clearly thinking about his mother.

'And the other?'

'You destroy him.'

*

Even as she admitted her visitor, Katy had second thoughts. 'May I see that ID again?'

The journalist handed it over without a protest. 'Ronnie Pierce, you may have heard of me?' she said airily.

Katy shook her head. 'I really don't see that I can help. And you'll probably understand that we don't want to get involved.'

'"We"?' The woman peered at the hallway behind her. 'Is your husband here?'

'No. At work.' *I hope he's at work*, she thought, and something must have shown in her eyes; a hint of weakness that Pierce was quick to spot.

'How very industrious. Now, Katy, I appreciate your unwillingness to speak, and I very much regret to say this, but you're beyond the point where you can plausibly deny what happened.' She indicated the lounge. 'Shall we rest our weary feet?'

Reluctantly, Katy let her pass, and sensed the other woman casting a quizzical eye around the room. After a close inspection of the sofa cushions, she shrugged off her coat and sat down.

'Please be assured that I am not, and never have been, some tawdry newshound. My speciality is long-form journalism, in major publications such as *The Times*, the *Telegraph*, the *Spectator*, the *Wall Street Journal* – you've heard of…?'

'Yes.' Katy gave her a glassy smile. 'Newspapers and magazines do manage to reach us out here in the sticks.'

Ronnie Pierce uttered a squawk of laughter. 'Excellent. Then you'll appreciate my pedigree. The material I'm gathering will form the basis of what I now envisage as a full-length book, covering the entire affair from beginning to end. If you wish, you and your family can appear under a pseudonym – since you are, after all, playing only a minor role.'

It sounded condescending, but Katy could hardly take offence. 'Yes, we would definitely prefer that. But are other journalists willing to—?'

'Oh, pouf.' She karate chopped the air. '*Other* journalists don't have this story, a state of affairs that I am ferociously keen to preserve.' A phone appeared from her bag. 'I'll record our conversation, if I may?'

Katy opened her mouth to object – then decided that it might protect her to have everything down on tape. 'All right.'

'Thank you. Now, events were set in train by a minor collision, yes?'

'Well, not even a collision, really.' Having gone through the story more than once with the police, Katy found it was becoming easier to describe. Against all the odds, she began to relax.

She thought briefly that Adam, when he came home, might well take the view that she should have refused to talk. *But you weren't here*, she would tell him, if he opted to get snarky about it.

You weren't here.

CHAPTER FIFTY-SEVEN

So far it had gone better than he could have asked for, but Jay knew he mustn't get over confident. There was still no guarantee that Adam would agree to help – and even if he did, it might not be enough.

There was a careful balance to strike here: he needed Adam to be convinced of the threat posed by Voronov, without sending him running in terror back to his family… and then to the cops.

He had omitted a few details about his escape, such as how, after calling a few associates, he'd ditched his own phone and bought a couple of cheap pay-as-you-go mobiles. He'd also drawn out all the cash he could get, knowing he wouldn't be able to use his bank cards for the foreseeable future. And this wasn't just to stop the authorities from tracing him: he suspected that Voronov had contacts who could also obtain such data.

The Russian was capable of vengeance on a grand scale, which was why Jay had repeatedly warned Maggie not to escalate the feud, or to think she could get the better of him. But she hadn't listened, and now it might already be too late to save her.

He still couldn't quite believe how fortunate he'd been in finding Holly. Replying to her texts, posing as Adam, had started as a bit of a laugh, something to pass the time. He'd quickly grasped how unhappy she was, and how much she wanted her ex-boyfriend back in her life.

Asking her to meet at the hotel yesterday afternoon had been the easy part. When she walked into the bar and found that she'd been duped, it had felt like his whole life was on the line.

In his favour, he was young, good-looking, charming when he needed to be – and he hadn't tried to bullshit her. He'd read her correctly and knew she would respond to a drama, one with plenty of scope for gossip and excitement. He'd persuaded her to sit down for a late lunch and hear him out; they'd gone through two bottles of red wine, softening her up nicely as he described his predicament, and how only she could help him.

She hadn't expressed much concern over the illegality involved – he'd correctly identified her as a classic middle-class rebel – and it had been her idea, when the wine had been drunk, that they should go to bed together.

'You seriously want to?' he'd asked, having just listened to her go on and on about how only Adam could fill the void in her existence.

'Just because he's the long-term destination, I don't see why I shouldn't enjoy the occasional diversion en route.'

'To seal the deal, then?'

'Precisely. Though one word to Adam and that deal is off.'

Discretion suited him fine, and Christ she'd been a live wire in bed. He'd never slept with a woman as old as her – fortyish – and even now he wasn't sure whether to envy Adam or pity him. No wonder it was Katy that the guy had chosen to settle down with. He reckoned Holly was the kind of woman who'd make you want to kill yourself if she left you, or kill *her* if she stayed.

In that respect, she was not unlike his own mum; he knew a few people who'd muttered that his dad had only copped so much prison time to get a break from her.

He was glad when Holly went for some food. It demonstrated that she was doing this of her own free will, and it gave Jay a chance to try some male bonding. He told Adam about his childhood, raised in a family devoted to criminality, but he was careful to play up the hardship and the violence done to them, while editing out the violence they had done to others.

The truth was, they'd never gone short of money, though the bailiffs were always round because his dad never paid the bills. Then there were the police raids – as if they'd be careless enough to keep drugs or stolen goods on the premises – and the heavy-handed arrests by a whole mob of cops, because Dad was never, ever taken down without a fight.

He tried to portray Maggie in a better light, though she'd never truly been a mother of the sort that Adam himself had undoubtedly had. For the most part she had left Jay and his brother to fend for themselves; it was always made clear that their father was her one and only priority.

When Dad was in prison she had pined so extravagantly that she neglected them all the more, and when the old man succumbed to cancer a year before he was eligible for parole, she had dedicated herself to what remained of the family business, on a mission to preserve his legacy.

'Thirty-five years they'd been together, and she had to live with knowing that he was getting his chemo while handcuffed to the bed, watched over by a screw who used to laugh at the pain he was in.'

'That sounds appalling,' Adam said. 'But surely it made you determined not to end up in the same kind of trouble?'

'Course it did – especially with a brother who's also doing life. We've got a minicab firm that was thriving, till fucking Uber came along. A couple of decent pubs, and one or two other things. Until all this blew up, my focus was on the legitimate side of the business.'

Not the whole truth, but close enough. He saw Adam buying it, and then ask, 'So what led to the dispute with Voron—?'

A knock on the door. Jay had half a second to tell himself his time was up – and he registered a similar, inexplicable alarm in Adam's eyes – before Holly called out, 'Well, let me in, boys, if you want to eat something.'

*

Holly was operating in a state of pure exhilaration, smoother and more intoxicating than any drug she'd ever taken. In the stultifying days and weeks since losing Simon, her own will to live had slowly leaked away. It had taken a jolt on this scale to demonstrate just how empty, how barren her life had become.

Yesterday, upon entering the hotel, the final text had asked her to call him. Thrilled at the prospect of seeing Adam, she'd brought up the number and instantly heard the trilling of a phone… held by a complete stranger.

If it had been anyone but Jay, it probably wouldn't have worked. Holly was a shrewd woman, not easily swayed by others, no matter what the circumstances. Jay was young – fourteen years her junior – and he was cute, but what had drawn her in was his vulnerability; she'd rarely met a man who exhibited such a beguiling mix of anger, pain, desperation and tenderness.

Holly liked it that he wasn't afraid to piss her off, even though right now he needed her so badly, and they both knew that one phone call would bring the police running.

It was that frisson which had persuaded her to take him to bed. How often did you get the chance to shag a decent man who was also a fugitive and a killer? It was crazy beyond belief, but she'd guessed that in bed he would be energetic, skilful and as rough or as gentle as she desired – and he hadn't disappointed in any way, shape or form.

Thank God she hadn't panicked, or let disappointment govern her response.

Before that, Jay had let her ask the inevitable questions: Where's Adam? Who are you? How did you get my number? To hear the answers, she had to give him time. She was in a public place, with staff and other guests wandering past, so there was no physical danger. After listening for an hour, she had agreed to book her own room for the night and begin an anxious search of the internet to ascertain whether her ex-partner had survived.

The first news reports were sketchy, and Jay seemed truly baffled that there was no mention of the family. Holly had applied her own resources, checking their Facebook pages, phoning Adam's office and the shop where Katy worked. She'd learned that they were absent, but had called in with an excuse.

'So they're alive?' Jay had been astonished, while Holly was both delighted and just slightly regretful. They didn't *all* have to make it out safely, did they?

A shameful thought, but that hadn't stopped it recurring a few times. And she was genuinely concerned for the children; had spent a good deal of last night fretting over the potential psychological effects, and whether those effects would make it more or less difficult to adjust to other major changes. Like emigrating, for instance.

Or having a new mother.

Her attitude towards Katy was complicated. The woman had done nothing to her personally, of course. She'd kept Adam happy for a number of years, and provided him with healthy children: all to her credit.

But Holly found it hard to accept that Katy had arrived on the scene at just the moment when Adam needed stability, following his break-up with Holly. It felt too serendipitous; a bit too goddamn fortunate.

The break up should never have happened. Yes, she had strayed, and the fact that Greg had been a mutual colleague (and a dick) made it more difficult to dismiss. But it seemed like the worst kind of double standards that Adam had reacted so savagely in walking out on her. He blamed that on his intention to propose, although she had no doubt that, as a man, he'd have expected to be given leeway for one last fling. They all did it, didn't they?

In recent weeks, having resumed contact in a less melodramatic fashion than last time, she had seen that the bonds were still there, and could only get stronger. It had helped to learn of the job offer in Vancouver, which meant she could steer their conversations in a direction that exposed the differences between Adam and Katy.

And where there was a difference, there was an opportunity to exploit.

Last night it had been Jay who finally advised her to send an email, correctly guessing that Adam wouldn't yet have his phone back. They'd debated what to say, and agreed it had to be cryptic: to lure him here, just as Jay had lured Holly.

Only, in this case, Adam had been aware that he was meeting Holly. He just hadn't known that Jay was here as well.

He came because of me. And so far Holly was delighted with his response. A lot of grumbling about the police and justice and so on, but that was to be expected.

There was a fair way to go, but so far the signs were encouraging.

Everything she wanted was within reach.

CHAPTER FIFTY-EIGHT

When Holly came in, the hot greasy smell of takeaway food made Adam's stomach rumble. She placed the bags on her dressing table and started removing polystyrene containers.

'Took an executive decision: burgers with skinny fries.'

'Great.' Jay moved in to help, and handed Adam one of the burgers, which was spilling over with salad and dollops of melted cheese. Before he started eating, Adam checked his phone. No messages, although it was gone three o'clock. The time had passed in a blur, and he was quite surprised that Katy hadn't been in touch.

Jay squeezed a sachet of ketchup on to his chips, and ate in frenetic gulps while he explained their history with Voronov.

'It was nothing to do with crime, or even business. It started a couple of years ago, with a kid called Ethan. He's a bit of a lad, to be fair, bit of a loudmouth. One night he's in a club with some mates in the West End, and they get into an argument with these guys – just a lot of mouthing off over a spilled drink.'

He paused for a chip. Adam took a bite of his burger, felt juice dribbling down his chin and in a flash Holly had reached over, napkin in hand, and wiped it away.

'The two sides face off, and then the guy that started it – a young Russian bloke – pulls a knife. Ethan and his mates back off, but outside they lie in wait, jump a couple of the Russians and give them a beating. About what they deserved, really,' he added. 'And that should have been the end of it.'

'But one of the Russians was Voronov?' Adam asked.

'Oh no, those fellas just worked for him. So yeah, it's a dent to his pride that they got spanked, but what's he gonna do? He has no idea who these other kids are.'

'Okay.'

'But over the next few weeks, our people start to feel they're being watched. We think maybe it's the cops, but no one gets busted. Then some kid at university in Surrey nearly dies after taking GBL and a video pops up on social media of one of our guys – one of the boys who'd been at the club – selling him the stuff. All hell breaks out in the papers, and he gets lifted and charged. While he's in custody, there's a visit from some cocky bastard in Major Crimes who tells him a "Russian birdie" is helping to bring us down.'

Adam had eaten more than half of his burger, and was rapidly losing his appetite. He put the remainder of it back and said, 'So it's a turf war?'

'Not quite. Voronov is a billionaire, and although he's got all sorts of links to organised crime in Russia, over here he doesn't need to steal, or sell drugs. Like I said, these guys use Britain to park their money safely.' Jay finished off his last chip. 'No, he just hated the fact that a couple of his men got "disrespected", so he tapped up the authorities to identify us, and then set about trying to destroy our livelihoods.'

Holly was nodding. 'If you've read anything about how things are in Russia, the crossover between the mafia, the government and the oligarchs, none of this will come as a surprise.'

'Except we didn't realise, at first, who we were taking on,' Jay said. 'Voronov keeps a very low profile, so even when we'd identified the guys who caused the ruck, it took us weeks trying to piece together who was in charge.'

He described how Maggie had authorised a series of attacks on property and businesses belonging to the Russian – burglaries, fires, vandalism – and how Voronov had responded with even greater aggression. 'They drove past one of our pubs one night and unloaded an automatic rifle into it. This was after closing time, but the landlady was inside. She got two bullets in the spine, and now she's in a wheelchair for life.'

'Jesus,' Adam exclaimed. 'Didn't you get the police to go after him?'

'No proof,' Jay said. 'Anyway, the cops don't listen to people like us. They took the line that, whoever it was we'd pissed off, we'd better make sure it ended, or else they'd be looking to shut us down. Revoke our licences, send in the tax man, all that kind of stuff.'

'Was that Voronov's doing as well?'

'Could be. Either way, Maggie saw we were headed for destruction, so she put the word out that we wanted to talk. There was a meeting, just her and Roger, with Voronov's right-hand man. A guy called Xavier De Vos – Belgian, I think he is. He took a shine to Maggie – or at least that's what we thought – and he started feeding her some inside info on Voronov and his setup.'

'Behind his back?' Adam queried.

'Yeah. It was Xavier who mentioned the affair with Carole.'

'And that's why you kidnapped her?'

Jay looked slightly ashamed. 'Only because we didn't know if they could be trusted – Voronov, Xavier, any of them. We wanted something up our sleeve, if Voronov tried backing out of the deal.'

'What was the deal?'

'My mum made a big decision. Basically, to get out. Shut everything down, sell off the legitimate businesses and retire abroad. Roger was gonna do the same – the two of them are kind of together but not together, if you know what I mean? Everyone on the payroll was in line for a windfall. Voronov was offered first refusal on our businesses, some of which can be quite useful for money laundering purposes. He also gets an end to the attacks on his people – and more than that, the satisfaction of knowing he's frightened us away.'

His lip curled in disgust as he said it, and Adam frowned. 'Surely it didn't have to be framed in those terms?'

'No. But we knew that's how he'd want it. Pride, you know? If you come up through a world of competition and violence, it's your status, your reputation that gives you power. That matters more than money. It's what made him so furious about a silly little bust-up at a nightclub. He has to be seen to come out on top.' Jay released a sigh. 'Just one problem with that.'

'Your mum,' Holly whispered. She'd clearly heard this story already, but sounded no less enthralled by it.

'Yeah. Because Mum, Roger, me – we all came up in exactly the same way as Voronov. To take the humiliation of being chased off our patch, it had to be some seriously good compensation.'

Adam nodded. 'How much?'

'Eight million pounds.'

'*What?*'

'Well, seven million, really, because we'd agreed a kickback of a million to Xavier.' Jay saw the shock on Adam's face, and said, 'You've got to understand, that's chickenfeed to Voronov. His main yacht is worth ten times that.'

'Then why wouldn't he just go ahead and do the deal?'

'Dunno. The truth is, we were never more than mosquitoes, buzzing around his world. All he had to pay out was the cost of a spray. Instead, he's come after us with a fucking flamethrower.'

'How did he find you? Did this Xavier know about the farmhouse?'

'Nope. I'm wondering if Voronov had a tracker put on one of our vehicles. It's possible he found out about Carole's abduction, and acted as a result of that, but more likely he'd planned this from the start, knowing he could draw us out somewhere to finalise the deal, then finish us off in one go.'

'Now do you see why we have to help?' Holly said to Adam. 'For all the wrong she did, we can't let Jay's mother be tortured to death.'

This isn't my problem, Adam was thinking, as selfish as that might have sounded. But equally, he knew what it was like to lose a mother, years before her time, so he could understand some of the anguish Jay was feeling.

'I'd still say that the police stand the best chance of saving her.'

Jay shook his head, chewing forcefully on his burger. 'I know it seems that way to you. In your law-abiding middle-class world, the police are always the answer. Running to the rescue, putting things right again. In our world, it doesn't work like that. Get a problem, you have to sort it yourself.'

'But you can't take on Voronov and his men. How many does he have?'

'Four or five really trusted professionals.' Jay nodded soberly at Adam. 'Don't worry. What I want from you isn't dangerous. Just a couple of quick errands, and then you can leave the rest to me.' A glance at Holly. 'Time?'

She consulted her watch, a TAG Heuer Aquaracer which had been a gift from Adam for her twenty-fifth birthday.

'Ten to four.'

'Shit.' He finished the burger, wiped his hands on his trousers and climbed to his feet. 'I need to get some stuff. Can you run through it for him?'

And before either of them could respond, he strode out of the room.

CHAPTER FIFTY-NINE

Ronnie Pierce listened intently as Katy described how she'd had to take Dylan to a birthday party, with one of the gang hovering in the background.

'Good Lord, what courage! To have freedom all around you, and yet be confined by your obligations to poor Adam and Freya.'

Katy smiled modestly. It was a struggle not to be warmed by such admiration, but she couldn't allow herself to forget that these compliments had a purpose.

It was as she moved on to the next stage of their captivity that the questions began. After answering a few, Katy paused. 'Sorry, I never offered you tea or coffee.'

'I'm fine, thank you.'

Since it had only been a ploy to buy time, Katy said, 'I'm going to get some water. My throat's quite dry.'

In the kitchen she ran the cold tap, listening for signs that Pierce was taking the opportunity to rummage around the room, and asked herself, *What am I so anxious about?*

She'd reached the point in her account where she and Dylan were back from the party, and Carole had been taken upstairs.

'And you still had no idea what this was about?' Pierce queried when Katy returned. 'Or had Adam gleaned any more from Carole?'

'Not really. Only something to do with…' Katy faltered. DI Branning seemed to have dismissed the idea that Carole's affair played any part in the kidnap, so was it right to publicise the woman's infidelity?

'With what?'

'I don't… I'm not sure…'

'Another relationship? That's the whisper I'm hearing.'

Katy tried to remain impassive. 'She had said something, but not in any detail, and I don't think it's related—'

'We'll all have opinions, of course.' The journalist's smile was cold. 'I prefer to marshal the facts. How long was Carole upstairs?'

'I've no idea.' She registered Pierce's exasperation and said, 'It was impossible to keep track of time. Anyway, my focus was on the children.'

'But when Carole returned, I take it you didn't just ignore her?'

Katy bridled at the remark, and wondered if Pierce was deliberately trying to antagonise her. 'She was in shock. We gave her what comfort we could, but she barely registered our presence.'

'Nevertheless, you must have asked what the gang had discussed?'

'Yes, but she wasn't very communicative. Nothing made any sense.'

'Such as?' Pierce was leaning forward, knees pressed together.

'Look, my memory isn't clear on a lot of things – because of the stress, I suppose.'

'Are you sure that isn't a convenient excuse?'

'I'm sorry?'

Blithely ignoring the offence she'd caused, Pierce said, 'We seem to be approaching the crux of the matter, and that's commonly when a witness becomes vague, hesitant, evasive. It's the subconscious at work, unwilling to be taken back to a moment of crisis.'

'Well, in that case you'll understand why I can't remember.' Katy's attention was nudged by the sound of a car manoeuvring close to the house. She willed it to be Adam.

'Oh, you *can* remember.' Pierce made it sound like an order. 'Carole had something to say about the reason for her abduction, and I'm sure you know what it is.'

Katy stood up in a rush, almost knocking her glass of water to the floor. 'I'd like you to leave, please.'

'Two minutes. Tell me what the gang said to Carole. Was it linked to her affair?'

'I want you to go. I'm not answering any more questions.'

Pierce chuckled, but her eyes were narrow. 'A foolish strategy. The people who come after me won't be so polite.'

Katy gasped. 'That sounds like a threat.'

'It's nothing of the sort.' A knock on the door startled them both. Ronnie Pierce stood up, eyeing the phone in her hand. 'One final chance. Why did they take Carole?'

'I can't answer that.' Katy blinked away a tear. 'I've got nothing more to say.'

A second knock, firmer this time. Katy kept the journalist in her sight as she stepped into the hall. She was bolstered by the prospect of some moral support until it struck her: what if this was another reporter?

Pierce loitered by the door, as if trying to gauge whether she could successfully refuse to leave. 'I'll get what I need, eventually. It's in your best interests to tell me now.'

Ignoring her, Katy opened the front door and could have collapsed with relief.

It was DI Branning.

Adam couldn't quite believe that Jay had left them alone. He stared at Holly, who regarded him with a placid gaze, even while one of her legs twitched with a barely suppressed excitement.

'So this is for real?' he asked. 'You're not being coerced into anything?'

Her laughter was unforced. 'Good grief, haven't we just explained it?'

'All right, but I still don't think you appreciate what you're involved in. You didn't see the dead bodies, the people pulling guns and opening fire. They threatened our lives, Holly. The lives of a nine-year-old, a seven-year-old. Innocent children. And Jay was one of the men responsible for that.'

'I know, but he insists that they never intended to hurt you, and I believe him. The real danger comes from Voronov.'

'Maybe it does, but we have to let the police take care of that.'

'Oh, you really have become so staid, haven't you? Middle-aged, middle class, law and order, safety first, tally-ho!' She made a hooting trumpet sound.

Adam sighed. 'This is real life, Holly, not a Liam Neeson movie.'

'Look, Jay's going to be the maverick hero, if there is one. You and me, we're just the sassy sidekicks.' A shrug. 'And yes, it might turn out to be an atrocious error and get him killed, but what do you care? After what you've just said, you'd probably welcome that.'

'Of course I wouldn't,' Adam snapped. Holly was never one for nuances in the heat of an argument. 'I want proper justice. Prosecutions, prison sentences.'

'Oh, please! As if the legal system is about justice, for one thing. For another, it rarely applies to men like Voronov. They enjoy their wealth and freedom on a licence issued by the Kremlin. When Voronov's day of reckoning comes, it's not gonna be PC Plod on the doorstep. It'll be a dose of poison, or an "accidental" fall from a balcony.' She sighed, glancing around the room as if infected by the same paranoia she was describing. 'Until that day, he's practically untouchable.'

'Even if it that's the case, I don't see that Voronov has any reason to come after us.'

'Don't you? Once he finds out you were talking to Carole, he'll assume that Maggie told her who Voronov really is… and that Carole might have told you.'

There was a moment of frustrated silence. Adam thought Holly was being sincere, but his doubts centred more on her judgement.

'What exactly does Jay want me to do?' he asked sourly.

'Not much. Just go and collect some things he needs.'

'Where? And what things?'

'I don't know, *exactly*.' She looked frustrated, or perhaps bored, by his questions. 'Stuff he'll need for the next stage.'

'Why can't he get it himself?'

'Weren't you listening? It's too dangerous to venture into any of his usual haunts.' She stepped close and raised a finger, almost but not quite touching his lips. 'Before you say it, we'll be completely safe. Nobody has a clue who we are.'

'You're going, too?'

'Bloody right I am. With or without your assistance.'

'Holly…'

'Don't get patronising. It's probably a couple of hours at most, and then you can toddle off home. I daresay you'll hear on the news whether he succeeds or not.'

Adam sighed. It still felt like she was treating this as a game.

'And what will you do, after we've run these errands?'

Her smile matched the glint of victory in her eyes, as well as something a little cheekier. 'I'll probably stay here one more night. Why – are you thinking of joining me?'

'No.'

She pouted. 'Shame.'

'Holly, don't start—'

'It's your choice. Just remember Seville…' She glanced around the room. 'Bit nicer hotel than this one.'

'What's Seville got to do with anything?'

'Our kiss, Adam. Don't pretend it hasn't stayed in your memory. It was that moment, that kiss, when I knew that you and I were truly meant for each other.'

'Stop it.' He gave an irritated twitch of his shoulders. 'Are you serious about doing this, even if I walk away?'

'Discuss it later, then?' She smacked her lips sarcastically. 'And yes, Jay needs me to drive him. My car has tinted rear windows so he can hide in the back.'

Adam put his hand into his pocket and felt the phone there. He had a lot of misgivings, but still wasn't sure if he would act on them.

'I need to call Katy.'

'Have you told her you're here?' Holly's brief, hostile glare was quickly replaced by a grin; it was as though she'd found a way to peer inside his soul. 'Ooh, Adam! She doesn't know, does she?'

'I had no idea what I was getting into. I didn't want to freak her out.'

He was expecting fiery sarcasm, but instead she changed tack. 'How were things going before all this?'

He shifted uncomfortably. 'Yeah, okay.'

'Because your texts have been so vague. And with this issue of Canada, and Katy's parents unwilling to travel…'

'That's all still rumbling on. Maybe after this she'll be keener to go…' He tailed off, reluctant to elaborate. With Holly, there was always the sense that anything he said could later be used against him; he'd once joked that she ought to caution him before a conversation began.

'But *you* want to go, still?' She lifted up on tiptoe, seeking to maintain eye contact when he was trying to look away. 'You really should – even if she doesn't. It's a fabulous opportunity, and I'm sure you'll make a huge success of it.'

Adam could tell his face was bright red. 'I'm not interested at the moment. Let me make a call.'

He turned away, reached for the door, and heard her say, 'You don't have to go out there.'

'I'd prefer to.' When he looked back she was pouting again, but not really cross with him.

'All right. But be vague, is my advice.'

CHAPTER SIXTY

DI Branning saw at once that something was wrong. His enquiring gaze moved past Katy, just as Ronnie Pierce glided insouciantly into the hallway, phone in hand.

'A journalist.' Boosted by the detective's presence, Katy was almost incoherent with rage. 'She's refusing to leave.'

'A mere misunderstanding,' Pierce declared, skipping past Katy, who pressed herself against the wall to avoid physical contact.

DI Branning blocked the woman's exit. 'What are you doing here?'

'Gathering some background… Detective *Sergeant*, isn't it?' From the sly tone, it was clear she knew Branning's correct rank. 'And please don't act mystified. You were never going to conceal something like this.'

'Let me see some ID. If one of my guys has been talking, I'll bloody—'

'Calm down, Detective.' She pressed a business card into his hand. 'Katy will explain my angle. If you feel like contributing, you know how to reach me.'

After a brief standoff, Branning stepped aside. The journalist strode haughtily along the path and got into an Audi parked across the road.

'Parasites.' DI Branning muttered as he studied the woman's card. 'What did she mean about her angle?'

Katy shut the door. Her whole body was still rigid with fury. 'She's writing a book, apparently. She tried to persuade me that she'll keep my details anonymous, and nothing will get into the papers.'

'What would be the point of that – from her perspective, I mean?'

'I expect she was lying. I shouldn't have told her anything, but she already seemed quite well informed.'

'I don't know how. I trust my team not to leak.'

'Unless she was bluffing? I mean, would she really be planning out a book this soon after it happened?'

'Who can say?' Branning was grinding a fist against his palm. 'A book might be her goal in the long term, but in my experience a journalist wants to be first to a story. That's where the money is, and the acclaim, so don't be surprised if this ends up splashed all over tomorrow's papers.'

Katy shuddered. 'Will we have to move out?'

'I hope it doesn't come to that. What exactly did you tell her?'

They moved into the lounge, where the lingering aroma of the woman's perfume turned her stomach. 'She was pushing me about Carole, and why they'd abducted her. I got the impression she might have known more than she was letting on, and was trying to get me to confirm it.'

'And did you?'

'Not really. After what you said about there being no trace of the Russian… and with Carole not around to defend herself, it didn't seem right to mention her affair.'

'Absolutely. The less you say, the better.' He looked around. 'Adam not here?'

'No. He's, uh, popped into work.' She gave an awkward laugh. 'Is that a problem?'

'I hope not. I have a couple of questions, if that's okay?'

'Of course. Do you want a coffee?' As she said it, the landline rang.

'Go on, then.'

He waved away her apology at having to answer the phone. Katy grabbed the cordless handset but didn't connect the call until she was walking through to the kitchen. Could this be another reporter? It surely wouldn't take long to find their number.

But it was Adam. 'Hi, I just wanted to see how you're doing?'

'Not too bad.' The sound of his voice was like a sneaky blow to the gut. 'How are you getting on? Will you be home soon?'

'Um… I'm not sure. Is that a problem?'

'Yes – I mean no,' she gabbled. 'DI Branning's just arrived. I think he was hoping to speak to you.'

'Was he? Why?'

The questions were too abrupt: they were both nervous, she realised. 'I don't know.' Katy lifted the kettle and poured the dregs into the sink. 'A journalist just came by. Quite nasty, but luckily Branning got here and made sure she left. He can't believe any of his team could have leaked—'

'Katy, I'm sorry. I'm not at work.'

'What?' She turned sharply to check the doorway, but DI Branning had remained in the lounge.

'I'm safe, completely safe. But I've got a chance to help sort things out, so I won't be home until quite late. I don't want you to worry—'

'What are you talking about? Sort what "things" out?'

'I can't explain now. Please trust me – and don't mention this to Branning. I'll be home when I can. I love you.'

'Adam, please…' Before she could say anything more, he rang off. Katy put the phone down, leaned over the sink and retched.

He had lied to her this morning. He'd taken her for a fool.

'Katy?' Branning's voice was soft. So was the hand that settled on her shoulder.

'I'm okay. Just had something in my throat.'

'Oh.' He backed off. 'Shall I make coffee, or would you prefer not to bother?'

'No, I'll be fine.' She composed herself, then turned and offered a smile. If his expression was anything to go by, she must look dreadful.

He indicated the phone. 'May I ask, was that...?'

'Oh, just my dad. They're bringing the kids home later this evening.'

'Right. So you'll want Zoe to come round?'

She nodded, thinking, *Oh God, yes*. 'Please.'

She filled the kettle, found mugs and coffee, apologising for the fact that it was instant.

'It's a big step up from a vending machine.' He chuckled, but the awkwardness was still there.

'What did you want to talk about?' she asked.

'It's a bit odd, actually. We've looked at the phone records, and Adam's mobile shows a number of SMS messages on Sunday.' He paused, frowning. 'What time was it that they confiscated your phones?'

'As soon as we got there. Probably no later than one o'clock.'

'And you didn't get access after that?'

She thought about it. 'Well, yes – because of the party. There was some contact with Suzy Chadwick.'

DI Branning nodded. 'We've allowed for those. But there's another number, with an exchange of messages going back several days, at least.'

'Prior to Sunday?'

'Yes. The initial search parameter was quite narrow, because frankly we didn't expect to find anything. We'll have to go back to the phone company.'

'But why?' Katy asked.

'Because those messages continue through Sunday afternoon and into the evening, when the phone was – presumably – in the gang's possession.'

'It was, absolutely. So who…' She felt her throat closing again. 'Have you been able to trace the number?'

'Yes. It's registered to a Ms Holly Wolstenholme.'

'*Holly?*' Katy thought she might faint. Branning clearly thought so too. He made a grab for her, but she turned and gripped the worktop. 'I'm all right.'

'Sorry. I should have anticipated that it might be a shock.'

'There's no reason why you should.' She coughed, took a deep breath. 'Holly's a… a friend of Adam's. An ex-girlfriend, actually.'

'*Oh.*' Branning managed to invest an awful lot of meaning in that one short syllable. 'I suppose the million-dollar question is, why would one of the gang be chatting to her until late into the night?'

Katy couldn't give an answer. Right now there was a much bigger question reverberating in her mind.

How many other secrets was her husband keeping from her?

Adam had tried to be as honest as he could, but knew he'd probably just made things worse. And it worried him that DI Branning was there right now. Given the anxiety he'd caused, he couldn't blame his wife if she chose to pass on what he'd just told her.

As a precaution, he switched off his phone. That only intensified his guilt, though it felt like the right decision when Jay came into sight and registered him standing in the corridor.

'What are you doing?'

'I had to call my wife. I didn't tell her anything specific.'

'Okay.' Jay glanced casually over his shoulder. 'If you've set the cops on my tail, they won't get here in time. We're leaving.'

He tapped on the door. Holly opened it, greeted Jay with a smile, then scowled at Adam. 'What did she say?'

'Nothing much.' He followed Jay into the room, and was told by Holly that he should use the toilet. It might be the last chance for a while.

'But me first!' she squealed, like a child about to go on a day trip.

Adam wandered to the window, and saw headlights on the main road, arrowing through the gloom. It was rapidly getting dark, and he wanted to be away from here.

He said, 'You talked about how Voronov might be torturing Roger and, uh…'

'My mum,' Jay said grimly. 'What about it?'

'Will they have told him about us?'

'I hope not.'

'But if he questions them about Carole, it'll come out that we were there.'

'Mum and Roger didn't know much about you. It was Gary and Dale that took your wife home, and I don't think they got asked any questions before they died.' He cracked a bitter smile. 'That's why this has to be dealt with now, for their sake, for mine – and for yours. Voronov has connections galore – cops, lawyers, politicians, the media. Once he knows about you, he'll find you easily. If I don't stop him, he could wipe out your entire family.'

'But I don't understand why. We're no threat to him.'

'He won't take that chance. It doesn't matter what you know or don't know, or whether you've already given statements. The simple fact is, if you're not around to attend court, or campaign against the politicians that support him, you're a problem solved.'

Adam had a nagging feeling that he'd missed the significance of something in Jay's words, but he couldn't pin it down. Ruefully, he said, 'You honestly think he'd go to these lengths?'

'Christ, yes. And probably done in a way that makes the cops think that Maggie arranged it. She and Roger – and me, if I'm caught – will take the blame. He'll dispose of our bodies so that they'll never be found, and once again… he's in the clear.'

They heard the toilet flush. Holly appeared, visibly nervous but also, possibly, a little wired. She caught Adam's frown, and blew him a mocking kiss.

Jay stood back and said, 'I'm not pissing you around, Adam. If you don't believe me, you're welcome to go.'

Holly nodded. 'It's the moment of truth. Are you helping us, or not?'

CHAPTER SIXTY-ONE

'Do you…' Katy began, then had to stop for a moment. 'Do you have the contents of the messages?'

When he nodded, Branning's demeanour was so sombre and caring that it made her want to scream. At least it gave her warning to brace herself for his next question.

'I'm afraid I have to ask this. Do you think Adam might be—?'

'Having an affair with his ex? I have no idea. What do the messages say?'

'It's, er… well, from what I've seen, there is a certain amount of… flirtation.' He blinked a few times. 'I'm sorry. This is very intrusive.'

She blew her nose on a piece of kitchen roll, and made a huge effort to recover. The children would be back soon: she didn't want them to think she'd been crying.

'What about talking to Holly?' she asked.

'It's an urgent priority. We haven't yet tried the mobile number, because I want someone to see her in person. An officer from Northants police is calling at her address this evening.'

She won't be there, Katy thought suddenly, though she didn't dare say it. *She'll be with Adam, wherever he is.*

There was a brief respite while she made coffee and they moved to the lounge. After a couple of minutes to reflect, she felt slightly calmer.

'We had to speak to Suzy Chadwick and then take Dylan to that party to avoid creating suspicion, so perhaps this was the same sort of thing.'

'I guess so. The difference is that this is one of the gang passing themselves off as Adam.' He took a sip of coffee. 'One wrong word and Holly might have realised it was an imposter.'

'But they took some crazy risks the whole way through. Hijacking our car in broad daylight. Taking us to Noah's party.'

'You're right. I suppose they mitigated it by using their most expendable people.' He pondered, tugging on an earlobe. 'It was obviously crucial that no one noticed you were missing. They told you they had something important planned for the next day – but why would a news story about a missing family jeopardise that?'

Katy shrugged. 'Because of the extra police presence?'

'Could be. Though their base was a few miles from where you were taken, and presumably their meeting wasn't due to take place at the Kirbys' house.' He drank again. 'It says to me that they were dealing with someone who was exceptionally cautious. Someone who'd cry off at the first sign of anything amiss.'

Katy nodded. She couldn't dispute that theory.

'And what that also indicates,' Branning continued, 'is that the meeting was more important to Maggie and her cronies than it was to our Mr X. Which suggests that he is probably rich, and powerful—'

'Like an oligarch? So you do think there's something in what Adam was saying?'

'Maybe. It's more that I'm at the stage where I'm throwing out ideas – though that still doesn't mean our Mr X attacked the farmhouse.' He sighed. 'I do wish I could put more resources into identifying this gentleman friend of Carole's.'

'Perhaps you should engage the services of my unwanted visitor?' Katy joked.

Branning smiled briefly, then checked his watch. 'When are you expecting Adam home?'

Katy tried not to squirm. 'I don't know. If he gets really absorbed he can lose all track of time.'

'Can't we all? Well, I'll see what we find out this evening, and speak to Adam tomorrow.'

'Are you sure? I can ask him to call you when he gets in.'

Branning considered it, and nodded. 'All right. Thanks.' He finished his coffee and stood up. 'Better get going – unless you'd like me to stay?'

'No, of course not.' She scoffed at his concern, but inside she was thinking, *Do I look that scared?*

They took the stairs to the lobby. There were only a few people around, fellow guests who paid them no attention, but still the presence of potential witnesses brought it home to Adam: he was working with a criminal, a wanted man.

Didn't that make him a criminal, too? At the very least, he was putting himself in jeopardy, risking arrest, violence or worse. But he was doing it because there was so much at stake – and because there was no other way.

He'd asked himself a couple of simple questions. Did he believe his family were in danger? *Yes.* Was he confident the authorities could protect them? *No.*

On that basis, he had no choice.

Jay didn't say a word until they were in the car park, which had filled up since Adam had got here. It was nearly six o'clock.

'You have a satnav, yes?' He followed Adam to his car and gave him a postcode. 'That's for Ebury Road, in Rickmansworth. At this time of the evening it's gonna take around forty or fifty minutes.'

Adam stifled a protest, partly because he was at least heading in the general direction of home. 'Okay.'

Jay produced a cheap Nokia phone. 'In Ebury Road there's a small workshop, Brayson Engineering. Use one of their parking bays, then call me for instructions.'

'What am I getting?'

'Plenty of time for that.' They both turned as a car approached, a white Lexus NS which drew up beside them. Holly was at the wheel.

'Drive sensibly,' Jay said. 'And keep your own phone switched off.'

As he climbed into the passenger seat, Holly leaned past him and raised a hand in farewell. For the first time, Adam thought she looked slightly pensive. Perhaps, now they were on the move, it was becoming more real to her. *Well, about time*, he thought.

But it did little to assuage his own guilt. *There's no other choice*: do I really believe that?

The answer was yes, and it brought a wave of despair as he drove out of the car park. Only time would tell if it was the right decision or not, but either way he had a horrible feeling that he might lose Katy because of his lies, his deception.

She'll never trust me again.

Holly wasn't accustomed to driving slowly. When they reached the M1 she tried to creep along in the inside lane, but they kept getting trapped behind lorries driving at forty or fifty: to Holly it felt as though they might as well be going backwards.

After a couple of miles, Jay said, 'You can speed up a bit.'

'I thought we had to stick close to Adam.' His Peugeot was three or four cars ahead. 'Aren't you worried that he'll change his mind?'

'Not really. Are you?'

'I'm quite surprised that he's agreed to this. I thought we'd have to work a lot harder to persuade him.'

Jay chuckled. 'Take it as a compliment. He's doing this for you.'

Holly smiled, but for all that she wanted to believe it, she wasn't sure it was true.

She drove on for a few seconds, gliding into the outside lane at a much more natural seventy-five, and said, 'I hope his family are going to be all right.'

'Depends on whether I can stop Voronov in time.'

'You don't think he'll have got anything out of… his prisoners?'

'Dunno.' He sounded pained, not wanting to discuss it. 'I'm gonna try to get the best possible outcome, yeah? For me, for him. For you. But nothing's guaranteed, is it? Just like I told you.'

'In other words: "Shut up and drive."'

A snort of laughter from the back seat. 'You really crack me up, Holly, you know that?'

'It was an observation, not a joke.'

'Ah.' Another laugh, a lot less certain. 'In that case,' he said wryly, 'shut up and drive, *please*.'

CHAPTER SIXTY-TWO

When DI Branning had gone, Katy immediately called Adam. There was no answer. She tried to compose a text, but wasn't sure what to say. This was more about talking to him, listening for the truth in his voice when he was asked about Holly.

She thought about last night, and remembered that he'd gone online to catch up on his work emails. If he'd lied to her about going to the office today, maybe he'd lied about what he was doing then.

She grabbed the iPad, but got no further than opening a browser when a car pulled up outside. Mum and Dad, bringing the kids home. As worried as she was about Adam, about their marriage, it would have to take second place for a while.

Her delight in seeing them was genuine, even if her smile of greeting had to be forced. Freya and Dylan entered the house without any hesitation, and both seemed glad to be home. It probably helped that they were fizzing with excitement about the animals they'd seen, the meals and the ice cream, the lavish toys they'd been bought from the gift shop.

Her mum caught Katy's frown of disapproval and snapped, 'Not a word! Your children have been incredible, and they deserve every one of these treats.'

With darkness outside, they drew the curtains and turned on lights and the central heating. The effect was to make the house feel cosy and safe, a cocoon from the outside world. Clive fussed over hot drinks, while Laura took the kids upstairs to see where the new toys would be living.

'A nice idea of your mum's,' her father said. 'Get them focused on something else so they don't even notice they're settling back in.'

'It's perfect,' Katy said. 'They actually seem fine, don't they?'

Clive agreed that they did. 'And you?'

'Not too bad.' She was reluctant to mention the visit by Ronnie Pierce, but needed to warn them, in case they were also targeted.

'Christ almighty,' Clive said when she'd told him. 'I thought that detective had assured you of their discretion?'

'He was the one who rescued me. And he can't understand where she got her information from.'

Clive chuntered on about it in a fatherly way, and then said, 'So what's Adam doing at work?'

She flinched. 'He missed a big meeting yesterday, you know what it's like…'

'Not really. After what you went through, I can't believe he thinks it's the best use of his time. Not when it means leaving you here alone.'

'I told him I was okay.' She gave him a serious look. 'Please, Dad. I don't want to talk about it.'

'Fine. It's between the two of you.' He shoved his hands in his pockets and gazed forlornly at the tiled floor. 'Be a relief to get away from me, won't it, with all my fussing?'

'No. We were very grateful to be able to stay last night.'

'Not that. I mean a new life. Vancouver.'

'Oh, Dad, that's just about the last thing on our minds.'

'All right. But it will be discussed, in the coming days or weeks. And when it does, I want you to do what's best for you, and Adam, and the children. No one else.'

Katy could feel tears welling up, and knew it would be impossible to convey the extent of the anxiety and confusion she was feeling right now. So she simply embraced her father, and then begged him to change the subject.

*

Living just minutes from his office, Adam had forgotten how frustrating it was to drive in the rush hour, particularly on a stretch of orbital motorway around one of the most traffic choked cities in the world. Through the long periods of stop start driving – stationary to thirty or forty miles per hour and back to stationary within a few hundred yards – he kept glancing at the mobile phones lying on the passenger seat.

It felt wrong to cut off all contact with Katy. Worse than that, it felt cruel.

Going back over their conversation, he regretted not finding out more about DI Branning's visit. What had he asked her? Had there been any new developments?

And this journalist: how on earth had she found them?

Guided by the satnav, he funnelled off the M25 at junction eighteen and slowly progressed through a prosperous-looking area busy with traffic. Holly's Lexus was no doubt nearby, but he didn't bother trying to spot it.

A couple of roundabouts and a short stretch of dual car-riageway led him to Ebury Road, a mostly residential street of modest semi-detached and terraced houses. About halfway along he spotted a single-storey building with a sign for Brayson Engineering. All the lights were off, and the three parking bays at the front were empty.

Adam slotted the Peugeot into one of them. He got out, grateful for some fresh air. He had both phones, and thought again about speaking to Katy, only to dismiss the idea. Get this done first.

He called Jay, using the only number programmed into the phone. 'I'm here.'

'Okay. At the end of the road you go left, through to the High Street. Then left again, towards the traffic lights. You want a pub called The Bull.'

Adam walked as he listened, quickly reached the corner and saw the lights of the High Street a short distance away.

'Go in and buy a drink. Stay at the bar if you can. I'm hoping you'll be served by a tall black guy with a bald head and glasses. That's my man, Dex.'

'What if I'm not?'

'Then wait till you can get his attention. Don't use my name – just say you're Holly's friend.'

Adam snorted. 'That's the code word, is it?' No response from Jay, so he said, 'Whereabouts are you two?'

'We've just driven along the High Street. There's a guy in a car, sat outside another business of ours, and I don't like the look of him. As far as I can see, no one's watching the pub, but there could be someone inside. Be careful.'

The call ended, and Adam shoved the phone into his pocket. All of a sudden he felt scared, out of his depth. Transferring that fear into anger, he told himself Jay was just trying to keep him on his toes.

And like they'd said, no one knew who he was. *I'm not in any danger*: that was the mantra he repeated to himself as he entered the High Street. It clearly dated back centuries, and had only a single lane of one-way traffic, which was queuing for the lights that Jay had mentioned. By now most of the shops had closed, but there were various bars and restaurants in sight, and therefore plenty of people about. It caught Adam off guard: he'd expected to be sent somewhere quiet.

He spotted the pub in what looked like a mock-Tudor building, next to a clothing store. He walked towards the junction and crossed the road, darting between a couple of stationary cars before the lights changed. The pub's stained-glass windows gave little clue as to what was inside, so Adam steeled himself and pushed the door open.

CHAPTER SIXTY-THREE

It was a locals' pub, that much was evident from the looks Adam received when he walked in. The decor was gloomy, with a lot of wood panelling, maroon wallpaper and a dark green carpet. The partition that once divided the saloon bar from the public bar had been removed, but that seemed to be the limit of its gentrification.

There were about thirty patrons, spread around an assortment of vinyl seated booths, small rustic tables and a row of creaky wooden stools. Rock music was playing at one end, which was home to a dart board and a couple of fruit machines.

Adam made for a gap at the bar, squeezing between a couple of the stools. A young woman with multiple piercings turned from dropping coins into the till and nodded a greeting. 'Yes?'

'Uh… just a Coke, please.'

There were no other staff in sight, and he felt his stomach lurch. Was Dex not working tonight? Had Adam misheard the instructions in some way?

He paid for the Coke, took a sip and half turned, taking in the people around him. There were two solitary drinkers at the bar, both male and elderly; four young guys at a table, laughing about a game of football; three middle-aged women sharing a large plate of nachos in one of the booths; next to them, a young couple glowering at their empty glasses, as if they'd argued over whose round it was.

Then he heard movement behind the bar; a man who fitted the description of Dex emerged from a doorway, carrying a tray of clean glasses. His gaze swept along the bar, registered Adam as a newcomer, then moved on.

Adam took a gulp of Coke, while reaching for the change he'd just been given. Realising it would look odd to drain the glass too quickly, he caught the barman's attention and asked for some peanuts.

'Sure.' Dex snatched up a packet and placed it on the bar. 'One pound ten.'

While sorting the coins in his palm, Adam mumbled, 'I'm, er, Holly's friend.'

'What's that?' Dex leaned in, a little aggressively.

The music was too loud to be subtle. Adam didn't want to shout, so he mouthed the single word: 'Holly.'

The barman frowned. Adam deflated again.

'You're Dex, though? Because Jay—'

'Too right!' Dex said, deliberately cutting him off. Before he turned away, his eyes flashed a warning.

Adam picked up the peanuts, wrestled them open and poured a few into his hand. *Super nonchalant*, he told himself. *Nothing to see here...*

Dex disappeared into the back, ignoring one of the men at the bar who was signalling with a five-pound note. He returned with a Tesco's carrier bag, apparently full of groceries.

'Here we go.' He handed the bag to Adam, plucked the receipt from the top and held it in front of Adam's nose. 'This all right?'

Adam had no choice but to study the slip of paper. A message had been scrawled in pen: *Young couple, here for hours, not drinking – might be Russian?*

Adam nodded, and had to clear his throat. 'Er, yes, thanks.'

His hand trembled as he took the receipt. He swung the bag off the bar, the plastic handles immediately digging into his fingers. There were bananas and a multipack of crisps on top, and clearly something heavy beneath them.

Dex was already moving to the next customer. Adam suddenly felt like an actor propelled into the limelight for the first time. All he had to do was walk out of the pub, carrying the shopping that had been put by for him. Could he do it naturally enough not to draw attention to himself?

Six steps to the door. A step back, to open it. The bag dragging his arm down: *Christ, what if it splits?* Then a clumsy move as he went through the doorway, trying to support the bag with his other hand and stumbling as the door struck his hip.

But now he was outside. In the clear. A few cars rumbling past, so no chance to cross the road. He started back towards the side street, Bury Lane. The bag was clutched tight to his chest, and he could feel his heart pummelling. But he had nothing to fear. He'd done it, hadn't he?

There was a break in the traffic coming up, caused by a bus pulling in to a stop. Although it was a one-way street, Adam reflexively glanced over his shoulder and saw the young man from the pub, dashing across the road in front of a slow-moving car. The woman was hurrying along the pavement behind him.

It couldn't be a coincidence.

They were on his tail.

His first impulse was to speed up, but even if he managed to sprint along Bury Lane, the man would easily catch him before he reached the car.

And he might have a gun.

The growl of an engine gave him an idea. The bus was preparing to pull out. Adam slowed his pace and tried to act as if nothing was wrong. By turning his head slightly, he could see that the man was now almost parallel with him.

Then the bus was rumbling past, and for a second the man had no sight of him, and no opportunity to cross. Adam broke into a run and went left at the next corner, following a much wider road up a gentle hill. The contents of the bag were jolting against his chest, and slowing him down; it was tempting to ditch the bag, but then all this would be in vain – and it still wouldn't guarantee his escape.

He had no idea where he was going, except that it was in the opposite direction to his car. He had to assume the woman was close behind, though he couldn't risk turning to look. Rather than outrunning her, he needed to hide.

Up ahead the road diverged at a mini-roundabout, with some sort of municipal building on the right. He followed the road round to the left, drawn by the darkness of the yards at the rear of the retail units. Most had cars parked in them, and there were plenty of commercial waste bins, but they offered only superficial concealment.

The panic was expanding in his chest like a balloon, adding extra pressure to his heart and lungs. He couldn't run like this for much longer.

A couple of teenage boys were ambling towards him, and weren't going to move aside. He darted round them, and caught a glimpse of the girl, further back than he expected; she was half-turned and gesturing, presumably to the young man. Was she urging him to go the other way and cut Adam off?

He faltered, just for a second, and noticed a builders' truck parked in one of the yards. It had a flat bed with drop sides, and he could see a cement mixer and a couple of stepladders in the back.

Adam dashed towards it and ran round past the cab, lifted the bag above his head and tried to set it down quietly inside the truck. He jammed his foot against one of the wheels, grabbed the side panel and scrambled over. He landed with a thud, but hoped the sound would be obscured by passing traffic.

The truck bed was covered in a layer of sand and grit. He felt it digging into his cheeks as he flattened his body and lay still, praying that the woman hadn't seen where he'd gone.

A moment later there was a lull in the traffic, and he heard running footsteps, which slowed, then stopped. Adam held his breath. There was enough light to make out a few bricks lying next to the cement mixer. If need be, he might have to use one as a weapon.

The whine of a motorcycle wiped out all other sounds; as it faded he heard voices nearby: an urgent question, asked by a woman in a language he didn't understand, and a reply from a man, in accented English, 'Lost him. Fuck it!'

He couldn't hear what was said next, but had the impression that they were walking away. Adam was still too frightened to move, until he realised that at any moment the truck's owner might appear, and perhaps drive off with him in the back.

Cautiously he raised his head and peered at the pavement. There didn't seem to be anyone loitering nearby, so he retrieved the bag and climbed out. He brushed off his clothes, hoping he didn't look too dishevelled.

So Jay hadn't been exaggerating. Adam dug out the phone he'd been given, and when Jay answered, he said, 'Where are you?'

'On the move. Why?'

'I was followed out, by a young couple. Russians, your friend Dex thinks. I managed to lose them, but I need a way back to my car. They might still be in the High Street.'

He described the route he'd taken, and Jay said, 'Carry on the way you were going, and you'll come back round to those traffic lights. There's an estate agents' over the road, and at one end there's what looks like a doorway. It's actually a passage that cuts through to Ebury Road. I take it they don't know where you parked?'

'No.' It was a good point. Hopefully the Russians would assume that Adam had been heading towards his car when he ran, rather than drawing them away from it. 'What next?' he asked.

'Back to the M25, and head for the Slough Trading Estate.'

'Oh, bloody hell.'

'Last favour, Adam. Once we're there I'll get the stuff and you can go.'

Adam sighed. 'What's the address?'

'Uh uh. No satnav this time. Just follow the signs and call me when you're there.'

CHAPTER SIXTY-FOUR

Zoe arrived at around six, to the children's delight. Katy's dad had insisted on cooking risotto for them all, which they ate in the dining room, and the conversation stayed light and easy – once Katy had conjured up an appropriate explanation for Adam's absence.

'There's a problem at work, and after missing yesterday he's trying to earn brownie points.'

'It's not his boss he should be worrying about,' Laura muttered, only for Clive to hiss her into silence: 'We've had that conversation.'

'He'll be here soon.' Katy was still saying that as six-thirty came and went, and her parents were quietly seething. They were deliberately delaying their departure, and by seven she'd had enough. Manoeuvring them into the kitchen, she said, 'You don't need to stay on my account. Zoe's here. We'll be fine.'

'It's not just that,' Laura said, her jaw tightening with disapproval.

'I know. But we both agreed to get things back to normal as soon as possible, and sometimes that means Adam has to work late. Okay?'

Although they didn't look convinced, they drew the children close for a lavish farewell, complete with the promise of more treats at the weekend. Clive suggested swimming.

'Or ten pin bowling?' Laura said.

'Let's do both!' Clive only grinned when Katy rolled her eyes at him.

'Can't we go tomorrow?' Dylan asked.

'Not really. We have to work,' Clive said.

'And you might have school,' Laura pointed out.

Groaning, Dylan turned to his sister for solidarity, but she shrugged. 'I'd like to go back to school tomorrow.'

Both then looked at Katy. 'Actually, I think that would be a good idea.'

After her parents left, the children returned to the living room, where Zoe had a game of Monopoly under way. Katy recalled how she had tried to interest them in playing it the previous winter, when they'd declared that it was 'boring' and 'rubbish'. Under Zoe's watchful eye, they rapidly turned into cutthroat tycoons and loved every second of it.

Katy declined an invitation to join in. 'You don't mind if I slope off for a bit?' she asked. 'I've got some stuff to do on the computer.'

Zoe smiled. 'No problem at all.'

Holly had an anxious wait, trying to make sense of only half a conversation.

'Is he all right?' she hissed, looking at Jay in the rear-view mirror, but he gestured for quiet.

She felt a twist of resentment. *I rode to your rescue, and now you keep telling me to shut up?*

She thought it strange that they'd left so quickly. After a circuit of the High Street, she'd passed the pub just as Adam emerged. Holly hadn't seen him, but Jay, crouching on the back seat, said, 'He's got it.'

Holly had expected them to rendezvous nearby, but instead Jay urged her to make for the M25. 'The next stop's Slough. Let's go.'

She hadn't questioned the decision until the minutes ticked past and still there was no message from Adam. Now, finally, he was speaking to Jay, and it seemed as though something had gone wrong.

After giving Adam the next location, Jay dropped the phone on to the seat and said, 'He was followed from the pub.' He punched his thigh. 'Shit!'

'But he got away?' The car swerved a little as she stared at the mirror. 'He's all right?'

'Yep, and he's got what I need. So fast as you can now, please?'

'I'm doing eighty-five.' The evening traffic was thinning out nicely, and the M4 junction wasn't far away. 'I assume you don't want me getting pulled over?'

'No. But time's running out.' Brooding, he muttered, 'And if I don't get this sorted, there won't be a place on earth I can hide.'

Holly said nothing. She wanted to see if Jay made any comment about Adam's safety – or her own. But the intense young man in the back seat remained silent, his gaze distant, even haunted, as he watched the streetlamps strobing past.

Holly sighed. After the four-year nightmare of her relationship with Paul, a building contractor from Essex, she'd sworn that she would never again succumb to any form of coercion or abuse – and she most certainly included deceit as a form of abuse.

At no point in the past two days would she have put Jay in the same category as Paul, despite the many crimes to which he'd freely admitted.

Now, though, she was beginning to wonder.

Katy took the iPad up to her bedroom, shut the door and logged straight into Adam's Hotmail. She felt no guilt or shame; just dread.

Anything incriminating and he'll have deleted it, she was telling herself. He's not stupid.

But maybe he was. Or careless, at least. Because the first thing she saw was Holly's name in a message at the top of his inbox.

In fact, there were several emails from her. She clicked on the top one and saw a chain of communications. She scrolled to the bottom and read the first message.

Adam, are you there?
Reply to me as soon as you get this. VERY IMPORTANT!

She sat back, stunned. After a few seconds she'd recovered enough to read Adam's response, and then the succession of messages that followed.

Her reaction was the same as Adam's. This was crazy. How the hell could this woman know anything about their ordeal, unless she was in some way connected to it?

She checked the Sent folder, and found that after Holly's final email Adam had pushed for more information, presumably without success – unless he had deleted a subsequent email, or switched to using the phone.

Was that why he'd taken the old mobile this morning? At the time she'd been touched, viewing it as an indication of his concern for her. It hadn't been anything of the sort.

The Skyway Hotel, Dunstable. That must be where he'd gone, either in search of answers, or perhaps just for a huge celebratory fuck with his former girlfriend...

She shut her eyes, muffled a sob by clamping a hand over her mouth, and her mind seemed to wander away for a time; to grieve, almost.

She was slowly crawling back when the bedroom door blew open and Dylan raced in. 'Zoe asked if we're meant to have baths or showers, and Freya said yes, because it's nearly bedtime, but I don't want a bath and I'm not tired!'

'Are you sure about that?' Katy produced a smile, but she could see that he had registered the tears, and was staring at her in alarm.

'I want Daddy to come home.'

'I know.' All evening she'd been lying quite glibly, but right now it was beyond her. She rose, shooing him out of the room. 'Have a shower, and you can stay up a bit later than normal.'

'A lot later.'

'A *bit* later. And only if there's no cheekiness!' She grabbed him as she said it, tickling him beneath the arms, and his squeal was both laughter and a protest.

Somehow it took more than half an hour to get them showered and ready for bed. It was when he had put on his pyjamas and joined them on the landing that Dylan's mood suddenly nosedived again.

'Where's Daddy? I'm not going to bed until Daddy comes home!'

Freya didn't join in, though her expression indicated that she felt just as strongly.

'He might be late,' Katy said. 'But you can watch a DVD or something for half an hour.'

'Under a duvet?' Freya said.

'And have chocolate?'

'Don't push it, Dylan.'

'Will you watch with us?' Freya asked Zoe, who was observing the negotiations from a polite distance.

'Happy to, but bedtime when your mum says – and no arguing.'

Her stern look at Dylan met none of the usual resistance. Katy said, 'Go and choose something. I just need to speak to Zoe.'

She retreated into her bedroom. Zoe followed, instantly serious. 'Is it Adam?'

'How did you…?'

'You've been stalling for a couple of hours. He doesn't strike me as someone who'd put work before his family.'

'He's not at work.' Shamefully, she confessed: 'He phoned me this afternoon, and admitted that he'd gone somewhere else. He wouldn't tell me anything, just begged me to trust him.'

'Okay.' Zoe's eyes narrowed. 'But this isn't to do with what happened Sunday?'

Katy nodded, and picked up the iPad. 'Do you know about the messages on Adam's phone?'

'DI Branning briefed me. A woman called Holly.'

'I came in here to check Adam's emails.' She swiped at the screen and brought up the Hotmail page. 'It felt horrible. Like I'm spying on him.'

Zoe said gently, 'In the circumstances, I don't think that's unreasonable.'

'It's not.' Katy sniffed. 'I think I've found out where they are.' She handed Zoe the iPad. 'And Holly knows about Sunday.'

CHAPTER SIXTY-FIVE

Holly left the M25 at junction fifteen and took the M4 towards Slough. Jay hadn't said a word, or barely even moved for about ten minutes. When she saw the sign for the trading estate coming up, she made her way across to the inside lane. Only then did he jerk into life.

'Not this junction. The next one's better for where we're going.'

So he said, but when they came off at junction seven, passed a couple of car dealerships and entered the estate via Dover Road, Jay seemed confused by his surroundings. 'All these bloody roads look the same.'

'But you've been here before?'

'Only once. And not at night.'

He leaned forward, peering at the map on the satnav screen. Directed her to take a left, and then a right, and they promptly came to a dead end.

As she did a swift three-point turn, Holly said, 'Was it Xavier who told you about this place?'

'No. We found it by following one of Voronov's guys for a couple of weeks.'

Holly was glad to hear that. Her own conclusion, from what Jay had told her, was that Xavier was a classic double agent, and had been deceiving Maggie from the start. 'But you still don't know for sure that they'll be here?'

'We took a good long look at his operations.' Jay sounded moderately offended. 'As well as the bolthole in Forest Row, he's got an estate in Scotland, penthouses in Manchester and Chelsea and a mansion in Virginia Water. This is the only suitable place for what he'll be doing – and he doesn't know that I know about it.'

But if they aren't there? Holly chose not to say it, since her preferred answer was unlikely in the extreme: *Then we'll just have to go home and forget all about it.*

It turned out they should have gone further before making the right turn. He directed her to a service road on what seemed to be the estate's western perimeter. At this time of the evening many of the units were closed up, the car parks deserted, but some were not. Huge lorries continued to rumble back and forth, and Holly wondered at Voronov's nerve to commit torture or murder in such surroundings.

Slowing to let a delivery van out, she thought she heard Jay's phone vibrate. She checked the mirror and saw him staring at the display; he did something and the phone was silent again. He looked up, caught her gaze and seemed to flinch.

'What was that?'

'Nothing.' He lurched forward, grabbing the headrests, and she jerked away, fearing he was about to lash out. A hand jabbed between the seats.

'Park at this one, on the right.'

A juddering breath escaped her, and she felt absurdly relieved. Of course he wasn't going to hurt her. Jay wasn't anything like Paul. Yes, there was a coldness that hadn't been present before, but that was understandable, given what lay ahead of him this evening.

She turned into the car park for a long, two-storey redbrick building that seemed to be divided into four or five units. The car park was screened by a line of trees and bushes, and Jay directed her into a particular space, offering them a discreet view of a warehouse across the road.

Switching off the engine, she glanced from side to side and checked her mirror. There were half a dozen cars parked in the vicinity, but no one in sight.

'Are we here? I mean, is that the place?'

'Yeah.'

She could have guessed by his body language, the way he had tensed as he leaned forward again, while simultaneously crouching, almost kneeling in the footwell.

The warehouse was a grey square box, about sixty feet wide and deep and perhaps twenty feet high, with a door and a row of narrow windows at the front. The left side of the building wasn't visible from here, but on the right-hand side there was a much larger roller door.

There was no light coming from the interior, and no vehicles parked outside. 'Looks empty,' she said.

'Yeah. Either because it is, or because that's how they want it to seem.' He gestured towards the front. 'That glass is what-do-you-call it…?'

'Opaque?'

'Yeah.' A moment later the suspension creaked; a click as he opened the door.

'Where are you going?'

'Reconnaissance.'

'But what about Adam? Don't you have to wait…?'

'I'll be back before he gets here.'

The door shut as a thought came to mind: *Adam doesn't yet know where 'here' is.*

Holly twisted in her seat to catch Jay walking fast and disappearing between a couple of the trees, heading away from the warehouse. From that direction it would take quite a detour to reach it, she thought, but perhaps he knew something she didn't.

That produced an involuntary shiver.

What was he really up to?

Adam followed the signs for the trading estate and parked in a McDonald's car park. It was almost eight o'clock.

He called Jay. The phone rang a couple of times, then went dead. Adam was immediately worried. What was happening that meant Jay couldn't answer?

He started to repeat the call, then decided to wait a couple of minutes. He could do with a breathing space.

He desperately wanted to speak to Katy, but feared her reaction, especially as he couldn't yet admit to what he was doing. When he called her, it should be to tell her he was on his way home… where he would beg her forgiveness, and hope that their marriage survived the pressure he had put upon it.

The bag of shopping caught his eye. He might as well check what was in it: he'd look pretty stupid if it only contained groceries.

He took out the bananas and crisps, and then a pack of five oranges and some cookies. At the bottom of the bag was a box of Rice Krispies. And that was it.

Just groceries. Everything looked brand new and genuine. The cereal box was sealed, and rattled convincingly when he touched it. Only when he picked it up did he register that it was far too heavy.

Would Jay be angry that he'd looked inside?

Did Adam really care?

He prised open the lid and found a bag of cereal, scrunched over but open. He took it out and found, buried amongst the cereal and wrapped in clear plastic, a Glock handgun and a box of 9 mm ammunition.

The weight of it in his hand came as a shock. It was the first time he had ever held a firearm. Had this gun already taken lives?

Whether it had or not, if a police car were suddenly to roll up beside him, he would go to prison. The stakes were as high as they could be – and while Adam had always known and accepted that, theoretically, he now understood it viscerally, in his gut.

People were going to die this evening, and for all Jay's assurances to the contrary, Adam might be one of them.

He noticed something else: a fat envelope at the bottom of the box. It wasn't sealed, so he tipped the contents on to the seat. There was a wad of twenty-pound notes tied up with an elastic band, plus a passport and a credit card which, when he studied them closely, had been issued in the past month to a Mr Jack Harper. The picture in the passport was Jay's.

Revenge, and then escape. Adam wondered if Maggie and Roger had been as thorough in their contingency planning, or whether it was just Jay.

He put everything back as he'd found it, placed the shopping bag on the passenger seat and picked up the phone. So now, a choice: try Jay's number again, or toss the bag out of the car and drive straight home to a wife and children who loved and needed him more than ever…

Then the phone rang in his hand. It was Jay: 'Are you there?'

'Yes. Why didn't you answer?'

'Busy. Now listen – here's where you need to go…'

CHAPTER SIXTY-SIX

Jay walked to the far end of the car park, keeping his head low while he checked the buildings for CCTV. He found a spot on the corner where there was no one in sight, but he could still see the warehouse, some fifty or sixty yards away. His neck was stiff and he stretched, gasping a little as he aggravated the wound beneath his arm. He probably should have got Holly to put a fresh dressing on it at the hotel, but it had slipped his mind.

The night was mild and still, but he was struck by the amount of noise: the drone of distant traffic, the roar of lorries on the trading estate, the clatter of a train and even a high-pitched whine from some kind of industrial drill. Given the location of the warehouse, it was unlikely that anyone would hear gunshots from inside.

Or screams.

The number he called was the one that Maggie had used to contact Xavier, who had supposedly betrayed his boss. If that were true, he would be dead by now, or at least in no fit state to answer his phone.

And yet here he was: 'Who is this?'

'Guess.' Jay kept a lid on his rage. 'So you sold us out?'

'*Non.* I drew you in.'

Jay felt sick. 'Was everything a lie?' he asked.

'Everything important. Voronov is a brother to me. I would not betray him to English scum.'

Silence, then a new voice. Jay had never heard Voronov speak, but the quiet authority left him in no doubt as to the man's identity. The Russian accent had been softened by almost two decades in the west, and he spoke with the kind of lazy drawl associated with the upper middle classes.

'You are the one who calls himself Jay?' A chuckle. 'You know, your mother wishes to see you.'

'I don't think so.' Jay felt his stomach tighten, an urge to double over as if winded by a punch.

'Oh yes. I am keeping her alive to be with you one more time. If you care for her, you will want an end to her suffering.'

'If I show my face, you'll kill me as well as her. And that's not what she would want.'

'You disappoint me, Jay. A son with courage would face up to his responsibility. Where are you?'

The question caught him off balance, as it was intended to do. Jay took an uneasy glance over his shoulder, as Voronov said, 'You sent someone to The Bull?'

'That's right. An acquaintance of mine got the stuff I needed to move on. A new identity, passport, money—'

'Not enough money.'

'No. Ideally I'd have more, just like – ideally – I'd track you down and kill you.' A pause. 'But I know you're too well protected. So I can't get at you, and I can't go to the cops, because I killed Brian Kirby. But I do have something to trade.'

Voronov didn't laugh, as Jay half expected: he only sighed.

'No trade. Deliver yourself, and I will make the end come quickly.'

'Listen to me. There's a family that got caught up in this. A mum and dad, two little kids. We stashed them in the cellar. Your boys didn't find them Sunday night because they found a crawl space and hid beneath the floor.'

He paused again. Encouraged by the lack of an interruption, he said, 'They were with Carole for hours. She talked about you.'

'Carole did not know my—'

'We told her,' Jay cut in, and he sensed the fury it caused: a man like Voronov wasn't to be interrupted. 'We told her who you really are, and then we put her in the cellar with this family.'

Silence for a moment. When Voronov spoke next he sounded slightly perplexed, as if he couldn't work out Jay's angle. 'Then the police will already know, too?'

'They don't. I managed to get a message to the family, warning them to keep quiet.'

'Why? How?'

'I had their phones. I took the numbers before I got away. I knew I might need leverage over you.'

'And this you would exchange… for your mother's quick death?'

'Plus a promise not to look for me.' Another confused silence, so Jay snorted. 'Hey, if you don't think that's enough, you can always bung me a couple of million quid.'

Voronov ignored the attempt at humour. 'This is no trade,' he said calmly, 'because we already know who they are.'

'Bullshit.'

'Adam and Katy Parr. Children Freya and Dylan. A home in Lindfield, East Sussex.' Voronov gave a caustic little laugh, and ended the call.

'Fuck!' Jay only just restrained himself from hurling the phone into the road.

Maggie or Roger must have given up enough detail to trace the family. Jay couldn't bear to think what might have been done to them to extract that information.

It was a blow, but not a fatal one. He wasn't going to give up now.

He phoned Adam, who sounded aggrieved. 'Why didn't you answer?'

'Busy. Now listen – here's where you need to go…'

*

Holly found herself back in the world of Paul, which was a nasty, squalid place to be. A place she'd sworn never to revisit.

He had been a pincher. Usually with his fingers, but not always. As a (self-titled) Hard Working Self-Made Man, he was proud of his viciously strong grip. But on one occasion near the end – before she finally emerged from the fog of insanity and fled from a house that she owned in order to be away from him – Paul had used pliers.

He'd been raging about her inability to lose weight, disgusted by her 'bingo wings', and to Paul the appropriate punishment was to fix the pliers to the soft, loose flesh of her underarm and squeeze until she felt the metal plates make contact—

A noise caused her to cry out. Somehow Jay had materialised by the side of the car and grabbed the door handle. She took a deep breath to quell the panic and unlocked the door.

He climbed into the back once again, barely acknowledging her presence. He looked immensely pissed off. Perhaps she was just being unduly influenced by a lot of dark and painful memories, but Holly couldn't help thinking: *This really isn't fun anymore.*

She gestured towards the warehouse. 'Is Voronov not there?'

'Dunno,' Jay said brusquely. 'I couldn't risk getting too close.'

'Oh.' In that case, what was he so unhappy about? 'Is Adam—'

'I've spoken to him. He'll be here in a few minutes.'

He slumped back in the seat, chewing on a fingernail with a disconsolate air. Something had happened to turn his mood, and it struck her that he hadn't gone off to carry out reconnaissance. It had been to make a phone call.

They were silent for a couple of minutes. Then he reached out and gently touched her arm. 'Sorry about this. I owe you a hell of a lot, no matter—'

His body seemed to spasm as his attention was caught by something across the road. Holly followed his gaze to the warehouse and saw that the big side door was rolling up. A Range

Rover emerged and drove towards them, then took a right in the direction of the motorway.

'How many inside?' Jay said, his voice thrumming with excitement.

'Not sure. Maybe three?'

'That's what I thought. Two up front, one in the back.'

'Where do you think they're going?'

'Dunno. As long as they don't return any time soon.' He clenched his fist and shook it, victoriously, though all Holly could see now was Paul, his muscles pumped, getting ready to hit her. 'My chances just got a hell of a lot better.'

CHAPTER SIXTY-SEVEN

After reading the email exchange between Holly and Adam, Zoe suggested that she would have to notify DI Branning. Katy couldn't disagree, though she was mortified by the implications of her husband sneaking away to meet his ex partner.

That Zoe was so sensitive to her feelings only made it worse, somehow. She remained with Katy while she made the call, and kept it strictly factual.

'He's going to get a local officer to check it out,' she reported. 'High priority, since Adam isn't answering his phone. We should hear something this evening.'

Am I going to learn that a cop walked in on the two of them in bed? Although unspoken, the thought was so vivid that Zoe might have read her mind: she clicked her tongue and said, 'In the meantime I'm not going to speculate, and I don't think you should, either.'

'But it's agony,' Katy whispered, the admission slipping out before she could stop it.

'I know. DI Branning asked that you keep trying Adam's phone.'

Katy picked up the landline and hit redial. 'Still no answer.'

Zoe spread her hands. 'All we can do is wait. I'll put the kids to bed, if you like. You could even get some sleep yourself, and I'll wake you when there's news.'

'It's only just gone eight o'clock. But you'd be a star if you could persuade them to turn in.'

'No problem. Let me sit with them for five minutes.'

'Thank you.' Katy yawned. 'I think I'll make some hot chocolate. Would you like a cup?'

Zoe's eyes lit up. 'Haven't had that for years. I'd love one.'

Adam tried to memorise the directions Jay had given him, but years of reliance on the satnav had made him lazy. He took a couple of wrong turns and then, because the Lexus was quite well concealed, nearly drove straight past the car park.

He pulled up alongside them. When Holly met his eye, he thought she looked uncharacteristically solemn, perhaps even a little scared.

Jay got out and moved round to the back of the Lexus, opened the boot and stood there, waiting.

That's me told, Adam thought, nursing his resentment as he picked up the bag.

'Got it all?' Jay asked as Adam stepped into sight. 'You did well.'

Adam grunted, thrust the bag at the other man and said, 'Why didn't you stick around to help me? I nearly got caught.'

Jay grinned, but without much humour. 'Let's just say I had complete faith in you.'

He emptied the bag into the boot, but his expression changed when he saw the cereal box was open. He turned slowly to regard Adam.

'I wanted to make sure I'd collected something with actual value.'

'Right.' Grim-faced, Jay stuck the envelope in his pocket, returned the gun and ammunition to the bag and tucked it under his arm. As he got into the back seat, he nodded at Adam. 'Join us.'

Adam stood his ground for a moment, before reluctantly climbing into the front passenger seat. Holly looked from one to the other. 'Was it wise to be arguing out there?'

'We weren't,' Jay said. He was hunched over, doing something with the Glock. Adam exchanged another glance with Holly, and again had the sense that all was not well.

'So is this the place?' Adam asked. 'And Voronov's here?'

'Yep,' Jay muttered, distracted by his task.

'Well, we don't know for sure,' Holly said. 'About ten minutes ago a Range Rover came out of that warehouse with three men inside.'

'And you think he only has four or five guys in total?' he asked Jay.

'For this kind of stuff, yeah. There's plenty more he can get for surveillance, and minor tasks – like the ones posted to watch our businesses – but hired killers who are trustworthy and reliable, they're not easy to find.'

'Just one or two left inside, then?' Holly said.

'Hopefully,' Jay agreed. 'Plus Xavier. And Voronov himself.'

'If he's there,' Adam said.

'He will be, if that's where Maggie is. He'll keep her alive until he finds me. He'll want her to watch me die.'

'You don't know that.' Adam couldn't hide his revulsion, but Holly gave voice to what they were both thinking.

'Do you say that because it's what you would do?'

Adam tensed. It seemed like a bold question to ask of a man who was currently loading a gun.

'You mean, do I judge him by my own standards?' Jay pondered. 'I dunno. Maybe.'

'Look, why don't you call the police?' Adam suggested. 'Do it anonymously, if need be. It's crazy to take them on alone.'

'You can come and help if you want.' He knew Adam would baulk at the idea, and snorted. 'Nah, this is something I've got to do. Right or wrong, live or die.'

Holly gave a tiny gasp, and Adam said, 'That's madness.'

'Yep.' Jay laughed, a little bleakly. 'Look, you two have been great, but I have one last favour. I want to give it twenty minutes or so, to make sure the guys that left are a fair distance away. When I go in, it's not gonna be more than ten minutes, either way. So I'm asking you to give me another thirty minutes of your time – and then, if I don't reappear, you can drive away and forget all about me.'

Adam was a little surprised when Holly didn't immediately agree. She glanced at him, a questioning look which seemed to say, *I suppose we could, couldn't we?*

Adam checked the time: almost eight-thirty. By nine he could be back on the road, and probably home before ten.

'Okay,' he said.

CHAPTER SIXTY-EIGHT

Zoe performed a near miracle, getting Dylan and Freya into bed without any quarrelling. Then she and Katy drank their hot chocolate at the dining room table and talked about families. Zoe loved children, she said, but only from the perspective of an auntie, or a friend; she couldn't see herself having kids of her own.

'Really? And how old are you?'

'Thirty-two next month.'

'Ooh, you're heading for the danger zone,' Katy joked. 'I know women who were adamant they didn't want them, and then it was like a switch being flicked.'

Dylan cried out once while they chatted, but he was sound asleep again by the time Katy had run up to check on him. She confessed to Zoe that she still had no idea whether to send them to school tomorrow – or what they should say about their absence.

'Perhaps another day at home wouldn't be a bad idea,' Zoe said. 'See how things play out?'

Katy knew she had to take the suggestion in the spirit it was intended, but the subtext carried a bitter sting. Would Adam even be home when the children woke up in the morning? How was his relationship with Holly going to affect them?

Zoe's phone rang while Katy was putting their mugs in the dishwasher. She'd been wondering whether to propose a glass of wine rather than another hot drink. Now she turned, squeezing her hands into fists. It was clear from Zoe's reaction that there was news of some kind.

After listening for half a minute, Zoe passed her the phone. DI Branning.

'Katy, I'll come straight to the point. There is a Holly Wolstenholme checked in at the hotel near Dunstable. She stayed last night and then extended for a second night. Unfortunately she's not in her room and didn't respond to a call over the PA system. There was also no sign of your husband, though I've asked my colleagues to wait at the hotel. They're going to check on the current guest list, and also take a look at the CCTV. Do you have a decent image of Adam to assist with that?'

'A picture…' Katy was struggling to process this information. *Adam must have met Holly, but instead of being in bed together, they'd gone out somewhere.*

'Of Adam?' Zoe saw her confusion. 'Did I see a recent one in the lounge? I'll take a photo of it on my phone and WhatsApp it to John.'

'Would they have gone for a meal or something?' Katy asked.

'Possibly. I'll ask what's in the locality.' Branning injected some energy into his voice. 'And try not to feel too despondent about this. I know it's worrying, but until we get an explanation—'

'His phone's still switched off. Why do that if he didn't have something to hide?' She was getting emotional; Zoe went to offer support but Katy waved her off. 'Do you know any more about the gang, and which of them might have been talking to Holly?'

'Not yet, I'm afraid.' Branning sounded chastened. 'I also read the riot act about this journalist, Ronnie Pierce, and every one of my team is adamant that there hasn't been a leak.'

'So what does that mean?'

'I don't know. Because I managed to spirit you away, there's only a restricted group that are aware of your involvement, and I trust them all. So either I'm incapable of spotting when one of them has lied to my face, or… well, maybe Pierce got her information some other way.'

'Like how?'

'From one of the gang, perhaps? Though I can't see why they would do that.' She heard a shout in the background, and he said, 'I've got to go. Call me if you hear anything, and I'll do the same.'

Katy returned the phone to Zoe, who said, 'Do you want me to stay and talk, or would you prefer some time alone?'

'You can stay here, that's fine.' Katy sat down, and reached for the iPad. 'But I need to check something.'

Jay was in the car for another fifteen minutes, but to Holly it felt like much longer. The atmosphere had turned unpleasant somehow, dominated by a tense, suspicious silence that none of them seemed willing to acknowledge.

It was probably to be expected in view of what Jay was about to do, but she was troubled by his behaviour, sneaking off for his so-called reconnaissance. And why had he been in such a hurry, back in Rickmansworth, to the point that they'd left Adam in danger, and yet now he was sitting here, stalling?

Finally, unable to contain her frustration, she said, 'I don't see that waiting makes much difference.'

Jay grunted. 'Eh?'

'Their Range Rover. If you don't know where it's going, you can't predict when it'll come back. Therefore another ten minutes, say, isn't any more or less likely than two hours from now. Is it?'

'Suppose not.'

Holly hadn't expected him to defer to her logic so readily, and said, 'Not that I'm pressuring you to go,' she said.

Adam nodded. 'There are better options than this. There must be.'

'Not for me,' Jay said darkly. 'I want answers. I want an end to this – for your sakes as well as mine. That's not gonna come from the cops, and if all I'm looking at is a life in prison, I'd rather take my chances here.' He checked his phone. 'Give me fifteen minutes. And don't, whatever you do, go anywhere near that building.'

'What if we hear gunshots?' Holly asked.

'*Especially* if you hear gunshots.' He forced a grin. 'Hey, for all I know the place could be empty, right?'

Holly nodded, but she thought: *You don't believe that.*

He got out, opened the boot again and collected the equipment he'd sent her to buy from a DIY store this morning: a crowbar, latex gloves, a Stanley knife and some plastic cable ties. Adam had also turned in his seat to watch, leaning close enough that she could feel his body heat. Holly felt a sudden, overwhelming rush of tenderness towards him.

This had been her dream from the start, the reason she'd bought into Jay's plan. A chance, if it came off, for her and Adam to be thrown together in adversity, at which point he would wake up to the truth: he needed her, and she needed him. The marriage to Katy had been a mistake – as had most, if not all, of her own prior relationships.

She'd been happy enough with Simon, who was probably the closest to Adam in terms of appearance and character. His calm, self-effacing manner had been so reassuring after the nightmare world of Paul. She'd been devastated by his sudden death in a car accident, and it wasn't really until this week that she had seen the truth. Simon had only ever been a pale facsimile of Adam; a little too reliable, a little too dull.

What Adam offered was a rebellious streak, an impulsive and somewhat fiery nature that made life interesting, without even the slightest risk that he would hurt her. In her fantasies they would go back to the hotel and spend the night together, discussing the practicalities of a new life in Canada, just her and Adam, with the kids visiting perhaps a couple of times a year…

Now those fantasies were evaporating; there was so much more going on, so much that she might have misjudged.

Nobody spoke as Jay put on some latex gloves, slipped the tools inside his coat, shut the boot, rapped his knuckles on the window in farewell and was gone.

Be careful what you wish for. That was the phrase that had come creeping into Holly's mind on several occasions over the past two days; now it was lit up and screaming like a digital billboard.

CHAPTER SIXTY-NINE

They clearly knew he was shit scared, but Jay didn't care. If anything, it probably helped – made them more inclined to be sympathetic. And if they were sympathetic, that hopefully meant they would do as he asked, and stick around.

Fifteen minutes, he'd said, but he intended to push that as much as he could. He didn't think they'd drive away on the dot of nine. They'd start debating it, and one of them – probably Holly, if he hadn't pissed her off too much – would argue that a few more minutes couldn't hurt.

It would come down to curiosity, as much as any sense of obligation towards him. That was what he counted on. And every minute carried Voronov's Range Rover a little closer to its destination…

Jay moved off in the same direction as last time, but continued well past the row of redbrick units before darting across the road and hurrying along the side of a warehouse almost identical to Voronov's. These units were the last ones on this part of the estate, and the service road at the rear was enclosed by a high chain-link fence, beyond which lay a patch of waste ground, overgrown with weeds and bushes. It was closer to the railway line here, judging by the noise. That was good news, too.

A few thin trees grew by the fence, like escapees from the wilderness beyond, and Jay decided they offered enough cover for him to hide his money, passport and his main phone. He didn't want all this stuff weighing him down, but nor did he feel comfortable leaving it with Holly and Adam.

Now he had his spare phone in a back pocket, along with the cable ties and the knife, and in his hands he carried the Glock and the crowbar. He was all set to go, though still he waited, counting off the seconds in his mind.

He tried to meditate, or at least blank out his thoughts, but it was hopeless. He felt feverish with excitement and fear. So much to do in the next few minutes; so much that could go wrong. He had only guesses about the number of people inside the warehouse. He knew nothing of the layout or where the occupants would be positioned. What he did have was an appreciation of Voronov's firepower, and knew the trouble he'd be in if the sustained shooting brought the police rushing to the scene, while Holly and Adam raced away.

Eight fifty-one: time to go. Holly was worrying him more than he'd have liked. He'd done his best to keep up the charm offensive, but after a day and a half the woman was really grating on him, especially now she was simpering over Adam.

Jay had seen at once that she didn't stand a chance, but clearly she was deluded. Still, that had served his purpose. It was probably only a matter of time until she worked out that Voronov was sending his men to deal with Katy and the kids. Maybe she would convince herself that only Katy would die: the poor bitch was in the grip of a fantasy about skipping away to a new life with Adam.

Jay didn't buy any of it. Voronov came from a country where blood feuds ran through the generations. Even if Freya and Dylan posed no threat to him as witnesses, he would want them eliminated – and in that scenario, Adam wouldn't be hooking up with anyone.

Not that they'd be getting a chance, if everything went to plan. As witnesses, they were far more dangerous to Jay than they were to Voronov – all the more so now that Adam had sneaked a look at his new passport.

Once Jay had dealt with the Russians, Holly and Adam would be the next to die.

Adam watched Jay until he was lost from sight, and only then became aware of his proximity to Holly. When she, too, turned away from the road, there was a second where he was convinced that she intended to pull him in for a kiss. Swiftly leaning away, he almost bumped his head on the door.

'So… nine o'clock, and then we leave?'

She nodded, but without much conviction. 'I suppose.'

'That's what he said. Whether he makes it out or not.'

'Do you think he will?'

'I don't know.' He visualised Jay tearing across the car park with armed Russians in pursuit, spraying gunfire into the road. 'We are horribly out of our depth here.'

'A lot of it's my fault. I'm sorry.'

Adam gave a start. 'You sound like you regret helping him.'

'You have to remember, I thought I was talking to you. I walked into that hotel, expecting to find you there, and instead there was this young, good-looking stranger, and he begged me to listen to him.' She shook her head, marvelling at the memory. 'I was so psyched up, disappointed, intrigued, excited – it was mental.'

She threw up her hands, just as Adam said, drily: 'And one thing led to another.'

That earned a sharp look. 'How did you know?'

'Actually, that's not what I meant.' He shook his head, incredulously. 'You didn't?'

'Why not? He seemed really cute. Can you believe he's only twenty-seven? And what a life! His father started out as an actual bank robber, sawn-off shotguns and everything. Blaggers, they were called. But honestly, if someone like Jay had been given the chances most of us take for granted, he could have ended up a CEO.'

'Well, he's certainly dishonest and ruthless enough for a busi-ness career. Are you sure you don't have Stockholm Syndrome?'

'I was never a prisoner.' Holly sounded wounded, though she then shrugged, a little hopelessly, and said, 'Though I'm starting to wonder how much he can be trusted.'

'What did I say to you?'

'Don't be lording it over me, Adam.'

'I'm not. Did something happen, while I was on my way here?'

'He's just been acting sort of strangely.' She described how he had left the car for a few minutes, ostensibly to check the warehouse. 'When he came back he was holding a phone, and said he'd spoken to you. But I just... I wondered if he had other calls to make, that he didn't want me to hear.'

'Calls to who?'

'How should I know?'

'But you've got a theory?'

'Not really. Just...' Her cheeks were bright red, and her eyes seemed to be shining with tears. 'When the Range Rover came out, it wasn't long after he'd got back. And he didn't seem very surprised to see it. If anything, he looked quite smug.'

'But how would he know...?' Adam had to pause, thinking furiously. 'Say he's in contact with Voronov... what would have persuaded the Russian to despatch half of his bodyguards away from where they're holding Maggie?'

'I suppose, with three people inside, it's going to be something that takes a while. For a really quick errand, you'd only send one or two people, wouldn't you?'

'Depends on the errand, surely?'

Holly said nothing, but then opened her mouth just as Adam hit on an idea: 'Unless he was drawing them away somewhere?'

'Yes.' She almost choked on the word, nodding rapidly as she cleared her throat. 'That's what I was thinking.'

He saw the horror on her face, and felt a deathly chill run along his spine.

'No,' he breathed. 'Tell me it's not that?'

CHAPTER SEVENTY

Jay started off lucky. Each of the units had a door at the back alongside a waste area, marked off with timber partitions, about eight feet high and home to a variety of dumpsters and other commercial waste bins. Security lights were mounted above each of the rear doors, but they were permanently lit rather than operating on sensors, which meant they posed little threat.

He was able to creep along the service road from one partition to the next, and then conceal himself with a good view of Voronov's building. It had only a couple of bins, and no discarded pallets or other loose waste. But there was a car parked at the back: a brand-new Jaguar XJR.

His heart seemed to stutter at the sight of it. Voronov was here, Jay was certain of that now.

There were a couple of ventilation grilles set into the wall, but no windows. As Jay studied the door, trying to calculate whether he could prise it open without making too much noise, his luck got better still.

The door opened.

The man who stepped out was about forty, tall and broad and unmistakably muscular beneath his dark suit. One of Voronov's principal bodyguards, Jay guessed. Invariably ex-military, and probably one of the men who attacked the farmhouse on Sunday night.

Jay held his breath as the man wandered over to the Jaguar and took out a cigarette. After lighting up he automatically relaxed and went to perch on the bonnet, only to swerve away as he remembered whose car it was. He took a casual look in both directions and then turned to stare at his own building. He must know he'd be in trouble if he was caught skiving.

It made Jay's life tricky. He had to opt for speed or stealth; he couldn't have both. And even with all the traffic noise, he didn't want to use the gun outside.

He realised there was a plane approaching, still low in the sky after take-off from Heathrow. He waited until the engine's roar was at its loudest and then crept out from behind the partition, half crouched with the crowbar in his right hand and the gun in his left.

He took a diagonal path across the space between the units, veering towards the rear fence to stay out of the bodyguard's peripheral vision. Satisfied that the plane was obscuring the sound of his footsteps, he sped up and reached the Jaguar. The bodyguard was another eight or nine feet further on. The man shifted position as he blew a stream of smoke into the cool night air. His other hand delved into his pocket, perhaps for a phone, and that was Jay's chance.

He leapt forward, two quick paces as his arm came up and back, then a third as he angled slightly to the right and swung hard and fast, his feet leaving the ground as he put his entire upper body into the strike, like a forehand winner in tennis.

The bodyguard had no time to move. The claw end of the heavy steel crowbar struck him on the temple and took him out so abruptly that Jay didn't get a chance to catch his body as it fell. The impact with the ground was louder than he would have liked, a thud as well as a metallic clatter as the man collapsed on to his own firearm.

Jay quickly knelt down and pulled some cable ties from his pocket. The bodyguard was deeply unconscious, with a dent in his skull and blood streaming from his wound, but Jay wasn't taking any chances. He wrenched the man's arms behind his back and bound his wrists together.

Poking from beneath his stomach was the unmistakeable folding stock of a Skorpion machine pistol. Jay dragged it clear of the body and checked it over. With a twenty-round magazine, and set to automatic, it was ideal for indiscriminate fire at fairly short range: a lot of fun to use, if you didn't care too much about the noise, or the mess.

Although Jay was tempted, he hid it from sight behind one of the bins, then moved towards the open door from the blind side. That little detour probably saved his life. As he reached the door and pulled it further out, another man stepped into view, squinting suspiciously at the yard.

With Jay suddenly in his face, one of them had to react instantly, or die. Jay rammed his gun into the man's belly and pulled the trigger. The man staggered backwards and fell, dropping the gun he'd been holding. Another Skorpion.

The element of surprise was lost now; nothing he could do about that. Jay switched the Glock to his right hand and fired again to make sure the man stayed down.

He was in a smallish room with a lot of metal shelving and a couple of benches, perhaps for maintenance work. A side door led to a rest area with a kitchenette, while another door straight ahead would take him into the main part of the warehouse.

He could see the room was brightly lit, and mostly empty, though there were a couple of vehicles parked inside: a Mercedes Sprinter panel van and a black Range Rover, identical to the one he'd seen earlier. He moved quickly but cautiously to the doorway, ducking back as he heard someone approaching.

It was Xavier De Vos, Voronov's right-hand man. He was of medium height, physically unimposing and stupidly not carrying a gun. Perhaps he'd assumed the bodyguards were arsing around, or perhaps he'd just acted without thinking, in the complacent belief that no one could seriously threaten them.

Jay ambushed him as he had the second bodyguard, but this time just drove his gun hand into Xavier's stomach, then butted him in the face as he crumpled. The Belgian stayed on his feet, so Jay spun him to face the warehouse and used him for cover, the gun pressed into his neck.

Xavier was choking on the blood pouring into his mouth, and his attempts at speech were unintelligible. Jay wasn't sure if he even knew who had attacked him.

He propelled Xavier towards the van, which offered him some cover on the left flank. He couldn't see any hazards to his right; no other rooms or hiding places.

It was the view up ahead that mattered. Beyond the vehicles, in the centre of the large open space, a cage had been constructed, like something for monkeys at a zoo. It was the shape of a cube, about twelve feet wide, with the latticework of metal bars forming six-inch squares.

Inside, there were two bodies, clad in what looked like rags, and covered in blood and bruises. One was Roger. He lay flat on the ground, on which a large black tarpaulin had been spread out. A slick of congealed blood surrounded his head and upper body, and most of it must have come from the gaping wound to his throat. The fatal wound.

The other prisoner, Maggie, was tied to a plain wooden chair. Slack and unmoving, her head was slumped down on her chest, and he could see where large clumps of hair had been torn from her scalp. What he couldn't tell was whether she was still alive.

CHAPTER SEVENTY-ONE

Katy went online with only a vague idea of what she was searching for. Zoe asked no questions; after slipping away to use the loo, she sat and browsed on her phone.

Ronnie Pierce didn't have a website. Her main focus was her Twitter page, which had plenty of updates, about half of which were retweets accompanied by brief, acerbic comments. She followed only a couple of hundred people, but had nearly twenty thousand followers.

Scrolling down, Katy found links to articles and interviews in the publications which Pierce had mentioned. She clicked on a few and scanned the stories; often there was a byline photo, and it was undoubtedly the woman who had come to her house this afternoon.

And yet, still she felt uneasy. If one of Branning's colleagues had leaked, why go to a feature writer based in London, rather than a news reporter? Unless there was money involved – a kickback from Pierce or whoever would publish the book. But that didn't sit well with Katy's impression of the officers who had helped them.

She'd remained on a magazine website, and idly clicked on a link to Ronnie's profile, which had a snazzy page of its own, with images and snippets of her other work for the site. One headline caught her eye: THE OLIGARCH'S DILEMMA.

She already knew not to expect balanced, insightful writing, and this was more of the same – a nonsensical puff piece that seemed to bemoan the lot of the lonesome, misunderstood Russian billionaire, exiled to London and forced to partake in a high society that was hungry for the investment but contemptuous of those who possessed such newly acquired wealth.

Perhaps because so much of it is *stolen* wealth, Katy thought. But Pierce hadn't shown any interest in that issue.

There were various unattributed quotes from supposed oligarchs, bitter at the snobbish attitudes of the British upper classes, but towards the end she referenced a couple of them by name, as examples of wealthy Russians who had elected to live quietly: 'men like Sergei Ledovskoy and Alexander Voronov, who recoil at the idea of owning a football club or a newspaper. You'll more likely find them sipping beer and watching cricket on a village green, wishing only to be respected in the country they have chosen to call their home.'

Alexander. She knew it was a common name, and yet even this tiny connection felt significant. She started a search, then wistfully glanced at the phone, praying once again that it would ring, and that it would be Adam.

This time it did. And it was.

Jay pushed Xavier forward, slamming his face against the bars. The Belgian screamed in pain and his legs started to give way. In a red mist of fury, Jay wanted to kick him to death, but instead he bore the man's weight, dragging him around to use as a shield. He felt sure Voronov was here, and the only hiding place was behind one of the vehicles.

A scuffing noise distracted him. Inside the cage, Maggie's right foot was brushing against the floor. Her head rose a few inches, enough for Jay to see the damage to her features.

She was unrecognisable. Beaten and smashed and torn, caked in blood and dirt, the wounds so large and inflamed that she probably couldn't see, or speak. A second or two was all she could manage, then she slumped down again.

'Where's Voronov?'

'Not here.' Xavier's voice was a cowardly squeal.

'Bullshit. I've been watching this place since I called you.'

'He left – in the Range Rover.'

Jay was about to lash out again, but hesitated. It wasn't impossible that Voronov had been one of the three men in the car, though he didn't think so.

More noise from the cage. This time the chair shifted on the tarpaulin. Maggie let out a weak but insistent groaning noise; it sounded like an attempt to communicate.

'Give me the keys,' Jay said.

When Xavier didn't respond, Jay pushed the gun harder into his neck, causing a shriek of pain. With his other hand he tapped the crowbar against the man's thigh, and heard the tinkling of metal in his pocket.

'Take them out, very slowly, or I'll put a bullet in your ear.'

'Okay, okay. I do this.'

His left arm dropped, his hand carefully easing into his pocket. At the same time he automatically glanced down, and his head turned a little, forcing Jay to shift position, trying to keep the barrel of the gun lodged against the Belgian's neck. But he also leant in the other direction, wanting to see that Xavier only had keys in there, and not a weapon.

His hand gave a spasm as he drew the keys out, and they fell to the ground with a tiny clatter. Xavier suddenly shoved his elbow into Jay's chest, wrenching himself free. He clearly didn't care about Jay's threat to shoot him, or perhaps reasoned that he had nothing to lose.

The Belgian wasn't a natural fighter but he was fast, and desperate. He got off a couple of weak blows, then snatched at the gun and jammed it upwards, trying to break Jay's wrist in the process. The only way for Jay to protect himself was by letting go of the gun, and he made a huge effort to hurl it across the floor, out of Xavier's range.

And he still had the crowbar, which the Belgian tried to grab, but this time he wasn't quick enough. Jay whipped it back and swung at Xavier's arm, causing him to flinch away, then he dummied a punch with his right hand and used the distraction to land a proper blow: jabbing the crowbar like a dagger into the other man's gut.

That took the fight out of him, but Jay wasn't satisfied. He started swinging wildly, and Xavier went down under a barrage of heavy impacts, at first trying to protect himself, and then in no state to do anything. Jay didn't register that the fight was over until a voice, barely audible, managed to form his name.

'Jay.'

He stopped, hunched over and exhausted, splattered with blood, and turned towards the cage. Maggie had lifted her head, and although her eyes were barely visible she must have been able to see something.

'Jay,' she said again.

But she wasn't looking at her son. She was trying to warn him.

He looked round. Voronov had emerged from behind the van, and he was holding a Skorpion machine pistol.

Adam watched Holly grow more agitated than he had ever seen her. His own urge to panic was becoming harder to resist, and he wasn't sure whether he could stay in control for much longer.

'It suddenly occurred to me – what if he's been manipulating us?' she said. 'Both of us, I mean. Getting us to wait here, in case he needs help to get away. But, in the meantime, if he wanted a decoy – something to offer to Voronov…'

'My family.' The understanding dropped on Adam like a rock, a crushing weight. 'When did they leave?'

'What? I don't—'

'Think, Holly! What time did you see them go past?'

'It was… probably around eight.'

According to the dashboard clock, it was a couple of minutes to nine. About an hour. At this time of night, with fast, clear roads all the way to Sussex…

It could be close.

He powered up his phone and stared at the screen, willing it to get a message through in time to save them, while praying fervently that he was wrong, and Holly was wrong, and those men were really heading somewhere else.

Holly gestured towards the phone. 'It might be dangerous to use that…'

'I don't give a toss.' He saw a cascade of missed calls from his home number and jabbed at the button to call back.

It answered almost instantly, which disorientated him, made him light-headed with relief.

'You're there?'

'Adam! Where are you? What's—'

'That doesn't matter. Katy, you have to listen. Are you and the kids at home?'

'Yes, and Zoe's here.'

'Zoe.' Another wave of relief. Zoe was a cop. His family weren't as vulnerable as he had feared.

'I've been trying to call you. This journalist who came here, she wrote about some wealthy Russians—'

'Katy, there isn't…' Midway through interrupting her, he finally made the connection, and understood which of Jay's comments had been nagging at the back of his mind.

Voronov has connections galore – cops, lawyers, politicians, the media.

Katy said, 'The name that caught my eye was Alexander Voronov, and since he called himself "Alex" …'

'Yes – that's him.' Now he tried to examine the problem from another angle. Had Voronov employed a journalist to press Katy for information about the kidnap? Why?

To see how much we know.

'Okay, this is even more important,' he said. 'I think Voronov might be sending people to get you. The men who attacked on Sunday.'

He heard Katy gasp, and there was a voice in the background: Zoe, probably trying to make sense of the sudden panic.

'Look outside,' Adam shouted down the phone. 'If it's clear to leave, you need to get out of there.'

'All right.' Katy's breathing was rapid; he heard a clatter as she started moving. 'Zoe's calling DI Branning for backup. And we're checking all the doors and windows.'

'They'll have guns, remember. It's better to get away if you can. Drive somewhere safe.'

'I've got to ring off. Will your phone still…?'

'I'll leave it on. Call me when you're out of there. Hurry!'

'I will.' A gulp. 'I love you.'

'I love you, too.'

He sat back in his seat, felt his heart hammering in his chest. But he'd reached them in time; there was a police officer in their house, and she was calling for support.

He took a deep breath. Now he could concentrate on what was happening here.

'Did you know about this?' he asked quietly.

'Of course not!' Holly sounded outraged, but was it genuine, or manufactured?

'Tell me that you had no idea at all.'

'I didn't. And that's a terrible thing, to imply that—'

'It's my wife and children, Holly,' he snarled over her. 'They mean more to me than anything, so no bullshitting—'

'I'm not!'

She shifted forward, clapped her head in her hands and started bawling like an infant. Adam regarded her for a moment, and found that a strange sense of calm had enveloped him; it felt as though all his thoughts, his movements and emotions were being directed by someone else.

He got out of the car and hurried away.

CHAPTER SEVENTY-TWO

Katy was glad she didn't have to explain anything in detail: Zoe had caught most of the conversation, and while neither of them understood what had prompted the call, she recognised that there was an emergency – that she would have to act first and get an explanation later.

While she called DI Branning, she was also testing the back door. As Katy hurried through the hall, she heard Zoe requesting armed police. Branning must have queried the reason, and Zoe said, 'After Sunday, I think there's a credible threat, sir.'

Katy drew the security bolt on the front door, then went into the living room, switched the light off and moved cautiously towards the window. She drew back a sliver of curtain and peered out. The street was well lit, silent, deserted. No unfamiliar cars, no one loitering in the shadows.

In the sudden turmoil, she hadn't had a chance to ask Adam about Holly. Was he still with her, and how on earth did she figure in these events?

Even more importantly, what had Adam done to learn of this latest threat, and was *he* in danger?

Too many questions. She returned to the hall and joined Zoe at the foot of the stairs. 'I can't see anyone.'

'Good. There'll be a car here within five, maybe ten minutes at most.'

That seemed a horribly long time in the context of their lives being at risk. But maybe Adam had got it wrong. Maybe he was overreacting.

'Is it best to stay here? He was urging us to get away.'

Zoe looked tense, but sounded calm: 'I'm sure we're fine, but it might be a good idea to wake the kids, in case we do have to leave.'

Katy nodded. 'I'll check the windows up there as well.'

She raced upstairs, and when Zoe returned to the kitchen, there was a rasping noise that took Katy a second to identify. It was the sound of a blade being drawn from the knife block.

Zoe was arming herself, just in case.

Holly didn't look up when Adam got out of the car. She knew where he was going.

Another disaster in the making, but calling him back would achieve nothing. He would probably never listen to her – about anything – ever again.

It took a moment to realise that she was weeping out of self-pity, and that disgusted her. Grief, remorse, even shame: those were valid reasons. But not self-pity.

She wiped her eyes and stared straight ahead as a lorry thundered past. By the time it was gone, Adam had vanished and the whole situation seemed unreal. With such a peaceful, ordinary world around her, it was hard to credit that so many lives could be in danger. Could be about to end…

Perhaps she had drifted into a trance, for suddenly she found that her seatbelt had been drawn across her chest and fastened in place. Her feet were poised on the pedals. Her hands gripped the steering wheel as if clinging to a life raft.

And she clung to words, as well: *I didn't know.*

Jay saw what I wanted, and nudged me into thinking I could get it, then used me to entice Adam. Deep down, I knew there would be violence, blood, death. But I drew a veil over who, exactly, might die.

Grief, remorse, shame: all for later. Holly blinked a few times, and her vision remained clear.

She started the car, and no one in the peaceful, ordinary world came to prevent her from driving away.

Jay had caught glimpses of Voronov before, during their surveillance, but never up close. The Russian was a burly man, not tall, with grizzled features and unkempt greying brown hair. His skin was pale and doughy, and only his sharp green eyes saved him from being completely forgettable. If you'd seen a picture of him with Carole Kirby, and knew nothing of his wealth and power, you'd conclude that it was Voronov punching above his weight; not Carole.

But in the flesh, Jay could feel how that wealth, that power carried its own aura. Voronov was a man who expected to come out on top, and the confidence he projected was intimidating in itself.

And then there was the machine pistol.

'Who is with you?' the Russian asked.

'No one.' Jay tried a grin. 'Who'd be crazy enough?'

Voronov grunted. 'And the man you sent to your pub?'

'He's low level. Not up to this sort of stuff.' That wasn't entirely a lie, at least. 'The ambush on Sunday night, was that planned from the start?'

'Naturally. I was never going to give you my money.'

'So it wasn't because of Carole?'

Voronov shook his head, curtly. 'This part of your plan was not known to us. Now you will suffer more because of it.'

'Her death was an accident, I promise you.' Jay couldn't ignore the flare of disbelief and loathing in the Russian's gaze. He tried to bump the conversation along. 'How did you know about the family in Sussex?'

'Roger told us they had been with Carole. I put my contacts to work. A friend in the media is skilful at extracting information. She visited the wife this afternoon, and told me she was not yet certain how much they know. She was due to return tomorrow, but after your phone call I changed my mind.' He dipped his head. 'It was a clever move.'

Jay shrugged off the compliment. 'Are you going to kill them? The whole family?'

'Of course.' Voronov was lost in thought for a moment. 'As for you, do I wait for my men to return, and watch them take you apart? Or do I finish you now?'

The Russian seemed genuinely to be waiting for an answer. When it didn't come, he gestured angrily with the gun, jabbing it towards the floor, where Xavier had dropped the keys.

'Get in the cage.'

Jay glanced at the keys, then at Maggie, who once again seemed to be unconscious. He was listening keenly, desperate to hear a sign that someone would intervene and save him, but the warehouse was eerily quiet.

'Do it.'

He had to buy some time. Straightening up, Jay crossed his arms and slowly shook his head. 'No.'

Katy went first to Freya's room, crossed to the window and checked that it was shut and locked. Her daughter stirred, mumbling something as she started to turn over.

'Can you wake up, darling? Sorry.'

'Uh?' Freya sat up in a rush, terror on her face. 'What is it?'

'Nothing. But we might have to go somewhere.'

'With Zoe?'

'Yes. Put some clothes on, quickly, while I get your brother.'

She reached the landing and realised that the trap window in the bathroom might be open: she diverted that way and saw that it was. She pulled it shut, telling herself this was just precautionary. There was nothing to fear.

Dylan's room next, where she found him lying awake, a bewildered expression on his face. 'What time is it?'

'About ten past nine. Can you get dressed quickly? We might be going somewhere with Zoe.'

'And Dad?'

'No. He's not home yet.'

'Why not?'

'Dylan, I don't have time to explain.' She grabbed jeans and a sweatshirt from the floor. 'Put these on.'

He was grumbling as she left the room, and wasn't sure if she'd heard something from downstairs. Had Zoe spoken?

She stopped in the doorway to her own bedroom. Both windows were shut, though the curtains hadn't yet been closed. Outside, instead of the darkness she'd expected, there was a white glare off to one corner, coming from a badly positioned security light on the house behind them.

Katy took a couple of steps into the room, but knew there would be little to see. The light didn't reach far enough to illuminate their own garden – and if she was worried, there were plenty of things that could have triggered the sensor: cats, foxes, someone popping out to have a smoke or put something in the bin…

There was movement behind her; Freya trudging sleepily on to the landing. 'Where's Dad?'

'He'll be home soon.' She glanced back at the window, just as the light winked off and the glass became a black mirror, reflecting all her uncertainty and fear. 'Can you get Dylan?'

'Where are we going?'

'Just get him. Please.'

Freya stomped off to her brother's bedroom. Katy turned towards the stairs, in response to a tiny clatter from the kitchen. It must be Zoe, fetching something else. But then she called out: 'Katy?'

'I'm here.' Katy grabbed the banister just as Zoe strode out from the lounge.

Not the kitchen.

She gazed up at Katy, both of them mystified for the half second it took to appreciate that neither of them had made that noise. Then Zoe turned towards the kitchen, let out a gasp, and yelled: 'Barricade!'

CHAPTER SEVENTY-THREE

'Pick up the keys. Slowly.'

At the second time of asking, Jay did as he was told. If nothing else, it gave him a weapon to throw.

Voronov was alert to that risk. He eased back a step and turned side on, to present less of a target.

'Now get in the cage.'

'No.'

Glowering, the Russian jerked the gun, but it was an impotent gesture. If Jay continued to refuse, he would have to shoot, or accept that Jay wasn't going to comply. A dangerous tactic, for sure, but Jay sensed that Voronov would feel cheated by a quick death. He wanted to stretch this out, relishing Jay's torment.

'Last warning.'

When Maggie made a sound in her throat, Jay fought an instinct to look round. Maintaining eye contact with Voronov might be the only thing keeping him alive.

'Your mother wants you,' Voronov said. 'Go to her.'

'*Don't.*' Her voice was remarkably strong. 'Don't let him… torture you.'

Jay fought back a sob. Mentally he thought he had written her off, telling himself he wasn't going to be affected by any of this – not until it was over, at least – because he'd never expected her to survive. But now, having seen how she'd found the courage to cling to life, defying Voronov to the last, he wanted her to come through it. He wanted a chance to repair things between them, if he could.

'I won't,' he told her.

'Roger…' she gasped. 'Roger died proud. You do the same.'

Jay had turned slightly in her direction just as Voronov strode forward. A few heavy steps to the corner of the cage, where he poked the barrel through the bars and fired a quick burst. Maggie toppled over, the chair collapsing as it fell, blood splattering across the tarpaulin.

Jay could only stare in horror. He might tell himself that she hadn't stood a chance, but now it was on his conscience. It was his refusal that had killed her.

Voronov backed away. 'She was a strong woman, your mother. Now, are you strong like her? Or are you weak?'

Adam wasn't thinking straight when he ran towards the warehouse. His mind was seared with white hot rage. Jay had manipulated him, which was bad enough, but then he'd put a death sentence on Katy and the children.

For that, he was going to pay.

The front door didn't move when he pushed it, and even with his face up against the glass he couldn't see anything inside. He ran round the corner and examined the roller door halfway along the side, but that too looked impenetrable. Slowing as he approached the rear of the building, he found a small yard area where a Jaguar XJR was parked.

Just in front of it lay the body of a large man in a dark suit. He appeared to be dead, though Adam didn't want to look too closely.

The back door was open. Adam crept inside and immediately saw another body, this one unmistakably dead. Lying at the man's side was some kind of compact automatic rifle.

Adam checked that he was alone in the room, then picked up the weapon and quickly looked it over. It had an extendable stock, folded over the body of the gun, and there was a switch just above the handle, with the option of single or automatic fire. He pushed it to single, and turned towards the main part of the building.

He could hear voices: two men. When he reached the doorway he spotted an unfamiliar figure about thirty feet away, holding the same sort of rifle and talking angrily to someone that Adam couldn't see.

The next voice was Jay's. A single word: 'No.'

The stranger looked furious. This had to be Voronov, Adam thought. He was a burly, thickset man in dark trousers and a white shirt. Adam couldn't make out what they were discussing, but Voronov had gestured towards a metal structure that looked like a cage.

So Jay had been right. The Russian had prisoners here.

There were a couple of vehicles parked by the left side wall. Adam moved out of sight behind them and was working his way closer when Voronov spoke again, and then another voice broke in. The tone was harsh, and desperate; it came from someone who was in terrible agony. Adam thought it was a woman speaking.

He made it to the back of a Range Rover and peered round it, just as Voronov opened fire on someone inside the cage. It was all Adam could do not to cry out in horror.

Maggie had been tied to a chair. Now she lay dead, alongside another body that might have been Roger.

Outside the cage, Jay stood helplessly. Voronov backed away, then spoke again. Adam was too shocked to catch anything but the final words: 'Are you strong like her? Or are you weak?'

There was going to be a bloodbath, he realised, and neither of these men would stand trial for what they had done.

He glanced down at the gun one more time, then switched it to automatic fire. Could he use it if he had to? More importantly, could he appear convincing enough to disarm the Russian?

He took a deep breath, and started to move into sight, but his leg gave a nervous spasm and he stumbled, bumping his knee against the Range Rover. Voronov reacted at once, swinging the gun round.

Adam froze, but it was too late. Voronov could see him.

Jay had no idea what had caused the distraction, and he didn't need to know; he just had to use the chance he'd been given.

He launched himself forward, slamming into Voronov, and his momentum took them both to the floor. Jay managed to prise the other man's fingers from the Skorpion's trigger, while keeping his head out of range as the Russian tried to claw at him. He drove his knee into Voronov's groin, and felt him instinctively try to curl up to deal with the pain. Jay made a grab for the gun, but that gave Voronov a split-second opening and he lurched upwards, toppling Jay to the side, the gun falling away as Voronov's strong fingers raked at his face and tried to burrow into his eye sockets.

Jay roared and fought with all his strength, but Voronov had the advantage now. He pinned Jay to the ground with his knees and pressed an elbow against Jay's neck, grunting and growling the whole time, an enraged animal, his saliva spraying over Jay's face.

And then there was a flurry of movement, a loud crack and Voronov fell sideways, blood erupting from his nose and cheek. Jay gasped and rolled in the other direction, but hit an obstacle. Blinking away tears of pain, he looked up and found Adam, holding another of the machine pistols the wrong way round. He must have struck Voronov with the butt of the gun.

'Ah, thank Christ.' Jay pointed at the Russian. 'Gotta restrain him.'

He sat up too quickly, his head spinning. Voronov's gun was out of reach; he couldn't pounce on it, and Adam was standing strong. He'd have to be persuaded.

'You do it,' Adam said, turning the Skorpion the correct way round.

'Uh, mate, it's probably best if I take the gun—'

'Just tie him up, or he'll finish what he started.'

This didn't sound like Adam. Jay knew he had to play along, at least for now. Voronov was stunned, but not out of the game completely.

'I almost had him,' Jay muttered, 'but thanks.' He took out some cable ties and started binding Voronov's hands. The Russian came to and struggled wildly until Jay grabbed a fistful of the man's hair and rammed his head on the ground. Adam recoiled at the sound of the impact, but didn't criticise Jay's actions. That gave him hope.

'He'd have killed you,' Adam said in a flat voice.

'Maybe.' With Voronov now restrained, Jay sat up and nodded grimly. 'If it matters to you, I'll admit it. You saved my life.'

'Wrong.' Adam took aim with the Skorpion. 'Your life isn't saved.'

CHAPTER SEVENTY-FOUR

Katy lost a second trying to understand what Zoe meant.

Barricade?

A shadow moved in the hallway, and Zoe ran towards it. Katy heard the sound of bodies colliding, then the louder crack of glass, coming from the lounge. There must be more than one attacker: Zoe couldn't possibly hold them all off.

Katy turned, saw Freya and Dylan clutching each other in terror. She pointed to the door just behind them, and yelled: 'In there!'

They bundled inside and Katy virtually shoved them across the room. 'Other side of the bed,' she shouted. 'Lie down on the floor.'

Slamming the door, she heard two quick sounds from downstairs: *pock pock*, like muffled punches. It was the same noise they'd heard at the farmhouse: gunfire, perhaps with a silencer.

Katy groaned. Was Zoe hit?

She couldn't dwell on it. Thankfully a new sound was drifting into the room: the slow wail of a siren: that had to be help coming their way. But would it get here in time?

Freya had a standalone wardrobe, gifted from her great-grandmother. It was six feet high and three feet wide, made of solid oak and filled with clothes, shoes, belts, jewellery and assorted junk. If at any other time you'd asked Katy whether she could have shifted it on her own, she would have laughed. *Of course not. Crazy idea.*

But now their lives were at stake. She was hideously aware that Zoe might have sacrificed herself to save them: if so, it was Katy's duty to make that sacrifice count.

The wardrobe was positioned against the same wall as the door. Dragging it around wasn't feasible: she didn't have the strength or the time or even enough space – it would jam up against the bed.

But she had a better idea. She moved to the far end, into the gap between the wardrobe and the adjacent wall. Knelt down, braced her back against the wall, lifted the wardrobe from its base and thrust it upwards.

The effort made her shriek. Something went in her lower back, and it felt like her arms would pop out of their sockets. But Katy kept going, even when the base of the unit was crushing against her abdomen, and she could hear shoes and hangers go sliding to the far end. She felt a pummelling vibration that meant someone was charging up the stairs – just as the wardrobe reached the point of equilibrium and for a moment became weightless, before crashing down on its side.

The kids screamed at the noise, and the whole room shook so violently that Katy feared the floor might give way. 'Stay low,' she warned them.

The wardrobe now blocked the bottom half of the door. As she watched, the handle rattled and someone tried to push it open. When it didn't move, there was another muffled gunshot: a hole appeared in the door, and a bullet struck the opposite wall in a tiny explosion of plaster and brick.

Katy dropped into a crouch. The gunman pushed at the door again, then launched a couple of kicks, hard enough to jolt the wardrobe.

The sirens were growing louder, with a conflicting pitch that suggested several vehicles were converging on the house. Katy thought she heard a shout from downstairs, and the man outside the door growled a response. He must be getting the order to run – surely?

The door shook as he kicked it again; this time there was a loud splintering. Then another: he was aiming higher, either kicking or maybe ramming his elbow into the upper panels. Katy was no expert on joinery, but she knew that most internal doors couldn't withstand a prolonged attack.

The split widened, and on the fourth blow she spotted the sleeve of his jacket as he broke through. The sirens were now so loud, the police had to be in their street, and yet this man seemed determined to carry out his mission. He must have lost his mind.

Then Freya screamed; 'Mum!'

Her first thought was that one of them had been hit. A ricochet, or shrapnel from where the bullet hit the wall. But when she glanced in that direction, her daughter was on her knees and thrusting something across the bed.

'Get down!' Katy roared, even as she grabbed the hockey stick that Freya had taken from beneath the bed.

By now a couple of savage punches had enlarged the hole. The man's hand withdrew, snapped off a loose shard of wood, then burst through again, this time holding a pistol with a silencer attached.

As Katy moved, acting purely on instinct, she was dimly aware of the terrified keening of her children, of sirens and shouts from the street outside. She gripped the hockey stick in both hands, lifted it above her head and brought it down on the man's wrist with all the strength she could muster. There was a loud crack, and a scream; he dropped the gun and whipped his arm away.

Breathing hard, Katy raised the stick again, but he was gone. She heard running on the stairs, an explosion of noise from the hall and shouts of warning – 'Armed police! Get on the ground!' – and then shots were fired, much louder than anything before.

Then silence.

*

Adam was ready to do it. He thought he was physically capable of working the gun, of aiming and firing it correctly.

And he felt emotionally prepared. Adam had agreed to help Jay, had ignored his deepest instincts and tried to trust this man. He had even offered sympathy – and in return Jay had sold out the three people that Adam loved most in the world. An act like that couldn't go unpunished, could it?

Jay didn't look as though he took the threat seriously at first. He sat still, but his eyes kept flicking to one side or another, searching for a weapon, a distraction; anything to help him gain an advantage.

Adam monitored him closely as he moved over and kicked Voronov's gun further out of reach. For the first time he registered that there was another body lying outside the cage, beaten beyond recognition. Jay followed his gaze, and said wearily, 'That's Xavier.'

'Your inside man?'

'Except he wasn't. He made us believe we'd sorted out a deal, when he was really just laying a trap.'

'But if Voronov knew everything in advance, why did he let you abduct Carole?'

'He didn't know about that. Although Xavier had mentioned her, we came up with the idea ourselves.'

'But the whole time, you were never truly in control? Voronov had the upper hand, and we were just…' Adam felt sick, realising how terrified they had been of their kidnappers, all the while unaware of the far greater danger posed by the Russian.

'It was seriously bad luck on your part, Adam. But you did well to hide from them – why not settle for that, rather than screwing up your life even more?'

'You don't think it's already ruined?' His voice broke with emotion. He was desperate to call Katy, and make sure that Zoe had led them all to safety.

He spotted a little twitch of alarm from Jay; he too must be wondering whether they were still alive.

'Look, Adam. Shoot me now, and you're going to prison. No doubt about that, even allowing for all the other…'

'Extenuating circumstances?' Adam supplied the phrase.

'Yeah. Exactly. So be sensible.'

'Oh, I've calmed down a lot, while we've been talking. And I still want to kill you.'

He took a step forward, and aimed at the centre of Jay's chest. Narrowed his eyes and steadied his breathing, and a voice said, 'Don't do it.'

Startled, he half turned. Holly was striding towards them, also holding one of the machine guns. Adam knew he couldn't afford to be distracted, but the damage was done. Jay hurled something at him; Adam only caught a flash of movement and tried to raise his arms as a solid metal bar struck him a glancing blow. He fell to his knees, not badly hurt but helpless as Jay threw himself towards Voronov's gun – only for a burst of automatic fire to chew up the ground in front of him. Chunks of concrete sprayed out like shrapnel. Jay shrieked, curling up to protect himself.

'Hurry!' Holly gestured at Adam. 'Tie him up before he tries anything.'

His ears were ringing, but he understood the instruction. Perhaps the throbbing in his arm had brought a new clarity, but it already seemed surreal to think he might have executed a man in cold blood. Could he really have done it?

He put his gun down next to the crowbar that Jay had thrown at him, took some cable ties from Jay's pocket and bound his hands behind his back. Jay whined about the minor cuts he'd received, but he didn't resist. Holly had the gun pointing down at his head, and he seemed to fear her a lot more than he did Adam.

'You're a fucking liability with that,' he complained.

'You should be glad I'm a poor shot,' Holly said. 'I was actually trying to hit you then. I won't miss again.'

Once Jay was securely tied, Adam stood up and took out his phone.

'Calling the cops?' Holly sounded forlorn.

'We've got to.'

'I know. I just wish I could run away and not come back.' She sighed. 'In fact, I very nearly did, a few minutes ago.'

'Well... thanks for staying.' Adam stared at the phone, longing to find a missed call from Katy, but the display was blank.

His physical pain was nothing compared to the agony of not knowing. He turned his back on Holly and rang the landline. If they didn't answer, he told himself, that might be good news. It meant they'd fled the house in time—

But the phone was answered on the fifth ring. By DI Branning.

His stomach lurched in terror.

Did that mean...?

CHAPTER SEVENTY-FIVE

Katy ran to the children. Dylan was sobbing in silence; Freya just gazed blankly at her mother, her body trembling uncontrollably. Katy pulled the duvet off the bed and wrapped it around them.

They heard footsteps on the stairs, and shouts of 'Clear!' Then someone cautiously tried their door.

'Don't shoot!' Katy cried. 'It's us. My children are in here.'

Reassurance was given, while DI Branning was called for, and finally it was his voice that said, 'Katy? Are you okay?'

'I think so.' Katy sniffed, and discovered that she was crying. She hugged the children closer, and promised them it was safe to get up.

The door tried to open; she heard Branning grunting with the exertion and told him: 'We barricaded ourselves in. There's a wardrobe in the way.'

'Good thinking.'

'It was—' she began, then broke off, heart in her mouth. It had been Zoe's idea, but she didn't dare ask in front of the children whether Zoe was alive.

'How do we get you out?' the detective asked. 'Can you shift the wardrobe?'

Katy gave it a try, and the children helped, but it was just too heavy. After a couple of minutes, and reflecting on the fact that the door was already damaged beyond repair, Katy got to work with the hockey stick and smashed the upper panel until the gap was large enough to climb through.

Dylan went first, then Freya. As Katy was lifted out, she heard more commotion downstairs, lots of running footsteps. There was an icy draught from the open front door, and blue emergency lights strobing across the walls. DI Branning read the question on her face and said, 'Paramedics are with her.' He crossed his fingers, glanced at the children, and then whispered: 'She got shot in the chest.'

Someone clattered up the stairs, a uniformed officer holding a ringing phone. It was the landline extension, which he offered to Branning. 'Sir, did you want to…?'

The detective turned to Katy, as if seeking her permission. She nodded. Right now she wasn't sure if she could speak.

'Hello?' He listened intently for a few seconds, then said, 'Yes. She's here, in fact.'

And he passed her the phone.

Adam was in a daze, and barely heard his own frantic questions or Branning's calm reply. But then another voice came to the phone: 'Adam?'

'Oh, thank God. Are you all right?'

'We're okay. They attacked the house, but the police are here now.' She stopped, overcome, and he guessed there was a lot that she couldn't say. 'What about you?'

'Yes, I'm fine.' The relief was so overwhelming that he couldn't stay on his feet. As he sank to his knees, he sensed Holly moving in and quickly shooed her away. 'It's over now. Voronov and Jay are both disarmed, and I'm calling the police straight after this.'

'But how did you…? Never mind.' She sounded flustered, tearful. 'Is it safe there?'

'I promise. You don't need to worry.'

'I can't help it.' She sounded bereft. 'Do you know when you'll be home?'

He gave a gentle smile, and suspected that Katy could sense it. He thought of the bodies everywhere: Maggie and Roger inside the cage, three more of Voronov's men dead in various parts of the building, plus Voronov and Jay tied up and awaiting arrest. 'It could be a while.'

'Of course. Look – can you speak to Freya and Dylan? I want them to hear your voice.'

'Yes, please,' he said, and a moment later, when a subdued Freya said, 'Daddy?' he had to fight back a sob.

He did his best to put on a reassuring demeanour, told them both that he loved them and would be back there as soon as possible. He could tell they were deeply shocked, and no wonder: an attack on their home might affect them even more profoundly than Sunday's trauma.

'Are they going to be all right?' he asked when Katy came back on the line.

'Too early to say.' She now sounded just as flat as they had done. DI Branning was talking in the background. 'I'd better go. There's a lot to explain.' More murmuring. 'He's saying we'll have to spend the night at my mum and dad's. Can you meet us there, once you're finished?'

'Definitely. I can't wait to see you all.'

'Same here.' There was a pause, and he braced himself for a question about Holly, but instead there was only a sniff, and then: 'I love you.'

She cut the connection before he could respond. Adam wiped his face, took a couple of breaths, then rose to his feet. Holly had her back to him, though she'd clearly been listening.

Now she turned. 'You know we might both end up in a jail cell?'

'Yep.'

He gazed around the warehouse, taking in the scale of the carnage. The smell of blood made him want to retch, and he said a silent prayer of thanks: a scene like this could so easily have taken place in the cellar. It could have been his wife, his children lying dead…

Jay had twisted round and was trying to catch his eye. He seemed to be contemplating whether to speak.

'We should wait somewhere else,' Adam said. It had occurred to him that Voronov might have other people on the payroll, and he didn't want any more encounters with armed men.

First he checked that Jay was securely tied, and for good measure dragged him closer to the cage, attaching several more ties between his wrists and the bars.

'Fucking hurts,' Jay growled.

'You can bear it.'

As they started to walk away, Jay made his final pitch: 'Come on, guys. Let me go and I swear you'll never hear from me again.'

'Ignore, ignore,' Holly said under her breath. After initially thinking it was meant for him, Adam understood that this was an instruction to herself.

A few more feeble pleas followed them out of the building. Adam rang 999 and asked for the police and ambulances to a major incident. The operator wanted to keep him on the line, but he cut the connection, and gestured to Holly's car.

'We'll wait till they've secured the scene, then walk over and introduce ourselves.'

'Okay.' She swallowed nervously. A moment later she thrust something at him.

Her keys.

'Take them,' she said. 'I don't trust myself not to drive away.'

'You didn't last time.'

'I was worried about you. Now I know you're safe.' She tried for a smile, but it died when she saw the look on his face.

At the car, Holly opened her door and started to get in, hesitating when she saw that he wasn't doing the same.

'I'd rather stay out here,' he said.

'Right.' She looked away. Her knuckles whitened as she gripped the roof of the car. 'Adam, I am *so* sorry. I swear that I didn't know what he had in mind. Maybe I should have guessed—'

'Forget it, Holly. I don't care what you knew or should have guessed. It doesn't matter. There's no apology that could ever make a difference to how I feel about this.'

'No. All right.' She nodded to herself, then got in and shut the door.

Adam turned his back on the car and gazed up at the night sky, contaminated by the eerie glow of light pollution. A jet was passing overhead, and as the sound of its engines faded, he thought he could hear sirens.

CHAPTER SEVENTY-SIX

The days that followed would be long remembered, they came to realise, in the same way that even a disappointing holiday can be recalled so vividly years later, simply because it represents such a departure from the usual routine.

There were hours of interviews to endure – preceded, in Adam's case, by an arrest. He couldn't blame the officers from Thames Valley Police for reacting as they did; when he and Holly identified themselves as key witnesses to a scene of absolute mayhem, the SIO considered it prudent to have them cautioned and taken into custody.

As DI Branning later explained, 'He was covering his back, which makes perfect sense on a case as big as this. And it worked in your favour, too. You had the right to legal advice, so you couldn't later feel you'd been duped into incriminating yourself.'

Even with the Sussex detective's assistance, Adam wasn't released until early afternoon on Wednesday. His interview had been delayed by a doctor, summoned by the police, who questioned whether he was fit enough to make a statement. Although he was exhausted, and psychologically wrecked, Adam had insisted that he felt well enough to cooperate with their enquiries.

It was about four o'clock when he was finally reunited with his family, having been unofficially reassured that he would not be facing any charges. Freya and Dylan were ecstatic to see him. Despite constant assurances from their mother, they seemed to be convinced that Adam was badly hurt – or perhaps didn't intend to come home the way he had promised. It took him a while to appreciate that Katy might have unknowingly transmitted her own insecurities there.

His first night in Lewes had been surreal: armed police guarding the house and patrolling nearby streets; the TV and internet out of bounds for fear of what they might see or read about themselves; Katy's parents veering between elation at their survival and neurotic meltdown at the thought of how narrowly they had escaped; all of the adults shattered but too wired to sleep; late-night pizzas being delivered through the police cordon and washed down with shots of some old brandy that all of them claimed to dislike.

In bed at last, in the early hours, Adam had told Katy the truth about Holly: their prior conversations, including some unwise flirtation, right up to the messages that Jay had sent on Sunday and Monday, luring her to the hotel in Dunstable.

He described how she had been persuaded to work with Jay, and how he, ultimately, had betrayed her trust. By this point he'd dismissed his own suspicion – that Holly might have gone along with Jay's plan to set Voronov on them, in order to clear a path for her to be reunited with Adam.

'But what was she thinking, to help a man as dangerous as Jay?'

'The impression I got was that she had a bit of a thing for him.'

'As in, *physically?*' Katy shuddered, but also looked a little relieved. 'If you ask me, they're welcome to each other. She can write to him in prison – and I hope she gets locked up as well.'

She didn't. The news came through after a couple of weeks that the Crown Prosecution Service felt there was insufficient evidence to charge Holly with any crimes. As they learned from DI Branning, this was largely a consequence of Jay Nolan's evidence, which absolved her of responsibility.

According to his testimony, Holly had been deceived and then coerced into helping him; his threats to harm Adam had made her too fearful to run out on him or alert the police.

'That's absolute bollocks,' Adam had exclaimed. But he reluctantly accepted that proving their case in court would be a struggle.

Quite rightly, achieving a watertight conviction against Jay was seen to be the absolute priority, since he was now the only person who would stand trial. Alexander Voronov had been rushed to hospital with a serious concussion, where he was held under police guard, but two days later he suffered a fatal cardiac arrest. Before long there were rumours flying around the internet of a Kremlin plot to silence him.

DI Branning encouraged them to pay no attention – the medical staff were satisfied that the death had been a natural consequence of long-term heart disease – but even he was dismayed when he learned that, after some shady manoeuvring by the Home Office, the two surviving gunmen who'd attacked the house had been spirited back to Russia, and would not be facing justice in this country.

'She was owed that,' Branning said of Zoe. She had fought bravely to protect the family, and Katy was in no doubt that they owed her their lives.

When the three men stormed the house, Zoe had tackled the first intruder and stabbed him in the leg. She was then struck by a bullet fired by the second man, but still managed to hinder him, giving Katy time to create her barricade.

The third attacker had been the most determined, trying to break through the bedroom door even as armed police pulled up outside. He was caught trying to escape the house, as was the second man. The first one, hampered by the knife wound, had gone for his gun and was shot dead by the police.

Zoe had sustained a serious injury, and might have died without the urgent medical treatment she received. The bullet narrowly missed her heart, but broke a rib and did significant damage to her lungs. By the following day the doctors felt confident she would survive, but expected some permanent impairment.

'Reduced lung capacity for sure, and maybe some nerve damage in her right arm,' Branning told them. 'For someone who prides herself on her fitness, this is going to be hard to take. I'm not sure if she'll be able to work again.'

He wasn't allowing for her extraordinary determination. When Katy visited her in hospital for the third time, ten days in, Zoe was breathing unaided, had recovered ninety per cent of her mobility and even regained some weight. She was playing down the extent of the pain, Katy felt sure, and she wasn't about to be deterred by the expert prognosis.

'If the bullet had been an inch to the left or a couple of inches to the right, on a more upward trajectory or a more downward one, it would have taken out my heart or a major artery, and I'd be dead. Instead I'm alive – and everyone agrees there's no better starting point than that.' Zoe grinned. 'I'm already walking sooner than they expected. Next step swimming, then running, and then back to work.'

Katy still feared she was being overly optimistic, but at least she had good news for the children, who couldn't wait to visit Zoe themselves.

'Not till you're sure it won't upset them,' Zoe had warned. 'They've already been through way too much.'

That was an understatement. The worst aspect by far in the immediate aftermath was the voracious media attention. The involvement of a Russian oligarch had the press salivating, and since Adam and Katy were practically the only living witnesses, they became the prime target of the tabloids.

With the family refusing to cooperate, the journalists were reduced to stripping private family photos from their Facebook profiles, and doorstepping their colleagues and friends. Fortunately the focus switched a little once Voronov died, and various conspiracy theories began to gain attention. And then, to their eternal relief, news emerged of a pregnancy in the royal family and it was as though a tap had been turned off. Overnight the story was dropped and seemed completely forgotten.

It wouldn't last for ever, of course. There was still Jay's trial to come. He was to be charged with the murder of Brian Kirby, assault and kidnapping of Carole, and kidnapping and false imprisonment of the Parr family. Many other charges had been considered, but the CPS feared the evidence was too murky, including the issue of Holly's possible coercion.

That lay some months ahead. In the meantime, normal life had to resume. The children had been reluctant to return home, so Adam and Katy decided to place the house on the market and find a property to rent in Haywards Heath. In the meantime they would stay with Katy's parents.

The children went back to school after two weeks. Both reported that it was 'fine', and wouldn't be drawn any further. Anecdotally the word from their school friends, via the parents, was that they had been regarded as quasi-celebrities for a day or two, until everyone grew bored and moved on to something else.

'Turns out that seven- to nine-year-olds have essentially the same mindset as tabloid editors,' Katy observed.

Adam had slotted back into work easily enough, but Katy found it more difficult. Whereas his office was protected territory, a shop has to actively encourage the public to enter, so for a week or two there were frequent visitors who had no intention of buying anything, and simply wanted to gawp at 'the woman who'd been abducted'. But that period, too, had passed, and Katy had been grateful for the support of her colleagues.

One of the customers had been her police officer friend, Leah, who by then knew that Katy had been forced to bring Dylan to the party in Burgess Hill. It turned out that she *had* spotted Katy in the Mazda, but hadn't thought anything of it. 'Henry's teething, and he'd kept us up most of the night. I was operating on autopilot that day, I'm afraid.'

'Don't apologise,' Katy told her. 'I'd never have forgiven myself if anything had happened to you or Henry.'

As a family they had had some group counselling, and when that proved beneficial Katy had broached the issue of relationship counselling.

'If you think we need it,' Adam said.

'Well, something can't have been right, if you'd had to keep Holly's messages secret.'

That was a fair point, and it became the launchpad for a forthright discussion about their future. The appeal of a move to Canada had grown on them both, aided by a lingering suspicion that only a dramatic change could cleanse them of the traumas they had experienced.

After three weeks, with the media interest having dwindled away and a rental property not yet finalised, Laura and Clive took the children to visit relatives in Dorset over the weekend and let Adam and Katy have the house to themselves. For a blissful couple of days they felt like tourists in Lewes, and realised just how much they loved this part of the world.

'You know, I'm really not sure if I want to move abroad,' Katy said. They'd spent the afternoon browsing in galleries and antique shops, enjoyed lunch at a quiet bistro and then drinks in the Rights of Man pub on the High Street; now they were standing by the town's war memorial, taking in the glorious pink and purple light of a winter sunset.

'Me neither,' Adam admitted. 'I thought I did, but now it feels like we'll be… admitting defeat, almost.'

'Like they've chased us away.'

'All that upheaval, and if we aren't any happier, then what do we do?'

'Plus it's not fair on your parents.'

'I don't want that to be the issue.'

He held her arm. 'It's not. Your mum and dad have been brilliant about it, and I don't think either of them would get in the way if it was what we genuinely wanted. But now things are settling down, it feels more and more like a kneejerk reaction, rather than a wise solution.'

She let out a sigh. 'I'm so glad you feel that way.'

'Still got to move house, though.'

'You never know. Last night Freya admitted to me that she's missing home, and isn't sure if she wants us to rent. I asked her if she would feel safe going back, and she thinks it would be okay. She's willing to try, at least.'

'Mm. So there's just Dylan to convince?'

'Or bribe. You remember that pool table we said he couldn't have…?'

Adam's eyes lit up. 'You were the one who vetoed that. I was up for getting a pool table – secretly.'

'Well, Dylan saw through you.' She nudged him fondly. 'I'm just saying, there might be a way to make this happen.'

'Have to give Freya something as well, in that case. But still a hell of a lot cheaper than renting, and paying all those fees.'

They embraced, both full of positive feelings, and then Katy murmured, 'Only one thing still to get through.'

'Yeah.' He sighed. 'The trial.'

CHAPTER SEVENTY-SEVEN

They knew they would be key witnesses – the most important of all, in terms of having been present, as victims, and certainly of most interest to the media. Rumours that Jay would plead guilty came and went but were never confirmed. It seemed to them that Jay didn't know himself which way he should plea.

DI Branning cautioned them to prepare for the worst. 'If he puts his hand up to it, the trial becomes a minor footnote. But for every charge he contests, you're looking at a full-on circus. Depending on what else is happening in the world, you could be all over the newspapers for day after day.'

He made it clear that the trial was unlikely to take place for months, which seemed like a double-edged sword. It gave them an opportunity to recover, to build up their strength and prepare; but with the knowledge that their emotional wounds would invariably be reopened at some point in the future.

They'd been back at the house in Lindfield for a fortnight when the detective called round unexpectedly. It was six o'clock on a Tuesday evening, the week before Christmas. This year they'd gone wilder than ever, with a six-foot Nordmann fir and several elaborate displays of LED lights strung around the windows and doors.

'Cosy,' Branning remarked when he came in, rubbing his hands together in cheerful appreciation of the warmth.

'It is – until you see the electricity bill,' Adam said.

Katy poked her tongue out. 'Skinflint.'

The banter was a consequence of their nerves, and Branning knew it. 'Some news,' he said. 'Let's take a seat.'

Adam coaxed the children into the kitchen with the promise of a sneaky taste of the chocolate tree decorations, then hurried back. 'We're good for a few minutes.'

'This won't take long,' Branning confirmed. 'It's about Jay.'

'He's pleading not guilty?' Adam guessed.

'Do you have a date for the trial?' Katy asked.

'Uh, neither. His body was found this morning. Probable suicide.'

For a moment they were both too shocked to speak. Then Adam, frowning, said, 'But he was on remand.'

'It happens – more often than it should, to be frank.'

'You say "probable"?' Katy queried.

'He'd used a makeshift shiv – the sharpened end of a toothbrush – and stabbed himself in the throat. Opened the carotid artery, and bled out before anyone raised the alarm.'

Katy and Adam shuddered in unison. 'Could he have done that to himself?'

'With enough determination, yes. There's got to be a full investigation, to rule out foul play, but I'm pretty sure that death came at his own hand.'

He looked from one to the other, awaiting their response. Later they would discover that they had both been thinking of Carole; if Jay was to be believed, she had taken her own life in an act of desperation. Had she provided the inspiration for Jay to do the same?

'Anyway,' Branning said gently, 'from your point of view it makes little difference either way.'

It took them a good ten or fifteen seconds for his meaning to become clear, but when it did they were stunned.

'No trial!' Katy said.

'Precisely. I hope that will be a weight off your minds?'

'Absolutely.' Adam pressed his hands against the beard he'd decided to grow in a bid for greater anonymity. There was other good news, too, which he would relay to Katy once Branning had gone. A colleague had just texted to say that Holly was taking a job in Australia.

'I can't quite believe it,' Katy said. 'We've both had to accommodate the idea that one day it would all flare up again… and now we don't?'

Branning nodded. 'Call it an early Christmas present. Which, if you don't mind me saying, I think you thoroughly deserve.'

He left soon after, with a promise to call in for a drink over the festive period. Adam saw him out, then rejoined Katy in the lounge. He saw at once that something was wrong.

'It's only a small thing, really,' she said when he asked. 'I was on Amazon today, and there's a book listed for publication in June next year. No title or product information yet, just the author's name.'

Adam was confused. 'Why's that…?'

'It's by Ronnie Pierce. The category is true crime.'

'Ah.' Adam took her hand. He knew how distraught Katy had been when Branning had to explain that there simply wasn't enough evidence that the journalist had colluded with Voronov. In their hearts, they felt sure that her visit had paved the way for the hit team that attacked the house later that night. 'I thought the book was only ever a bluff. If she was Voronov's accomplice, surely she wouldn't risk exposing him to publicity?'

'Maybe she doesn't care, now that he's dead?'

'Good point. Or perhaps she was always going to gloss over his part in it?'

Katy agreed. 'If she chooses, I daresay she can portray him as a victim – and who is there to contradict her?'

Only us, Adam thought sadly.

'It's sickening,' Katy went on. 'We ought to take legal advice, see if we can stop it.'

Adam shook his head. 'I think that would be a huge waste of time and money, and it would just give her more publicity. We don't even know what she's written yet – perhaps we'll only be minor characters, like she said to you?'

Katy scowled at the memory. 'Even so, she shouldn't be allowed to profit from this.'

'In an ideal world, no. But who cares? What we've got right now, against all the odds, is a happy, healthy family.'

'Freya is still having nightmares. And Dylan's only just stopped wetting the bed.'

'Yes, I know. But they're getting over it. Week by week, they're improving.'

She nodded, a little reluctantly. 'True. I've certainly never seen them so excited about Christmas.'

'There you go.' He took her hand, and they embraced. 'Nothing she says can hurt us unless we let it hurt us. And we won't.'

After a moment, Katy seemed to chuckle. 'Minor characters? I suppose I'm okay with that, if it means a peaceful life. You and me, Freya and Dylan.'

As she drew him in for a kiss, Adam smiled. 'That's a deal.'

A LETTER FROM TOM

Thank you so much for reading *One Dark Night*. If you'd like to keep up-to-date with all my latest releases, just sign up at the website link below. I promise to only contact you when I have a new book out and I'll never share your email with anyone else.

www.bookouture.com/tom-bale

The initial idea for this book came to me while I was swimming in the sea on holiday in September 2017. It started with the image of a car swinging from a junction, almost but not quite striking another car which held a young, innocent family. From the father's justified rage, and his determination to confront the offending driver, came a story of kidnap, imprisonment and murder.

Quite why an idyllic morning on the beach brought forth a desire to put a family through such misery, I couldn't begin to say – though I do have form in this area. Plunging ordinary people into deadly predicaments seems to be what I gravitate towards in my fiction (though not, I hasten to add, in real life).

As ever, the only reason that I'm able to continue writing is because of the support from my readers, many of whom have been kind enough to write reviews and to talk about my books on Facebook, Twitter and elsewhere. If you have enjoyed this novel, I'd be very grateful if you would consider posting a review or recommending the book to your fellow readers. Thank you.

If you haven't read any of my previous thrillers, you can find them here:

Each Little Lie
All Fall Down
See How They Run
The Catch
Blood Falls
Terror's Reach
Skin and Bones
Sins of the Father

I'd love to hear from you – so please get in touch on my Facebook or Goodreads page, Twitter or through my website.

 www.bookouture.com/tom-bale

 tombalewriter

 t0mbale

 www.tombale.net

Thank you so much for your support, it is hugely appreciated.

Tom Bale

ACKNOWLEDGEMENTS

Firstly a huge thank you to my editor, Keshini Naidoo, and the brilliant team at Bookouture, including Kim Nash, Noelle Holten, Lauren Finger, Alexandra Holmes, Jon Appleton and Natasha Hodgson.

Thanks also to my agent, Camilla Wray, as well as Mary Darby, Emma Winter, Kristina Egan, Rosanna Bellingham and Roya Sarrafi-Gohar. I am indebted to everyone at Darley Anderson for the work they do on my behalf.

As ever, thanks are due to my wife, Niki, and to all my family and friends, not least the many online friends I have made over the past few years from within the vibrant community of crime fiction bloggers and reviewers. It has been a delight to meet many of you at the Harrogate Crime Festival and other social events, and I can't thank you enough for the time and effort that you put into sharing your love of books.